HIGH PRAISE FOR KIRK ALEX

Throwback & Backlash
Love, Lust & Murder Series

"I enjoyed the risqué nature of the books and was drawn to the ensuing hilarity and creativity of the story and characters."

—Hidden Gems Review

Lustmord: Anatomy of a Serial Butcher

"Great book. Dark—yes. Grotesque—certainly. Sexually explicit—without a doubt. And the writing is excellent. Character & dialogue, is as real as it gets. A terrifying, non-putdownable horror."

—Jeff Bennington, K/Book Review

Zook

"**Zook** was a zoo ride! All of the characters were well written and you find yourself unable to put the book down! You might even find it a little sad. ***** out of 5 stars."

—NetGalley

"A very good book that will leave you on the edge of your seat. If you make it through the first 2 or 3 chapters, you will not want to put the book down. **** out of 5 stars."

—NetGalley

Ziggy Popper at Large:
14 Tales of General Degeneracy, of Mayhem & Debauchery – for the Morally Conflicted & Borderline Criminal

"Gruesome, violent, awesome! I absolutely LOOOVEEE Kirk Alex. I am always ready for his next book!! Extremely entertaining. A whole lot of violent, and just what I was looking for. Private detective Felix "Choo-Choo" Buschitsky and Ziggy Popper are now my two favorite characters. ***** out of 5 stars."

—NetGalley

nonentity
–A Rant For Those Who Can't–
Presented as a Novel

"This is a quick read and engrossing. I found myself wanting to know what happened. Many of the situations were funny in the way they were presented. Fast, easy read."

—NetGalley

"Author Kirk Alex loves Bukowski and Kerouac and it shows; his prose is swiftly moving and terse and dark and angry and ugly. There is no wiggle room in what he writes and what he sees; bad is bad and good is rare. Apparently the writer has struggled a long time to get this book published, and it's a good thing he did. This will grab you by the heart and choke the breath out of you—and by book's end, you'll thank him for doing it."

— Steven Rosen, Curled Up With A Good Book

"This is another well done, honest and heartfelt piece of writing from Kirk Alex. At one time or another, everyone can identify with Chance, being unemployed and very low on funds. It's short, easy to read, and well worth the reader's time."

—Paul Lappen, Dead Trees Review

**Working the Hard Side of the Street —
Selected Stories / Poems / Screams**

". . . this is a nicely put together piece of work."

—BookLore

"City of Angels? Maybe for that couple of percent of people who get anywhere near that thing called 'fame and fortune.' Everyone else is just trying to get by in a place where, if you don't have the right job and a flashy car, the odds are very much stacked against you.

"This book is excellent. It's full of honest, heartfelt writing that certainly shows a very different view of Hollywood."

—Paul Lappen, Dead Trees Review

"**WORKING THE HARD SIDE OF THE STREET — Selected Stories / Poems / Screams** is an anthology of powerful, caustic, original tales and poems by Kirk Alex about the ups, downs, and hard knocks of Hollywood's seamy underbelly. The perspective of a "fly- on-the-wall" cab driver provides a piercing realism and insight into the vicious clashes and personal struggles that lie hidden underneath the entertainment capital's glossy, photo-touched exterior. **WORKING THE HARD SIDE OF THE STREET** is recommended as a gut-wrenching read for both its candor and bravado."

—The Midwest Book Review

BLOOD, SWEAT and CHUMP CHANGE –
Taxi Tales & Vignettes

"After reading BLOOD, SWEAT AND CHUMP CHANGE — Taxi Tales & Vignettes by Kirk Alex you understand why the American Dream needs liposuction. It's all here: Hate, poetry, sadness, hope and the ache of an aloneness that never goes away. Belly up!"
—Dan Fante, author of Mooch & Spitting Off Tall Buildings

Fifty Shades of Tinsel
A Novel

"This story is a bit dark and to say there is a lot of sex is an understatement. Jimmy's journey is an interesting one. **** out of five."
—NetGalley

BY KIRK ALEX

Crime Fiction:
Throwback: Love, Lust & Murder – Book One
Backlash: Love, Lust & Murder – Book Two
Disturbed: Love, Lust & Murder – Book Three
Ziggy Popper at Large – 14 Tales of General Degeneracy, of Mayhem & Debauchery – for the Morally Conflicted & Borderline Criminal

Horror:
Lustmord: Anatomy of a Serial Butcher
Zook

Erotic Romance:
Fifty Shades of Tinsel
(graphic carnal situations not meant for prudes)

Chance "Cash" Register Tucson Working Stiff Series:
Take This Job & Shove It!
Loopy Soupy's Smut Asylum
Journey to the End of the Week
A Confederacy of Mooks
nonentity

LA Cab Exploits:
**Working the Hard Side of the Street — Selected
Stories/Poems/Screams**
Blood, Sweat & Chump Change — Taxi Tales & Vignettes

Eddie "Doc" Holiday Contemporary Mystery Series:
Hush-Hush – Holiday #1
Hubba-Hubba – Holiday #2
Hard Noir – Holiday #3

LIKE A BLAST FROM A DOUBLE-BARRELED SHOTGUN,
TWO HARD NOIR LA NOVELS
IN *ONE* BLOOD–STAINED VOLUME:

THROWBACK
&
BACKLASH

LOVE, LUST & MURDER SERIES

KIRK ALEX

TUCUMCARI PRESS

Tucson — 2018

ISBN: 978-0-939122-63-9 (6x9 pbk)

Contents

THROWBACK
Love, Lust & Murder
Book One

KIRK ALEX

TUCUMCARI PRESS

Tucson — 2018

Throwback: Love, Lust & Murder — Book One is a work of fiction. Names, characters, places and incidents are either the product of the author's imagination or are used fictitiously. Any resemblance to actual persons, living or dead, or to actual events or locales is entirely coincidental.

ISBN: 978-0-939122-54-7 (6x9 pbk)
ISBN: 978-0-939122-55-4 (ePUB)

Dedicated to the late, great Dan Fante for creating the unforgettable Bruno Dante series of novels, as well as the exceptional murder mystery entitled *Point Doom*. RIP.

"I zigged when I should have zagged."
—Ernest Hemingway

Chapter 1

Sure. Peeps kill for *love* and *money*. Nothing unusual there. Pick up a paper, any paper—any day of the week—and there it is: Hubby walks in on wife with her lover & blows them away. Turn the tv on & it's: Hubs shoves his Significant Other down a precipice to gain full access to her Benjamins.

Then you have the type of situation fueled by some of this, and some of that, as in: Jilted wife and one-time socialite breaks into her former spouse's home in the middle of the night with a loaded .38, strolls into the master bedroom, where the ex and his new bride are sound asleep, and sprays them with lead.

Yep. At times can be a mix of both, with a bit of nitro called *lust* tossed into the cocktail to make it entirely combustible. In this particular case that's exactly what it was: combo of all three. *Love, Lust & Greed.* Triptych of chaos. Flammable and deadly. About the only thing 'unusual' about it, and makes you shake your head, is what set the nightmarish chain of events in motion. A dead car battery. An effing DB.

What caused the DB? Loose nut under the brake pedal in this used ten-year-old Toyota that belonged to the woman I was shacked with at the time. The bitch of it was it didn't matter if you turned the lights off, because the brake lights would stay on. What you had to do was jiggle the goddamn brake pedal with your foot a bit and make sure *all the lights were off* when you cut the engine. If you didn't, you were in deep shit—because that was all it took to drain the effing battery.

But hey, who can remember to do that every time? Especially after pulling a long-ass night delivering pizza for your measly bread and butter. I mean that was the last thing on my mind, the brake pedal and to check and make sure ALL the lights were off.

It was 2 a.m. by the time I got home. And it wasn't until three and a half hours later, when I was awakened by Monica trying to start the car, did it occur to me what I may have done.

I was having the usual money issues. My meager take-home consisted of tips mostly and was never steady like hers. She never said anything about it. If I was short on my end, Monica would come through without a word. She was always great. Still, it was something that nagged at me.

I'd been trying to land a job driving a truck for the studios (as I'd heard how well it paid), or maybe I could do stunt work, it didn't matter to me—as long as the money was there. But it was hard. The unions wouldn't let you in. It came down to nepotism, who you knew. I'd been trying to break in for two years, ever since coming out to LA from the Midwest. It wasn't until I'd met Monica at a party I'd crashed in the Hollywood Hills eight months before and talked to her about it that I even thought I had a chance. She was a secretary at one of the production companies in Burbank. As far as she was concerned, persistence was key, and not to get discouraged. All I was after was a fresh start, a chance to get somewhere. I had a history I wasn't proud of, runs-ins with the man, in and out of jail. I needed to get away from the craziness of it, because I knew it would lead to no good. You know?—a dead-fucking-end. And so that's how I wound up in the Valley, spinning my wheels.

I didn't give a shit for movies or actors; I wasn't out for fame or to make a million bucks, just a regular job that paid a decent wage. That's what I saw the truck driving gig as: a way to put a few bucks in the bank, buy a decent used car, maybe a trailer to live in, maybe even a house of my own. Give myself a shot at the 'American Dream.' Was it pie-in-the-sky? Were the odds against it? That's yes—to both. Millions of peeps were in the same boat. But when you're young, and I was young at the time, you do your best to cling to a bit of hope, feel like it might be worth having something to strive for, as in a better life, a way to improve your lot.

So now, with the car not wanting to start (and Monica possibly missing her early a.m. aerobics class) and all of it being my fault, it made me unhappy.

I got the bathrobe on and staggered into the living room. Chambray, her Pyrenees mix, barked as the front door opened. She hadn't expected it to be Monica. Chambray can be a mean mother who barks only at strangers and what she perceives to be sounds made by strangers. She hadn't been fully awake or something, so she barked. Once she saw that it was Monica, she settled down.

"It won't start."

"It's the battery."

I was the desperate one and no doubt sounded like it. Monica had a way of remaining undaunted when life's many little nerve-racking problems would crop up. I liked that about her.

"Damn. I forgot to check the brake lights when I came in. What probably caused it."

I felt bad about it. Couldn't help being pissed. I had Triple A, but unless you were stranded on some deserted road, late at night, you didn't call Triple-A—not unless you wanted your membership to go up. So when she suggested the auto club, I nixed it.

"What are we going to do, honey? I'll be late for work."

I kept cursing and shaking my head. It never solved much. That's the way I was back then. Monica tried to calm me down. I cursed.

"Can you call one of your friends to give you a jump?"

"Not at this hour. Besides, there's no room for another car in our yard, let alone a pickup truck or a van." That's what the guys I knew drove, of the few people that I knew in LA.

We lived in a modest, one-bedroom California bungalow in the back. There was a two-car garage to the left of our bungalow, a stall for the guy who owned the small photography shop in the front, and a stall for us. It was too early for the shop to be open.

Lambert Miles owned the real estate both properties were on, and came in to work when he felt like it, which was usually around ten, other times he didn't go in at all. Ten o'clock would have been way too late, on the outside chance he showed, so that was out. Opening, and then closing the creaky old garage door, if we wanted to use our stall, seemed like more trouble than it was worth, and so, as a matter of convenience, we parked the bucket in the small yard that separated the shop in front and the house we lived in in the back. There certainly would not have been enough room for a vehicle to pull up next to ours to jump it. Also, some of these guys I was acquainted with lived in their junkers, no access to a phone. Like yours truly used to.

I was too upset by then to think of pushing our car into the garage, therefore creating enough room for another short to get in there and give us a jump, but all this would have taken time, and time was something Monica was running out of. She would be late.

While I paced, bitching and grumbling, she got on the phone and dialed a co-worker's number.

"I hope Sally hasn't left."

A moment later, and her friend Sally answered at the other end.

"Thank God. Sally, it's Monica. Can I get a ride? My car won't start. Thanks, Sally."

We were both relieved. Sally lived in Studio City and would be able to swing by our place easily enough and drop my girlfriend at her job in Burbank. I still looked pretty miserable.

"Oh honey, don't worry. It'll be all right."

"I know. I'm just angry with myself for blowing your aerobics class."

She gave me a kiss. "As long as I get to work I'll be all right."

Who could ask for more? She was a gem.

"I'm sorry."

"Honey, you worry too much."

"I'll be okay."

We hugged, kissed again, and she went outside to wait for Sally.

Chapter 2

My weary body was sending desperate signals that I needed to return to bed and get caught up on sleep. Instead, I got into a pair of jeans, my old army shirt, and went out to the car and adjusted the nut under the brake pedal. Two minutes later and it was taken care of. The lights went off. I tried starting the car. The juice that remained in the battery was not enough to do it.

I staggered back to the house for the shuteye I needed and didn't get up again until about 2 in the afternoon. That's what a night job did to you—ruined you and your days, too.

The solution to the car issue was a simple one really: the battery needed recharging. I popped open the hood, checked the brake fluid—it was low. Refilled it. Checked the oil. Oil was good. Checked the water in the battery. *There was no water in the battery.*

Nothing.

We took such good care of that car. Battery probably hadn't been tended to in months. Yes, we took great care when it came to that car.

I poured water in, two full *Dr Pepper* bottles, let it sit a while, and tried again. No go.

So I removed the battery, put Chambray on a leash. During the day I was a babysitter: Chambray couldn't be left alone; she was neurotic that way. Even though we had reinforced the bit of backyard fence between the house and the garage, she always got out—and when she got out she attacked people. And if we left her inside the house she would tear up the place. The only solution was to always have one of us with her.

I didn't have the heart to leave her in the car. Chambray was an all white, half Great Pyrenees Mountain Dog/ half something else, who had sunk her teeth into three people, that I knew of. She didn't usually go around biting people at random; she just didn't like strangers to approach either Monica or me. In the 8 months I'd known Monica this dog had come to accept me as part of the family, and I had to admit I felt the same way about her. But yes, it hadn't been easy going in the beginning for us. She'd attempted to lunge at me a couple of times, until I finally had to stare her down and make sure she understood: If I got bit, there would be consequences.

Yeah, I knew she had her problems, but she was just a dog, after all. Still, if we wanted to keep her we had to be extra cautious. Living in this area of the Valley in particular, we wanted to keep her. Too many burglaries committed by hard up druggies, too many assaults on women, and other crimes. With my working the graveyard shift and Monica all alone at night (back then she preferred not to have guns around), a dog like Chambray was the only reasonable solution. She'd brought her down from Phoenix when she moved to LA six years before we met.

I swung the car battery up on my shoulder, wound the end of the leash tightly round my right wrist, and walked the two or three blocks to the gas station.

Chapter 3

"Yes, we charge batteries." The gas station attendant was from the Middle-East and spoke with a heavy accent. "Four dollars."

I left the battery there and let him know I would return in about an hour. Chambray and I crossed the street, headed north. Reached the neighborhood park. Park was huge. Had a baseball field, tennis and basketball courts, monkey bars and olympic rings. I decided I wanted to do some pull-ups for a while to kill the time. It was a warm, sunny day and I wanted to enjoy what was left of it before returning to the pizza joint later that evening where I worked.

The dog and I got on the gravel path and took it toward the monkey bars. The only thing I did not like about the park, although a city facility, they had like a daycare center for young kids housed in one of the buildings and there were always kids around, playing in the sandbox, throwing rocks and empty pop bottles and cans around. I didn't like it because it would have been nearly impossible to so much as do a single pull-up without fearing some kid might go up to the dog and start petting her. It did not matter to the Pyrenees how young or how old the individual was, if the person approached her and Chambray did not know him or her, she would bite. Period. This was the great fear. What had made the dog this way? I didn't know, and neither did Monica, and she'd raised her from a fairly young age.

Fact was, Chambray didn't cotton to strangers. Gender made no difference or who the person was. Without warning, without anything, other than a low growl maybe, other times nothing: no growl, nada—if they attempted to get near her, or me, she'd bite.

So I was worried, especially when this five or six-year-old kid refused to keep his distance, even after countless warnings. He was determined to play with 'the pretty dog.' I was doing chin-ups on the monkey bars and had Chambray tied to a post when this kid kept getting closer and closer.

"I'm telling you she bites. Stay away."

"Why?"

"She bites, that's why."

I thought I better get down and walk over. I'd had my sunglasses on and the kid wanted to know if I was a movie star.

"No, I'm not. Don't go near the dog."

"Take your glasses off."

"Stay away from the dog."

A blond-haired girl, a little older than the boy, came by with a handful of sand and flung it at him. The kid picked up a brick and was about to retaliate. I stopped him.

"What's your dog's name?" the boy wanted to know, and got real close.

"Chambray. Now, will you stay away?"

"I want to pet her."

"No, you don't."

The kid insisted.

I couldn't reason with him. Chambray growled. I held her down. The kid got real close and put his hand on top of the dog's head.

"Get away. She bites."

The kid shook his head, and continued to pet the dog. "See, she won't bite me."

I kept my hand by Chambray's jaw. The girl had a little more sense than the boy: she didn't get too close.

"My father says if a dog bites you, you can sue."

"Sure you can sue. That's why I say stay away."

Chambray continued with the warning growl. I held her down.

"It's all right, Chambray. Calm down."

The kid continued to pet her. He had both hands on Chambray.

"Please don't do that. I'm telling you *she bites.*"

The kid smiled and shook his head, and briefly took his hands away from the dog. Because Chambray had stopped growling, I had allowed myself to relax. I knew I shouldn't have, but I did. That was when the Pyrenees snapped at him. It had happened so lightning quick I hadn't even been certain I saw it take place. The kid jumped back in shock. Not a sound came out of him for about two or three seconds, then he let out a wail. He screamed at the top of his lungs. I tied the dog's leash to the chain link fence in back of us. Went over to the boy.

"She didn't bite you, did she?"

I wasn't sure. It had happened too damned fast. The kid continued to scream. It was then I noticed the blood on the kid's neck. Not a lot of it. A dot. In fact, it was barely visible. One quarter of an inch in diameter. I wiped it with my hand and the kid got louder.

"I'M BLEEDING! I'M BLEEDING!"

I was all nerves, but did my best to maintain. "Did you fall?"

Kid shook his head. "SHE BIT ME! SHE BITTT ME!"

"What happened? The dog didn't bite you. You must have tripped or something."

The kid kept shaking his head and was screaming. *"I'M BLEEDING! I'M BLEEDING!"*

More blood appeared. I glanced at the teenagers shooting hoops about sixty/seventy feet from where we were. No one paid any attention to us.

They were immersed in their game. I walked back to the fence, untied the leash, and walked as fast as I knew how (without running) in a westerly direction. I could feel my heart pounding. My throat had gone dry on me.

Goddamn it, I knew it was the wrong thing to do, but we couldn't afford another medical bill. The last one had cost eighty dollars. I couldn't afford to buy a pair of pants. We didn't have money in the budget for doctor bills. Worse yet, I was worried the dog might get taken away. I knew in time the boy would be okay, after the initial shock wore off. Chambray didn't have anything. She was clean. The boy was going to be all right.

We crossed the street, and just before ducking behind a building on the corner there I turned my head and could see one of the women who worked at the daycare, with the young vic and his sister in tow, questioning the basketball players.

We made it to the gas station. I paid the gas station attendant four bucks for the charge. Asked him to step back so that I could pick up the battery.

"She bites."

"She bite?"

I nodded. *"She bites."*

I wished people would take my word for it.

He stepped back. "I think this kind of dog do not bite."

"They do."

He gave me room.

I lifted the battery, thanked him, and left.

Chapter 4

By the time we got back to the house I was sweating, I was sweating like someone who had just participated in a twenty-six-mile marathon, and it wasn't entirely from hauling the heavy car battery,

either. I could still hear the kid's voice screaming in my head. *"I'M BLEEDING! I'M BLEEEEEDIIIINNNNNG!"*

The kid was going to be fine. I knew it. But I couldn't get his voice out of my head. What I had done was wrong. No one had to tell me that. Not going back seemed like the best solution. No one had to tell me I was wrong in that respect, either. But, dammit, I couldn't go back. I didn't want us to have to deal with *Five-0* again, or the kid's parents. I didn't want to give Monica more problems to worry about. Little, every day things she could cope with better than I. But everyone has their limit. I didn't want to see Monica fall into another depression. I wanted to spare her that. Because the dog was actually hers, whatever she did, she felt responsible. She would have felt responsible for it this time, too. The last time Chambray bit an old woman Monica was in a funk for two weeks straight. She was too good a person to deserve it. I wouldn't tell her, no matter what.

I left the battery on the front porch, chained Chambray to the post in the yard, and went looking for the nearest bar. I needed a beer.

Chapter 5

Bunch of keys dangled from a carabiner on his belt in the right hip area. There was a chrome chain that was attached to the keyring at that end and was attached to a loop near the silver belt buckle at the other. There was a second chrome chain with thicker links that went from his hip pocket and the billfold in it to the same loop in the front of his jeans.

I recognized the sweat-stained Stetson wearing macho blowhard from his numerous appearances on news programs and tv talk shows throughout the Midwest. He loved publicity. Whenever he had a bail jumper that he was bringing in there always seemed to be a camera on the event. The showoff thrived on it. How did I know so much about him? I had been one of those bail jumpers the mofo bagged a few years back. I hoped the mother wouldn't recognize me, and he might not have if I hadn't opened my mouth. He not only nailed the Midwest accent right away, but noticed the name on my army shirt. In my rattled state I'd forgotten to take it off back at the house. I was done. No way around it.

"I know you from somewhere?"

There he was, acting like he didn't.

"It's quite possible, sir."

He was one of those middle-age a-holes who got rowdy when drunk; big and loud, a real ass-kicking type I never liked being around, and he had a bushy, walrus type stash that lots of folks, myself included, were inclined to find repulsive.

I asked where his videographers were. He was known for having his own personal camera team with him when he went out on hunts. Like the time he bagged me in Santa Fe and hauled me back to where I'd jumped bail: there was a married couple with him, filming. So I wondered about that.

"Publicity generates income, jobs. My videographers got kids. Didn't want to leave the Midwest. Like me, hate LA. Only reason I'm in this sewer is because my wife's got this bug up her ass: wants to be in the movies. Been here before, on business; was also a tech advisor on a couple of cable shows. It's a cesspool. Hollywood is full of Commie scum. Can't stomach 'em. But it comes down to making my young wife happy. Now, my other wife, the ex I had two kids by ain't too pleased about that, having the kids two thousand miles away. Tried to tell her it's only temporary. This thing with Marge wanting to make it in the movies is pure bullshit and won't last."

He wanted to know what made me trade my home town for LA LA. I couldn't tell him I needed to get the hell away from the likes of him and rollers with a chip on their shoulder and a hard-on for me and maybe try for a new start on the west coast.

"Couldn't take those winters anymore. And job prospects. Union studio drivers make good money."

"You figure you might do that here in LA?"

I just got through telling him that I did.

He shook his head. "Now, this might sound cynical, but them union jobs are locked up. Gotta know peeps. Outsiders rarely, if ever, get in. Just the way it is. Hate to break it to you this way. Same goes for ingenues. Tried to tell my young wife: Only way good looking young hotties like her get in is by gettin' down on their knees and blowing tubesteak. How Marilyn Monroe did it; how so many of 'em got their first break: Suckin' dick. Siphoning nutsack chowder. Now, if some son of a bitch tries that shit with her all she's gotta do is let me know, and I'll deal with the motherfucker personally. I told her that. Sure did, Alf. Come to Daddy, and Daddy will take care of it." He paused to think about something for a minute. "Been here less than a month this time and bad shit's already begun happening to further feed '*bad vibes*' about '*this diseased whore of a town*'. Had nothing but bad vibes about this snake pit all along. And so far I've been more than spot-on." And another double went down his gullet. "Now, my young wife Marjorie, I call her Marge, she don't feel that way at all. She likes it."

"She likes LA?"

He nodded. "Believe it or not, Freddie Reed. My young wife just loves LA. She loves it here. Loves the rotting palm trees, mansions crawling with rats, polluted beaches, flash floods and quakes, the flakes. Mostly the flakes." He ordered another double. Turned to face me again. "My wife is going to be a '*movie star,*' Freddie Reed. That's why we're in this fuckin' toilet. That's the *only* reason we're here."

The double arrived. Frank only sipped at it this time. "I'll tell you something else, Freddie Reed, just between you and me, she don't give a damn about the kids. And I know that for a fact. Between you and me."

I didn't say anything because I knew I had no right to.

"She don't care. Why should she? They're not hers. Why should she give a damn? She wants to act, be a star; she don't care about nothing else. Goddamn fame-struck opportunist."

Next thing I knew, it was the photo. Out, it came. From his wallet. Laminated. A raven-haired, mixed-race looker with a clear complexion;

full lipstick red mouth and large sultry eyes that you were immediately drawn to. No doubt he feared he might lose her in this town known for its glitz and glamor, known also for how quickly it devoured and spit out wannabe starlets like this woman he was married to.

"Is she a beauty? *Or is she a beauty?* One third Swiss or maybe Italian, one third Rican, and the last third negro. Lookit that natural tan. Bronze skin made my mouth water first time I laid eyes on her; still does. She a good looking negro wench, or what?"

"She's a beauty, Mr. Graham."

The photo went back in the wallet and the wallet was jammed back in the hip pocket.

"I don't know if she can act or not. Hell, she could make it on looks alone. Good lookin' mixed-race number like her. More and more lately, studios see there's real money to be made by making roles available to ethnic types. Explains why we're seein' so many all over the tube. Can't get away from it. Most of 'em got no talent to speak of. Colored and wetbacks. Ruinin' the country. Fuckin' Mexicans. Illegals. Criminal pukes. But they're in. Marketplace makes it possible. Networks and studios never miss an opportunity to make a buck. And Marge, with that body and face, has better than an equal shot. What I'm afraid of. Then, of course, we'll stay put for good, or at least until her career gets under way, and then we move back. Gonna be hard, though. Dealing with all this Holly-weird scum; Lefty slime bags. Can't stomach the bullshit. Every asshole you meet is a producer. Only thing most of them can produce is a business card. It's a con. Pissants rent a small office on some half-ass movie lot, put a sign on their door: *Blow-Me Productions.* They're a producer now. Horseshit. Pay some artist a few bucks to sketch up a movie poster, run ads for ingenues in movie publications to make it look legit on the surface, but they still ain't produced a fuckin' thing. Business cards. That's all most of them ever produced. Buncha *pimps and whores. Fruits and nuts.* Phony cocksuckers."

I didn't know, didn't care. All I wanted was a regular job that paid real money, maybe buy a decent pre-owned car. Do my best to put my past behind me.

Chapter 6

It was getting to be 8 o'clock and we were both pretty soused. I knew Monica would be worried, and that I should have called to let her know, but didn't. Drunk, laughing, shouting and cursing, that kid was still on my mind. I would be late getting in to my job. If I got in.

Frank Graham asked what I did for a living these days, while waiting for the driving job.

"I deliver pizza."

"That's nothing to be ashamed of. Takes a good while for a man to get his bearings."

"I'm closing in on 28. It's no gig."

"You'll do all right. It takes time to figure things out, what you want to do with your life."

He made a suggestion. Maybe he could work it out so that I might go along with him on some of the hunts, soon as he got situated. Tape his exploits. Maybe one day he'd be able to sell the lot to a cable network. There were nibbles. Nothing worth his while. *Yet.* What the hell? Could be a few dollars in it for both of us. Besides, it promoted work. Bail bondsmen saw him on tv and got in touch. Just like back home. He'd been out this way a few times in the past and knew enough people in local law enforcement.

"Appreciate the offer, but you wouldn't need somebody like me."

"Sure, I would. You know the city better than I do. I could go out and hire one of these Pinko movie people, or some wannabe actor former cop—but I wouldn't like to. They make me puke, most of 'em around here. Besides, you're from the Midwest and a war vet to boot. You deserve a break."

Even after close to two years of kicking around in LA I still hardly knew Southern California. Place was way too big and spread out. I was familiar with Hollywood and the San Fernando Valley well enough, I supposed.

"I guess we can try it."

"There's money in it, Freddie Reed. I guarantee it. It's dangerous work, can be, but it pays well when it pays."

He pulled up his shirt to reveal several old bullet scars, dagger scars, surgery scars. He was proud he'd lived through it all.

"Why do you think I do it? It ain't just the thrill of the hunt that keeps this *old dawg* getting up every morning."

I didn't know what to think. It was past 10 o'clock by now and he had trouble sitting up. The barkeep kept hinting I take my 'friend' outside. I tried. Frank Graham wouldn't hear of it until I gave him my home phone. He insisted he wanted me to work with him.

A guy like me couldn't afford to be rude to a guy like this. Besides, guys like this had connections, and it wouldn't have been tough for him to track my number down. It made it easier all around just to let him have it.

"Not many young people your age who got their head on right."

I thought maybe he was putting me on, only he'd meant it.

"We all make mistakes, so long as we learn from 'em. Looks like you learned from yours. It's in the past."

I hoped so. Then thought: If I had my head on right, what the hell was I doing being a pizzeria delivery flunky at my age? I was no kid, that was for sure. Thirty was but two years away.

Well, I had a record. For this and that. It was enough for most employers to hold it against you. Not all. Most. Who could blame them? Only I had to get money in my pocket. I had to get something going. I was desperate for it. Without money you might as well be dead; without money you ended up sleeping in the park like all those homeless people living out of cars and spending their days on park benches.

I had this fear of it happening to me, and in fact, I had been sleeping in my Buick, before it gave out completely, when I met Monica and then moved in with her. So Monica had been a real lifesaver in more ways than one. The other thing was: I wanted to stay out of stir. I'd had enough of that scene. And was determined. No matter what it took. All I had to do was walk that straight and narrow. Pizza delivery was one way, while waiting for the break.

Finally, I got Frank Graham to stand up, and managed to help him walk outside in search of his van. He kept pointing out the van had signs on the sides and back that said *Throwback's Ready Rooter*, or some such, and to look for pipes on the overhead rack.

I spotted the van. It was an ordeal getting him to it. Frank Graham was no little guy. Built like Duke Wayne and just about as tall. He had a good 60 pounds on me. I'm 6ft, tops, and weigh 170. It was an ordeal.

I got him inside the back of the van. He was unconscious, but kept mumbling. *"I catch him, I'll kill him with my bare hands. . . ."*

Chapter 7

I drove the late model van to the address he'd given me earlier. It made me edgy and nervous because the house was directly across the street from the park. I kept hearing the kid's voice over and over in my head. Having consumed beer after beer hadn't helped wash it away.

I parked in front of the house, slumped against the steering wheel, wondering where the boy was and the hell his parents must be going through. They had no way of knowing that the dog was disease-free. I hoped they wouldn't force the kid to undergo the rabies shots and waited a while to see that he was going to be all right. Tetanus? Yes. You knew they had to do that, but the other? A week's worth of rabies shots? It bothered me.

The light came on in the house and I sat up and slowly turned in its direction. It was typical Southern Cal. Spanish style. Maybe two bedrooms. Nothing fancy. It looked gray in the evening light. There was a lawn in front that hadn't been tended to in weeks, and a picket fence just as neglected.

The front door opened and a female stood on the other side of the screen. "Frank? Is that you, Frank?"

It took me a moment to snap out of my stupor.

"Yes, it is. I mean, it's your husband, Frank."

I staggered out of the van and made it to the back door and leaned against it and didn't move. I just stood there. My skull was tight, pounding. Getting drunk never agreed with me.

I threw my head forward and it came up, all of it. I heaved and I coughed and when I was through I fell back and staggered against the tire. My eyes closed, and I wanted to sleep.

Her voice shook me awake. It was pleasant-sounding, angelic. She had a handkerchief in her hand and was wiping my mouth. I looked up and could see that the back doors to the van were open. It was a kind of blurred image. That was all I could get for a couple of minutes, the doors and this female figure in a night robe looking inside the van and looking down at me.

"Jesus Christ, Frank."

She shook her head in disgust. I mumbled an apology and explained that I usually didn't get like this. I didn't hear the lady say anything. When my vision cleared, I saw her wiping tears with a Kleenex. She was in her early or mid-20s, dark hair that was long and wavy. From what I could see in the night, her eyes had a mesmerizing indigo tint to them. To say they were hypnotic would not be far off. The moonlight bounced off her hair and gave it a kind of shine. She had the type of face that wasn't cute or pretty, but made you want to get a better look all the same. That photo of her Graham carried around in his wallet didn't do her justice. Not even close. Sitting down there on the pavement and looking up at her, she reminded me of a Greek goddess, something like that. It wasn't often that a face, just the face, brought about carnal desire in me, especially not the shape I was in, but this face did. I was hard down there. I felt sick, but I was as hard as the curb I was sitting on.

"I'm sorry, Marge." I found myself apologizing for the condition her husband and I were both in. Never having met the woman, addressing her by her first name showed how out of it I was.

She kept wiping her eyes and not saying anything. I rose to my feet.

"If you can give me a hand. I think we can get him inside."

Then I toppled back down, my head pounding away like a jackhammer. I continued to apologize and explain that I hadn't been like this in five years and that something had happened that made me want to tie one on.

She blew her nose and stuffed the Kleenex in her pocket.

"Once every five years? With Frank, it's every five days."

She helped me up. We soon realized that attempting to lift her husband was going to be impossible. So we didn't even try. Closed the van doors. She mentioned that they had hydrogen peroxide and Band-Aids in the house and that she'd be right back to help take care of my cuts. I nodded, appreciating the kindness. As she stepped away, she did a sudden about-face and suggested it might be easier if she didn't have to come back out carrying the items with her.

Chapter 8

She offered a shoulder to lean on and I limped along with her to the front door. A mean, muscular Dobie was at the fenced-in gate to the left of the front entrance. He wasn't barking, but the growls were a clear sign that he meant business. Not unlike Chambray, he was ready to tear you apart, if only given the chance. Figured it was Graham's dog that he took on some of the hunts with. Didn't have him years before when he bagged me, though. I believe he had a Rottweiler back then. Equally mean, to be sure.

We were inside the living room when I was reminded that she had kids sleeping in the back and that we had to keep it down.

"Thank you."

"For what?"

I shrugged. "Helping."

She shrugged her own shoulders and put a Band-aid on a cut I had on my forehead. It was here I noticed she had a small strip of a Band-aid over her left temple, and another just below her left ear. I paid no mind or knew what it was about. Could have been scratches caused by the Dobie, or was a battered wife. Wouldn't have surprised me, just from seeing the type of redneck bully she was married to. I didn't know and had no right asking. She set about to make some coffee. That's when she broke down again.

I had mixed feelings as to what to do and half-nervously put my arms around her and attempted to console her. She wept in my shoulder. I guided her to a chair and we stayed like this for a few minutes until she'd had time to regain her composure, then she broke away and poured coffee for us. I took mine black, and let her know how ashamed I was about the whole mess.

She said it wasn't my fault.

"I know. Still feel kind of bad about it."

She wept. Never making a sound.

I found myself apologizing. Explained that it came down to her husband and I talking about the part of the Midwest we were from.

She looked up. Surprised to hear I was from there. Asked what part.

"North Side."

She wanted to know how far north.

I told her.

Turned out she'd gone to high school in the area.

"Really?"

Mentioned the year she graduated.

The only school I graduated from was hard knocks. Didn't matter, because from then on, it was much easier to talk. We sipped our coffee and reminisced about the various neighborhoods, one in particular. She wanted to know when I had been there last. I told her it had been a while. And she said that it had changed a lot.

"That's what I hear. Old Town is not Old Town anymore."

"Nope. It's a high-class neighborhood now. Gentrified. No more street thugs. Practically crime-free. That area, anyway. It's clean, and it's nice. But I don't miss it. We were there during the last blizzard, and I don't miss it one tiny bit. I'm glad we're on the West Coast this winter."

I wanted to say that I was glad she was spending the winter on the West Coast, too, but didn't. It might have been out of line.

Chapter 9

We talked way into the night. Well, she did most of it, I listened. She touched on her dreams of becoming an actress, about her *Italian* stepfather and mixed-race mother, about her marrying Graham against her instincts and because her widowed mother had practically coerced her into it because he had money in the bank and his home paid for, and because she had been pregnant at the time (knocked up by an eighteen year-old drop-out she had been dating) and the subsequent miscarriage, and the fact she never wanted kids. Had nothing against them, but merely felt she wasn't capable of being a good mother; wasn't qualified, that's all. She had dreams and goals and kids would've made it nearly impossible to do anything, get anywhere. She didn't like her life with Graham, didn't relate to his offspring. But she made it plain enough that as long as she was his wife she wouldn't stray.

I stayed aroused the whole time. The womanly smell of her being behind it. She was the type I'd always had fantasies about. I wondered what she would look like in a dress and high heels, hair all done up.

And it wasn't before long that she had her high school album out, showing me pictures of her in various school plays she'd been in. If she didn't have talent, she sure could make it on looks alone. And stone drunk Frank Graham lying out there in that van knew it, too, and it worried him. And I understood fully why. Every Tom, Dick and Harriet in Hollywood would be out trying to bed his beauty down. I wasn't even in show business, but I was already thinking about it: me and Marge; kissing, embracing, undressing each other; naked in that bed in back.

She was a big-breasted woman I could easily tell even with that robe she had on. I wondered just how big she really was. I wanted her. My balls were beginning to ache. I got fidgety and stood up. I think she knew what was happening because she smiled.

"I should be going. Thanks for the coffee."

"You're in no condition to walk."

"You ain't just whistlin' Dixie."

This made her chuckle. "That's not what I mean."

"You're a good looking woman."

"What's the rush? Frank is out."

"Thought you weren't the type to stray?"

She walked over and gave me a good, hard slap that drew blood. She pulled back for another one. I grabbed her arm and held it there.

"How dare you talk to me like that? You're no gentleman; you're no gentleman at all."

"Never claimed it."

"You try to act like it. You're no gentleman."

"I got a rule says don't mess with no woman married to a guy like Frank Graham. I try to live by that rule."

"You don't know what it's like living with that. He's no good. He's tired."

"He's the type who can get pretty mean, too."

"You scared, Reed?"

"Yup."

"You're fag, ain't you? Ain't you?"

"That's a wedding band on your finger, Mrs. Graham."

"You're queer, aren't you?"

I tugged gingerly at my aching loins. "Right now, maybe I wish I was. Maybe." I opened the front door. "I'll see you sometime."

"You're a dead man, Fred."

"How's that?"

"Should I tell him now, or wait until he wakes up?"

I just looked at her. She wasn't making sense. Then she said to follow her.

"Don't worry, Alfred. I won't try to seduce you."

I followed to a bedroom in the back. She flicked on a night light and stood by a set of twin bunks. There were two kids asleep in those bunks, and one of them was the dark-haired boy Chambray had sunk her teeth into at the park.

Chapter 10

"Need I explain?"

"No."

"I saw the whole thing from the living room window. The way you scurried out of sight."

"The kid will be all right. The dog is clean."

"You sure?"

"Sure, I'm sure."

"Frank don't know it. You think maybe we should tell him?"

I didn't respond. Asked her to show me where the john was. I grabbed at the bottle of mouthwash and gargled plenty, spit it out, then gargled some more, then pulled her toward me and kissed her hard on the lips.

We broke, and made for the other bedroom. I didn't have time to get out of my clothes, nothing, just unbutton my fly. She went for it, like a mad woman. The assault threw me off balance and I staggered back against the bed, landing on my back. She was on her knees, going at it. I lifted my head to watch. She was one hungry wench. Goddamn. It was unbelievable. I watched that head of hers go up and down, bobbing. She'd look up from time to time with those manic eyes. Seemed to turn her on that I was watching. It was almost scary. In fact, it was. Scary to witness. Seeing a woman this needy; scary and the best kind of turn on.

I unbuttoned my belt buckle, undid the top button on my trousers. I wanted them down, all the way, to give her easier access; only she had her hands on either hip and tugged on them before I'd had a chance to. I lifted my legs, and she yanked the pants off, tried to. Sneakers were in the way. She got them off in a fury, and attacked my privates with a continued frenzy.

It was stunning to witness. I was effing speechless. Made you wonder where the bitch learned the business, because I'd never experienced anything like it, not with this type of intensity.

I reached for one of the pillows to my left, shoved it under my head and dropped my head back. Heard her spit. I Glanced down. She was spitting right on the head of it, and stroked. She spit some more. Damn.

She lifted my legs, then started licking. Then her tongue went down and under. Get it, I thought. Get it, babe. This was one desperate female in need. Then she was back on the pole, her tongue circling the head; took it inside her mouth and inhaled it like a Mega-Vac. Unbelievable. I was wincing. It felt that great. Found myself gasping as I exploded.

Chapter 11

She shed her clothes while I rested, taking in her body—and what a body it was. Before I knew what was happening, she straddled me: a thigh at either side of my face. It was time to reciprocate—and reciprocate I would. She was moaning. I looked up to see that she had her eyes closed, head tilted back, and she was making sounds.

I wanted to give back in kind. The broad had given me one incredible blow job and I wanted to see her get off. The way I was. Some mofos never want to take the time. Have to admit, I'd been this way now and then. Not here; not with this insatiable ho.

I proceeded with every bit of passion I could muster and felt her begin to quiver, her entire body quivered. She was shaking and wincing, making way too much noise, I thought, and had to remind her about the kids. She did lower the audio, but not altogether; she hadn't been able to. Then she screamed; covered up her mouth but continued screaming and creaming. I stayed with it until she could no longer take it. She climaxed time after time. Then she rolled off, collapsing beside me.

Chapter 12

We did more, a lot more. She acted as though she hadn't had any in months, or longer. Probably longer. She had mentioned that Graham was 'tired.' I believed it. Said he'd hardly touched her ever since the miscarriage years before. Marge was making up for it. I believed this as well. We did everything you can imagine. Miscarriage didn't hinder me in the least. Nope. Didn't think about it. That was Graham's hangup, as well as loss.

His lady and I even picked up the last act back inside the tub. She wouldn't let go. Couldn't get enough. It got kinky. Hot and kinky. Most of it her doing. I lost count after the fourth or fifth time. And we would have kept on if exhaustion hadn't finally kicked our butts and I did need to get back.

We broke. I pushed her away long enough to finish my shower and get into my clothes.

"Will I see you again?"

I couldn't say. "Hubs wants to hire me."

"To do what? Track down the beast that mauled his kid?"

I didn't think that part was funny. I kissed her good-night, and left.

Now here was a woman who needed to get laid on a steady basis. As much as I was inclined to oblige, I wondered if I could. Graham sure as hell wasn't doing it. Besides, I was clearly being coerced.

Chapter 13

It was unusual for me to come in this late. Monica was up when I walked in. She looked concerned, as though she'd been crying.

"Your boss called. Wondered why you weren't in."

"Ran into someone from my home town. We had a few drinks."

"Till 4 in the morning?"

It's against the law to sell booze after 2 in LA, so I had to correct that real fast.

"After the bar closed we went over to his place."

I considered fabricating some tale about him being an old army buddy and how he'd saved my life in 'Nam, but then thought better of it.

"Hon, few hours after you left for work, I thought I better get the battery charged; and did. Took Chambray with me. Dropped the battery off at that gas station near here. Guy said it would take a while to recharge it, so I thought I'd take the dog for a walk and maybe do a few dips and chin-ups on the parallel bars at the park."

I had wanted to spare her by not telling her about her dog snapping at someone else. Hell.

"Long story short, hon: Chambray attacked a kid; this little boy. Nothing serious, but serious enough. I panicked, and got out of there. I couldn't risk seeing the dog get put down. I know how much she means to you, so I took off. Got back here with the battery, all sweaty and feeling shitty. I had to go find a bar, get a drink. I met this guy from my home town. After the bar closed we went to his place and drank a few beers. Well, I had beers, he had the hard stuff. He was too drunk to drive himself, and I drove him home. The irony is the kid is his. The whole thing is just one big mess."

"Does he know it was Chambray who attacked his son?"

I shook my head.

"No. Not yet, anyway." I looked at her, stood there and just looked at her. She had stopped crying at this point. "He doesn't know, but his wife does. She saw the whole thing from her living room window from across the street."

"My god. . . ."

"Yep. Could be we're fucked."

She heaved a sigh. She was shaking her head.

"What do we do, Monica? If we don't say anything the kid faces a bunch of rabies shots; and if we do, Chambray gets put to sleep. She's got a history."

"She's clean, Fred. Chambray is clean. Does the man's wife know this? Did you tell her? The kid has nothing to worry about."

"We know that. So does the man's wife. I pleaded with her to give us time. The kids aren't hers biologically. They're his kids."

"Where there other witnesses? Anyone else see you?"

"There was the boy's sister, about the same age. A bunch of guys were playing basketball over at the basketball court, but were into their game to notice anything else."

She nodded. Said she'd figure something out. She hugged me and said how much she'd missed me; realized what I'd gone through was to protect her and the dog. She had been worried that something might have happened to me when I failed to show for work.

"I wasn't going to tell you. . . . I know how much Chambray means to you. I'm sorry. It's my fault. The whole thing is my fault. I know it."

We held one another. Monica's eyes were welling again.

Chapter 14

I couldn't get Marge out of my head. I kept seeing her in my mind's eye, diving for my Jones as if her life depended on it. I couldn't stop replaying the image: Marge panting and slobbering and sucking cock like some mad woman, then draining me as though dying of thirst. Then came the other: not wasting time tearing off her night robe, then the gown;

ripping her panties off, massaging her heavy breasts, the mound between her thighs, and climbing on top of my face with that beaver right up against my mouth.

Getting her off, licking that hot cunt, for me, had been as great as my own release. Other images came into play: the writhing she went into on that bed, rubbing her open cunt and sucking her own nipples and begging me to fuck her. . . . She was like a tigress, a wild, ravishing storybook beauty in heat. Uninhibited and kinky to the max. I'd never even thought of some of that stuff she came up with, but had to admit it definitely added a new dimension. And I also had to admit I'd liked enough of it to want to go back for a second helping, no matter how dangerous. I risked getting my nuts shot off, for sure, and yet I was drawn. The power of amazing sex. We were doomed. The crazy bitch, and I got the idea she was effing half-crazy, and her wanton ways had me. Could be that's what it was. The loony tunes aspect scared the shit out of me, and yet there was no denying I wanted more.

That was the difference between her and Monica. Monica Frances Gooch was shy in bed, even at 36 years of age and having been married once and given birth to a kid. Her son Modigliani was 13 and living with her parents in Phoenix. In spite of all that, she was always reluctant to try anything new, anything different. She had no way of making you desire her, of making you want to give it to her. She was just there. Although Monica was easy to please, she never brought a thrill to it. She could never make it as exciting an adventure as Margie. Monica had even refused to be talked into wearing black stockings and garter belt. I suggested getting a pair of those crotchless panties at Frederick's on Hollywood Boulevard.

"That's for whores. I wasn't raised that way. I just can't."

I had clung to Margie Graham with all my might during our last go-around and had to cover my mouth to subdue my screams; it had felt that good with her. No one had ever been able to do that to me before. No one.

Chapter 15

Monica was up by 5:30 for her early morning jog. She alternated between jogging with Chambray at the park, and aerobics near the studio. But what good was all this exercise when sex with her was too straight and lacked passion?

When she was through with her jog forty minutes later, sans Chambray, she came back for her shower, kissed me, and left for work.

The phone rang.

"Freddie?"

"Who's this?"

"Have you forgotten already, old buddy? This is Frank Graham."

"How are you doing, Mr. Graham?"

He insisted I call him Frank. Said he'd be by in five minutes.

"You will?"

"I got a job for you."

"This soon?"

"You got something against making money?"

"Feel kind of groggy, Frank. Hungover. Can't handle that stuff like some people."

He explained what had happened to his son and that he needed to find the dog and the owner real bad. I gave him the address.

"I'll meet you out front, Frank."

There didn't seem to be any other way. If I'd said no, he would have been around anyway and seen Chambray and heard her bark and that would have been it. No telling what Graham might have done.

I took the curtains down, closed the windows. Got some chairs and placed them as close to the front door as possible, so as to keep Chambray from tearing up the carpeting (this was always her favorite spot; always trying to dig her way out from under the front door), and went outside to meet Graham. I had my ball cap on, different shirt for sure, no dark glasses. Someone was bound to remember the sunglasses.

Chapter 16

Four minutes later exactly, Frank Graham was pulling up to the curb in the *Ready Rooter* van and was honking his horn. Man was completely sober and in a pissed mood.

I got in.

"I'll pay you for this."

"Glad I could help out."

We pulled away from the curb. Van was equipped with a police scanner. On a stand below the dash I noticed a portable phone, couple of walkie-talkies. In back of us was a dark curtain made of heavy material. Part of the curtain at his end had been brushed back just enough so that I was able to take in a shotgun secured vertically to the panel, next to it was a black, foot long, stainless steel flashlight secured to the panel in the same manner.

He noticed me glancing around.

"There's scum and then there's scum. And this low-life bastard is the lowest of the low."

"He shouldn't have taken off like that. Probably panicked."

"Panicked? You think he panicked? My little boy was in shock. The doc had to put him under. So far they don't think there's any real damage. They got no way of knowing for sure. If my boy dies. . . ."

"He won't die, Frank."

As soon as I'd said it, I felt a wet tongue licking my left hand. I glanced down. The same vicious Doberman pinscher who had growled at me that night from Graham's fenced-in yard was trying to determine if he ought to sink his fangs into my arm. I think my heart skipped a couple of beats. Dobie looked like he'd kill at the snap of a finger, and really enjoy it. Son of a bitch was so well trained that I'd never heard him poke his snout from behind the curtain to check me out, determine if I were friend or foe.

I withdrew my hand, slowly.

The beast's name was Thor. Frank ordered Thor to get in the back. Thor got in the back. The bounty hunter fired up a Cuban cigar. Asked if I wanted one. I didn't. He sucked on the Cuban.

"You just don't run off when a kid's in a state of shock like that. You just don't do it. There's no excuse for it. None."

"I agree."

"Even if the kid isn't subjected to the rabies shots, it's something that will stay with him the rest of his life. It's a mental scar that will never leave him."

Chapter 17

The first stop we made was that very same gas station where I'd had the battery recharged. While Frank questioned the gas station attendant, I made an excuse to use the john, and didn't come out until he was through.

"What'd you find out?"

"Plenty."

I wondered if the gas station attendant remembered that I'd had on that army shirt that day, the one with my name on it? If he did, I was in trouble. Frank wasn't talking.

We drove to the 7-Eleven across the street, and a couple of other liquor stores and shops in the area. With my ball cap bill low over my face, no one recognized me.

By 10 o'clock Frank wanted a beer. He kept saying how much he hated LA. All he could talk about was the Midwest and getting back to where real people lived. We went to his place. Frank lowered himself in the recliner in the living room there by the coffee table, I sat on the sofa to his right.

Margie walked up from somewhere in the kitchen part in back of Graham. She had makeup on, hair combed and shining. The dress she had on was yellow terry cloth, tight-fitting, and had slits on both sides. My groin stirred inside my trousers. To me she looked better than any *Playboy* centerfold I'd ever seen. She was wearing high heels, too, and black hose. My mouth got dry. I noticed that the Band-Aids: temple and below the left ear, were no longer there. Must've been scratches caused by Graham's dog, after all, and had healed and Band-Aids not needed.

Goddamn, but she had some rump on her.

Frank introduced us.

"Meet a buddy of mine, Margie. Alfred Reed. Alf, Marge—my beautiful wife."

Margie reminded him that I'd been the one who'd delivered him the night before. Frank acted like he couldn't recall. Margie and I shook hands all the same. Our palms equally damp.

"Friends call me Fred."

"The pleasure is all mine, Fred."

"What are you all so dollied up for, honey?" Graham was on the verge of chuckling. "Going to a damn Hollywood premiere or something?" And then did chuckle.

"For your information, Frank . . ." She slammed a prescription down on the coffee table in front of him. "That's what I'm all *'dollied up'* for!"

Frank nodded. Stuffed the piece of paper in his breast pocket. "Fetch us something to eat. I can get this."

"We need groceries. Who'll stay with the kids?"

"Have it delivered."

"I didn't go to all this trouble for nothing, Frank." She indicated the time it had taken to get dressed, brush her hair and do makeup. *"I want to get some air."*

"You want air? You got air." He opened the front door and sat back down in his recliner. "Except I got news for you: That ain't air you're breathing. Another Code 2 Alert today."

"Don't give me a hard time, Frank. It's just as bad where we come from."

"No place is as bad as LA. Ask Alf. Alf'll tell you."

I didn't say anything, just kind of nodded my head. I had fallen for her so hard I couldn't think straight. It wasn't easy trying not to show it. I couldn't keep my eyes off her. It bothered me the way she was being talked to. She didn't deserve it.

"Now get out of that fancy dress and fuck-me pumps and fix me and my friend here some breakfast, hear? Make it snappy, hear?"

Margie slammed the front door shut. "You go to hell, Frank Graham! I'm not one of your Kentucky Fried redneck sluts!" She started to walk away. Graham spun in his chair. I didn't think a man his size could move as fast as he did. He reached out with a quick fist for the dress, grabbed the bottom of it, that resulted in a long tear that went up to the hip; then yanked on her arm, pulling her to him as he rose to his feet. Now, I had no idea what the man had planned on doing next, but whatever it was, I didn't think I'd be able to stand it. I saw no point in smacking a woman like this for no real reason; no point in damaging the goods. It's also true that I wasn't thinking clearly, because I shot up and gripped him by the shoulder. He grabbed me by both arms and flung me clear over his head and back into the sofa against the wall.

"This is a domestic quarrel, junior. Stay out of it."

He straightened his collar, fired up another Cuban. He was looking at her. "You gonna get us that chow now, Margie?"

Margie, eyes burning with hatred and rage, went in the back. She reappeared a few minutes later wearing the night robe, and started fussing with some kitchen utensils.

I got to my feet, said something about not being hungry, and stepped outside. Frank was on my heels. Apologized for tossing me.

"A domestic quarrel is a domestic quarrel. These things happen. I might add: I might be a Commie-hating right-winger and a redneck, and proud of it, but I don't believe in beatin' on women. Oh, some might deserve it now and then, surely do, especially one like that. Baits me all the time, her and her psycho mama—after all I done for 'em—but I never laid a hand on either one. Self-defense? That's another matter. That's different. Now then: I'll give you a couple of hundred bucks if you help me out. *I got to find the bastard who hurt my kid. I got to find him, Fred.*

I walked back in with him. Frank had his arm around my shoulder. He was smiling as though nothing had happened. Two cups of black coffee waited for us on the kitchen table. Marge asked how I liked my eggs.

"No eggs, please. Coffee is fine."

The phone rang.

Mrs. G. picked up the receiver. She looked at Graham.

"Lieutenant Grozewski."

"I'll take it in the bedroom."

Frank left us to go in the back. She waited until he left the kitchen and replaced the receiver, then she buried her eyes into a Kleenex and wept. I put my arm around her.

"He's an animal, Fred. He's an animal."

"That's why I don't think I should work with him on this thing."

She looked up. "How will I see you?"

"We'll think of something."

She shook her head.

"He means business. I don't have to tell you that. He finds the guy responsible for doing that to his kid . . . he'll hurt him."

"He'll never find out. He's too stupid."

She held on tight.

"Who's this Lieutenant Grozewski?"

"Fat dick. Bruno Grozewski. As corrupt as they come. Another so-called Midwest buddy. They were on the force together."

"Why didn't Frank get him to help?"

She shrugged. "Something about Grozewski not having the time. He's trying to get his family situated out here himself. He relocated his family to be with Frank."

Chapter 18

For a long moment neither of us said a word. We just stared at each other. I don't know, she had those indigo eyes I couldn't get enough of. They were large and hypnotic, unlike any eyes I'd ever seen. And it was rare for me to go on about a woman's eyes. Women always did it. Talked about the man's *eyes*. "They're so blue. They sparkle."

I'd gotten it myself from time to time. Or when you weren't within hearing distance, they'd go on about your action in bed, the size of your groin, and the rest of it.

But there I was, noticing a woman's eyes, eyebrows; the contours of her face, the teeth that should have been on a *Cosmopolitan* cover. She should have been on the cover of a high class fashion magazine like *McCall's*, only they seldom used women like Marge on their covers. Her nose wasn't the perfect, Hollywood cutie type, either (courtesy of some high-priced Beverly Hills plastic surgeon); no, it was a full, strong nose, but on her it enhanced her looks. It went well with the wide face and thick hair, all that thick, silky hair, and made her that much more alluring.

It was happening. Whatever it was, it was happening. There was no need for words.

Chapter 19

Frank made his way back to the kitchen and we broke just in time. He appeared to be complaining, if to no one but himself, it seemed, about not being able to urinate.

"I go when I go, yet don't feel like my bladder's completely empty. Oddest thing. Ever experience it, Fred?"

I shook my head. Pretended I'd been about to reach for either the cream or sugar or both, after all, to add to my coffee.

"Is that any way to treat a guest? Get him what he needs."

"I'm all right, Frank."

"I don't want to hear it. Sit down."

He pushed me into a chair. Marge poured cream in my coffee. He asked if I took sugar and how much. I usually drank it black, no sugar. Not this time.

"Teaspoon should do it."

Next thing I knew he was reaching back inside the fridge for a box of doughnuts. I couldn't eat a doughnut and let it go. Frank pointed out they weren't his. Said he got them for the wife and the kids. Evidently Margie had a sweet tooth she was dealing with.

Chapter 20

We spent the rest of the day asking around some more. I kept the bill down over my eyes. Frank smoked his stogie and didn't say much. He was worried about the kid, it was obvious. But what puzzled me was this: If he loved his kid so much, why was he treating Marge like dirt? Why'd he have to tear her dress and be abusive? What was he trying to prove? That he was a real man? He didn't have to do that. One look at him and you knew immediately you did not hassle Frank Graham about anything. Maybe it was because he couldn't get it up anymore. I didn't know what the story was.

Around 4 o'clock we drove up to the North Hollywood police station and I got to meet the homicide dick, Lt. Bruno Grozewski, a 5'10 tub of dook who never so much as cracked a smile. I don't think he liked my looks. You could tell that he and Frank went way back.

After the initial intro, he and Frank went off to the side and talked. I couldn't make it out. They made a deliberate effort to keep it down to a whisper. I wondered if Grozewski had dug up some info on Chambray? He had the type of dyspeptic face you could never read and were always skeptical of. The fat cop had probably located the other victims Chambray had had her fangs in.

I remained calm and waited.

Frank gave me the keys to the van, the prescription, and said to get it over to the house.

"Me and Bruno got some old times to go over and a few bottles to uncork."

It was fine by me. Uncork all the bottles you want, I thought. "As long as you take Thor with you."

He had the pinscher get out of the van, and I left.

Chapter 21

I fetched the medicine as fast as I could, and got back to Margie. She put a finger to her lips and said that Butch was wide awake. Evidently the kid had been resting up, taking a nap.

"He might recognize the sound of your voice."

After I told her where I had left Frank, she arranged for a babysitter to come over and we went out.

"What if Frank shows up and you're not home?"

"No way. When those two start drinking they don't know when to stop."

From what I had seen of Frank, I believed it. The man drank like a fish. Beer, wine, whiskey. Whiskey was a man's drink all the way—and Frank Graham was all man, except in one department—and that worked in my favor. That's why I didn't care for hard booze or heavy drinking in general. It interfered with a man's love life.

We picked up a 6-Pack and I took her to the top of Mulholland drive. The skirt she had on was hiked up to about mid-thigh and I noticed the bruise. On the inside of her right thigh. I leaned over, taking a closer look. Right ankle was bruised. What the fuck was this Kentucky redneck asshole doing to her? I asked. Insisted on knowing. She didn't want to discuss it. Claimed it was too painful, and preferred to cherish the moment and insisted on being positive. I hadn't cared for it, but went along.

"Thank you, Fred. You're a sweetie."

"Me?"

"That's what you are: a true sweetie."

I nodded my head. I had flaws. Shit, too many, but when someone you had the hots for saw you as unblemished, you went along. Why not?

She said that she always knew that Los Angeles could be beautiful and that people like Graham never gave it a chance. They were always quick to knock it.

With me, I told her that I had always had the attitude: I could take it or leave it. And that I had come here looking for a job that paid a fair wage and made it possible to have a life. Not too much struggle and strife.

"Driving for the studios seemed like a good notion, a good way to get my foot in—until something better comes along." Bottom line: I was looking for a way to get over and stay out of jail while doing it. You read about the way the Kennedy's did it: from bootlegging to the White House. And there were others. Break every law in the book, not excluding murder, to get the brass ring, then fix it so that they appeared legit, made it by being law-abiding—*on the surface*. Sure. That was me: law-abiding. *On the surface*. I wanted the easy life for a change. Of course, this part of it I kept to myself.

We drank beer and got off on the view below that was the LA basin and stretched all the way out to the ocean. The Santa Anas had swept the smog away the night before and the scene was close to breathtaking.

"This is paradise, Fred. If there is such a thing as paradise on earth. This is it, Fred."

A teardrop formed in her right eye as she looked at me, so angelic and pure. "Don't worry. . . . That's a tear of happiness."

We kissed, and we both wept because we were relieved that it had finally happened: we had found each other. The heart connection was real and true and no one was going to take it away from us. *No one.*

Chapter 22

We shagged in the van. She was back on that dream she'd had ever since she could remember. She'd always read movie magazines and her mother's tabloids as a kid in school, read about Hollywood, and the other kids had put her down for it. Even her mother had teased her about it; kept urging her to do the right thing and be a good wife to her husband. Her mother's reason for having so much affection for Graham? Years before, not long after her hubby, Margie's step dad Mario passed, she'd been delinquent on her mortgage, the bank ready to foreclose, and saintly Frank Graham had stepped in and bailed her out.

You see, Mama Rossi had had a nose problem. Woman would've ended up homeless, without Frank Graham's kindness. Had been but an inch away from a park bench. This is what I was told. What I was led to believe.

"I always knew I would get out here one day—and here I am."

Presently she needed pictures, 8 x 10 glossies, and to sign up for acting lessons.

"He keeps stalling; stingy with the funds needed for quality glossies and portfolio, my acting classes. You have no idea how humiliating it is to show up for an interview on a studio lot in a shitty Ford Fiesta, while everyone else is there in a new Mercedes Benz or Lexus, or some other fancy ride just to rub it in and make you feel inferior. He keeps hoping I'll get discouraged and won't lift a finger to help. He'll come around, though."

I was tempted to ask why stay with him if he was treating her so effing rotten? But the answer was obvious: funds. Everything costs, and it took money to get anywhere and make any kind of headway. Same reason I'd been spinning my own wheels all this time. Working shit jobs for shit wages. The fat fucks who had money were determined to hold on to it. Gave you a crumb here and there only when they had to. Truth was, if you wanted it you had to take it.

I had to ask, though.

"Why stay in the marriage?"

"It's hard to get out of a marriage when you're Catholic. Ask my mother about that. But that was the plan: to hang in as long as I could, study— make it on my own, and leave him. He's mother's Plan-B. Only real source of income. She's goes through money like there's no tomorrow. Besides, if I had left him before we'd have never met."

She was right about that.

Chapter 23

After the beer was gone, and we were sitting up front again, and were both quiet, but had the same thing on our minds.

"What do we do about him, Margie?"

"Nothing. . . ."

"Nothing?"

"Nothing—for now, anyway."

"It's not going to be easy, sneaking about like this. Just because the man might be a redneck doesn't necessarily mean he's automatically a fucking idiot. If we're busted and dealt with, then it's us who are the fucking idiots, not him. I mean initially, yes, I thought he was just another redneck halfwit. Don't know anymore. You can't be stupid and survive as long as he has in his line of work."

"Let's not dwell it."

I asked if she would reconsider divorce.

"I want to."

"Will you?"

"It's not that easy."

"People do it every day."

"I'll have to think about it."

"Do you love me?"

"You know I do."

"What's there to think about?"

"I'll have to think about it."

Chapter 24

We drove to a doctor I knew at the free clinic on Vineland to have her lip looked at and to make it seem like she had a legit excuse for leaving the house, just in case Frank happened to beat us back. I also requested some type of skin balm for her bruises. She rejected it at first, insisting she had stuff at home. I insisted she accept the doctor's suggestion and she had no choice but to go along. When the doc asked what had caused the welts, Margie was evasive, but then offered a vague response: her husband's unruly and vicious Dobie had been the culprit that had caused her to trip against the cocktail table in her living room. I didn't buy it before when I first heard it and didn't buy it presently in the doc's office, but let it go. This was no time to be giving the woman the 3rd degree in front of this stranger, no matter how well-meaning.

Chapter 25

When we pulled into the driveway we could both sense Graham was inside. He was sitting in the living room, a beer in his hand, half dozing/half watching raw VHS footy of himself going after baddies throughout the U.S. He didn't say anything. Didn't bother to so much as look up. Some of the footy did get to me, because it was of my own ass getting busted and then smacked around by him. Yeah. Made me get tight inside my belly. I did what I could to turn my eyes away from it.

"I had Fred drive me to a clinic to take down the swelling."

"What swelling is that?"

"You know what swelling, Frank."

"I didn't lay a hand on you, Marge."

"I never said."

"You're making it look that way by omission—in front of company, no less."

"You're putting words in my mouth, Frank."

He looked my way.

"This is what I get for being kind, helping out. Kept her mama out of the poor house when Margie's step-daddy unexpectedly dropped dead and this is the thanks I get."

She leaned over and kissed him on the forehead.

"Sorry, hon. Mother is grateful; we both are. For all that you've done for our family."

"You give Butch the medicine?"

"Yes, I gave Butch the medicine."

I told Graham I'd see him in the morning. He let me know he'd be there, same time. His eyes back on the idiot box.

I was playing with fire. Guilt-ridden and frustrated. That's why I had mentioned divorce. The idea of sleeping with a married woman gave the sex that extra edge, only there was too much risk involved. Especially when the other guy was Frank Graham. The thought of losing my precious testicles didn't appeal to me one bit.

Chapter 26

When I got home the phone rang. Monica was on the living room sofa taking a nap. Two things that were off about it: her to be home this early in the afternoon and taking a nap like some middle-age broad with tired blood.

I lifted the receiver in the bedroom. Kept my voice low.

"I can't talk right now, Margie."

"Frank's passed out. Let's meet."

"Not now, sweetheart."

"I have to talk to you, Fred."

"Why now?"

"He knows it's you."

"What are you talking about?"

"The dog, Fred. He knows it's your dog."

"Sure?"

"I'll meet you in front of your place."

Chapter 27

We drove to a coffee shop at Burbank and Lankershim.

"Was it Grozewski?"

She nodded.

"I knew it, I knew it."

"What do we do, Fred?"

"I don't know."

"Monica has no idea what's going on, does she? You never told her, did you?"

"I don't want to talk about it."

"What will you tell her when Frank kills her dog?"

"He might not."

"He wouldn't?"

"He's a dog lover."

"What makes you think that? Because he's got Thor? That dog is with him for one reason and one reason only: to cover Frank's butt and protect him from the countless enemies he's made all over the country."

"Look—you're excited.

"Damn right, I'm excited. I've waited so long—I don't want anything to happen to us. He'll ruin things, Fred. He'll take our happiness away."

"No one is going to do that, Margie. I guarantee it."

"I love you, Fred. I love you more than anything in the whole world."

"I feel the same, Margie."

"The racist bastard is twice my age. What am I doing married to a bigot like that?"

"I want us to be together. You know that. It comes down to what we discussed earlier. Divorce."

She shook her head.

"I get that same reaction every time I mention divorce. What the hell is it?"

"It's just not done, that's all."

"I guess I don't understand."

"My family, goddamn it. It's my Catholic family."

"Try explaining."

"You don't know my mother. It's the reason I married Frank—to keep my mother happy."

"You going to let your mother tell you how to live your life?"

She wouldn't say.

"Are you?"

"No."

"Get a divorce, Margie."

"I want to, Fred. I want us to get married as soon as possible. What are you going to do in the morning when Frank comes calling?"

"I got it coming, I guess. Face the music."

"He'll hurt you, sweetheart. You'll end up in the hospital."

"Won't be the first time."

"It's not worth it. There's nothing wrong with his kid. Butch was never in shock. Frank was exaggerating. I know him. I've lived with him long enough. The way he goes on about those kids like he really cares. He doesn't. I know. Frank Graham don't give a damn about nobody. He's got two grown kids from a previous, previous marriage. They refuse to have anything to do with him. Oh, yeah: they call when they need money. They can't stand him, his own flesh and blood. What does that tell you? A brute like that shouldn't be allowed to live. You've seen the way he treats me. I put up with that for six long years, Fred. I can't take it. I can't take it, sweetheart. I want us to be together. He would never consent to a divorce."

"You don't know that for sure."

"He'd rather see me dead than let me go; see me run off with someone else. He's a walking time bomb. It's scary."

I suggested she was getting all worked up and looking at it from a negative angle.

"What if he consented? You've been battered all this time. Got a good case to present. Any legit court of law would side in your favor. They would have to. People aren't blind. You can't say divorce is far-fetched and beyond."

"And then what? Spend the rest of our lives hiding out? Looking over our shoulder? He would hound us, Fred. I know him. He's the type. He wouldn't let up. His macho image of himself wouldn't allow it. Don't you see?"

"You're not thinking what I think you're thinking?"

She didn't say anything.

"Because if you are—forget it. That's out."

"He's a pig. I don't want to live without you, honey. I couldn't. . . ."

"This kind of talk is just a little too much, if you ask me."

"Know what he does for a living?"

"I know what he does for a living."

"He kills people, Fred. That's what he does for a living. He kills. It gives him a rush. The money is nothing more than icing on the cake. Hunting humans is how he gets his rocks off. This is exactly it. Instead of getting off in bed like normal people, like most people, these sorry asshole bounty hunters with pathetic penises do it by beating the shit out of skips, and often, way too often, killing them. Hunting two-legged animals beats hunting the four-legged kind any day of the week. I've heard him say it hundreds of times over the years. Tracking 'reprobates' and taking the 'motherfuckers' out gives him the biggest rush."

"You don't have to convince me of anything. I was laid up in a hospital bed by the time he was done with me. All the more reason why we should forget it. Didn't you notice the footage when we got back from the clinic? That was me, that time he bagged me, getting my butt kicked by him and his partner. You saw it."

Her eyes welled. We embraced.

"I didn't mean it that way, Margie. I could never let you go."

"There's no other way for us, honey. I hate the thought of us having to do something like this. It's dreadful, I know. I would do anything to keep you. Anything."

I wiped the tears from her eyes, and asked her to let me sleep on our problem.

Chapter 28

The next morning Frank appeared bright and early. I climbed in the van, sat there waiting for either the shit to hit the fan or for us to get going. One or the other. Instead we sat and waited, neither one of us saying anything. It made me nervous. You bet. Graham pulled out a fat stogie and fired up. He puffed on that thing, blowing smoke out the window on his side. What was peculiar is that he was right-handed, but held the cigar in his left. It got mighty uncomfortable, I can tell you that. Felt I had no choice, and got to it.

"I might as well own up: I was the one with the dog; the coward who took off after my girlfriend's Pyrenees mix snapped at your son. I'm sorry. It was a chickenshit thing to do. It's been eating me up all this time. I just didn't know how to come clean."

"I was waiting for you to confess."

"You knew?"

"Soon after."

"But how?"

"Not important."

"For what's it's worth: I ran off to save Monica, my girlfriend. Dog belongs to her. Chambray's been in trouble before, and yet I can't help it: I've grown attached to the animal. I'm a dog lover, Frank. It would be really hard if she got put under. It would destroy my girlfriend."

"Feel the same way about Thor. He's family. Love him as much as I do my own kids. Almost. Not quite, but close. I do get it."

"So we're okay?"

I didn't see it coming. His right fist came up, the knuckle side, fast and hard, that he sent into my jaw that sent the back of my head bouncing against the head rest. Then he did a repeat. And I was out.

Next thing I knew, what tasted like raspberry iced tea was being splashed in my face from a thermos.

"Now we are."

"I suppose I had it coming."

"Sure did."

"I expected far worse."

"Confessing spared you. Thor and I decided to give you a break for handling it like a man."

"Thank you—I think. You and Thor."

He handed me the box of Kleenex to wipe the blood and raspberry tea off my aching face with.

"Where's the dog, Reed? I won't hurt her. Lemme see her."

I did.

"Mean mother, ain't she? It's perfect."

Chapter 29

I didn't ask for what. Before I knew it, we were in a seedy area near Echo Park. This was where the Judas had called from a phone booth. We pulled into a taco joint parking lot. Frank decided to let me have a look at a picture of the man we were on the trail of, a USC film school student evidently. The sneering face I was looking at was rough around the edges, and that's putting it mildly. Mid-30s, lumps and scars. Gold front tooth.

"Now, I ask you, Fred, does this scumbag look like a 23-year-old college student to you? Someone who might be interested in the creative arts in any way?"

"Can't say, Frank."

"Well, I can. Munoz is not his real name, either. Got a history of run-ins with the law. Been busted by border guards a few times, running illegals, guns, dope. This is how this kind of slime sneaks into the country: wants to study filmmaking, interested in pursuing his education, all that shit. Lefties like to call them 'Dreamers.' It's a load. Why can't he pursue his 'dreams' south of the border? Bunch of shit."

"What makes it possible for dudes like that to keep doing this?"

"Fucking Lefty libber assholes doing it for votes, and to spite the Republicans. Now, me, I don't give a shit for politics, Fred. You've got assholes on both sides, in both parties, but this is wrong the way they're destroying the country by letting slime like this in. He couldn't be interested in getting a degree in cinema no more than I would be in being a tree surgeon, or you would be in being a Buddhist monk. Now, I don't presume to know what makes you tick, but I'm guessing you're not interested in spending the rest of your life in a monastery."

"You're not wrong, Frank. I'd make a lousy monk. No question."

"That's what I'm saying." He stowed the pic. "His real name is Quintero; Fidel Cipriano Delmar Quintero. That's the *Reader's Digest* condensed version."

Graham had to use the john and had me stay behind while he went inside. From there we drove to an East LA police sub-station. Said the smart thing to always do was to give the cops a heads-up on things. He did that, and then it was on to a neighborhood mom and pop type grocery store. According to Graham, the dirtbag's wife or girlfriend, one of them, worked here. My part was to cover the rear exit. He reached back for a flak jacket and handed it to me. I asked if I should get into it.

"Up to you. Keep in mind: the jumper is armed and is not inclined to go back to jail."

I slipped my arms through the sleeveless vest. He reminded me to use caution, stay on my toes.

Since haste makes waste, I didn't feel a need to rush to get to where it was I needed to get. Wondered if it was worth risking my life for what the man was paying me. By the time I reached the area in back I noticed a junker of a Mustang idling in the alley with a *Los Cochinos* gang member at the wheel. Hair cut close to the scalp, the wifebeater he had on revealed enough familiar prison tats on his neck and elsewhere to confirm what I felt the dude was about. Seconds later Quintero was running out the store's rear exit. Saw me, raised the hand that he had the gun in. I ducked in time, even though I didn't hear him fire, and watched him jump in the car. By the time I stepped out from behind the building they were tearing down the alley. Graham staggered out not long after with blood below his right ear and back of his neck. The look on my face told him what he already knew: the skip had skipped.

I apologized for not having been able to do much.

"Forget it. Wasn't your fault."

When I asked what happened, he wasn't saying. Instead, did an about face, and walked back inside. I heard a woman scream, a loud thud, then what sounded like a bunch of cans hitting the floor from a display stand.

Graham called my name, and I followed him through the store, with fruit and vegetables, busted-open watermelon all over the floor, canned beans and cracked jars of salsa. There was a Latina of about 30, hard looking, with a bloody mouth, out cold among the tomatoes and canned goods. I made it out to where we had the van parked.

Chapter 30

We drove to a Mickey D's so Graham could get cleaned up, wash the blood off, apply Band-Aids to his cuts. He was experiencing cramps in his belly and did not order anything for himself to eat, but did offer to treat me to a Happy Meal. With my nerves pretty much shot and dealing with thoughts of Marge and our situation, I had no appetite for anything but her, so I passed.

We walked to a table. He unscrewed the top on the thermos and poured himself some of that raspberry tea. He sipped. Looked at me.

"It's the girlfriend, the wife, you got to watch out for. Come up from behind, sneak up on you. Can't hear 'em, and *wham*. How it usually works. Gotta have eyes in the back of your head. Trouble is sometimes they're not open wide enough. Not being able to take a leak is what's caused it; the runnin' shits. Drinking this tea ain't helping."

He didn't say anything for a while. I asked why he drank the tea if he didn't care for it. There was a shrug.

"Margie trying to keep me 'healthy'; tryin' to make me 'eat right.' Cut back on red meat. This is part of it. Don't believe in it myself. Prefer a good, strong cup of coffee any day of the week, well, whiskey actually, but not when working. Never while on a hunt."

He asked if I wanted any.

"Go grab a cup. I'll pour you some. Got more than enough here."

I declined. I'd had my share of it in the van after the knuckle sandwich.

"You're getting a pretty good idea what this is about, Fred. Money to be made, but a man can get hurt. This one's worth 20k to me." He said most of the time there wasn't anything to worry about. "Most of the time. Not much happens. But then there's times like this."

At least he wasn't worried about his kid anymore and hadn't mentioned another word about it. He said because of my experience in 'Nam he felt I had potential. Also, I worked cheap. This was the main factor, no doubt. Besides, we were both from the Midwest and Thor and Chambray got along pretty good.

Said he had to go take a dump. Cramps in his belly refused to go away.

Chapter 31

He did his business in the men's room, came out. Not in a good mood at all.

"Goddamn chorizo."

His beeper went off. He looked at the number. Got up to make a call. Graham's tip came from a consistently reliable Judas. He had them, snitches, in practically every city he spent time in.

He was back.

"That's a huge part of it, Fred. Money talks. One hand washes the other. I'll have to get this Judas a new refrigerator—if his info helps me nail the skip."

Was I surprised? Hardly.

"People are strapped for cash, Frank. I get it. I relate."

He said, according to his source, our fugitive was at a Santa Monica Boulevard adult movie theatre in Hollywood, hanging out with the projectionist, a film school buddy who worked there part-time.

We pulled up to the Hollywood PD and he went inside to give them a heads-up. When he stepped back out a moment later he was shaking his head.

"They don't give a shit. Ain't about to help."

We drove west. Spotted a couple of cops sitting in their squad car in a doughnut shop parking lot. Graham parked next to them and let the two cops in it know what was about to go down. They were familiar with Graham and his situation and didn't raise a brow. Cops were nonplussed. Graham suggested they might want to back us, mentioned that he had been one of them at one time, and then clearly requested assistance. They weren't interested. What it came down to. We were on our own. Graham didn't haggle. Pretty much what he expected. We got out of there.

"The way it is, Fred. Typical reaction. Cops do not care for bail enforcers. They're not going to help. Just so's you know, should you decide to pursue this line of work. Don't expect help from law enforcement. Period. The fact that I was a police officer once upon a time makes no difference. Now and then you might meet a cop who may be sympathetic, but it's rare."

Chapter 32

We got on Santa Monica and drove west. We parked around the corner from the movie house on a dark side street, in a quiet residential neighborhood. The raincoat Graham wore concealed the shotgun well enough.

"Let's go dance with the devil."

We walked up to the box office. He slipped a tenner to the fat broad for two tickets, and we went in. The lobby reeked of Lysol and stale urine. I followed Frank to the manager's office on the second floor.

Upstairs reeked almost as much: it was a combo of reefer, ammonia and moth balls. Carpeting was worn, walls had cracks throughout from having survived a multitude of quakes over the years. Cobwebs up in the corners with dead moths and flies in them.

Graham knocked, and we entered. The bail enforcer explained the situation to the rail thin, cross-eyed dude with the lopsided toupee and crooked teeth and uneven stash. Room was small, dingy, stacked cans of 16mm and 35mm film and reels everywhere; movieola. All types of posters and one-sheets on walls with dry and peeling paint, from *Debbie Does Dallas* to *Deep Throat*; from *The Magnificent 7* to *Citizen Kane.*

The manager was willing to cooperate. Said that Munoz was not the regular projectionist, merely hanging out with a friend named Tito from USC film school who was. Graham asked the manager to get the friend to step into the hallway under some pretext. We needed Munoz/Quintero by himself.

He did that.

We moved out of the office. I followed Frank into the hallway, the manager followed after me. The mid-20s Hispanic named Tito emerged from the projection room and followed the manager back to his office.

"Filmmakers are like flies, Fred, feasting on the same turd—celluloid being the turd."

I already got it: he didn't care for Tinseltown. Didn't matter to me one way or the other. We made it to the door to the projection room and paused there. Graham had me lower the video camera and gestured he was going in alone.

Tito, the friend, wanted to know what was going on? Who were we? He kept looking at the manager. The manger gestured that he stop with the questions.

"These gentlemen are bounty hunters. Your friend skipped bail. He's being taken to jail." He gestured they keep quiet, and closed the office door behind them.

Graham wanted to make sure I had my piece with me. I nodded.
"I'll give a holler should I need a hand."

It was his call. He walked in there, quiet and calm, the black 12-gauge, pump action Beretta RS200 at the ready, and closed the door just as quietly behind him.

Hey, it was his life. I didn't like risking mine for the chump change I was being paid and was okay with doing as asked. I had my piece out and held at my side just the same. Skip was armed. I knew as much from our earlier encounter with him.

Chapter 33

I couldn't say what happened in there, all I know is when Graham called me on the walkie-talkie I had the video camera up and running and went in.

Quintero's wrists were cuffed behind his back, and the fugitive's face was a bloody mess. Broken nose; blood dripped from his lower jaw; eyes swollen and bloodshot. Looked like he'd been hit by a freight train. It was unnerving to look at—even through the lens. I also noticed blood oozing from Graham's nostrils. He had cuts above both brows.

He wanted me to turn the camera off. I did. Noticed he had the skip's gun jammed in his waist.

"Too bad we didn't get footy of the dirtbag getting bagged."

I reminded Graham he was the one who told me to stay put in the hallway.

"I'm well aware of that."

The manager opened his door and stuck his head out as we walked past, saying nothing.

I asked Frank how he was doing.

He didn't want to talk about it.

"This is how these dirtbags slip into the country: false papers and pretenses. Interested in getting an education. What a crock; what a load. Then smuggle contraband in across the border to poison our youth: white, black, Hispanic, Asian. They hurt all of us. This is exactly what fuels my rage."

"Gotta admit the demand is there, Frank: from all races and backgrounds.

If the demand wasn't there, there wouldn't be anyone to sell dope to."

"I'm not disagreeing. Doesn't make it any less offensive. Both sides are at fault, are part of the problem. This turd has a bounty on his head; and we're bringing him in so I can get paid so I can pay for Rinelle's pain pills and acupuncture sessions, and Margie's acting classes and elocution lessons. Never mind that it's nothing but a waste of money, all of it. Waste of funds. Flushed away."

I asked how Quintero was doing.

The only thing that came out of Graham about that was that he had to take another dump, bad, and that his belly was in turmoil. That was it.

Chapter 34

We made it to the john downstairs. I had no choice but to go in with them. Somebody had to keep an eye on the skip while Frank did his business inside the booth. You heard a lot of noise and wincing. Sounded like Graham was shitting his guts out. It went on and on; the stench really too much. Like I said, no choice.

Finally, I heard him flush the toilet several times and he stepped out, shaking his head and looking non too-happy.

"I'm pissing in dribbles—throughout the day. Not able to take a real good piss no matter how much I need to. Feel it backing up into my bladder. Mighty uncomfortable."

We walked outside. He tossed the van keys to me. Threw Quintero against the van and started beating on him, knocked him down and kicked him in the face and neck. I had no choice but to pull him off.

"You can't kill him, Frank, and leave Margie a widow."

"Like she would shed a tear."

"What about your kids?"

I helped Quintero get in the van. We climbed in, with the fugitive ensconced in the back away from Thor and Chambray. To be on the safe side and to keep Chambray from making any sudden lunges, I had her secured to the leash and the leash tied to my seat. Graham informed Quintero that his dog would not bother him, so long as he did not make any sudden moves. This did not keep the canines from growling and bearing their fangs. Looked like the mule was about to take a dump in his panties himself.

I asked what it was Frank felt like doing. He said we were driving to the Hollywood station to drop the dirtbag off, and that we'd stop by the bail bondsman's later after a visit to the VA hospital in West LA.

And that's what we did, with Graham squirming in his seat as we pulled away from the curb, all that water backing up. I could see him sweating, clenching his jaw. Graham needed me to find the nearest men's room, pronto.

Chapter 35

I got us headed south toward Santa Monica Boulevard. Made a right, and got us heading west. I Pulled into a mini-mart parking lot not long after, and watched Graham hurry inside the store with his trusty shotgun.

There were the usual punks hanging around outside: nightflies, pushers and dope fiends, low-rent hookers, male as well as female. I didn't care, so long as they stayed away and that they did.

Bounty hunter was gone a long time. When he finally stepped back out he had that same grimace on his face as before: no luck. Hadn't been able to relieve himself. He limped to the van, pausing at the passenger side. Heaved himself in, and we rolled.

"I don't get it. I need to piss but can't. And my balls hurt. Actually no, the pain is in my bladder. I know it needs emptying, but simply can't. There I stood over the urinal, with my dick in my hand, for what seemed like forever, but I couldn't make it happen. It's the damnedest thing. I don't understand it. Can't be my prostate. I ain't that old—yet. They say late 50s is when it starts to happen. Prostate starts givin' us trouble. Late 50s, early 60s."

He tried to forget his discomfort by pulling out a stogie and lighting up. He had the window on his side down and blew some smoke out. He was rather quiet, still wincing from time to time, but all in all quiet and calm.

I asked how he was doing presently.

"Like I said: Need to make a pit stop and not able to."

He wondered if Margie might've been stepping out on him & gave him something.

"Social disease."

"Margie?"

He came right out and asked if I was doing her. I looked at him, and held it like I was shocked that he would even think it.

"We're partners, Frank."

"Fuck that 'we're partners' shit. Partners is the ones you got to watch closest. Your partners, main amigos. Always."

"She's not my type. I like 'em petite—and white. Never went for colored."

"She's mixed."

"Same thing."

"Funny. Didn't figure you for a bigot."

"Never been. My daddy was from Bogota."

That was a lie, only because I had no idea who my daddy was or where he was from. My mother was a common street whore. The trick who knocked her up could've been anybody.

"What about your mother? What was her race?"

"Never asked."

"What color paint job she have?"

"Looked caucasian. That don't mean nothin', though."

"Was raised by bigots and rednecks myself down around Bowling Green. Kentucky. Later on moved north. More bigotry and bullshit everywhere. Never had much use for it. Hatred is stupid—and a waste."

"Except when it comes to pushers, illegals and other criminal types."

"You got that right, sonny."

I watched him wince some more. Indicated his swollen belly. It was huge by now. All that urine with nowhere to go but back up.

"Can't be a good thing, Frank."

"Hell, it's life threatening. A dummy would know it. Urine is toxic. If it backs up into your kidneys it's over. Pretty much. That's serious shit."

Chapter 36

Frank requested I step on the gas.

"VA Emergency."

"You got it, Frank."

I picked up speed, taking us toward West Hollywood, and beyond. He leaned back, his head against the backrest. We drove through Beverly Hills and that cluster-fuck of BMWs and Mercedes Benzes and Rolls Royces.

"My gut feels like it's about to explode."

Some celebrity BH a-hole in a white pickup ran a stop sign on our right, made a right turn there at the corner. I tapped my horn. The cocksucker had the nerve to flip us the bird.

"Real nice of him. Don't you think, Fred?"

Graham adjusted the shotgun in his grasp so that it could easily be discerned by the jerk who just dissed us, and the pickup truck took off like a rocket ship. Graham wanted me to step on it for a stretch, make it look like we were going after it. I did as asked. Must've scared the crap out of the driver, because he fled like the chickenshit punk that he was.

"Armpit of the world, Fred. Like I said. Right here. Beverly Hills. Asswipes and degenerates."

Chapter 37

We reached the part of BH where Wilshire and Santa Monica intersect, made a right on Wilshire and kept going. It was a long drive, past the country club, Holmby Hills, congested Westwood Village.

We got there eventually. Pulled into the hospital parking lot. I hopped out. Helped him disembark. We made it to the entrance.

Waiting area was empty. It was late. Way past midnight. The only one there was a sole male clerk behind the plexiglass partition. In back of him were some nurses, hospital staff walking around, engaged in tasks, etc. Guy seemed relaxed, in his late 40s. Graham already had his VA ID out and was presenting it to the man.

"How can we help you, sir?"

"Not able to pass water, sir, and it's mighty weighty."

The clerk's fingers worked the keyboard. He typed it in. Handed Graham's ID back to him.

"Please have a seat, Mr. Graham. We'll have someone see you shortly."

"Thank you kindly, sir."

I helped Frank limp to the waiting area in back of us. We both sat. There was a pile of magazines on his side: *Time, Life, New Yorker*, the usual crap. Graham picked one up, but then quickly dropped it back down on top of the stack. Not able to stay put. Restless. Stood up, and started pacing. The pain showed on his features. Back and forth, he limped in the waiting room. A nurse stepped out, made a left, and entered a door on that same side.

A man in civilian clothes hobbled in from outside on crutches. Made it to the clerk's window. Soon after, another nurse stuck her head out, called Graham's name.

"Right here, ma'am."

He followed the beefy, plain Jane in, and I followed him. Woman did the usual: asked his name, last four digits of his social, date of birth; asked what the trouble was.

Graham went over it. She had him roll his sleeve up and she took his blood pressure; then she had him get on the scale. Checked his height even. It was routine, but had to be done. I'd gone through it myself for one thing or another over the years.

She asked who I was. Before I could answer, Graham claimed I was his son. I guess it made him feel better if I hung around to keep him company and he wouldn't be left by himself. I had no problem with it.

She attached a plastic strip to his right wrist with his name and something else on there, and we followed her out of this room, took a left, passed a couple of small rooms with a single patient in each, until we got to one that was vacant, with the usual: bed and whatnot. She indicated politely we go in and have a seat and that another nurse would be along shortly.

Chapter 38

Graham's situation was getting downright unbearable. He was lying on his side on the bed, in the fetal position. He had his arms folded across his lower belly and he was clutching and un-clutching his jaw repeatedly. His knees were bent, up into his lower belly and he must've been in incredible pain. It was getting to him, no doubt, but he did his best to maintain. This was a real man handling it. You had to admire him for it. For twenty long, excruciating minutes this went on; his agony intensifying and becoming more and more pronounced. I did not envy him one bit.

I'd heard about the prostate and the trouble it could cause a man and thought nothing of it. Didn't concern me because it didn't mean much, frankly because it was something for old dudes to worry about, and here it was: witnessed to it up close and saw it was nothing to be taken lightly.

Made me wonder: was this what I had to look forward to? If so, how did one go about circumventing the situation? Keep one from having to deal with it? I knew nothing about it, and evidently, neither did Frank. We ignored shit, all kinds of shit, until it struck home and we were knee-deep. Of course, by then, it was too late to think about preventive measures.

I watched the man suffer, toss from one side to the other and back again and I hated to see it, after all. I wanted him helped. What to do? I stepped into the hallway, looked around in the lobby type large room. There were nurses, male and female, a doctor or two walked by. None appeared to be aware of what was going on. This was no slam against the VA, far from it, merely an observation—because most all of them were exactly aware of what was happening. But there must've been other patients there and things got taken care of at a pace that was conducive. I understood.

I looked at the nurse at a desk to my right, down a ways a bit, typing away on a keyboard; I looked at a couple of female nurses in the center of this area behind a plexiglass partition that went up to the ceiling, doing something; all tending to a particular task before them: talking on the phone, typing, exchanging paperwork. Who could fault them? Certainly not I, and I stepped back inside the room.

Graham was on that bed, in that fetal position, tossing about, unable to stay still. Pain was eating him up. And yet, you had to admire the guy for doing his best to keep it under control.

Chapter 39

A pretty brunette nurse appeared with a clipboard. Asked Graham a few questions; asked if he would be against the nurse applying a catheter to deal with his situation.

"Of course not, ma'am. It has to be done."

She asked if he wouldn't mind lowering his trousers, not now, but for the male nurse, in a moment. Graham was fine with it. Did he wish for privacy? Graham gestured in my direction.

"My son Fred stays."

"Your nurse will be in to see you in a few minutes, sir."

"Thank you, ma'am. Appreciate all that you're doing here for me."

"You're welcome."

She was gone.

The male nurse, Rene, a bespectacled Hispanic man in his mid 50s who appeared far from healthy himself, walked in, announced himself; described the procedure that was about to take place and if Graham would consent to it.

"Absolutely, sir. I need to have this done."

The nurse came across as a compassionate gent and had a kind smile for him. Somehow or other, we discovered that his wife was battling lymphoma. It was easy to tell he was under a lot of pressure; personal problems.

"Life, Rene. Sooner or later something or other, be it a health issue, death in the family or finances, or some other damned thing hits every one of us and we find ourselves dealing with it as best we can, trying to cope, trying to beat it, and live for as long as we can. Life is still worth living."

"Exactly right sir."

"We're all in the same boat. Only some of these young thugs, gang bangers, don't get it; until it's too late. Ingest all kinds of drugs; have a reckless, devil-may-care attitude, thinking they're invincible. Only nobody is. Not a one of us, sir, is invincible. Can't make 'em see the big picture, what matters."

Rene needed Frank to lower his trousers down to around his knees. I turned away.

"Okay, sir."

Graham had completed this part of it and awaited further instructions. When I turned back I saw the man unpack what looked like a large plastic bag with a hose. There was a long tube about one quarter of an inch in diameter at the end of the hose. He had his back turned to Graham the whole time he did this. Just by seeing this thing and adding it up, it was easy enough to deduce what was about to transpire: it was not going to be pleasant at all for the patient, this was plain enough.

Was I glad I was not in Graham's shoes? That long tube was going to be inserted deep into his penis, and way up into the bladder. This was what the nurse's explanation amounted to. The prostate (inside the bladder) was swollen and was pressing against the urinary tract from either side and preventing the flow of urine.

All Frank could do was sweat and sigh and nod his head. He was gasping at this point, the agony too much. Chills ran down my spine just contemplating what was about to be done to the man. Hell, it was true: I didn't know him, was not tied to him in any emotional way at all. Still, the idea of something like this being done to you was painful to consider even in a hypothetical way.

Graham did not seem perturbed in the least. And even if he was, he kept it to himself. Besides, what choice did he have? Seemed to be his attitude. The nurse liked that.

"It really does help, sir. Sometimes certain patients make a fuss, so it does make the job a lot easier whenever we get someone like yourself who is eager to cooperate. We do appreciate it. Frank, is it?"

"I'm glad you're here, Rene; hospital staff; all of you. All I can say, sir."

Now, mind you, Rene's back was turned to Graham the whole time as they were talking and the tube was kept out of Graham's sight. It was intentional, no doubt. If Graham had got a good look at the tube he might not have been as non-plussed about the whole thing. Doctors and nurses were hip to this little fact.

"I'm not going to ask if it's going to be painful, Rene, only to what extent."

"Not inordinately."

There was no mistaking Rene, the nurse, had suppressed the slightest trace of a grin as he sold Graham this white lie. He knew, all too well, how agonizing it was going to be for the patient, but chose not to dwell on it.

I got it. I understood. So did the patient.

He turned, at last, holding that foot-long plastic tube in his right hand.

"Do you wish for me to proceed, sir?"

"Of course."

Graham's bloated belly made him look like a pregnant woman in her second trimester.

"At the count of three: take a deep breath."

The nurse counted off, and just as he did, I turned away, as Rene jammed that plastic tubing deep inside the center of Graham's groin, and up into the bladder. I heard the bounty hunter grunt, repeatedly, and had me wincing with each sound he made. Rene said he would be back later.

Chapter 40

The urine traveled down the length of the hose and into the plastic bag that sat inside a tub at the foot of the bed. You could see Graham's anguish abating by degrees. His face covered in sweat, but there was no mistaking the relief he was the recipient of. By the time he was empty and done, the full bag was about the size of a gallon milk jug.

"That's a lot of fuckin' urine."

"Sure is, Frank."

"I could kiss these folks, the lot of 'em."

"We tend to take people in the medical profession for granted—until we need them."

"I never have. No, sir."

The cute female nurse was back to check in, and left; then Rene showed to see how everything was working out. He seemed pleased.

Graham was thanking him all over again, letting him know how much he appreciated what they did for him.

The bag was disconnected, and a new bag was attached to the hose. Graham was asked which leg he wanted it strapped to. He decided on the left, since he was right-handed and would make it easier to be able to reach across to make adjustments later, if need be. This was done, with an explanation how to us it. Rene pointed out the release lever below the bag.

"When it fills up, you flip the lever to empty it out. The urine will flow out, and you flip it up to close it off. And there's an extra bag for you here also should you want to replace the current one eventually."

There were some other details. Graham needed to know how long he would have to walk around with this bag attached to his leg.

"About two weeks."

Graham revealed what he did for a living, and asked if he would still be able to do his job.

"I don't see why not? We have a doctor who's got one of these strapped to his leg, and it's not keeping him from getting around, coming in every day."

"Encouraging to hear, Rene, sir."

Frank's pants were soiled in the crotch region and he requested something like a small plastic sheet to possibly cover the vehicle seat with later. He was given what looked like a large diaper.

Rene said the doc would be in to talk to him for a bit in a few minutes, and he was gone.

Frank dressed himself. That hose ran up alongside his leg, inside the pant leg, and he buckled up.

"I don't mind sayin': feels like I got a new lease on life."

"You look it."

"Hope you never have to go through what I just went through, Fred. I've weathered a few episodes in my time, but that certainly was a new one. Different kind of pain altogether."

Chapter 41

About fifteen minutes hence, the doc walked in. Tall fellow with a positive demeanor. About 49, 50. Fair-haired. Thin in the face, with a bit of a gut on him, but nothing too serious. You got the idea the dude was partial to cocktails. Hey, nobody's perfect. These are observations, nothing more. The bell tolls for every damned one of us eventually. Health goes (mind & body), dreams go; all that. Disappointments.

Sure, I was still clinging to a dream or two at this stage. It was tenuous, yet undeniable.

You got the idea this doc was an okay kind of guy. Likable. Had a smile on his face. He shook hands with us both, pulled up a chair so he could be closer to the patient when he spoke.

"It's hard to believe not being able to relieve yourself can cause so much discomfort."

"You said it, Doc."

Graham was still looking for assurance that he'd be able to return to work, do his job, even with this damned bag on there. Doc nodded.

"Yes."

Graham mentioned what Rene had said a moment ago, about one of their own in this same situation showing up for work every day without a hitch.

"Shouldn't be a problem at all, Mr. Graham. Come back in two weeks and we'll see about removing the catheter. The nurse will be in shortly with your medicine and instructions when to take it, how many a day. It's very important that you take the medicine at the same time every day."

He rose. We shook all around, and he was gone.

Chapter 42

I didn't start out wanting to be able to relate to this old man, but it was possible it was happening all the same. And because of this undeniable little fact it was going to be that much tougher to kill him. But kill him we would. Not because I wanted to or would find any joy in it, but because there was no other way for us. I wished I could've used vengeance as a motive for when he put me in the hospital years before, it would've helped, but there was hardly any of that, not presently. Not much, anyway. No, I'd never forgotten it; but it was also true I was the cause & had pushed him into it by trying to make a run for it. And he beat my ass when he and his partner at the time caught up with me, and was thorough about it, too. A mite too thorough, you could say. Well, he was doing his job. And he'd warned me: "You'll be treated with respect, but if you get out of line, you won't like how I react. Painless—or painful. Up to you entirely."

A different nurse came in, blond white lady. Cute and friendly, with an engagement ring on her finger. She had the paper sack with the *Finasteride* and *Tamsulosin.* Opened the sack, pulled up the instructions and reminded Graham to read them carefully, and to never take more than one pill at a time. "Should you skip a day, say forget to take them, do not take two the next day. Never take more than one pill each per day, Mr. Graham. Your doctor's appointment is set for approximately two weeks from today. The time and date is on there. You'll also be sent a reminder in the mail. Should you not be able to make the appointment, please notify the VA."

Graham let the lady know how grateful he was to all of them for what they've done for him.

"We appreciate that, sir. It means a lot."

We got lost trying to find our way out. Were directed to the correct door by a volunteer worker, and we made it outside to the parking lot.

Chapter 43

We pulled up to the house. Light was on in the living room. Graham wanted me to take Thor by the leash, the items from the hospital, while he reached for his shotgun, and limped toward the house, with me following closely behind should he need an assist. I guess it took getting used to walking with a plastic sack tied to your leg and a tube running down into it from your groin.

He paused at the stoop, gave me the key to the gate and had me unlock it and let Thor in the yard. I did that, locked the gate back up and returned the key to him.

"What makes it worse, Fred, there's no way to control your bladder at this point. The urine just flows right out on its own and it burns like a bitch every time."

I'd had no idea.

"I'll need bigger pants to make room for the bag and the hose. Not even sure if I'll be able to do any contracts this way. We'll see. Can't really afford to sit around the house doin' nothing. Bills don't suddenly stop appearing in your mail box 'cause you're having prostate issues."

I helped him up the stoop and we entered. Margie was on the phone to her mother. Sounded like a heated discussion they were having. Hell, this was clearly another red flag and all I did was ignore it. How bright was that? Never under estimate the power of pussy. That's all. Beaver and bunghole. Suckable hangers. And her wearing a practically see-thru negligee readily underscored it.

Graham and I sat at the kitchen table. A few minutes later Margie joined us. She kissed Graham on the forehead.

"You look terrible, hon." She noticed my swollen lip and asked if I wanted a Band-Aid or something for it.

"Thank you, but no. I'll take care of it when I get home."

"You sure?"

I nodded.

"Margie, you have no idea what I just went through."

"Tell me, Frank."

"Was at the VA. Enlarged prostate. Out of the blue. Had trouble going to the bathroom all day; actually, more like last couple of days. It wasn't pretty."

"Could've called, you know. I'm your wife."

"Didn't want to worry you. Like I said: was far from pretty. In fact, downright debilitating. Fred and I had it under control. Didn't we, Fred?"

Frank didn't want to go into it. Instead suggested she get into a robe, cover up a bit.

"Seems unseemly for you to be strutting your stuff in an undergarment like that in front of company."

"I don't *strut*, Frank. That's your mind in the gutter, where it usually is."

She moved off in the back. When she returned she had a robe on. Frank wanted to know what it was Rinelle was after this time.

"She's not *after* anything. Could use new dentures. The ones she's got now are practically useless to her. Falling apart."

"What happened to the money we gave her for dentures a month ago?"

"More like three months ago. Dentures have a way of chipping. Goes for inferior quality to save money; only she can't save a dime to save her ass. She needs to watch what she puts in her mouth."

"Yeah. Fewer nuts wouldn't hurt."

"Took some doing: money went toward replacing that old car she had that kept breaking down. You know this already."

"She got enough money to buy a car; enough money to get her a good used car *and* dentures both."

"This gets us nowhere."

"Your mother is draining me."

"We can afford it."

"I'm working myself into an early grave here. Now I've got this prostate situation to deal to with."

"You're taking on way too much, Frank."

"Got no choice. Everybody's got their hand out. I'm the cash cow here. How much money I bring in depends on how many jobs I take on. The only reason we're solvent is due to the sound investments I made over the years."

"I've had enough. Really, Frank. Send her the damn money already or don't send it. I don't care anymore. Get her off my back. If you love me, you'll do this."

"I've got this bad case of the runs on top of everything else. Couldn't pass water, and the shits won't stop."

He dropped his pants, then the boxers—and it was some gruesome site: that tube that ran from inside his penis and down his leg and into the bag strapped to the calf already had urine in it. Fortunately, the shirttail had flopped over his privates and we weren't exposed to that ignoble site.

"See what I'm dealing with here, honey bunch? Rinelle is under the impression Frank Graham is Ft. Knox. Would love for her to take a gander at this. Maybe should take a picture and send it to her, just to show her I'm not a damned bank, honey. I'm not made of money."

"That's seriously gross, Frank. Please pull your pants up. I can't stand to see it."

"Take a good look, and next time Rinelle calls explain it to her. Your glossies cost a pretty penny, your drama classes ain't free; your wardrobe and hairdos;

pedicures and manicures, none of it free. Babysitters and day care. Then there's auto insurance, dog biscuits and bullets. I won't be able to stay as busy as I'm usually used to now because of this fucking bag I'm pissing into."

Thankfully, he yanked his boxers up, then the baggy Wrangler jeans. He reached for the paper sack with his medicine. Unraveled the top, reached in for one of the containers. Read the label.

"Finasteride."

Pressed down on the lid, unscrewed it. He asked Marge to fetch him a bottle of water from the fridge. He shook a tiny powder blue pill into his right palm and washed it down with a swig of water. He replaced the lid. Had the other container and did the same with it.

"Tamsulosin."

Capsule was the color of jade. Not exactly the size of a horse pill, but large enough. He popped it in his mouth and chased it, then picked up the packaging the spare plastic bag was in, turned it over to read what was on the back.

"Bard Latex-Free Urinary Drainage Bag. With anti-reflux chamber and Bard EZ-Lok sampling port."

I let him know I had to get going. Both thanked me for helping. Graham especially was grateful that I had been there for him.

"I'll make it up to you, Fred. Hang tight. You'll do all right eventually. With or without a license. Saw it for yourself: man can make a good living, if he applies himself."

I reminded him I still had that record.

"There's ways around it. But these things take time. You have to be patient. People make mistakes. None of us is perfect. What matters is that we learn from our missteps, and move on, move forward—and see to it we don't repeat. Up to you entirely. Or you can move to Idaho. Training not required. You can be a convicted criminal, been busted for DUI, and have a rap sheet a yard long and still be a bail enforcer."

I walked outside.

Chapter 44

It wasn't long that the door opened in back of me, and I heard her run up.

"He doesn't want you to have to walk to your place, not after all you did for him today. I'll give you a ride back."

"Like hell you will."

"What now?"

"Nothin'."

"What's the matter?"

I didn't want to say. Hated the circumstances. All of it. Made me feel downright shitty. She climbed in her Ford Fiesta parked at the curb. Sat there, waiting for me to get in. It was not easy, but I walked past the car and kept going.

I could hear her cursing back there, saying my name and cursing. I turned my head just then, not to look at her, but in the direction of the house. I'd been right: Graham had parted the living room window curtain and was watching.

Yeah; he suspected. Had a hunch. Even with that catheter in his joint he was not a man to be trifled with. I was aware of it just as I was aware of my loins aching for her; perhaps even more so.

Chapter 45

I walked in and heard Monica call my name from the bedroom. I told her I'd be there as soon as I got out of my street clothes. She had been worried about me.

I took my time getting out of my shoes and the rest of it. Stepped into the bathroom and took a look at my swollen lip in the mirror. The dog had walked up and stood there in the open doorway. I looked at her, pointed at my lip in a calm enough way.

"All your fault, you know? There was no reason to go after the kid. He was not a threat to you. Those kids were harmless. The boy just wanted to pet you and he was gentle, so gentle, Chambray."

Monica called me again. Asked who it was I was talking to. I took a quick shower, applied some balm to my swollen lips, and joined Monica in the bedroom. Got into bed. She rolled over to hug and kiss me. I held back. She wondered what was up. Turned on the lamp on her side of the bed and saw it.

"Oh, honey."

"Bounty Daddy found out."

"How?"

"Long story. Point being he figured it out."

"The wife?"

"Not quite. He's got a friend on the police force. With Chambray's illustrious history, wasn't all that difficult to add 2 and 2. And I got smacked pretty good."

I sat up. Chambray was lying at the foot of the bed in her usual spot. Taking it easy, not a care in the world.

"I hope you can appreciate what I did for you, Chambray."

Her ears perked up at mention of her name, but that was it. Dog didn't get what was going on.

"Does he still want you to work with him?"

"Looks like."

"Really?"

"Said he appreciated my confessing, being a man about it, and all that sort of thing. Otherwise might've been a lot worse all around."

"And the rabies shots?"

"Nope. There weren't any. Marge, the wife, convinced him to forego."

"Oh good."

"Yeah. Kid got a break. Looks like we all did."

I asked her to do me a favor and turn out the light. She did, wrapped her arms about my neck, snuggled against my chest, and she was out. Not I. Couldn't sleep. Marge was on my mind. What else? I needed to cut her out of my life.

Chapter 46

This is where I was going to do it. Escape the pussy trap, before I got in too deep. I had gotten my taste of it. Now was the time to call it quits; now, before emotions began to run wild. Only I was in a fever over her. I lay awake that night and other nights thinking about her. I'd see a dark-haired woman with Margie's ebony skin tone and figure walking down some street and I'd be seeing Margie. The pain in my gut gnawed at me like an anxiety attack and wouldn't go away. The longer we had to stay away from each other, the more it hurt. I'd go to their house after a day with Graham for coffee and pie, the rare job he would take now, and there she would be, the woman of my dreams, and I couldn't touch her. The pain turned me into a wreck and was becoming just too damned unbearable. I didn't know how much longer I could go on like this. A day would go by, and another and another and I thought I'd flip out of my mind.

I lost weight. No appetite. No interest in anything. The sole reason I continued to go on those track-downs with the bounty hunter, the few that he did on account of the prostate issue, was to catch a brief glimpse of her, just for that, and it would make the pain in my guts that much worse.

Monica noticed. Not only my weight loss, but I had begun to neglect her in the sack. Women are sensitive to that sort of thing. She knew something was not right. I covered up by claiming to be worried about not making enough money, being always broke at my age when other guys a lot younger were well on their way up. They owned homes, Jeeps, and whatnot. She reminded me that I was doing much better now that I was working with Graham, even though things have slowed down quite a bit, and that I needed to be patient in this regard and that it would pick up for me once the man recovered and was back one hundred percent. She also suggested I make the effort to be more positive in general. She felt that things would break for me and that I needed to give it time.

Sounded like what Graham was saying. Hell, I was not ignorant; no dunce here. How could I not agree with what they were pointing out? Truth was, patience was never a virtue I could lay claim to. Was not proud of it. Merely stating a fact.

Chapter 47

We did local jobs, for the most part. One in Santa Barbara; another in Bakersfield, the times we worked. No work meant no money for either of us. It also meant I now had no reason to go over to Graham's place, which meant I couldn't see Margie. It was excruciating.

Then early one morning I get a call from him; he had a couple of loco twins he was going after: Tasty and Nasty Tadeo.

"Tough numbers. *Los Cochinos* punks. Like that Quintero cretin. East LA; where they were seen last."

I did the driving, as usual. An acquaintance of Frank's, Walt Spunkmeyer and his girlfriend Loretto, were to meet us near the location.

Only a block before we got to our destination, an old brownstone in the barrio, Graham insisted on getting to the nearest men's room: gas station, coffee shop, hotel, didn't matter, so long as we made it. ASAP. He had to go.

"Could be this prostate medicine they got me on what's causing the shits, else it's the fuckin' street vendors. Can't say for sure."

I reminded him that he'd had the runs before he started taking the medicine. He agreed.

"Why I say can't say for sure. Been staying away from Mexican fly-by-night burrito vendors for the most part, so it's a downright mystery to me, not to mention a great nuisance."

We pulled into a Jack-in-the-Crack parking lot and I watched Graham hurry inside, did his best with that plastic bag that he had attached to his calf inside the pant leg.

It took him a long while, but he made it back, limping up to the van.

"How about taking time off, Frank, until they remove the catheter?" Hell, it was just something to say and show a degree of concern. I couldn't afford him taking any time off, period. That was the truth.

"Bills. What I've been saying: Got family members with their hand out. Getting tugged at from all sides. You saw it: the wife on my case to continue supporting her mother's reckless life style. Can't afford *not to work*."

"You got investments, Frank—by your own account."

"Can't touch my retirement. Also got to have bucks for the kids should they want to go to college. Got two in college at the moment as it is, always needin' cash. About the only time I hear from them."

"I had no idea you had two in college."

"From my first marriage. Margie's my third. You know what they say: three strikes and you're in the outhouse. Hell, I'm already in it half the time, with the runs. I'm hopin' this marriage'll stick. Tryin'. It was probably a mistake to marry someone considerably younger. We got next-to-nothin' in common. Refuses to relate to my kids. Won't make the effort. It's been rocky every step of the way. We'll see."

He yanked up on the diaper. Did some adjusting.

"What a fuckin' pathetic joke this turned out. Gotta be a first. Diaper-wearing bounty hunter. Only I ain't laughin'." He looked at me. "I don't want this to get out. If it does, I'll know where they got it from."

"That limp is hard to miss."

"They don't know what's behind it."

"What if your wife talks?"

"Margie? She best not wag that tongue of hers about this. Rinelle's money tap gets turned off. Just like that."

"Could cost you contracts, work—if word got out. There's that, too."

"Of course. I have a solid rep—but one never knows."

Chapter 48

We were parked in a liquor store parking lot across the street from the grotty brownstone with the litter in front and graffiti-covered entrance. This was supposedly where Nasty's woman was staying. Graham didn't seem to like the looks of it. Lifted his worn Stetson and wiped his brow with a neckerchief. "Keep this in mind: broads who run with types like the slime we're after are usually addicts who would slit your throat soon as look at you. I prefer to snag them where they work or in a parking lot. The last thing you want to do is this: arrest them where they live."

"So why do it?"

"Don't have much choice."

I didn't say anything.

"If Spunkmeyer's girlfriend looks familiar it could be because she used to blow dick for a living; would also, as a sideline, defecate and/or urinate on actors and studio executives. Looks much older than her actual age; hard, too. Just to give you a heads-up."

I was tempted to ask if he saw it with his own eyes, or was it merely hearsay he was repeating, but decided to let it go instead.

Walt Spunkmeyer and his girlfriend pulled up in a van designed to look like something a professional electrician might use. Man and woman alighted. Both in jeans and black Ts, Kevlar vests, with windbreakers over the Kevlars.

Loretto looked tough enough at 5'8. Been around the block a few times, this much was obvious. Walt was as big as Graham: burly, with a full dark beard. Back of his hands covered in tats. You got the idea he had plenty elsewhere: chest and elsewhere. Part of the chest tattoo was visible above the T's collar.

Graham passed out photos of the twins, and he had a plan.

"Fred over here gives Nasty and his brother a call to give them a heads-up on *Five-0* about to roust them. You know how the rest goes: Somebody should be on the roof lying in wait, someone else needs to be on their floor to grab 'em when they run out to either head down the stairwell or fire escape in back."

"The last place you want to arrest a skipper is in their home."

"Just got through telling Fred that very same thing, Walt."

"And we're still doing it?"

"Skips don't live there. According to my Judas, Nasty's girlfriend stays there."

"Same difference, Frank."

"This is a good opportunity to bag 'em, Walt."

"Just remember one thing: Judge said to bring 'em in alive to stand trial."

"Sure, I'd rather bring them in alive."

Spunkmeyer reminded us both that if the twins were not brought in breathing we wouldn't get paid, none of us would see a dime, and the bail bondsman would get stuck holding the bag. "It'll be a real bitch for him to get the court to release the 200k he put up."

"You worry too much, Walt."

"Working with you, Frank, is reason enough to worry."

"Who twisted your arm, Spunkmeyer? I asked if you wanted in on this; it was your choice. Now you want to back out?"

"I'm not backing out."

Spunkmeyer and Loretto noticed Graham limping and had too much class to ask what was the matter. They simply offered to go knock on the twins' door.

They looked at me.

"What's he gonna do with that effing camera? Ask the skips to grin and bear it when we snap the bracelets on 'em?"

"I'd like him to get some footage of this, Loretto. For the documentary."

"What '*documentary*' is that, Frank?"

Graham looked away. Walt Spunkmeyer shook his head.

"This need for 'exposure' will do your ass in one day, Graham. I hope I'm wrong. I think you're taking it too far. This constant hunger to be on tv comes with a price."

"I can use the money, Walt. Everybody's got their hand out: I got family all over the place and all of them got one thing in mind: gimme money."

Loretto was agreeing with her guy.

"Spare us, Frank. We know you. Always have to be in the limelight. Legend in your own mind."

"You were in the real movies, as I recall, honeybunch, not me."

"*Fuck off, Frank.*"

She and her man walked away. Said to let them know when he was ready on the roof. Graham cursed under his breath.

"Two-bit slut. Broad was in porn for years, fucked thirty guys a month. Made hundreds of videos. A rich relative dies, an uncle, I believe, leaves her a few bucks. She takes some Mickey Mouse private eye course and suddenly she's a 'recovery specialist.'"

"Used them before?"

"Only when I had to."

"Does Walt know she did porn?"

"I hope so. He was the instructor at the bullshit private eye institute. Bitch gives him herpes as a way of thanking him for passing her. So yeah, you would imagine he knows. Don't seem bothered by it. It's all about 'love.' Fucking Hollywood. I used Walt before; he's okay actually. I can't figure him ending up with a big-time whore, though."

Graham indicated he needed to take a dump real bad, but would forego it for the time being. Reminded me again to wait for his signal. He limped toward the building, his shotgun, as before, concealed within his tan raincoat.

Chapter 49

I waited for all concerned to be in place.

Graham called me from the roof on his walkie-talkie. Spunkmeyer and his girlfriend were ready and waiting on the second floor. I dropped my dime, made the call to the apartment where the twins were holed up.

"*Five-0* coming up the front and back. You can thank me later."

"Who are you, man?"

"Just a grateful dude you sold some fly shit to and my bottom bitch when we was low. Even though we was needy, your attitude was: I ain't greedy. A friend in need is a friend indeed. Know I'm sayin', bro? Tryin' to do the right thing, homie. Else it don't make me no nevermind."

I hung up, and hurried on over to the building. Had the camera running. It was tricky trying to watch where I was stepping through the B&W viewfinder. I did what I could. Did my best. Climbed up the stairs to the second floor. Heard shots. Saw the first twin limp out of the apartment. Looked like he'd been shot in the foot; then the other *cochino* punk hurried out after him, helped his sibling up the stairs to the next level. Saw Loretto rush inside the apartment, calling Walt's name. I followed after her.

Place had next to zero furniture. Odor caused by exotic spices was heavy in the air. Walt Spunkmeyer was on the living room floor. He'd been hit in the side or leg. Couldn't rightly tell from all the blood. The former porn queen, Spunkmeyer's squeeze, was down there helping him sit up and doing what she could to stave off blood loss, while at the same time dialing for help.

A screaming baby coming from my left drew my attention and I swung the camera at the corner by the door. There was a young hispanic woman huddled there, cradling her screaming infant. Woman was sobbing hysterically herself and was practically unhinged.

I got it, but I also was hired to do a job, so I kept shooting video of the scene. My eye glued to the viewfinder, to the left of mom and her child, I sighted in on a couple in their 30s, a man and a woman. So stoned out of their minds they had no idea what was taking place. The woman had one of her breasts out, hanging loose there, that the guy in a stained Che Guevara T-shirt was sucking on for nourishment. Seemed like it to me. In fact, dude had milk dripping from his mouth and chin. It was unsettling, you might say. I was disgusted by it. Found it more troubling even than seeing this guy Spunkmeyer losing blood.

"What do we got here?"

The woman never opened her eyes. Said something that sounded like ABR. I'd read about it in the joint, although I doubted there were actual couples like this in real life, until now: Adult Breast Feeding Relationship. The guy was sucking on the breast for milk and the woman whose breast it was hardly flinched.

Spunkmeyer's lady was done talking on the phone. She looked up and she looked pissed. Had every right to be, no doubt.

"Hey, *Fellini*, did it occur to you that Graham might need help up there?How about if you put that fucking movie camera down and get your ass to the roof?"

"I'm not allowed to make arrests or use a piece. Just sayin'."

"Get your ass up there, *asshole*! We know you got a piece. A piece of shit faggot like you always carries a piece and knows how to use it. *Use it or don't, but get your stupid ass up there!*"

She was right. I didn't care being called a faggot, but she was right: someone should've been up there with the big bad bounty man. Had been my plan all along. You might say the ABR couple had caused the distraction.

I slipped on out and made it up the stairs, working the camera still. If I didn't, I didn't get paid. It was that simple.

Chapter 50

There were shots as I reached the door to the roof, then a loud shotgun blast. Graham was leaning over one of the twins, lying there, and looked like he was relieving the dead man of his Rolex. Bounty hunter had no idea I was watching and I thought to leave well enough alone, and made it back down a dozen steps, did an about-face, and thought to call his name, make it look like I was just coming up.

By the time I got there Graham was at the roof's edge jamming the watch inside his flak jacket and looking over the short wall. The twin, who went by Tasty, was lying on this side of a pigeon coop in a puddle of blood and a hole in his chest the size of a Frisbee. You guessed it: dead as a doornail. I got footy of it. Graham seemed okay, in that he was leaning over the edge, looking down. I walked over, shooting tape the whole time, to take a look at what he was looking at. The other punk: Nasty, was a splattered mess in the alley below.

Graham asked about Walt Spunkmeyer and his woman, the former porn slut. I told him his friend Walt had been wounded and that Loretto had called for an ambulance. He nodded.

I asked what happened.

"That one down there tried jumping to the roof next door and come up short by a foot. I emptied my 12-gauge into the other skip—after he shot at me a bunch of times. So we got a stiff down in the alley, where trash belongs, and one on the roof here lying in pigeon waste and feathers. Both with their maker."

Graham crossed himself. Told me to stop filming, then he hurried over to the other side of the pigeon coop at about the middle of the roof to take that much-needed dump.

I lingered where the stiff was, bent down, got my hand about the gold chains round his neck and yanked them off and jammed them in my shirt pocket. Damn right. I was looking out after my own retirement. Nobody else was. I got out of there.

Chapter 51

Walt Spunkmeyer limped out of the apartment building with his girlfriend's help. Sirens wailed in the distance. Spunkmeyer was seriously pissed.

"I don't see the skippers, Graham."

"One of 'em is in the alley in back, the other's on the roof lying in pigeon poop."

"Dead?"

"Yep."

Spunkmeyer broke away from his girlfriend, moved up against Frank's face.

"Both? Dead?"

"Nothing I could do. It happened."

"I got this for what', Frank! Look at me! Shot in the leg! We don't see a dime for the blood I lost. Judge wanted these two brought in alive to stand trial."

"I do know that."

"I'm glad."

"You're not even going to ask what happened?"

"Gung-ho, Graham. Seems to me you'd rather deep-six 'em than collect the bounty!"

"Not quite."

"Yes. Quite!" It was the girlfriend. Put her two cents in.

"I'll make it up to you, Walt."

"By not calling next time you need backup, Graham."

Of course, Spunkmeyer and his chick had no way of knowing, but Frank Graham did get paid: liberating the dead punk of his wristwatch covered it well enough. Got something for my own labor myself.

Chapter 52

The ambulance arrived, as did a couple of squad cars. Loretto helped her man make it to the ambulance where the EMTs were opening the rear door and did their part. Graham handed me the van keys, his flak jacket, and hinted I should make myself scarce. More than likely he'd be taken to the station to make a statement. He'd call me to come get him in a couple of hours. Thor was a concern for me. He reminded me that the pinscher knew me by now and to relax, take him back to the house if I wanted, or follow him to the station and wait. I decided I'd follow him to the station. Graham walked toward the cops at the curb.

I stayed back, and could hear Frank talking to them.

"I do all I can to get you guys involved, for what good it does. It didn't have to turn out the way it did. A fugitive recovery agent is on his way to the hospital for surgery as a result."

A small crowd had gathered. The cops were busy handling that. Graham was informed that a homicide dick was on the way to talk to him and not to go anywhere.

Chapter 53

Later in the van the bond recovery agent looked at me. I had an idea what he was about to bring up.

"That answer your question?"

"Why bounty hunters are rough on skips? Yes. It does, Frank."

"We're dealing with *cochinos.* Subhuman pigs."

I wondered if all were *'cochinos.'*

"I never said. Just about, though."

"What percentage would you say?"

"You don't seem to get it. It's you versus them. They break the law, but don't want to go back for the court date. Tough shit. Living by the rules ain't easy—for any of us, but we do it. If you can't play, better yet: Refuse to play, you pay."

"With due respect, I never laid a hand on you, Frank, or your partner—when you guys caught up with me that time—only because I knew better. Had I attempted anything I knew I was toast."

"You fled. After we had you. Seems to be a character trait. Resisted arrest. Nobody laid a hand on you. Another time: same thing. Another skip. Gave us the slip. Took off after we had him. My partner, Mario, yes, that Mario, Rinelle's husband, Margie's step-daddy, got run over as a result. Ended up in a wheelchair. Then later on, some years later, drops dead from a heart-attack, or some such. He was a good man. Loved him like a brother. Went way back, he and I. High school buds."

I asked if that was how he got into the business. Not sure why I was probing, because it was going to be that much tougher to take him out later, if it came to that. You got to know someone, and very often, it made it difficult to betray the dude, or do anything: rob 'em, take from him. I was already carrying on with his woman. Probably it was bad enough.

"No. I was a cop. Mario already had the bail bond business; took over from his daddy who was ready to retire. I got shot in the line of duty. No choice but to leave the force with a pension. Mario needed help. Had a couple of knuckle-draggers working for him, caused him all sorts of trouble. There were lawsuits. The neanderthals he had working for him were practically illiterate; not even high school graduates. Well, they had GEDs; two did, the third not even. So to help out I went in. Was freelancing anyway, on top of owning my own bail bond business. I helped."

"And Rinelle? She a bounty hunter?"

"You're joking."

"Just asking. What do I know?"

"There was always a certain toughness to Margie's mother, for sure. She's got a mouth on her and can throw a punch; only it takes more than that, a lot more."

I had nothing to come back with.

"Go ahead and ask. I know you're curious."

I had no idea what he was getting at. Figured he'd get to it eventually. And he did. But first he wanted to stop by his bank not far from where he lived.

We pulled into the parking lot. He grabbed his flak jacket before going inside. Now, I found it curious that he would take his flak jacket with him to do his banking business; that is, until I got out to stretch my legs and was able to see that he walked past the tellers and disappeared inside the bowels of the bank. Safe deposit box, was my first guess. Good enough place to keep the Rolex, among whatever else he had stashed in there: other items of worth he'd picked off other skips.

His business, no doubt. Who could fault him? The dead skipper he'd liberated the Rolex off of had been paid for with drug money. Who was I to judge? My only complaint was that Graham was able to get to it before I could. I did have the gold chains. Had to be worth something.

I walked back to the van so it wouldn't look like I was spying on the man and sticking my nose where it didn't belong.

Chapter 54

He was back soon enough, wearing the flak jacket this time. Got in.

"Feel like getting something to eat, Freddy?"

I shook my head.

"You sure? Earned it."

"I'm okay."

He looked at me as we pulled out of the lot.

"No doubt you must've wondered why I went in there with the vest."

"Never crossed my mind."

He grinned.

"Had a Rolex in it, worth ten K, easy. Can't bring valuables home with me. Marge waits till I'm passed out, then goes through my pockets. She finds anything worth anything it gets sent to Rinelle pronto, to keep her in dope." He fired up a stogie. "I help myself to bling every now and then. I don't work for nothin'. You heard what Walter said: judge was withholding bail. We wouldn't get paid on account the slime bags bit the dust."

"I don't judge, Frank. I'm the last one to judge."

"Just sayin', gives me great pleasure to relieve some of these sacks of waste of their ill-gotten gains. They push the shit on our young, poison society with their killer toxins and make bank doin' it, as opposed to going out and working for a living. So, as a result, whenever the opportunity presents itself, I liberate these assholes of the bling they love to flaunt at every opportunity and shove in my face."

"I don't see anything the matter with it."

"Of course not, since you ended up with those gold chains worth plenty."

Now, I was the one grinning. We both were.

"What good is all that bling to a lowlife stiff like that anyway?"

"I like your attitude, Alf. Yes, sir. You're okay."

I had a question for him. Off topic. Only before I could even get it out, he was already responding. Never mind that it wasn't what I had in mind. One thing was certain, though: by the time he was done, my train of thought was off the rails, in that I couldn't recall what it was I'd wanted to ask him.

"How does an ugly old fuck like me end up with a hot number like Margie? It happened. I never went chasing after it; not in the habit of running after young babes like her. Sure, I look; we all look. Ain't blind, but I never went out of my way."

He pulled out a stogie and fired up.

"My friend Mario, who was married to Margie's mother at the time, came to me—after his accident. Pleaded with me to make it with Rinelle.

I refused. Outright refused. He wouldn't let up. She had a powerful sex drive and was frustrated and started to take it out on him verbally. She can be mighty abusive. He begged me to go ahead and take her to a motel. Offered to pay me. I wouldn't take his money, but finally said I'd see what I could do. Rinelle and I talked. Went out for a drink. Next thing you know, we're checking into a no-tell motel. I explained what I was doing and why. I had a wife. Couldn't afford to get involved. This was my second marriage. Besides, Rinelle was not my type; never was or could be. We had our fun and I thought that would be the end of it. Well, Mario comes to me, and offers to pay an all-expenses trip to Vegas, if I would only take Rinelle with. Again, I refused. Wanted nothing to do with it. He insisted. Then she starts buying me gifts and such. I gave in. We made it. Spent a weekend in Vegas. Saw Elvis. Live. Again, I thought that was the end of it. I wanted nothing else to do with her. And she knew it. She became obsessed. Wouldn't let go. Got nasty with my wife at the time. Told her everything. My marriage came close to falling apart. Somehow it held. My wife loved me enough to forgive and forget, especially after Mario explained it all to her. She felt sorry for him, and let it go. Well, Rinelle was not about to let *me* go. She brings young Margie in to help out around the office wearing mini skirts and short pants. Now, Margie was/is a jaw-dropping hot piece of ass, to put it mildly. But I kept my distance. Never came on. In fact, had given my notice that I was leaving. Rinelle wouldn't hear of it. More gifts and flowers. She was relentless. Now, she goes all out: pushes Margie on me. I had no idea how old Margie was, not certain. She had ID that said she was of age. Well, one night the three of us are watching a movie, having a drink, and Rinelle dozes off; soon after so do I. When I wake up, my pants are unzipped. Evidently Margie had helped herself to my privates. That was the beginning of the affair. I got involved. Ended up falling for her. Who wouldn't?"

"Rinelle did all this to keep you from leaving?"

"Yes, sir. Sure did. And then some. Of course, she'll deny it every time. Had to do them both for a while. Never at the same time. No *ménage* type thing. I don't do those. I'm Old School, I suppose. Never was interested.

Made me sick to do Rinelle the few times we made it. You'll see why when you meet her, should you ever be so unfortunate. I could no longer abide by her wishes, and dropped her completely. She starts doing meth; some of the skip punks and their relations slipped her some meth and other drugs and she got to likin' it. Margie's pregnant, evidently. Seems like. My wife decides she's had enough. Wants a divorce this time. Couldn't take my sleeping with Margie. Mario passes. Margie and I marry. We keep the bail bond office going a while longer, but Rinelle's drug habit finally wrecks it. To keep her from ending up homeless I help pay her mortgage, do as much as I can. She refinances, stays afloat a while longer, then spends that on drugs. You name it: crack, coke, meth, liposuction and cosmetic surgery. Didn't take. Not in her case. You've seen pictures of her. Her ugly is bone deep. And I watch her slide further and further down into the gutter . . . to the point where she's at now. She had a breakdown. Spent time in the bug bin. Could be where Margie's headed: loony ward, if she's not careful. Thanks to loony Rinelle. And there's the whole sorry scenario."

Whatever it was I had wanted to bring up, before he got into this thing about Rinelle, must not have been very important, because it was gone, my train of thought having been completely derailed. Like I said: must not have been worth bringing up even. Sometimes these things happened.

Chapter 55

It was the next day that we went on to pay this two-hundred-and-fifty-pound skip named Lotta Fish a visit at her favorite East Hollywood ice cream parlor, where the Judas who'd tipped Graham off this time claimed she'd be. She was seated at one of the tables inhaling a banana split. Graham bought us each a chocolate Sunday, and we sat at a table behind the big woman. We timed it so that we'd be done at about the same time she was, and followed her outside.

He had the one thick wrist cuffed before she knew what hit her, and Graham had been in the process of doing the other, when the beefy mama head-butted him with the back of her skull. She'd jerked her head into his face, spun and did her best to kick him in the groin and took off. Even though she'd missed his jewels by a considerable margin, the hose connected to the plastic bag on his leg got disconnected and he'd been unable to chase after her. Nothing kept me from doing it, though.

I traded a sleepy-eyed wino sitting on the sidewalk with his back against a utility pole a dollar bill for his nearly empty bottle of rotgut and pitched it at the back of the broad's neck. Bottle smacked her somewhere below the right ear, causing her to falter and stagger into a transient's cart overloaded with empty soda and beer cans. She got cursed out and whacked across the face with the man's staff and I caught up with her before she was able to recover and told her in a nice enough manner to cuff herself behind her back. No way was she about to. I thought I'd give it a try.

"Turn around, mama. I don't like doing it, but I need to cuff your wrists."

"Fuck off, asshole. You got no right."

Seemed like she wasn't interested, even after I threatened to taser her, and did. That dropped Ms. Fish to the ground and I got the loose bracelet on the other wrist. Assisted the plus size lady to her feet. Then I did a quick look around to make sure no cops saw me arresting her. With my history, I had no right doing anything of the sort. Graham had pointed it out to me probably a couple of times already. On the other hand, if I didn't make the effort to do my bit to help out, I wouldn't have felt right about hanging around with him and expecting to be paid. I figured he appreciated the effort.

"Okay, *mamita*, be nice and we'll get along just fine."

"Police harassment, what this is."

"I ain't no oinker, sugar. I'm one of the good guys. Civilian like you."

"I give amazing head, baby. Give you the best blow job you ever had, if you let me go."

"Love to do it, gorgeous, but that puts me in a situation."

"Just another motherfucker."

"Kind of language is offensive to these virgin ears, mama. Ain't you got no manners?"

She tried spitting in my face. I ducked in time.

"I got manners, faggot. You like my manners?"

I yanked her arms way up between her shoulder blades and had the bitch gasping.

"Just 'cause you look like a porker don't give you the right to act like a pig."

"Yo mama's the pig, asshole."

"I'll pretend that kind of talk don't bother me."

I guided her back to where Graham was standing in a doorway, doing his best to reattach the bottom of the hose to the bag. Plenty of urine had poured right out onto the sidewalk. Bertha was chuckling.

"Mucho macho pissed himself. Ain't that some shit?"

Graham looked up. Wiped blood from his lower lip with a hanky.

"I suggest you shut it, sister, or it gets shut for you."

Unfortunately she didn't get the message, and attempted for another kick, which he easily sidestepped. Graham grabbed her by the cuffs in back and yanked her inside the doorway there. They were out of sight for five or six minutes. I have no idea what had gone on, but when they stepped back out Lotta Fish was as docile as a kitten. Ms. Fish even went so far as to address him as 'sir' whenever he spoke to her.

Chapter 56

We escorted the beefy *mamasita* to the van. Frank asked me to drive.

Sometimes as you got to know people you didn't like to begin with, your resentment and/or loathing went ever deeper. In this case, in light of what I continued to see & was learning about the man, it became increasingly more difficult to resent him—about any of it. In fact, if anything, my attitude toward him went the other way. There was a certain respect that could not be denied, which made it increasingly tougher to consider taking him out. But there I was, pondering how to do it, even as he produced a thick Cuban and proceeded to fire up. He rolled his window down. Blew clouds of smoke out there to add to the haze.

As before, he thought to offer me one. As before, I declined.

"Your choice. Only you're missing out on one of life greatest pleasures, my friend."

"Better than trim?"

"No contest."

"Hard to believe."

"Sex is overrated. Of course, I'm twice your age. Could be part of it."

"And the catheter."

"No doubt. I have no choice. Even after they take it out, won't be able to get an erection for a while, let alone maintain one. Doc tells me I won't be able to ejaculate, either—for a while. Course, if you can't ejaculate you can't feel nothin'."

"What good is that?"

"Exactly what I said: What good is it?"

"For how long?"

He shrugged. "Could be months. Could be permanent."

"About the worst thing could happen to a man. Seems like."

"No, actually having the running shits beats it."

"I'd rather be dead than not be able to feel anything while doing my woman."

He needed me to locate a men's room. ASAP.

Chapter 57

The two long weeks finally crawled by and it was time to return to the VA hospital in West LA. I drove us down. We checked in at the front desk and found seats in the waiting area. We were on a different floor now, and no longer in that same waiting room as before. It was past noon and there were a dozen people waiting, sitting in chairs and waiting calmly, men and women Graham's age, some older even. Graham picked up the *Wall Street Journal* to see how his stock was doing. He seemed pleased. Sweeter than that even: this was the day he would be liberated from the catheter. Hallelujah.

The nurse called his name. We both rose. I helped him make it over. We crossed the fairly large waiting area to where the nurse stood outside a pair of double doors. Lady was short, with a short 'do. Late 30s.

"Mr. Graham?"

"Yes, ma'am."

"And this is . . . ?"

"My son Fred. He's been invaluable to me during this rather difficult phase."

This made her take pause, then decided it was okay to have father and son go inside the corridor, while holding the door open for us. Frank thanked her, and so did I. I usually did my best not to take acts of kindness for granted, no matter how seemingly insignificant.

We were guided along, past a 40-something nurse in her white uniform sitting at a table on our right, her back to us, as she tapped away on a typer keyboard. We passed another woman, good looking brunette, possibly Latina, in civilian clothes, half her age, at another table tending to paperwork.

Our nurse had us enter a room on our left, with the usual bed, chair, and hospital-related gizmos.

She asked his name, last four digits of his social, date of birth, mailing address, etc. She needed Graham to lower his trousers and that she would return shortly. I turned away, while he did that, which left him in his boxers, plus the shirttail over the front. I turned around when he said it was okay to do so.

"Think this'll be any worse, Frank?"

"I imagine it won't be fun."

"You ready for it?"

He looked at me.

"I'll be happy to get the tube out and the bag off my leg and be able to go about my business like a man again."

Chapter 58

Nurse was back. She had latex gloves on.

"When I asked the male nurse before he applied the catheter if it was going to be painful—his response had been, I quote: 'Not inordinately.' Now, I'm posing the same question to you, ma'am: Will there be pain?"

"Some. Yes, sir."

"Fair enough."

"I need you to lie back on the bed sir."

Graham had been sitting up on the bed, and leaned back at this point, resting on his elbows. The nurse sat at the other end of the bed, her back to him, same as the male nurse that time. There was a reason for this, no doubt. They were always turned a certain way.

This was merely my guess: my gut feeling was this was going to be far more excruciating than what the bail recovery agent had been through before when the thing was jammed in. Just a guess. You could tell Frank was bracing himself for the worst. Tense in the face, jaw clenched. He was an old worrier, been through some heavy shit in his time. I was half his age, and already been through my share of crap. He'd been through a lot more, no doubt.

I did my bit, by turning away as before. Wondered how she was going to go about it. Not a big woman at all at about five-two, but seemed quite capable. You sensed she knew what she was doing.

"On the count of three, Mr. Graham, I want you to take a deep breath. Ready?"

"Yes, ma'am."

She counted off. On the count of three, he inhaled and held it. And like the other fellow in her field, the male nurse, woman was quick and efficient. Did not waste time at all and yanked the tube out, and the combo grunt/gasp I heard Graham make this time far exceeded the reaction he'd made when the tube had been inserted.

I turned. Graham showed signs of trembling. It seemed he couldn't move, frozen, and stayed this way, even after the nurse requested that he stand up. About all he could do was sit up. He was no longer making any sort of sounds, not so much as batting an eyelid. Then there were deep gasps, eyes welling and tears flowing, the upper body shaking. He sat this way for what seem like forever. The nurse was on her feet, taking it in, waiting patiently. She knew; she'd witnessed it before with other patients.

He nodded eventually, indicated he wanted to stand up but could not do it by himself. At some point after, the nurse and I, taking him each by an elbow, helped him rise. Graham, although standing on his feet, remained frozen, head and shoulders bent forward, began to quake; his entire body was quaking, the tears pouring. He was not crying, not sobbing, nothing of the sort; they flowed of their own accord and flowed freely, silent tears brought about by indescribable pain.

Fuck. Is this what awaited me and my gender down the road? Was it? Once we got to be Graham's age? Face-off with the prostate?

Nurse and I stopped whatever it was we were doing, as the only civilized recourse, while he shook in place, wincing in agony, not able to take a step or so much as lift his head. His tears flowed like a river. It certainly left an impression and it was scary.

The nurse looked at me.

"Your father needs to use the bathroom so we can determine the extent he is able to empty his bladder."

I nodded. She spoke to Graham.

"Are you able to go to the bathroom, sir? If not, we can get you a bottle of water."

"I can go."

She pointed out where the bathroom was at the end of the relatively short corridor. Let us know she'd be back, and she left the room.

Chapter 59

"Frank . . ."

His eyes were on me. He wanted to respond, wanted to speak. His arms, head and legs continued to shake in that leaning forward stance that he was stuck in. I figured he might topple over and was ready for it, but it didn't happen.

After a while, I reached for the box of kleenex and held it out to him. He yanked a few out and wiped his eyes and face. He took a few deep breaths, then nodded his head.

"Let's do it, Mr. Reed."

"You sure?"

"They need me to."

I placed his Stetson appropriately on his head and helped him out of the room. We made a right and walked down the end of the corridor to the john. He entered, and closed the door behind him. When he was done, he stepped out.

Chapter 60

Back in the room the nurse did an ultrasound of his bladder to determine how much urine remained. According to her the results were encouraging. He had passed eighty percent of his water. She let us know the doc would be in to see him in a few minutes.

The doctor was a man of about 60, medium height, not in the greatest of shape, either. He went over some things. Reminded Graham that he wanted him to come back for a checkup in thirty days.

Frank asked how much longer he needed to keep taking the medicine.

"Rest of your life, probably."

Graham hated to hear it, hated to take any kind of medicine at all. Never even cared for aspirin.

"You don't have to take it, Mr. Graham. Entirely up to you. Only you could find yourself going through what you just went through all over again."

Graham mentioned the desire for sex was no longer there. Was it typical? And would it return? Would he be able to achieve an erection? The doc mentioned that if the problem with the prostate returned, the only solution might be to have it removed.

"This is what some patients have opted for."

"So that means no more sex?"

"That's right."

"What the hell, Doc? Other men gone this route?"

"They have."

"How are they coping with the fact they can't make love? Have to live without being able to have sex with their wife or girlfriend?"

The doc shrugged. "They live with it."

"That's no good."

"They're alive."

Graham asked the doctor if he'd ever had any trouble like this with *his* prostate.

"No."

"I don't mind telling you, Doc: not knowing if I'll ever be able to make love to my wife just ruined my day."

Doctor had no comment.

"Life goes on, huh?"

"The way to look at it. Then again, we just might take you off the *Tamsulosin* in a month or so, and things could return to normal for you. We'll have to see. Can't promise anything."

"And I'd still be taking the other?"

"*Finasteride?* Yes."

"I talked to a few people who like their John Barleycorn like me, and they never had any trouble like this. Alcohol is supposed to prevent it. I guess not in my case."

"Evidently not, sir."

The doc reminded him that it would not be a good idea to imbibe at this time, not while taking the medicine.

Graham inquired if there was anything else he might take, non-conventional. The doc had no patience for it, but listened, and responded.

"Some of my patience take Saw Palmetto, pumpkin seed oil. But it's not medicine. Entirely up to you, sir. I'm not trying to dissuade you and/or convince you of anything."

Graham said he understood. The Doc reminded him to renew his prescription when he ran out. We walked outside.

Chapter 61

We were at the van when I thought to mention that I had to run back inside to use the john. I had no idea how exactly we were going to kill him just yet. Did think of cyanide for some reason. It being quick and hard to detect. And if we didn't feed it to Graham, so be it. I might want to have it on hand for my own use. One never knew. This was how serial creepo Leonard Lake took his own butt out while in custody & the pigs in charge were about to nail his sorry ass. Like I said: I'd wanted to have some on hand, or else SUX, just in case the shit hit the fan.

Once inside, I waited for a gullible nurse type, or a lowly worker, or even a volunteer to appear. An older soul brother finally did make his appearance, pushing an obese white dude in a wheelchair past me, and was about to enter the room where the blood testing was done.

"Excuse me, sir. May I ask you something when you get a free moment?"

"Soon as I help this gentleman inside."

Couple of minutes later he was out.

"What can I do for you, my man?"

"Well, blood; it's like this: I got this ailing friend who's tired. Wants out. She's had it."

"Sounds bad. She try the Lord?"

"Yes. Nothing seems to work. Did my best to talk her out of it."

"Some folks is real bad off, can't take it. Want out."

"Exactly, my friend. Well, she, the both of us, came to the conclusion that cyanide might be quickest and the most painless; either that or SUX."

He knew what SUX stood for and I was glad I didn't have to go into an explanation."

"I can get anything you want: cyanide, SUX, Fentanyl, potassium chloride, ricin, botulinum toxin, arsenic, Rohypnol —"

"You can get *roofies?*"

"Yes, sir. Castor beans, mercury—and even *Liquid Plum'er.*"

"*Liquid Plum'er?* I can walk into any minimart and get *Liquid Plum'er.* That's one excruciating way to check out, blood, and can take days."

"I can dig it. So which is it?"

"Cyanide."

He quoted me a price.

"For a single cyanide capsule?"

"Take it or leave it."

"How about half now, and the rest when you come back with it?"

"You ever sold used cars? If not, you should. You a born used car salesman."

It was pure bullshit, but I let him have the paper money.

"Wait right here."

And he was gone. About fifteen minutes later I see the soul brother at the end of the corridor walking this way with a tall, slow moving hospital cop. Evidently the cop, or he could have been a security guard, couldn't quite tell, was over-the-hill and so out of shape that it looked like he was moving in slow motion. I hurried out of there just the same, a few bucks lighter.

Chapter 62

Graham wanted a few days to rest and recover. It was costing him, but he wanted to celebrate by taking it easy at home not doing much, spending time with his kids by taking them to the LA Zoo, Disneyland, the Universal Studios tour. There was nothing I could do about it. Margie wouldn't go to any of these places with them and would stay home and sulk, or else she'd be calling me up, upset because we hadn't been able to spend much time together at all.

After almost a whole week had gone by like this I got the nerve to go over. My excuse being I wanted to see how Graham was doing and when we'd be able to return to work. Marge answered the door, nearly in tears when she saw me. Hell, I was close to it myself. The ache inside was unbearable. And yet we were too afraid to touch, other than her daring to put her hand over mine when I had it on the door knob to close the door. Just this simple connection, flesh on flesh, felt like a current of electricity rushing through me. My heart pounded inside my chest. And there was no denying the growing erection inside my trousers.

"He's in the back with the brats."

I nodded.

"Can I get you anything?" She glanced at my crotch as she said it. Could not resist placing her free hand over it. I brushed it away.

We were whispering at this point. Everything spoken in cautious tones.

"I only wish."

She had a hanky out and was dabbing at her eyes, then blew her nose. It was killing me. Not being able to hold her in my arms was pure agony.

She led me through the house to the rear porch. Enclosed. Butch was tinkering with what looked like a brand new train set, and the girl was happily focused on what appeared to be a recently purchased Barbie doll. The new box it had come in was nearby. Frank was sitting comfortably in a lounge chair cleaning that mean-ass looking shotgun to a country tune playing on a boom box. He had a stack of cassettes sitting next to it.

He paused to take a pull from his beer bottle. I recalled medical peeps at the VA saying he wasn't supposed to be consuming alcohol, not even beer, while on the medicine. It was his business, I supposed, and I kept quiet about it. Watched him wipe his mouth with the back of his hand. Asked if I cared for one.

"I don't mind, Frank. Thanks."

He gave the order to Marge to fetch it. Indicated the cassette player.

"Know who that is?"

"Can't say that I do, sir."

"George Jones. Greatest country singer who ever lived."

"I agree. He's good."

When Jones was done, Graham put a woman singer on. Now this one sounded familiar.

"You must know who that is."

"Yes, sir: the one and only Patsy Kline." Some of the bulls and lifers at one of the joints I spent time in had been partial to her.

"Died young. Plane crash."

"Always liked her voice."

Marge was back with the bottle, that I nearly dropped because she'd unintentionally rubbed a thigh against me on her way back inside, only it had been more intentional than she let on with Graham there. He'd been focused on shining his shogun and hadn't noticed, or had he?

The perfume aroma of her, the nearness. I was walking on eggshells. Nerves and thumbs that I had failed to conceal one hundred percent. Frank had just laughed and blamed it on 'Nam. I had never told him that all I'd done the whole time in Southeast Asia was drive a truck. My unit was responsible for transporting grunts out to the boonies from the base camp. The grunts were the ones who did most of the real fighting, not that we didn't receive our share of NVA mortar attacks and weren't exposed to our share of Agent Orange when out in some village somewhere near the sticks.

He said that I was a good ol' boy and that 'Nam was a son of a bitch to recover from, but that I was doing great. He was in Korea and understood.

I asked Frank how he was making out, and when did he think we might return to work.

"Soon. As much as I'm enjoying spending time with the kids, I'm not one to sit on my behind doing nothing. Got to keep money coming in. Hopefully quicker than it's going out. Always on a man's mind."

"Exactly."

We raised our beers.

"To good health."

"To good health."

I asked permission to use the john and mentioned that Chambray was all by herself and that I needed to get back. He said to ask Margie to show me where the john was.

Chapter 63

Marge was sitting at the kitchen table eating a doughnut with a sadness to her that clawed at my insides. The need was so great. I stood there. My heart aching and my Jones stiffer than a billy. She noticed. Tried, but could not suppress a grin.

"When do you return to chasing skips?"

"Soon."

"Thank god."

I mentioned the need to take a leak. She ignored that. Took me by the sleeve, away from the corridor that led to the rear: my right/her left, toward the fridge and sink, and we embraced. Her tears flowed, while she squeezed me with all her might. We kissed and could not stop. I could not get enough of her. I kissed her eyes and the tears that flowed from them. It was nearly impossible to break free, but we did, we had to at the sound of the porch door slamming shut. It was the little girl. Wanted *Kool-Aid* and cookies for herself and her brother Butch.

Marge took care of it, had them on a tray that the girl carried back. She walked with the kid to hold the porch door open for her, and returned soon after.

"Where's the head?"

"What I would love to do right now: give you amazing head."

"It'll have to wait."

"I can't sleep. Can't eat."

She indicated the half-finished doughnut on her plate on the kitchen table behind her. I had my hands on her rump, then pressed her hard up against my bulging crotch. And we started grinding away this way. And the only thing it did was to make us both hotter and the situation totally unbearable. There was nothing to do, but stop. Either that or I got blue balls and/or Graham walked in on us.

We broke. She pointed out where the john was down the short stretch of hallway behind me, and I forced myself to walk to it.

Chapter 65

Next thing I know Margie's in the hospital for attempting to take her life. Graham was out of state on a job and had called long distance. Sounded like he gave half a damn.

"Want you to look in on my kids, Fred. They're staying with Bruno and his wife. Would still like for you to make sure they're taken care of."

"I can do that, Frank."

"Loony Rinelle is responsible, bet you anything. Pushed my baby over the edge. Margie couldn't take it anymore and saw suicide as a way out."

"What're you saying, Frank?"

"Has to stick her nose in our marriage. Always been that way. One of the reasons Margie had us move to California, to get away from her busybody mama. She claims it's the acting bug, but I suspect it's really to break free of Rinelle. She's impossible. Enough to drive anyone to drink."

"That what drove you to it, Frank?"

"Me? Hell, I always drank. She done it to her daughter, though. Every one of Rinelle's adopted kids is messed up in the head. Every damned one, Alf. No shit. In and out of therapy. Broad's been hitched and divorced too damned many times. In and out of rehab for years."

I didn't know what to add to it. He said he was flying in first chance. Asked me to check in on Margie, be there for when her mother showed to give her a hard time about what happened, and to blame him for it, too. I said I would.

As I hung up the receiver I could not help but notice that my arm was shaking, then the other joined it. Trembling. Christ. Why, Margie? What are you doing? Did she want to get out of the marriage this bad? Margie, Margie. . . .

Monica stepped out of the john and saw the look on my face. I attempted to rub at the welling tears by pressing my thumbs against my eyes.

I looked up. Cleared my throat. After I explained what had gone down, Monica offered to go to the hospital with me. I didn't think it'd be a good idea. Besides, someone needed to stay with Chambray.

Chapter 66

I was at Margie's bedside, practically a wreck. She looked like she was dozing. I reached out to her. Her eyes opened, and she was squeezing my hand in both of hers. Had it to her lips and was kissing the palm, then the back of it. When she had the tips of my fingers inside her mouth I thought it was a bit much. Gross even, and I withdrew my hand.

"You're the one good thing that's ever happened to me."

"Suicide? I'd be lost without you, baby."

"I'm so sorry. Can you ever forgive me? I. . . ."

"Don't."

"I feel awful about all the pain I caused you, Fred honey."

"I'll do it."

"No."

"If that's what you want; if that's the only way to make sure we have each other, so save what we have."

"Not if you love me. No. We can't be talking like this. Not now. There has to be another way."

"Not for us."

"What good will I be with you in prison? Good as dead, that's what good."

"Look what he's doing to you, to us. It can't go on. I can't stand it; I can't take it."

She clung to me. We were both weeping. That's when the beastly female in what appeared to be a fright wig barged in. Only it was no fright wig, it was her actual hair. Rinelle. Gaudy earrings and all. Rings on her tattooed fingers. TRUS TNO1 is what the crooked upper case letters and the number spelled out. Only it was clear enough to anyone who saw her that she was the one not to be trusted.

I knew her from the photos. Not an appealing looking woman at all. Only here, now, she looked like hell. Severely bruised and on edge. Her appearance raggedy. Some of it may have had to do with the long flight. Some of it. Not all; not by a long shot. The emaciated mixed-race punk who showed with her looked like shit himself. Strung out. Hype, no doubt. I'd been around enough to smell them.

Rinelle was glaring at me.

"*You*. What're you want with my Margie? What're you doing here?"

"I was concerned."

"You're not family! She's not married to you. She has a husband!"

"Leave him alone, ma. He's a friend. He was worried about me."

"Friend?"

"I work with Frank."

"Who's talking to you, asshole? I'm here to save my little girl."

"Okay."

"Not okay. Kindly get your nose out of my backside, mister, before I get security to throw you out."

I raised my hands, conceding, and me and the quiet junky punk stepped into the far corner.

Chapter 67

"My God, ma, you look worse than me. Who's been beating on you? Jamal?" She looked at the stringbean just then. Jamal never batted an eye. Didn't give a damn. He had nose trouble, it seemed. Sniffles. Constant and annoying. I watched him light up a smoke in this no-smoking zone.

"Hush, child. You need to conserve your strength."

"You're the one should be in this bed 'stead of me."

Margie's eyes were on the verge of welling.

"Ma, why are you letting them do that to you?"

"I'll be all right, honey. It's you I'm worried about."

"Face it, Ma: We ain't got such great luck when it comes to men."

"Men are no damned good. Not a one."

"Fred is good, ma. He respects me."

"He knows to go downtown. He licks and he's good at it. Only sex ain't everything."

"Not sex! It's not always about sex! It's respect. He treats me with respect."

"'Respect?' What's that? Besides, I've heard plenty from you about what a great licker he is; what a tireless tongue he has. He loves going downtown, and stays there until you're thoroughly exhausted."

"Sound jealous."

"He eats you out until he's exhausted you with multiple orgasms; so many orgasms, in fact, that you aren't able to budge, or only to nudge him to stop, because you're way too sensitive down there and can't be touched anymore. You prefer to just lie there afterwards. You've told me about it until I'm sick of hearing it."

"Shut up! Just shut-up, ma! Fred is standing right there, and you go on like he's not even in the room. Show some class. I know it's not easy for you, but try it; you should try it sometimes. Nobody said a damned thing about sex. You're obsessed. Always gotta bring it up. I never mentioned sex just now, not once."

"I'm sorry, baby. You tried to take your life. I can't believe you would do something like that to me. I raised you better than that. We're tougher than to turn to suicide when life gets us down. We are not weak; the women in this family are not weak. We can't be. That's for all those spineless wimps out there. Not us! Never us, honey. It comes down to survival of the toughest. Haven't you learned anything by now?"

"I love him, ma."

"It's lust. What's caused all this. And you're married to Frank. Having a dalliance now and then is one thing, but to let it go beyond is unacceptable. Stay true to your husband. I know he's older; it shouldn't matter. Some of those jerks I married were way older than me. Your stepfather Mario, rest his soul, much older. Then again, some have been younger. What's the difference, anyway? My point is: You are a married woman, Margie, and have no business getting yourself emotionally attached to this Fred character; to this drifter."

"You refuse to get it. He cares; he's good to me. I finally have a man who needs me and wants me; all of me. Accepts me the way I am, flaws included. Do you hear me, ma? Accepts me the way I am. *He's right there.* You can ask him yourself."

"For how long, baby? Meanwhile, you're wrecking a good thing that you have with Frank Graham. We had a plan; we had a goal to make your life better. This can't be happening now; not when things are finally working out for this jinxed family. I feel the curse is finally lifting, and you had to get involved with this Reed loser."

She glanced at me. Volunteered an apology that was as genuine as a counterfeit Benjamin.

"Stop it, ma."

Margie was on the verge of tears. They embraced, sobbing. I pulled out a couple of tissues from a box there and passed them out.

"Thank you." It was Rinelle. Thanking me. Then apologizing again for earlier. She even went to embrace me, but there was something peculiar about it. Call it disingenuous. She had her face turned away, even as she pressed herself against my chest. I let it go. Woman was trouble. And she had plenty to spare. No way to avoid her now that I was involved with the daughter. Too late to walk away when your heart was in it. Effing hooked emotionally.

Then she turned to face Margie. Asked for a smoke. Margie had none, and pointed out we were in a smoke-free zone. Rinelle turned to the zonked-out dude and got her butt. Fired up. Dragged long and deep, then released the smoke in my face. I don't mind admitting I felt like shoving that cigarette right down her throat.

She asked for privacy so she and her daughter could have a moment.

"Please close the door on your way out."

We stepped out, the punk and I.

Chapter 68

It wasn't long before mother and daughter were raising their voices, screaming at each other, trading expletives. It all came through the partially open window above the door.

"Whore!"

"Bitch!"

"No wonder you can't hold on to your men, Rinelle! Quit trying to run my life!"

There was major cursing going on, and soon enough escalated into what I feared most: hair pulling and shrieking; all out trading punches. Sounded like it. We thought we better get in there, for what good that notion did us. Someone, the mother, no doubt, had braced one of the desks, plus a chair against the door and we could only open it part of the way. She'd also managed to angle the bed and used it to support the desk and chair. The catfight took place on the other side of the bed, for the most part. The mother had managed to limb up on the bed itself, leaned over to kick at the daughter with a bare foot, in the face, repeatedly, viciously. In the head and face. Didn't matter. She meant business. Margie managed to grab at the foot with both hands and bit down on the big toe. Rinelle screamed, pulled back. Reached for a vase, poured water on the daughter, pulled the flowers out and thrashed Margie across the face with it, then pitched the vase at her, missing. The thing bounced against the window sill behind Margie, shattering in many pieces.

Margie swung her right arm against Rinelle's lower legs, throwing her off balance. The mother went down, and Marge grabbed at her locks with both hands, spitting in her mother's face. She yanked so hard, she pulled her off the bed. Now both were on the far side of the bed, on the floor. More punches were exchanged. Then Margie crawled up on the bed and was the one kicking at the mother this time, kicking and cursing, calling her all sorts of names.

"You sold me to him, cunt, when I wasn't even of age. I was just a kid!

Sold me to him so you could get your fucking drugs, bitch!"

"He helped us; all of us, after Mario died. We were destitute, about to lose the house, default on the mortgage."

"*Liar!* Mortgage was paid off, *lying bitch!* Who twisted your arm to refinance? Fucking coke-addicted ho!"

"I'm your mother! I had mouths to feed, kids to put through school. Ungrateful slut! You're the slut! Not me! Born slut! Your *mother* was never a slut! *Never!*"

"*Professional slut!* I hate your fucking guts, ma! You *ruined* my *life!*"

We kept pushing, shoving, heaving. Made progress, but hardly enough. Looked like the ladies were about to kill each other if we didn't get in there to stop it. It was evident that they were running out of steam, too. Pretty soon it was down to slo-mo for both. They were that exhausted. Both collapsing. Rinelle had her arms out, requesting to be pulled up.

"I don't want to fight with you anymore. No more, Margie. You're my daughter. I'm your mother, Margie."

Margie sat there, looking at her. She helped her mother climb up on the bed. They were sobbing again, embracing and sobbing. By the time Frank Graham showed, and was able to shove the desk out of the way, Margie had poured water from a pitcher there into a glass and handed it to her mother. She poured water into a second glass and drank it down. It was plain both women had wet themselves. Bed was drenched. There were possible signs of excreta.

Chapter 69

Graham must've said something to Rinelle that I missed, and suddenly Rinelle reached over and punched him in the mouth, giving him a nose bleed. Must've been caused by the gaudy and elaborate rings on her fingers. She tried for a second go, and Frank grabbed her by the wrist, forcing her to sit back on the bed.

"Are we calm now, Rinelle?"

She nodded. He let go, and she attempted to slap him. Only Graham was too quick for her & stopped her in time. He stepped away from her.

"Is it any wonder Margie's as fucked up as she is?"

"The mother is always blamed."

"In this case. Who else? All her daddies are dead and buried."

"Implying what, Mr. Graham?"

"You tell me, lady."

"We were in love once."

"I was never in love with you."

"We were friends."

"With friends like you, who needs a viper?"

"I'm a snake now?"

"Worse."

"Than a snake?"

"What I said, Rinelle. Far worse. Your kids are ruined."

"You were having carnal relations with Margie when she was under age."

"Did I know it? She had ID showed she was of age."

"She was not of age, you fucking degenerate! You're a molester! You should be locked up."

"She was of age. No way she was under age!"

"Under! Ask her! Go on, asshole!"

Graham looked at Margie. Margie wasn't saying.

"She's lying, Marge. Tell me what your true age was."

"I was not of age."

"You won't say how old."

"What difference does it make? Not legal is not legal."

"What difference does it make? It makes a heap of difference, Marge."

Rinelle had to jump back in.

"You bet it does, Frank."

"You schemed the whole thing, too, Rinelle. Set me up."

"How so, Frank? You're too smart to let anyone con you into anything, remember? You're the macho bounty hunter."

"You know exactly how, Rinelle. Opportunist. Squeeze him for all you can. Ain't that right? Ungrateful. After all I did for you and your family to keep your business going after Mario passed on, and you still let it go under."

"I did what I could. I did my best."

"Running around with meth addicts and dealers?" He glanced at Jamal. "You call that your best? Why I carried you for as long as I could; I gave a damn. Had to leave or go under myself. You broke every law there was. It's a miracle you're not in prison."

"Smoke and mirrors. To change the subject."

"I don't play games like you, Rinelle. Don't have time for it."

"Thank your lucky stars I didn't press charges."

"You pushed her on me to keep me from leaving. To this day I have no idea what exactly took place that night. I passed out. Next thing I know she's carrying my kid. Supposedly. I did the honorable thing and married her."

"You have ways of coming up with millions of excuses, only your excuses will never cover up the fact it happened."

"What happened?"

"You did everything you could to get to her young pussy. You can't deny it. Should've had you thrown in the can, where you belong."

"Like I would've done you much good as a source of funds behind bars. You needed money, always in need of money—and I gave. More to you and Mario than to my own family."

"Vagina costs, Frank. You ought to know. Especially *sweet-tasting, under age vagina*."

"I've been around vulgar types—you meet all kinds in my business, but you're about the nastiest; with the foulest mouth."

"Miscarried. Due to your abuse."

"Lies!"

"Make me want to vomit. All of you bail enforcers; no better than the scum you chase after. Lie, cheat, break every law in the book that you can get away with and that's the truth. And I mean every fucking law there is and got gall to act like you're law-abiding. Like I said: make me want to vomit. Exactly why I lost interest in all of it. Criminals chasing after criminals, when you're no better than the slime bags you run after."

"Never laid a hand on her the whole time you two claimed she was pregnant."

"Puke."

Margie was shaking her head. Raised her arms. Looked like she was about to start crying again. "Hey, need I remind you people? Who's in here for attempting to take herself out? One of you, or me? As I recall, I was the one who was fed up with everything and ended up here for trying to ace myself."

A nurse walked up, wanting to know what was going on. There was a security guard with her.

Chapter 70

I walked to the car in the parking lot, got in and couldn't move. I sat there in a daze. I was in shock, frankly. I'd been in situations, but nothing like this. My life's goal was to stay clear of shit like this. And I was in it—knee deep. I should have walked when it was still possible. I considered it. Was it an option even at this stage? Was it? I was fucked. It seemed that way. Not only slave to the *culo* and pee hole, but something far worse: heart connection. I was in love with her.

I drove out. And drove aimlessly. Like it was supposed to solve anything. Down to Sunset Boulevard, and out to the ocean. Stayed north on the PCH, out Malibu way, and further: Zuma, and kept going. I was halfway to Santa Barbara before I realized it, pulled a U-ey, stopped on the shoulder and got out to take a leak. Zipped up, and headed back.

I was in too deep and needed to extricate myself. If I didn't do it now I'd never get out. It was as clear as the ocean waves slamming at the shore below and the seagulls fighting over edible morsels they dug up along it. I was doomed. Addicted to the BJs and that brown butt crack that I couldn't get enough of. I'd always had a low tolerance for addicts, anyone with a habit, any kind—and look at me now. As pathetic as the worst of them.

"What happened to *Hit it & Quit it?*"

I gripped the steering wheel with all my might.

"Fuck!"

Chapter 71

I picked up a 6-Pack somewhere along the way and drove home. Chambray was quiet when I walked in and left me alone. It was late. I sat on the living room sofa in the dark and cracked the top on one of the cans. Had a good pull. Monica walked out from the bedroom in her nightgown. Flicked on the light. She stood there, not saying anything. She walked over and sat beside me. I offered her a beer. She passed.

"Is it that bad?"

"Worse."

"She tried to take her life?"

"Yes."

"She say why?"

"It's complicated, hon. A real mess. And I used to think what I lived through was bad. Some peeps had it far worse."

She slid her arm around my neck.

"I'll have that beer, after all."

"Help yourself."

She did. Swallowed brew.

"What will you do now?"

"Do?"

"Does your work situation with Frank change any?"

"Dunno." I looked at her. "The mother, Rinelle, is the thorn in everyone's side. Responsible for quite a bit. Appears that way. Hell, I can't say for sure what's going on. What pushed Margie over the edge? Frank's abuse, the mother's craziness—or both. More than likely—combo of the two. She's being ganged up on—and I hate to see it. So help me, I hate it. Looks like Margie was pushed into marrying Graham by the mother's need for him and his bank account. Greed. Like what else is new? Margie moves to the West Coast to get away from her family, maybe pursue a dream, get into the acting, only the mother won't stop calling, interfering—constantly, demanding cash for one thing or another. No matter how much Margie sends home, it's never enough. And Frank is getting tired of being used. Frankly, who can blame him? Put the brakes on it—and Margie's melt down/crack-up is the result. Pressure. Attempted suicide."

"Sounds like it would be a good time to start looking for another job."

I looked at her.

"Exactly what I was thinking." And it was. Only I doubted I was capable of it at this point. Monica had another pull. Lowered the beer and rose.

"I've got to get some sleep if I intend to get up in the morning in time to get a workout in. You coming?"

"Soon as I finish this."

Only I didn't. I had another beer, and kept drinking until I passed out on the sofa.

Chapter 72

Things returned to 'normal.' For a while anyway. Graham kept taking jobs & I went with him. Some were out of state: Arizona, Nevada, New Mexico, Colorado. We drove to the ones close enough; he used people he knew for the rest. Because of my past, I'd never be allowed to carry a gun 'legally' or make arrests in California and some other states. Mainly he had me running the camera, and I carried pepper spray, Taser, spare cuffs, etc. If additional manpower was required, he knew where to go.

And then Marge had a relapse. Rinelle's badgering never let up. Frank would be passed out in the back at the end of the day, the kids asleep in their bedroom, and Marge and I would be on the living room sofa trying to get something started. Just at about the time we'd get going, the phone would ring. I'd urge Marge not to take it. She usually insisted she had to in case it was for Frank. Only, almost invariably, it would be Rinelle, giving her a hard time, asking Marge to send money or else pumping her about me, wanting to know what was going on. Most often, though, Marge would take the phone into the closet with her or the bathroom and speak in hushed tones, so that I couldn't hear. When finished, she'd step out, looking frustrated and flustered. Certainly anxious. I'd ask what it was her mother wanted. Margie would shrug.

"The usual."

"Meaning?"

"Likes to give me a hard time. How she gets off. Can't get her boyfriends, who are younger than me, to fuck her, so she calls here to get off. Always probing into my sex life. She's perverted that way."

It was shortly after that Margie checked into rehab. It wasn't as bad as the suicide attempt, but bad enough. Claimed Frank's drinking drove *her* to drink. Rinelle wasted no time flying out—on Graham's dime. Alone this time, only because Graham refused to pay for two fares. She looked like hell. Frank and I drove out to Pasadena to the place. Margie's status was eventually changed to 'exhaustion.' Nurse said she needed rest, before walking us outside to the manicured grounds and a picnic table where Marge and Rinelle were having a heated discussion. Par for the course. They usually tended to be in one of those.

"Mrs. Graham is suffering from extreme exhaustion caused by extreme duress."

She left. Rinelle wasted no time pointing the finger at Frank and me. Graham suggested the three of us walk to a tree about thirty feet away. No sooner were we in back of said tree and out of Margie's sight, did Frank clamp his hands about Rinelle's throat. Looked like Graham was close to choking the shit out of her, and might have if I hadn't stepped in & reminded him his kids needed him. He released his grip. Left for the cafeteria. Rinelle spun in my direction. Instead of thanking me for saving her butt, she was glaring.

"I warned you this would happen. He's blaming me. When you and I both know I had nothing to do with it. She can't be in love with anyone but her husband! That's what's caused all this. You want to have your fun? You can have your *sex-capades*, rolls in the sack. You like the BJs Margie's so great at? Understandable. It's only natural. You like fucking my daughter—who wouldn't? So long as love stays out of the equation! Love is no fucking good here. Love causes nothing but problems. How many different ways does it have to be spelled out? You can't be that stupid. No one is that fucking dense!"

"Evidently I must be."

"No. What you are is stubborn! You want to see her dead, is that it? She's already attempted suicide, now it's exhaustion. And it's all your fault. Not Frank so much; it's you."

"How do I turn off what I feel about her?"

"You're a grown man! Do it! It's that simple."

"Even if I did—turn it off, how do we know that Margie will be able to? What would it do to her if I walked away?"

"She has the support of her family; she has her husband."

"I see: You're not capable of being reasonable, are you?"

"Tell her you don't love her. Don't drop her cold turkey. Just let her know the thrill is gone."

"Like that B.B. King song?"

"Yes."

"Too much."

"Listen, you bastard, we may not be able to save her next time. She's not as tough as I thought. I had hoped some of my character to have rubbed off—evidently not enough has. She's not nearly as tough."

"You just got through telling me to turn her loose."

"The bullshit heart-connection part, jerk! Have your occasional fling, but you need to start withdrawing emotionally. Do it gradually—but do it."

"If you were Dr. Ruth, to offer some sound advice in this area . . . I might give it a go. Thing is, you have no idea what you're asking. It's not clear to me. In fact, I'll say it: *You're not even sure what you're after.*"

"Want me to articulate it *again,* motherfucker? How often do you need to hear it?"

"What a bitch you are!"

She raised her arm to throw a punch. I grabbed her by the wrist & twisted it behind her back.

"You gonna cut it out? Huh, cunt? Like being abusive? Like hitting people? I've taken my share of punches, lady. You want a battle? I'll give you a battle."

She farted. Not once or twice; it was a bunch of farts released at about the same time. Fucking tweaker. I pushed her away from me and watched her land on the ground. She rose, loosening her arm to promote circulation. She attempted to spit at me, but I ducked in time. At least she wasn't throwing punches. I walked away from her.

"Where you going? Hey! What in the fuck do you think you're doing, loser?"

"Let's see what your daughter thinks of your idea."

I rejoined Margie at the picnic table.

Chapter 73

I put the question to her daughter: plain and simple.

"Want me out of your life, babe? Just say the word—and I'm gone."

"I never said to walk away just like that—*not cold turkey!*" Rinelle had to put her two cents in. Yelling from where she stood by the tree.

"You've had your say, Rinelle—now let Margie talk. Fair enough?"

"What would you know about fairness?"

"Ma!"

"I have a right to speak my mind, so long as my daughter's wellbeing is at stake here."

"Enough, ma! Please."

Rinelle dug around inside her purse for a pack of smokes. Fired up, and squatted at the base of the three. Then she did the unthinkable: lifted the hem of her skirt and relieved herself. Yes, the perverted witch was pissing.

I looked at Margie, waiting for her to say something. She offered a sip of her lemonade. I passed. She sucked on the straw. Lowered the cup.

"Well, babe."

"It's like this: we love each other and that complicates things; that's the fly in the ointment."

"What the fuck is that, Marge? We going to speak in riddles now?"

"It bothers her. The love part. Not the fact we have a great sex life, which she's jealous of—but the love part, which could kill the golden goose—and Frank is the golden goose. If my husband decides he doesn't love me anymore and wants out, there goes the gravy train. Money. That's what scares her. She's a fucking addict and would die without Graham's support."

"She wants I should tell you, rather convince you: I'm not in love with you—like it's something you can just turn off."

"She hasn't got a clue when it comes to matters of the heart, Fred. You can see that, can't you?"

"What I see is her *squatting* out in the open."

"Ignore her."

"Easier said than done."

"Fred!"

"All I know is I'm lost. I've never been in one of these."

"What?"

"Ménage."

She sucked on the straw, draining the cup.

"Neither have I. And it's too much. Pressure is too great."

"Would've been tough enough. Your mother sticking her nose in makes it impossible."

"Why do you think I'm here? There's no getting away from her."

"What's the answer?"

"You're asking me?"

"Who else?"

"Double-suicide."

"After what I just got through? Fuck that. I don't have a death wish. You might. I don't."

"Divorce Graham."

"And end up with a pot to tinkle in—if we're lucky."

"At least Mommy Dearest would have something to *tinkle in.*"

"Stop it."

"What then?"

"Keep doing what we're doing—and hope things change for the better."

"Or else go for what you were after initially."

"Oh, no. That's suicide for sure. If you get sent up I'm done. I wouldn't want to live. I couldn't."

"How about if we whack Rinelle, then?"

"Hey fuck you, Fred! She's one crude bitch and I hate her guts, she's still my mother."

"Not biologically."

"Yes, biologically. Shit; I'm not sure. I've never been one hundred percent certain. What's the difference? She raised me."

"She used you. Your mother. To bait guys like Graham. Put the bitch out of her misery. Let's ice the bitch."

"How about if we put *your mother* out of *her misery?*"

"You'd have to find her first."

"We need to get off the subject. I don't like this kind of talk."

"Lookit all the trouble she's caused us."

"I'm not taking Rinelle out, Fred. I might hate her guts and we have our share of disagreements, but I'm not killing my own mother. So you can get *that* sick thought right out of your mind. You like to claim *she's* sick? What you're *suggesting* is sick."

"What would work for you? You tell me. Give me something to go on. I'm not a mind reader."

"I'll tell you what would help right now." A grin crossed her lips. "Eat me. Lick my pussy and butt."

"What?"

"I mean it. No one's looking. I could raise my skirt. I'm wet. Lick me, my lover man. All this fighting makes me hot. We could go behind that tree. It would drive Rinelle crazy to see it. It would be a good way to get back at her for all the shit she's caused us lately. Let's do it."

"Know what? *Fuck you both.*"

I walked off.

"Wait. Fred. Don't leave. Fred."

I'd had it and was determined to stay away from her. What a crock that was. What bull.

Chapter 64

Margie would call me from time to time when it was safe enough for her to do so and the pain was the same for both of us, in that it continued to escalate and increase in intensity. She threatened suicide unless we got together.

"I can't go on like this, sweetheart. I'll kill myself."

"I hurt, too, baby. Toss and turn. Your face is everywhere. I see nothing else. Not to mention that tight *culo* that I ache to get back to, and those amazing hips."

"What about my tits? You don't miss my tits?

"What kind of question is that? Of course I miss them. I miss everything about you, Marge."

She was crying and that got to me. Nearly had me weeping right along with her. There was no controlling how we felt. I'd never been there before.

"Frank's passed out again."

"He's not supposed to be drinking."

"Either you come over or I drive to the Palomino and go home with the first cowboy who hits on me."

"You wouldn't."

"Try me."

"First cowboy?"

"The very first."

I didn't like hearing it. It was enough to get me moving and take the risk. We got together in her garage in the back. She had bundles of movie magazines and industry type publications and tabloids stacked along one side of the wall. We made a makeshift bed of them and placed a sleeping bag over it. We crawled inside, zipped it about halfway, and proceeded to make up for the time we'd lost. At that point, in each other's arms, we didn't care if he charged in with that intimidating 12-gauge. That was the level of need and intensity our love-making had reached. Of course afterwards, I sighed with relief when a semblance of rationality crept into my head, that Graham hadn't busted in on us. Margie and I had too much to live for.

"Are you ready now, Fred?"

"I can't stand to be away from you. I just can't stand it, Margie."

She unzipped the bag and sat up. I watched her roll her blouse up, over her head, and take it off. I had no idea why, because we'd already made it. And then I saw it: more welts and bruises. Along her arms and neck.

"He did this?"

"I can't live without you."

"Margie, did Frank do this to you?"

"I need you so much, Fred honey."

She held me tight, weeping in my chest. I cursed under my breath.

Chapter 74

At this point we were back to our original plan as the only solution. I mean we looked at it from all possible angles and nothing seemed remotely viable. Not putting the mother on ice, which I would have preferred, but the hubs. Hubby had to go. Other people in predicaments similar to ours had gone this route and gotten away with it. Our love was more important to us than this out-of-control abusive creep's life. It came down to that.

Margie had a suggestion.

"I'd double up on the antifreeze, if I thought it would work."

"Huh?"

"His raspberry iced tea. In his thermos."

"Goddamn. Explains the mother-humper complaining about belly cramps and back pain all the time, the runs."

"I've been spiking his rotgut and the iced tea off and on for months. Only it's not doing much. It's like trying to take out a horse. Fucker's too big; his system can take a lot and it could go on forever. Eventually he'd get wise to it. I thought maybe switching to rat poison might do the trick."

"No good. The autopsy would hang you for sure."

She insisted that it wouldn't, so long as she didn't overdo.

"Who would suspect it? His liver's probably shot anyway from all the boozing over the years. It's what finally killed Mario."

"Mario?"

"My stepfather. Rinelle's fifth husband."

"Fifth?"

"Fourth or fifth. What difference does it make?"

"I don't like it. It's chickenshit."

"If it works, what's the difference? He's not supposed to be drinking anyway, not while taking medicine for his prostate. Am I right? Doctors at the VA even warned him about it. More than once, I might add."

"Rat poison is *chickenshit*, if you ask me."

"It's easy to get. What's the problem?"

"You don't understand."

"Try me."

"I've been working with the guy over here. We, ah; there's no denying we connected on some level. . . . It's not easy."

"Oh shit. You never had a daddy. So now he's a father figure? Frank Graham? Because you apprehended a couple of low-grade skippers together? *Spare me, Fred.*"

"You weren't there, at the hospital; you didn't see what he had to go through."

"So what? What about *what I'm going through*? Years of it. You either care—or you don't. Which is it?"

"Why would it have to be *rodent killer*? He needs to go; no denying it. . . . We're equating him with sewer dwellers. And he's not. Shit; he's a human being. I hate the way he treats you, I do; but he's also got those kids that he gives a damn about. . . . Nobody ever bought *me* a train set."

"I never got a *Barbie doll. So fucking what?*"

"Just sayin'."

"And I'm sayin' I'll buy you *a fucking choo-choo train* once this is behind us, the best they got, and you can buy me a Barbie doll. How's that sound? That work for you? Because it works for me."

Then she suggested I might like this next idea she had of dealing with our situation a little better.

"He could have an accident on the job. It can be arranged so that we don't have to get our hands dirty. Before you go out with him on the next one, give Quintero a ring to let him know when and where Frank will be. Let him and his friends take care of the rest of it."

"Not bad, *except* I have no idea where the skip is staying. Frank is being tight-lipped about it. All I could get out of him was that the guy's name is De Amato, and that he's from the East Coast. Jersey area. Hiding out in some fleabag downtown. Probably using a fake name."

That's when I got the stunner. She jammed a piece of paper in my hand with the name of the fleabag written on there, room number and alias De Amato was using.

"How?"

"Judas left a message with Frank's service. Said Frank might want to be extra cautious on this one. And to use backup."

"Extra cautious."

"What he said." Marge was grinning. "And that he could use a new color tv."

"Extra cautious." I couldn't help repeating it. "And backup."

"I love you, Fred."

"I love you."

Chapter 75

The next morning, I phoned the Mexican market in East LA and asked to speak to the woman. Let her know I wanted to leave a message for Fidel and she promptly hung up on me. I didn't know what else to do at this point. And then later on in the day I got the notion to phone the adult movie house in Hollywood and asked to speak to the projectionist.

I left the number to a pay phone that his friend Fidel could reach me at and that I had some life-saving information for him and that I would wait no longer than thirty minutes.

Thirty minutes later the phone rang. Quintero's 'friends' had taken care of everything, the court date had to be extended due to his injuries, and all was *'bueno.'*

I told him I was calling to see how he was doing; and thought that he had been harshly treated by the bounty hunter. Then I told him where Frank Graham would be later that night, just for his information.

"Who is this?"

"All you need to know is that I'm no friend of the walrus."

"I want to show my appreciation. How can I do that unless I know who this is?"

"You can do it by making your very best effort to spare his partner.

Graham's the one you want."

"Graham is the one we want, for sure." Then he laughed. "Don't worry, amigo. No one is going to harm his partner—who has no business being in Graham's line of work, by the way. He's better than that. My friends and I equate bounty hunters with dog shit. The partner saved my life. *Pendejo* Graham would have deep-sixed my Mexican ass for sure."

"Well, his partner couldn't just stand there and do nothing."

"My associates could use someone like his partner."

"Your 'associates'?"

"My *friends*, hombre. Lots of easy money to be made. Practically risk-free. His partner can use a few dollars, I'm sure."

I was salivating at mere mention of money. But I was also smart enough to know that kind of 'easy money' and associating with the kind of cartel scum he ran with lead to a dead-end for certain, or prison, at least.

"Maybe somewhere down the road when his partner is hard up for cash."

"The partner must be hard-up for cash as we speak, amigo. Why else would he be running around with a *cabron* like Frank Graham?"

"I will pass it on, my friend."

"No problem, amigo."

It was just as well Quintero knew who I was. The odds that I wouldn't be getting hurt increased considerably. I hoped so, anyway. None of this came with guarantees. And Quintero couldn't rat out anyone later without incriminating himself and his 'associates.'

Chapter 76

I wore an old army helmet that night, plus a stainless steel cup over my trousers to protect my balls. Frank saw the cup strapped to my crotch and the helmet on my head and laughed.

"Man wants you dead, that won't stop him."

"Helmet saved me in 'Nam on more than one occasion. Cup did its share to protect the jewels. Not many guys wore one, but I did. Didn't feel ridiculous doin' it, either."

"This ain't Viet Nam, Fred. No shrapnel comin' at you, just bullets, well-aimed bullets at your head. Or your balls. That cup won't do much."

I could've cracked wise, but decided to let it go instead. Could not help but wonder if he was hinting. Was he onto Margie and me? And was waiting to catch us in *flagrante?*

He chuckled, and fired up one of those smelly horse dung stogies. He decided we needed backup on this one.

Frank gave Walt Spunkmeyer a call, who said he was in no condition, and as far as Loretto was concerned, Spunkmeyer didn't want her involved. Graham decided he was okay with it, because it meant he wouldn't have to share the bounty with anyone and said we were handling it ourselves.

Bounty hunter had a 9 millie Glock in a shoulder rig, another inside his hip, a .32 in the ankle holster, not to mention the pump action 12-gauge that he carried out in the open this time. All I had was the .380 in my pocket. Hardly felt adequate.

Chapter 77

It was around 1 a.m. when the van crept into the skid row area. Frank's back was troubling him, the belly cramping, and he needed to make a pit stop in a hurry. So he made like someone desperate to win the Indy 500 and we sped on down to the Holiday Inn on Figueroa, south of Wilshire.

When he emerged finally, there was no denying he looked worse for wear. Graham limped in, and we drove back to the Nickel. A group of winos stood around in front of this boarded up liquor store haggling over a bottle this one wino was unwilling to share, something like that. The man we were looking for was 'Loose Lips' Lou De Amato, aka Lenny Ditzler. Jumped bail back east (on what charge Frank wouldn't say). Well, he did say that it made no difference. Bounty on his head made it worthwhile. Word was the jumper was connected. Frank insisted on being tight-lipped about it. Said he didn't want to rattle me, so he kept things hush-hush.

For the hell of it, or maybe I was looking for a way to deal with my own guilt caused by what Margie and I were planning for him, I asked Graham how many peeps he had deep-sixed over the course of his career. It hit me just then, this was the very thing I'd meant to bring up that time we stopped by his bank so he could drop the Rolex off, before losing the thought.

Graham gave me this stare.

"How stupid of me would it be to discuss something like that with someone like you?"

"I respect that, Frank. Just sayin': Long Arm of the Law never came knocking on your door about any of it?"

"Why the hell should they? I help do their job. I'm ridding society of psychos, dope pushers, pimps and punks like Nasty and Tasty. Garbage. Every one of them sons of bitches I *'deep-sixed'* had it coming; every damned one, Fred. I never killed an innocent man, law-abiding citizen. Remember that."

I mentioned Quintero, and that he had nearly put him out, too.

"I was a little rough on him, I admit that. Thing you're overlooking: he's one of them *Los Cochinos* pieces of shit who bring in drugs what poison our society. They're destroying our country, or are you fucking blind to what's been going on? You weren't in that projection room and have no idea what took place, do you? Exactly why I didn't want you in there. POS was armed and I didn't want to see you risk your life for what I was paying you. That simple. Punk refused to go peaceful; resisted arrest, and paid the price. You saw my face when I stepped out of there. Cartels are scum and should be nuked and the bags-of-shit who do their dirty work should be executed on sight. Period. Law should be passed: You get stopped with crystal meth on you: cocaine, crack, Ex, PCP—any of that shit. You fucking die on the spot. End of story. You get nabbed crossing the border illegally, *you're history*. Dead on the spot. Busted carrying contraband? Guillotined on the fucking spot. No questions, no trial. We set up guillotines at every fifth of a mile or so along the border. Over 17, your head gets sliced off; under 17 you get sent back the first time. Second time it's a ten-year prison sentence, hard labor. No fucking around with this smelly dog shit subhuman scum. You get busted using illegal substances— death & burial—on the corrupt Mex government's tab. Free of charge. You want to get into this country and do it legally? I have no problem with it. Get on the list and wait your turn to be screened and admitted. We have laws that we live by. You don't do whatever the fuck you feel like doing. And I don't give a shit what your fucking reasons are: your mommy is here, your cousin is here, your *'hoes'* are here. Can't make it where you live; don't blame us, blame the government in your own fucking country! Overthrow the fascist maggots who won't let you start a business and prosper; who refuse to allow you to have any kind of rewarding existence. Does it make me sound like a Nazi? I hate fucking Hitler and what the Nazi scum did to millions of Jews and others. There are Blacks in this country, Hispanic-Americans in this country and Asian-Americans who feel this way right now, *in this country*. We don't hate Jews, Mexican-Americans, Muslim-Americans, Catholic-Americans, you name it: African-Americans, Asian-Americans; none of that bullshit. What we can't stomach are cartel scum and their underlings; the drug lords who exploit the innocent and push drugs over here to destroy us. No other reason; Ruin us and get fat while doing it." Then he looked at me. "Whose side are you on, anyway? Quintero has *raped, killed and/or maimed* more people—on either side of the border—than you and me can count on both of our hands. You think about that for a while before you start putting labels on Americans who love their country."

Admittedly, that pretty much shut me up.

Chapter 78

We pulled up to the fleabag and got out. Frank decided not to take Thor with him, so as not to give anything away. I refused to go in the back alley without Chambray. Fucking area was a crime zone. Damn right. He had his shotgun out, the badge, warrant for the skip's arrest, and changed his mind about not taking the Dobie with him and proceeded up the front way, while Chambray and I made it down the gangway toward the back of the building.

We were maybe about halfway to the alley, when the explosion rocked the area and had me hitting the ground. Old habits die hard. Chambray was going nuts; jumpy and freaking. I'd barely been able to hold on to her leash.

I did what I could to calm her down, and we made it back to the front. Origin of the blast definitely appeared to be somewhere on the ground floor. Hotel entrance and glass facade were blown out, along with a number of windows along the left side. Lobby was in shambles. Rubble and chunks of drywall and whatnot dangled from the ceiling above. Black smoke and dust so thick you could hardly see ten feet in front of you. There were bodies about: tenants, others.

Frank had staggered into the lobby with his right side looking as bad as Quintero's face that night. Blood streamed out of him, loose flesh dangled from his upper arm and leg. Thor was in his arms, head hanging down, what was left of it: jaw and a good portion of his chest having been torn off by the blast.

"Set-up." Frank was in a daze, eyes welling with blood and tears. *"Set-up."* And he would have dropped if I hadn't grabbed him and his dead dog in time.

After a while, his eyes opened briefly. He was trying to say something. I couldn't make it out, so I leaned in. It had to do with the RS200. Shotgun had cost him plenty and he wanted me to retrieve it.

"Forget it, Frank. We got to get you an ambulance."

He insisted. The pump action had sentimental value to him. He wanted it buried with him, along with the dog. Hell, it seemed outlandish.

Just a bit. But a dying man's last wish ought to be honored, I thought.

And so while waiting for the ambulance to show, I found a sofa cushion, wiped the dust and rubble off, and gently placed it under his head, and then I cautiously made my way down the corridor, shoving drywall and pieces of brick out of the way in search of the Beretta shotgun.

It took some effort, but I found it, buried under a pile of debris. Stock and barrel had its share of dents and scratches. Only a closer look, after I'd wiped it down, revealed that the damage was superficial. And that made me feel pretty good. By the time I had it stowed away in the van the ambulance was pulling up.

Frank came to briefly while they loaded him onto a gurney. He wished to be taken to a Valley hospital, so he could be near his kids before he shuffled off this mortal coil, just in case. I gave him my word that's what we would do, as the EMTs carried him outside. I followed the ambulance in the van.

I called Marge from the hospital. We met in the lobby. She performed wonderfully. The distraught wife.

"Save it, Margie. It's not that bad."

"It isn't?"

"Actually, it's bad enough."

"Which?"

"He'll live. . . . Looks like."

"Looks like?"

"Hard to say."

Chapter 79

We spent hours waiting for word in the waiting area. Nothing; we got nothing. We both could have used some strong coffee and a bite to eat. Only instead of a sandwich, Margie opted for a doughnut. I made it downstairs to the cafeteria, got the items. As I was paying the cashier Margie walked up. We found a table. She told me the doctor finally came out to see her.

"Critical."

"Huh?"

"His condition." She was smiling. "*Critical.*" Took a bite of her doughnut and chased it with java. "This has got to be one of the best."

"Coffee?"

"Doughnut. Coffee ain't bad, either."

I got into my ham and cheese sandwich, sip of joe. She mentioned something about him being in a coma.

"Medically induced."

"Medically induced?"

"What he said. To give the brain the rest it needs."

"So he's brain damaged?"

"He always was."

"How long?"

"What?"

"How long is this 'coma' supposed to last?"

"Specifically?"

"Yes."

"Didn't ask."

"Maybe you should've."

"Could be days, weeks—could be months. Depends how much rest the brain needs."

I'd never heard of it. Didn't know squat about it. Couldn't shake the apprehension. On the one hand there were pluses: he might not get through it and we wouldn't have to do anything else but wait things out and let time take care of it. The other side of the coin was my conscience continued to nag at me. I'd hoped for a clean job, at the least a cleaner hit.

"Who decides?"

"Who do you think? They do. Like I said, or he did, the doc did: There's brain damage. Coma is supposed to prevent the brain from swelling by slowing down blood flow and forcing the brain not to work as hard. What I was told. Shit, I'm no quack. Telling you what he told me. I say we take advantage of the situation. Make sure he never wakes up."

I bit into the ham and cheese sandwich. Found myself chewing aimlessly, trying to put it all together, make the parts fit.

"'His life is in the balance, Mrs. Graham.'"

"What the doctor said?"

"His exact words. *'In the balance.'* I like the sound of it."

I didn't say anything.

"What is it?"

"Rat poison."

"Not that, Fred. Not again. Don't ruin my day; don't spoil it. This is good news. Only thing that could make it better would be for the motherfucker's condition to stay critical, and then tips over into: Mrs. G., your husband flatlined. His luck ran out."

"What about Butch and his sister?"

"There's Carol. Their mother. They're better off. Lots of single moms are raising kids out there and doing a pretty good job of it, by the way."

It bothered me. There was no denying that it ate away. The man hadn't deserved this Mickey Mouse method of being whacked. I mean, sure, I did get my butt kicked by him that initial time, and smacked for running off with Chambray, but he'd also shown me some genuine decency. Hired me when he didn't have to, let me keep the bling I took off the dead punk. His motive? Who knew? Didn't matter to me what his motive had been. A break is a break.

"You know what, Fred? I'm ignoring this."

"What?"

"You. I'm not letting you piss on my parade. You're not spoiling this victory for me."

It was scary in a way: how hard she could be. Scary and impossible not to pick up on. What was I doing? She ate her doughnut and watched me, studying me scrupulously. I knew it. Let her.

"Critical is good, Marge. Look at the bright side."

"Dead is better."

"It's on the way."

"Let's hope."

It was at this point a soul brother walked in who either looked like the mook back at the VA who I'd tried to buy cyanide from, or else it was the same dude, who went from hospital to hospital doing who knew what kind of work: selling medical supplies, latex gloves, dish soap—or just liked being a volunteer for something to do. Who knew? Or maybe I was being paranoid myself here.

"Shit."

I turned my head away, grabbed her by the sleeve and guided her out of there.

"What is it?"

I told her.

"That was dumb. Really Fred. When Rinelle can get anything. Well, her friend Jamal can."

"Anything?"

"Anything."

"So. . . ."

"Got my heart set on rat poison, that is, should he survive. The beauty of it is hard to let go."

"The 'beauty' of it?"

"Okay, I'm romanticizing just a touch. You can give me that. I've waited years. If we have to go to the next level."

I loved her enough at this point to let her have her fantasy. I was in it. Up to my balls.

Chapter 80

We were back the next day. Spent hours. All we got was that the condition remained. Kept despair at bay. We were in the cafeteria, for the coffee and a bite. Marge mentioned that one of the neighbor's, an occasional drinking buddy of Frank's, had mentioned that he was interested in buying the van, along with Frank's shotgun and gun collection.

"What'd you tell him?"

"That he ought to be ashamed of himself."

I looked to see if she was saying this with a straight face. She certainly was. Hell, maybe she could make it as an actress. I'd seen far worse.

"My husband's not even buried yet, and this so-called buddy of his can't wait to get his hands on his possessions."

"I can see that it rubbed you the wrong way, Marge."

"It pissed me off. It really did."

"The audacity of some people."

"You said it."

We were deciding on a table when Grozewski walked in with the young doctor. The doc left the dick at the food counter and walked over to us. The medical professional struck me as arrogant. Hardly older than me, wearing black leather ankle boots with straps and buckles.

"Your husband's condition remains critical, Mrs. Graham. He sustained a concussion and some pretty serious lacerations. His right side will be scarred the rest of his life: face and neck, ribs, arm and leg will be scarred."

"Any chance that he'll get through it, doctor? Will he live?"

"Hard to say at the moment. We should have some indication by tomorrow, one way or the other."

"Thank you, doctor."

"Not at all, Mrs. Graham. Now if you'll both excuse me."

And he bounced off to rejoin the detective.

No word about the coma. It would've been nice to know, 'one way or the other.' I came close to mentioning it, instead watched her fold her hands, close her eyes. Her lips were moving and she was mouthing words, but I couldn't tell much else.

"Marge? What are you doing?"

"What's it look like? Praying for the motherfucker to expire."

Chapter 81

It was the following day that the shit storm we feared struck and struck hard. We got word that Graham's condition shifted from critical to stable. He was out of the coma. Tentatively scheduled to be released in three to four weeks. We pondered our next step over coffee in the hospital cafeteria. Marge had a cheese danish with hers. Claimed nerves made her crave something sweet. There were a few other folks present. Not many. Didn't spot the dick this time, either. No loss there.

"Maybe it wasn't such a great move after all, Marge. Still, we get four whole weeks together."

"Three weeks, sweetheart. *Possibly four.* And then we're back to sneaking around, hiding, lying, taking a chance on getting caught—and when we do get caught . . . I don't have to tell you what he'll do. And Frank's got ways to make it all nice and clean. That *Five-0* buddy of his would see to it without raising an eyebrow."

I told her what Frank's last words had been in that fleabag lobby before he passed out.

"That's what I mean, Fred. He'll add it up."

"It's going to be tough."

"I want us to get married, Fred darling. I want it more than anything."

With me, it wasn't 'marriage' so much that mattered, that I was after, but the need to have easy access to her pee hole and butt, those fabulous tits and BJs whenever the need arose—and it arose 24/7. I mean it was always there: wanting to either bang her or eat her out; smell her butt hole or watch her lick my asshole or slurp cum. Why deny it? Desire was a bitch, the ache for it so bad that you were willing to do anything to get it. Sex was as powerful as any drug out there. It was plain as day. My prick never went down. All I had to do was think of her or be near her and the pole stood straight up. Stiff, rock hard, needing it. Even now as we discussed how to spend the man's money.

"We'd be able to take that trip to Hawaii. I'll have enough money to cover everything. He's got more than enough saved up. He would never let me spend any of it. We're renting. He wouldn't buy the house we're staying in. He wouldn't sell the property he owns back home. He figured we'd be moving back eventually anyway—once I've gotten this silly notion of being in the movies out of my system. See the shitty Fiesta I'm forced to drive? It's pathetic. The whole thing. He never took anything I did seriously. I can't return to that." Her eyes filled with tears. I handed her a napkin to wipe the tears away.

"The bastard is cheap. It's just as well, Fred. It'll mean that much more for us, a nice nest egg to start over, a fresh new beginning. Suddenly I feel so exhilarated, baby. Life can be wonderful."

I mentioned his safe deposit box. Asked what was in it. Any cash?

"How am I supposed to know that?"

"You got his keys."

"His keys? Not to that. I got no idea what's in the bank box."

"Makes no difference anyway. For now."

Chapter 82

I leaned in, holding her hands in mine.

"I wish I could bend you over this table right now, lift your dress up over your ass and pull your panties down and just bury my tongue deep inside your butt-crack, honey. And then after I'd gotten a good taste of it lower my tongue down there and lick your hot pussy. Then turn you around, lift you up on the table, spread your legs and tickle your clit with the tip of my tongue and drive you crazy with multiple orgasms. . . ."

I watched her jaw drop as she hung onto every word. She squeezed my hands. I believe she was orgasming on the spot.

"I'm staining my panties. . . . Oh, Fred darling. . . ."

I looked about the cafeteria. Did I have the balls to do what I ached? Right there? Right then? One thing was for sure: my ploy to make her tears go away had worked. Made me feel real good inside.

"Do it, Fred. . . ."

"I would eat you out and have you explode about a dozen times, you unbelievably hottest of hot sluts, then I'd slide my cock in your mouth and watch you tongue it, play with it . . . then I'd drive it inside your wet joy box . . . and take my time stroking the shit out of your cunt. I'd have you spit on my cock for lube and slide it inside your tight brown asshole . . . then guide it back inside your mouth for a major explosion of scrotum lava."

The perspiration across her brow was easily visible. She was making faces, her lips twisted. She was not only planting kisses all over my hands, but leaving a trail of hickeys all over them. Then I watched her take the middle finger of my right hand and suck it as though it were my boner. I could tell there were things taking place for her down below: she was orgasming. Over and over, and making sounds. I had to remind her to keep it down, as it was making me nervous. The thought that we might draw undue attention from the few customers and employees in the place made me nervous.

I leaned in and kissed her on the cheek, whispered in her ear to calm down, that we had to show some control here; we had to behave, no matter how difficult it was.

We leaned back in our seats. I handed her a napkin to wipe her forehead with, then I handed her another so that she could wipe herself down there. She was discreet about it, and proceeded to do just that—and was able to get away with it, since that part of her anatomy was concealed by the tabletop. When she brought the napkin back up it was sopping wet. She held it under her nose with a grin on her face.

Jesus Christ, it damn near made my balls ache with desire. This was exactly the type of kinkiness that had been missing in my life. This bitch's notion of nasty drove me nearly out of my mind. As if this were not enough, she held it out to me. Stuck it in my face. I inhaled, hard. Clamped both of my hands around her wrist and inhaled the aroma of her cunt. I was damn near tempted to shove the napkin in my mouth, savor it this way, then gulp it down. If it hadn't been for the Mexican broad in her white frock eyeing us from behind the counter, I probably would have. I did the next best thing: kissed the wad of paper and told Marge to save it for later, and she stowed it in her purse. I must've cursed under my breath. Winced, no doubt as well.

"What's the matter?"

"Blue balls."

"Now?"

"Yes. Now."

"No."

"It was the napkin. Strong cunt aroma. I'm fucking doomed."

"We both are."

"Don't talk like that."

I could hardly move in my seat. Pain was acute. Margie was amused. I was glad one of us was, considering what transpired next.

Chapter 83

The same doctor passed our table on his way to get himself a cup of joe. He still had those ankle boots on with the buckled strap. That was something I had a hard time accepting, period: a medical doctor in footwear like that. I don't know exactly why it struck me as oddball, but it did. Adding to the annoyance was the fact the son of a bitch was my age and already established, had a career and was upwardly mobile. There was a young giggling nurse with him this time.

A moment later, on his way out, he walked past our table again. Felt a need to make our day with further good news.

"Your husband's condition has stabilized. That's a good sign. Looks like he'll get through this, Mrs. Graham. He's a tough old dude."

"When will he be released?"

"As I mentioned earlier: Three weeks. Give or take. The way my colleagues and I see it."

He exited the cafeteria afterwards, the same upbeat nurse by his side.

Hell, I could have stomped those ugly kicks he had on his feet and liked it. Margie's smile dropped. The tears were back. It killed me to see it. The pain in my scrotum was not easing up any, either.

"We'll do it before he checks out, Margie. In fact, we'll see to it he checks out permanently this time."

"You're everything I ever wanted out of life."

"You are my life."

Chapter 84

It was during the drive over to her place that I decided I wanted to get my hands on Graham's arsenal. Baretta 12-gauge, guns, ammo, Maglite, cuffs, sap, and whatever else there was to be had of value that was in that rectangular metal box inside the van. Why? I'd had no idea. There was no purpose to the notion other than that I might be hard up for cash somewhere down the road and might be able to sell the lot for a quick buck. Nothing more to it.

I pulled the van into the driveway, and we went in. She couldn't wait to show me the sex toys. I suggested she go in the shower and wash her cunt and bunghole real good before we did anything else.

"I have a better idea: Why don't you get in with me and you do it; and I'll do you?"

I said I loved the idea, but that I wanted to make a quick beer run.

"I'll be back before you know it."

She was in the john and had started to take her clothes off, then suddenly threw her arms around me.

"Hurry back, hon."

We kissed, and I was out one door, the front door, and opening another: door to the van. Realized I'd need a shovel or hoe, something to dig with. Did a quick look around in the backyard, found nothing I could use, and drove to the nearest hardware store. Paid for a shovel, enough good, strong plastic to wrap the weapons in, and headed out to the park. There was a cleaning kit inside the toolbox, so that was one less thing to be concerned with. I would clean and oil the whole lot some other time.

I pulled up to the sidewalk that the trees were on, and went to work wrapping the shotgun and handguns in the heavy plastic. Coast appeared to be clear. I slid the side door open, grabbed the toolbox, the shovel, and disappeared into the thick brush and trees. I had a hole dug deep enough in no time. Dropped the toolbox in, and covered it up. After I carved an upper case 'G' into the nearest tree, I got out of there and made the beer run.

Chapter 85

By the time I got back, she had stepped out of the shower and was drying her hair. She dropped the towel, practically tore my clothes off and shoved me in the shower and followed suit herself. We were both in there. She couldn't keep her hands off of me, not that I minded it one bit.

I couldn't stop her from following up on what she had wanted to do earlier, and had no intention of it. I let her do whatever it was she wanted, short of making me blast. That was when I did stop her, as I'd wanted to save it up for the bedroom, whereby we'd take our time. I wanted it to last; I'd wanted to prolong it. Margie was all for it. Grabbed me by the groin, and was eager to lead the way to the master bedroom in the back.

"Follow me, Sweetmeat."

She pulled out the works this time: a canvas bag she'd kept hidden away from Graham the entire time they'd been together: sex toys. All types: thick vibrators for vagina penetration and narrow ones for anal stimulation. Butt plugs, handcuffs, cat-o'-nine-tails, bottles of lube, and porn; a variety of porn on VHS tape: gay male, lesbian, straight; gangbangs and *bukkake*. She asked if I wanted to watch men sucking each other.

"*You nuts?* I don't get off on that shit."

"You should see the big cocks they take up the ass."

"No, thanks."

"How about lesbians? With strap-ons? Taking massive silicon dicks up their booty?"

This was how she'd been getting off for years, usually, watching porn and masturbating while Graham was out getting *his rocks* by either beating up or killing skips, which was most of the time. The only way she was able to get any sexual relief—until I walked into her life. So she claimed.

Did I want to see the lesbians?

"Go ahead."

She shoved the VHS cassette into the video player. Built, the porn starlets were built; tanned, wearing huge strap-ons. On this round bed. One of the blonds was on all fours, ass stuck out, while the other large-breasted slut slid this nine-inch dildo up her crapper.

Fuck. My jaw dropped. My prong was like *effing steel*. Then Margie shoved that damp napkin from the hospital cafeteria in my face. I jammed it in my mouth, chewed to drain her cunt juice out and swallowed, then spit the paper onto the floor.

I looked over at her. She had been lubing her asshole, and wanted to do mine.

"Why?"

She held the narrow anal vibrator and was interested in sliding it up my rectum. I shook my head. *"Nothing goes up my shitter.* Ain't no port of entry. Its sole function is expelling waste. I use it for defecating, and do not allow for any sort of invasion."

"But it's okay for the woman to be plowed in her *culo?*"

"Of course."

"You're a chauvinist."

"You got me confused with hubs."

Margie grinned, then slid that effing thing up her behind and turned it on. I heard it hum. Ho was pleasing herself, and needed my tongue on her cunt; the clit, especially. I did not hesitate to oblige here. Sure. Why not? She also desired my member in her mouth to work on. I went for it, all the while we watched the well-built lesbians take turns drilling each other in the ass with the strap-ons.

Goddamn. It was too much. Margie was getting off, as before, repeatedly. Took pause, withdrew the anal vibrator, and slid a butt plug up her crapper. In and out. Slowly. Gradually. She freed up her lips, withdrew the butt plug from the orifice down there, and slid it inside her mouth, sucking. Damn. Bitch was kinky as all get out. Insisted I park my Jones in her backside.

This was some amazing reaming taking place on the screen. She ditched the butt plug and had a pocket rocket against her clit. Climaxed, repeatedly; wincing, making noises. I traded the butt hole for the cunt hole. She asked if I was ready to cum; to make sure to give her notice before I blew my load. I said I was getting here. It would be soon.

"Let me know."

"Yes. *Nearly there, baby.* So close. Almost. *Yes.*"

I pulled out, and watched her spin around and dive for my prick with her open mouth. Shit. This was amazing. It was both disgusting *and* thrilling beyond anything I'd ever experienced.

Did anything top it? Could it? I didn't know; because I couldn't even think straight at this point and just dropped beside her, clinging to her.

Spooning. That's what it was: we were spooning. We were happy. Needed it so damn bad. It was nothing less than addiction. One of the strongest. Had to be. When sex was this fabulous. You couldn't go without. Wouldn't want to. It was a need. Powerful. And it had us in its vice grip.

Chapter 86

We rested up, and did a *three-peat.* You bet your sweet ass. It was never enough. Orgasms? Too many to keep track of. Especially that last one. Involving the *cat-o'-nine-tails.* She wanted to whip my ass. Guess what? No way. Like with the butt plug she wanted to shove up my crapper, I didn't feel like being whipped. I'd had enough of it as a youngster. No, thank you. Since I wouldn't let her beat my ass, she requested I beat hers.

I'd gone this way once or twice in the past with some of the whores I'd been with, but usually tried to steer clear of it. Why? Fear. That it would escalate into something else and land me back in stir. It was simple. Shit like this was easy to become addicted to. So the fear was there and I managed to keep away from it—for the most part, that is. Unless the ho insisted on it like this one was. Some bitches were like that. Liked it rough and real dirty. The rougher and dirtier the better. It could be scary. She kept asking for it. What was a man to do?

I went for it. My bone was all wood. Felt like it. She tapped it with her fingers and it put a grin on her face because it confirmed what she had known all along: I was as perverted as she was. There was no use denying: a couple of degenerates were about to venture into some pretty dangerous territory.

I gave her a lash or two. Followed up with a couple more. Watched her squirm in ecstasy with each whack. She was gasping, craving additional lashes. I did hesitate when she insisted I put more force into it. She wanted me to be vicious, at least pretend to be. Made me apprehensive. As much as I was enjoying it. This kind of thing can get out of hand real quick, and before you know it, someone ends up in the hospital and you get nailed for domestic violence.

"Fuck that."

Her buttocks were streaked plenty, yet there she was demanding I deliver the encore. She had the largest vibrator up against her muff while I whipped her ass. When I refused to up the ante, she insisted I choke her.

"Huh?"

"Do it. Choke me, sweetie. Please."

I didn't care for it. She kept pleading I do it. I shook my head. What was I getting myself into here? Only she wouldn't shut up about it. Wanted it. Just to get her to clam up, I went with it. Had my hands about either side of her neck, while pumping her backside; and the whole time I was doing this, she had a vibrator with a bulbous thing on it to massage the clit with, getting herself off multiple times, and all the while insisting I choke the shit out of her.

"No."

"Don't be a pussy. Make me gasp. *Do it, Fred.* Make it hard for me to breathe. *It'll intensify the orgasm.*"

Goddamn; it was too much for me. I'd never gone with the choking aspect with any of the broads I'd been with and didn't like it, but went ahead all the same just to shut her up. Little did I know that eventually I'd be considering doing this exact same thing—for real. I'd be so sick and tired of her that I'd be planning to crush her out of existence, just to be free of her.

She exploded. We both did.

Like before, the only reason we stopped was because we had to: exhaustion kicked our butts finally; exhaustion and sweat, trying to catch our breath. We were spent. I had no juice left in my nutsack and she was sore all over: *cunt, butt, lips;* her entire body. Too sore to continue. So we stopped. Forced to.

I remember lying on that waterbed afterwards, staring, just staring at the rotating Casablanca fan overhead. She wanted to know if anything was the matter.

"There's nothing like it in the whole world, this feeling of just being with you. *I want nothing else; I ask for nothing else.*"

"If we can't be together, sweetheart—I wouldn't want to go on. Knowing what we've got, I couldn't do without it. Life would be meaningless."

It had all sounded so romantic, maybe even sentimental. How was I to know it would turn to crap eventually?—and that I wouldn't be able to stand her a mere handful of months down the road?

Chapter 87

We crawled out of bed at 11 the next morning. We could have used a little more shuteye, but we both felt restless. We had plans to make, stuff to do. Late breakfast was grilled cheese sandwiches and a bottle of inexpensive wine at the park.

Thinking about it, it wasn't much, a poor man's meal—but with her everything was perfect. It could have been bread and water and it would have been fine. We would have acted like it. I'd never felt so good about myself. It was like looking at the world through new eyes. Happy to be alive. I was on a natural high every minute, every second I was with her, and it would be this way as long as there was 'us.' The euphoria would last, without pills or drink. We didn't need anything artificial and/or manufactured to keep us this way. I appreciated everything: rodents, bugs, snakes, loud kids, filthy bums. Everything was beautiful. That's what love did to you.

Most of my sexual encounters up to this point had been with hookers, when I had it to spend on them, or else if the women weren't working girls it amounted to me getting mine and making myself scarce afterwards; to hell with them. I never cared how they felt, or what they wanted or if they even enjoyed it or wanted it. Easy trysts. It's called getting yours. Period. Wonderful, sweet Monica included. Even though she was easy to please and was a good friend, the problem was that was all she was and ever would be: friend.

All your life you went around searching for that someone special, meant for only you; a life of searching for that magic *key* to the magic door, the portal you would someday walk through and your whole life would change for the better, leave you optimistic about everything, never cynical, always happy; in a virtual state of happiness.

I lunged at her and we rolled in the grass. The perfume of her, the sex of her, the tenderness.

She was all woman. She was more real woman than any fifty LA bimbos put together; than any hundred. I think I would have died for her and thought nothing of it. At the time.

We made love right there out in the open, uninhibited, unafraid; completely free. It was a back and forth giving, always giving; the way I'd heard it was supposed to be. You gave and got plenty in return. Like putting money in the bank and watching it draw interest; that's what our love-making was like. I was sure no one else had it as great as we did, no one else had ever loved the way we loved.

What did I know?

I know that it was ironic with all this love in the air that we should be planning as dreadful a deed as murder. To us it was something we had to do to save 'our world.' It was going to be a fight to save and keep what we had sought both our lives.

"First, we'll both have to work out alibis. Grozewski may look stupid, only he's far from it. It won't be long before he's onto us."

"He'll always be onto us, Fred. I know that for a fact. We can't let it stop us. As long as he can't prove anything, that's all that matters."

"What can you do about an alibi?"

"I can say I was with the kids. Put them under, leave the house, as long as I'm back before they're up and about."

"Good. You'll have to make sure they're out for the duration."

"They'll be out. Don't you worry."

"I can do the same with Monica. Knock her out with sleeping pills, wait for her to doze off. Sneak out, do it, and get back."

"It's great, Fred. We've been racking our brains all this time and it's so simple, so damn simple."

"Let's hope it works."

"Why wouldn't it work?"

"Grozewski."

"He can question them all he wants. What would he find out? Nothing."

"We'll need at least an hour. I'll have to arrange it so that she doesn't catch on she's been asleep that long."

"How will you do that?"

"I don't know yet. You'll have to do the same. I don't know if you can. If the kids let it be known they had dozed off, you're sunk."

"I can have the babysitter come over."

"It doesn't solve it."

"Sure it does. The sitter would make a more reliable witness."

"Why would you have the sitter over, unless you're planning to go out?"

"Because I'm too much of a wreck to deal with the kids by myself. My husband being hurt, laid up in a hospital bed and all. I can unplug the clock before I leave the house, plug it back in when I get back. When the sitter comes to, it'll look like she'd dozed off for no more than a few minutes."

"What if she should check the time at the other end? Where she lives; before she steps out? She wear a wristwatch? There's also that."

"What do you suggest I do? Go to her parents' house and boost the batteries from the wall clocks?"

"Can you?"

"How about if I punch you in the nose, Fred?"

"Loose thread. I don't like it. And the sitter's wristwatch is an issue that needs to be addressed."

"Of course. I'll think of something, and if I don't . . . no plan is perfect."

"I don't like the sound of that."

"All you have to do is see to it that Monica ingests the sleeping pills."

I didn't respond.

"Or else I stay with the kids. Let you go alone."

"I wish you didn't have to come along. I'd need a look-out."

"I wouldn't miss it for the world."

Chapter 88

After a protracted and heated back-and-forth on what type of poison was most effective and quickest and easiest to lay hands on: ricin, LUX, potassium chloride, Devil's Helmet, et al., it came down to antifreeze and rat killer. She wanted the latter & practically insisted on it. Her reason being: rat poison for a rat. I was favoring antifreeze. My reasoning being, that I kept to myself, she'd been using it all along, and should the shit hit the fan I'd be able to legitimately claim: Look, I'm a Johnny-come-lately in all of this. Frank was being fed the tainted tea long before I appeared on the scene. In fact, it could just be I'm the patsy, fall guy, not unlike Oswald for the JFK hit. They were waiting for a *scapegoat* & I was ready-made.

So I kept liking the idea of antifreeze more and more, and Margie liked it less and less. Maybe for the same reason I had: looking ahead, down the road. Hey, love can be great when it's great, only love had a way of turning ugly, too. Been there. So had she. What happened between her and Graham was a perfect example of that.

Sure, you wanted to be optimistic, upbeat, when you had someone in your life, only it didn't pay to be too effing naive about things, either.

To end the stand-off, and keep the relationship from unraveling, we settled on rat poison. You had to choose your battles. Nobody ever got everything to go the way they wanted. Nobody. Ever. Of course, the downside to using rat killer, no one had to tell me, was that any reasonably talented ME would be able to spot it easily enough. I pointed it out to her. She came back with: What was it to keep them from discovering the antifreeze? What's to keep them from discovering no matter what we went with? If they suspected foul play they'd look for anything and everything, wouldn't they?

"Besides, I already have it."

"You have it?"

"I've had it. Yes. Rodent poison and syringe."

It didn't matter. We had to get with it. This was our one chance to deal with the problem Graham's very existence caused. Get rid of the bounty man & our troubles were over. When you're stressed and panic-driven this is how the mind works: seeking the easiest solution. I didn't like it, no doubt was being pushed into it by the stress-inducing dynamic of it.

We would give it to him intravenously. A shot in the arm. Marge begged me to let her do it. I consented.

Chapter 89

What we were planning on doing finally, actually, dawned on me and worked on my conscience harder than ever. Truth was I didn't hate the man; truth was I continued to find it difficult to drum up enough loathing to justify and accept the fact we were about to inject him with rat poison. What was the linchpin that nudged me over to seeing it her way? Narrowing it down was problematic and probably could've been attributed to more than a single factor: love and money. Not necessarily in this order.

But the one thing, if you had to boil it down, that made it difficult for me came down to Graham. Even though he'd just had that catheter removed, taking the time and making the effort to take his kids to the zoo.

The fact that he'd loved his son enough to be angry enough to want to find the asshole, me, responsible for letting the dog attack him. Then there was the train set and Barbie doll. It added up and was hard to ignore. Hence, I did my best to push it aside. Had to. What choice did I have at this stage of the game? But it bothered me (and would continue to do so the rest of my life). Yet, we still went ahead.

I gave Marge enough pills to take care of her end, suggested she use the Fiesta for our date later that night, and went home. Monica was in a romantic mood, all the more in my favor. It was perfect. Even though I hardly felt like making love to her I knew that I would have to and followed through by conjuring images of Margie's naked tits up against my face, conjuring images of Margie's luscious thighs wrapped around my neck and her asshole pressed hard against my nose. It was all in my mind's eye, making love to Margie Graham, the woman that I loved. Monica had no idea at this particular moment what was going on. All she knew she was getting the ride of her life and enjoyed it for all it was worth.

I gave her a workout like never before. She said she wished it was always like this. I didn't say anything. She was ready to go to sleep afterwards; so was I. She usually liked a glass of water post bop. I said I was thirsty, too, and got a glass of cold water, crushed a few pills down to powder, poured the powder in and stirred, and brought the concoction to the bedroom. She drank half of it, set it on the end table by the bed and was out soon after.

I lay there beside her for a while to make sure, then quickly got dressed, yanked a handful of Latex gloves from a box in the cabinet under the bathroom vanity, and waited out front.

Not only was Marge late when she pulled up, but she was in the effing *Throwback Rooter* van with the pipes on top. I didn't like the idea of using the van for the obvious reason that it would be far easier to remember by someone than the nondescript Fiesta. She claimed the car wouldn't start and that she'd had no choice.

I told her to scoot over and that I was driving. She did that, and I got us going. There were some other issues she went into as to why she was late.

"I didn't have any trouble with the kids. The sitter was a problem. Had to make sure the radio and the tv weren't working. She would have been hip to the time laps for sure."

I asked what the sitter did to stay occupied.

"She reads. She's a reader. Bodice rippers. She smokes pot. Doesn't think that I know. I smell it every time. Dumb young chick."

"Was she wearing a wristwatch, Marge? Did you happen to notice?"

"Her wristwatch won't do her any good. You see, I 'accidentally' dropped it, then just as 'accidentally' stepped on it."

"You 'stepped' on her wristwatch?"

"We'll have to replace it."

I handed her a pair of latex gloves.

"What's this for?"

"I don't know about you, but I'd rather not leave my prints behind."

She slipped them on, and looked kinky doing it.

"I ever tell you you're beautiful?"

"Not often enough."

"*You are the most beautiful woman I have ever seen.*" I gave her another kiss. This time a wet one on the lips. "*And you're mine. All mine.*"

"*I love you, sweetheart.*"

Chapter 90

We pulled into the hospital lot. Paused in an area close enough to the front entrance to be able to see inside the lobby and sat there taking in the male nurse behind the desk. We hadn't thought about that and the night security guard.

"What now, Margie?"

"Why ask me? I'm no criminal. I don't do this for a living. You're a man; you're supposed to know these things."

"Thanks a lot."

"I didn't mean it that way, sweetheart. I'm so tense right now. Look at my hands. My hands are shaking."

I held her hands. Hugged her. Until she had calmed down. I got us away from there and took my time cruising the lot and settled on a safe enough parking spot under a tree.

"Smocks, Fred. We walk in like a couple of doctors."

"That won't work. Nurses know the doctors."

We decided we would wait for the guard to go on his patrol of the parking lot and grounds and then draw the desk clerk out, and I would knock him out. I ripped the top of her dress.

"You're a rape victim. Make sure he doesn't get a good look at your face."

She ripped the bottom of her dress, revealing a lot of thigh.

"That can't hurt, either."

She donned a wig, and scarf over that, while I dug around inside the gym bag making sure the rubber mallet was there. (Anything else like a hammer or crescent wrench or tire iron would have left too much of a visible gash.) We weren't pros. We weren't entirely stupid, either.

Chapter 91

It wasn't until we walked up to the door that it dawned on me how weak the whole plan was. You didn't have to be Einstein to see that the alibis wouldn't stick. None of it would work. Not only that, but there were security cameras all over the place. And if that weren't bad enough, I noticed about a dozen patients sitting in the waiting area just beyond the front desk. The utter folly of it dawned on me. It was sheer suicide. I did an about face and walked back to the van.

"What the fuck are you doing, Fred?" She followed after me. *"We had a plan."*

"You didn't see the cameras in there? Peeps in the waiting room?"

"We're wearing disguises. Beaners are half-asleep and too busy to notice a couple of goofs dressed like us."

"Yeah, well, the plan needs an overhaul."

I unlocked the van, climbed in. She got in on the other side.

"What are you talking about?"

"It's October."

"Meaning exactly what?"

"Halloween is a few days away. I say we wait until then and really do up the makeup and wigs. Hospital employees will come to work with outlandish makeup on. You can get away with layers of war paint and no one would give a damn or look twice. Peeps, young and old, visiting patients will be wearing all types of weird shit and no one will blink an eye."

I looked at her. She wasn't saying anything. Margie preferred to fume. It made no sense to me just then. Only later would I be able to put it all together. But that was later.

"Or else we wait for Christmas and go in dressed like Santa and his inordinately tall elf."

"Christmas? Christmas is too long to wait. *Fuck waiting until Christmas. And I'm not dressing up like a fucking elf!* And besides, he'll be out and about *way before Christmas!*"

"I was teasing, babe."

"At a time like this?"

I had to agree. Started the engine up.

"*Flowers*, Margie. What we need to do: stop by a flower shop tomorrow and come back here with flowers. You're the wife, I'm the crook-catcher's backup. We stop by to see how he's doing—with blooms, and a get-well card."

I got us out of the lot. I could tell she was staring at me, pissed to the max, and shaking her head.

"Stop shaking your head. You know I'm right."

"We had it planned out. You agreed. Now you're saying we're idiots?"

"Why not?"

"You might be, I'm not."

I glanced at her out of the corner of my eye. She was fuming; staring straight ahead and fuming.

"Stepping on the babysitter's watch? Knocking her and Monica out with sleeping pills was lame. Would never hold up under the weakest scrutiny."

She looked at me, then pulled the mirror down to check her make up. Yanked the scarf and wig off and tossed them in the back. She said she needed coffee and to take her to a doughnut shop. Then she cursed under her breath.

I found a doughnut shop. A bum sat at one of the tables at one end. We took a booth at the opposite end. Marge was still pissed, red-faced and pissed. I paid for a couple of coffees, couple of chocolate doughnuts sprinkled with nuts. It was fitting. The frustrated nuts ate their doughnuts. I figured she'd come around once she concluded that my thinking made sense. We needed another plan. Marge wanted another doughnut.

"That's your *Plan-B? Halloween costumes?*"

She took a bite of her doughnut. Sipped her coffee.

"Got something better? I'm all ears."

If looks could kill. That was what I got from her.

Chapter 92

We got together the next day, picked up a bouquet at a flower shop— and we still hadn't decided on a backup plan. What we had was Halloween. That was it.

I suggested we take the kids with.

"No."

"This just might be their last chance to see their father alive."

"Why complicate things, Fred? Aren't they complicated enough as it is?"

"Where's your heart, Marge?"

She cursed.

"What would it hurt to bring them along? Wouldn't it look better all around? To have the girl, Liris, walk into the man's room with the flowers?"

The extent of her response was to give me the side-eye.

Chapter 93

I drove us over to the hospital in Monica's car. We signed in at the desk as required, took the elevator up to Graham's room.

The first shocker we encountered was a rent-a-cop sitting in a chair outside Frank's door. I asked the guy who was footing the bill. He said he didn't know, or just plain wouldn't say. Requested to see some ID, and jotted something down in his pocket notebook. It was right then that I gave Marge a look that said: I was right. I was so right not to come in here last night. If we had, we would have been busted—big time. Only Marge, still pissed, wouldn't give me the satisfaction by acknowledging any of it.

I asked the guard if anyone was in the room with Graham. He nodded his head. We had the kids stay with him, and Marge and I went in. For the second shocker.

"Ma, what're you doing here?"

Clutching a Bible in her hands, sitting in a chair by the side of the bed as if in prayer, was the clearly rough around the edges broad in her 50s I'd had a close encounter or two with before.

Mixed race, dyed hair, bruised neck and face. Standing by the window, his back turned to us and toking on a joint, was that punk Jamal. Half the mother's age. Tall and wiry and looked way older than he should've looked.

Seeing him again only confirmed what I'd already pegged him as. Probably another user. Meth-head or crack addict. Uppers missing. Just another low-gauge mook Margie's mamma dug up somewhere.

The mother looked up from her Bible.

"I figure prayer can't hurt."

"When did you get in, Ma?"

"He has no one, you know. The exes hate him. And those grown kids of his only call when they need money. You're busy with the youngsters. I didn't want to see Mr. Graham leave this world without knowing that there are people who care."

It was Margie's turn.

"*Spare me, Rinelle.*" She looked at the punk, and back at her mother. "What's he doing here?"

"You've met my friend Jamal. He's been a big help to me. When I heard what happened I, well, basically had a collapse. Jamal here picked up the pieces, booked us the first available flight out . . . and here we are."

Graham's eyes were closed. He was not exactly asleep. Not awake, either. He just didn't look half as good as I expected, not after hearing the thumbs-up from the arrogant doc the other day.

I thought: *If you die, Frank, I wouldn't have to participate in this scheme to knock you off. I wouldn't have to be party to murder. So why don't you effing die, man?*

Only Graham wasn't talking, and the mother and daughter hated each other way too much to be able to have a civilized conversation, so I saw no point in sticking around. Left the room and ushered the kids inside.

I was making steps down the hallway when Marge caught up, calling and cursing at me to stop. I did. Looked at her.

"I'm no good here. What you two need is a referee."

"That's our way. I try. Ma's not the easiest person to get along with."

"I got better things to do."

I walked away.

"Where you going?"

"Chambray shouldn't be left by herself."

She called my name. I didn't stop this time.

Chapter 94

The phone rang the next day at noon, waking me from a sound sleep. It was Marge. Itching to get back to the hospital and take care of Graham. Even after I insisted that he would expire on his own.

"You saw him. On his way out. A day or two and you'll be able to stick a fork in him. He'll be done."

"No, he won't be. Bigot's bouncing back, recovering. I spoke with Rinelle. He'll be back and the abuse will continue. Not only that, he'll take us both out once he finds out we tipped Quintero off and that we've been carrying on behind his back."

I didn't like it. She insisted on getting together. Had to see me.

"Your husband's on his death bed. You're being watched. We probably both are."

"The kids are out of the house. Use the alley. Come in through the back."

There was no way to reason with her. Not only that, that tight pee hole was not easy to stay away from. No denying I was addicted to the cunt and *culo* and needing to blast a load in her. No matter how hard I tried to convince myself that I could do without, it was no use. Images of the kinky encounters we'd experienced up to this point kept replaying in my mind's eye.

"You can do whatever you want. I'll be your sex slave; or we can reverse the roles." She mentioned having picked up additions to the sex toys, plus a hot vid or two.

"I have to see you. Fred darling, I . . . Do I have to beg?"

"It might help. Beg, bitch. Let me hear you beg. Tell me you can't go another day without."

Then she proceeded to do just that. That's when I stopped her, and told her that I'd only been teasing. There was no need to beg; because I was as needy as she was. We agreed on a motel. I reminded her to make sure she was not being tailed before hanging up.

Chapter 95

She had the works: porn, lube, fishnets and skimpy silk panties, plus lingerie. She wanted to model the various items for me to get me hot. Only there was no need, because my Jones was like a steel pipe. And as far as bringing porn vids along? No need there, either, because porn played on cable 24/7. All types. You name it. Lesbians eating each other out, shafting one another with massive dildos, orgies and gangbangs.

You had one chick being done by a gang of dudes with huge dicks, or else it was one dude being serviced by a number of babes with big tits and hairy beavers. There were cum showers—and other types of showers. Hoes and moes. Creaming and screaming. *Bacchanals à la carte.*

We went at it half a dozen times, then were forced to take a breather and have a bite to eat: grilled chicken that we had brought with, washed down with a fine German beer. We showered, and were back at it on the bed for a few more rounds until we both passed out. Shagging was work. We napped for a while afterwards.

When we awoke, we were in agreement: *Graham had to go.* We had to make sure the cocksucker was history, and would never be able to come back and disrupt our lives ever again.

"Only what do we do about your mother and her boyfriend?" I was sitting up in bed, chowing down on a drumstick and pulling on that good

German beer. "What if they're there like the other day?"

"We'll have to create a distraction."

"For instance?"

"I'll think of something."

"It better be good, Marge. It has to work. And then there's the rent-a-cop. Probably put there by Growzewski."

"*Tub of shit*. Only that won't stop us. We can't let it."

Chapter 96

It was Halloween and we were in our getups. Mine was weak: pirate with a black eyepatch, fake beard, blackened teeth, sword in a scabbard. Margie wanted to go dressed as a cross between a witch and a zombie from one of those '*Living Dead*' flicks.

We were in her place. Kids were with the babysitter. Margie was still applying finishing touches to her makeup. I'd helped myself to a beer in the fridge and walked to the living room. I sat in Graham's recliner. Cracked it & hit it. She walked out, stood in front of me and wanted to know what I thought. She spun around, wanting my honest opinion. I told her it would do, without ever looking at her.

"What is it?"

"Nothing."

"I know you well enough, Alf. What's going on?"

"Let it go."

"No."

"I don't feel right about it being rat poison."

"Not again."

"What it implies bothers me."

"You're bothered? It implies what it should imply."

"Man's better to his kids than mine was to me."

"Because he took them to the zoo once?"

"Don't forget the studio tour. And we both know how much he despises all that 'dream factory' bullshit."

"There's no time for this, Alf."

"I still don't get why it has to be rat poison."

"He put you in the hospital the first time, and then knocks you out over nothing, because a dog you don't own snaps at his belligerent kid, who, by the way, wouldn't stop petting your girlfriend's psycho animal— *after you warned him*—and you want to start behaving like a pussy at a time like this?"

"I never said I wouldn't go through with it, just that I didn't like it. It bothers me."

"I don't like it either, but we have no choice. When he recovers, and he will recover, we're as good as dead. It's over. All of it. Our plans, the future. Over. Taken from us. That's not me sounding paranoid, but a fact; a fact, Alfie!"

I cursed under my breath. Finished off the can, and rose.

Chapter 97

I insisted we stop by a flower shop, and were at the hospital with the blooms. Front desk was busy with all types of hurting peeps. Couple in a wheelchair, a dude on crutches, an elderly lady using a walker; plus they had either family or friends or both present. Since this was also the information desk, people were asking about this and the other. In our favor, though, was the fact more than a few of the visitors were attired in all types of off-the-wall cinema icon outfits: from Frankenstein to the Wolfman, from the Mummy to Zorro, and even one steroid-bloated gym rat type wearing a loin cloth and some type of viking get-up. This was the Valley, after all; this was 'Hollywood.' Why not?

We strolled through without a hitch. Made it past the desk without signing in, and on up to the floor Graham was on. Getting off the elevator we noticed it right away: picked up on the ruckus, and it was loud. Marge gave me a knowing look. Margie's mother Rinelle and her punk boyfriend, no guises used here, were arguing with the same security guard. Had to do with Jamal having smoked weed in Frank's room.

"The man is sick. Want to get arrested? Want me to call *Five-0?*"

The boyfriend hadn't cared for the threat.

"*Five-0?* You serious? Over smoking a joint? Nobody gets arrested for smoking pot these days. Nobody! Hear? *Wannabe-pig!*"

"Not for smoking a joint, but for smoking it in a room with a sick man in it!"

"Still ain't got the right to make a big deal out of it!" Rinelle was cutting in now. The guard had his arms open wide, and was half-guiding/half-shoving them away from the door and down the hallway. Jamal didn't cotton to this one bit.

"Get your fuckin' clammy paws off me! *Now, motherfucker!*"

"Don't you dare lay a hand on Jamal!"

Rinelle then proceeded to slap the guard, who slapped back, and decided to radio for backup. Grozewski could be heard responding at the other end. That's when the boyfriend let go with a fast flurry of punches that knocked the man down. He got his hand on the Maglite and hammered him in the face with it, knocking him out. The boyfriend grabbed the guard by the feet and dragged him to the doorway that was the stairwell exit, while the mother held it open for him. They made it through, and the door swung shut behind them.

I stood there, kind of stunned by what I'd just witnessed. Margie, not perturbed by any of it, grabbed me by the sleeve and yanked me inside Graham's room.

Chapter 98

Graham was semi-conscious. Which was okay, but dead would've been preferable. Made no difference, really. We had our latex gloves on. Margie reached inside her purse for the syringe. Searched for a good spot to stick the needle in. She was going to go for a crook in one of the arms, an obvious spot. I nixed that.

"Where, then?"

"Under the tongue; or else one of the eyeballs."

"Under the tongue? Or one of the eyeballs? *That's gross.*"

"Not the eyeball itself, but the tear duct. Better yet, to the right just a touch. If you could aim for the nodule in the corner there by the bridge of his nose. It's not ideal, but it may have to do."

The swelling round the eyes, nose and mouth had gone down considerably. Only what remained was still daunting to look at, in that the discoloration was plenty evident: dark purple and black blotches throughout. The goal, when attempting something like this, was to hit the bloodstream directly, if possible. Going for one of the eyeballs was second choice; even under the tongue was.

"That's gross. I can't do that."

"Yes, you can. Else we're fucked. Autopsy will reveal where he was jabbed. They don't miss a trick. The obvious spots is what they check first: arms, toes, between the knuckles, lower legs. Any part of the anatomy with easy access to a vein. No different from when hypes look to hit a spot that will deliver the quickest rush."

"How do you know so much about it?"

"Spent enough time in the company of dope fiends."

"And you never mainlined?"

"We're wasting time, Marge."

She said she couldn't do it.

"You were the one who insisted on this."

"I was the one who tried to talk you out of it."

"Did you expect it to be easy?"

"Easier than this."

I suggested she go for the neck instead, the bandaged side. She stood there, undecided, while Graham's eyes opened. He was looking at us, seeing the needle and looking up.

"The fuck are you two up to now?"

He must have been under heavy sedation or something. For the pain.

"I'm talking to you fuckers. First your whore mother comes in here with that strung-out meth-mouth guttersnipe, now I gotta deal with you two assholes."

Margie told him to shut up, and reminded him that he was the only *'asshole'* in the room.

"I'll get you both for this shit, soon as I'm back on my feet. You can count on it. . . ."

"Oh yeah? You're not laying another hand on me, ever again, Frank."

"Lying bitch."

He wanted to know where his kids were. Who was watching them. Kept babbling about it, while vomit, mixed-in with blood, bubbled up. We ignored it. Had to. I urged her to hurry it up and get it over with. She hesitated. Tested the needle. Made sure it was not clogged. It was at this point the redneck's left arm came up and he grabbed her hand and those powerful fingers of his squeezed and squeezed hard, and that's when I whacked him with the mallet. *Pow!* Against the right temple. And she dropped the fucking needle. No way. Not that. She had dropped the needle.

"Who's being the 'pussy' now, Marge?"

"I'm no criminal. I've never done anything like this before."

"So who is? Who has?"

"I think my hand is broke."

"You think? It is, or it isn't."

"The motherfucker broke my hand."

"We have to get out of here before reinforcements come up. *Guard radioed for help.*"

"How can I?"

She fumbled. Managed to collect the syringe. Barely stuck the tip of the needle into the gauze, acting like she was having second thoughts, wavering. Said her hand hurt. I held her by the wrist to keep her steady, while she injected the strychnine. She stowed the needle back in her purse, and we got out of there.

Marge was about to make a run for the elevator, until I called her name. Gestured we take the stairs down. Not the same way her mother and the punk went, in case the guard had come to, but at the other end. And we did.

Deed was done. There was no way Graham could survive the toxins we pumped into him.

Chapter 99

A day went by, and another and another. No word. About any of it. Nothing in the papers or tv. It was not only troubling, but nerve-wracking as hell. I couldn't sleep a wink. Didn't think about tits or pussy the entire time. Not like me at all. Too much on my mind. Monica wondered what was up one morning, as she sipped her coffee at the kitchen table. I'd spent the night tossing and turning, and decided to get up with her. I'd fed Chambray, poured myself a bowl of *Cheerios*, and couldn't touch it.

"Nothing, other than losing out on the money I made while with Graham ever since he got laid up. Not seeing tips like I used to. Porn crowd is mighty tight with their cash. You wouldn't think they would be with all the bucks that business pulls in, but they are. *Tight.* And I'm not talking about their bungholes, either."

She reminded me I had to hang in, and that a studio driving job would eventually happen.

"Sure."

She gave me a peck on the cheek and left for the gym. The whole act of murder fucked with my head and left me jumpy. I wondered if Graham was even dead; if we had injected enough of the poison in his tough-as-rawhide ass? Who knew? No one was saying anything.

I decided to take Chambray for a walk. We got as far as the nearest phone booth. I dialed Margie's number.

Chapter 100

"The hospital contact you?"

"Not yet."

There was shouting in the background. A real back-and-forth verbal slugfest. I asked what was going on.

"Rinelle and Jamal."

"What caused it?"

"The usual: money. And dope."

Evidently Rinelle had just spent a good chunk of their funds on what turned out to be mostly baking powder.

"He's pissed because I refuse to let him have Frank's guns in order to recoup the loss. Asshole's blaming me for my mother's fuck-up."

"You can't give those guns away, Marge. They're worth money. Frank bought quality when it came to his weapons."

"I wouldn't give him shit. Besides, they're missing."

"What's missing?"

"Jesus. What the fuck are we talking about, Fred?"

"You look in the van?"

"Yes, I looked in the van."

"Frank kept them in a metal tool box, and the tool box was usually in the van."

"So where is it?"

"You're asking me, Marge?"

"Don't play fucking games with me, Fred."

"I'm being accused and I don't care for it."

"Feels like I'm stuck refereeing a wrestling match with a couple of maniacs, and you're not making it any easier."

I apologized. Asked how long the battling guests were staying.

Margie couldn't say. Hoped the windbags would be leaving town—and soon.

"I'll keep in touch."

"I love you."

"Likewise."

"*Likewise*?"

"What do you want from me, Marge? Blood? You want a pint of blood? That's all I've got left to give. Fine. I'll give you a pint of blood."

"What am I? Vampire?"

I had no response.

"Because that's what you're implying. I'm hungry for a little affection and suddenly I'm a vampire? My fucking right hand and wrist are in a cast because of that son of a bitch and I get called a bloodsucker!"

"Nobody called you a bloodsucker, Marge."

"You can't say that you need me the way I need you? Is that so hard? A word like love. It's a word, Fred."

"It's more than that. And my nerves are shot at the moment, babe. You get what I'm saying?"

"I've got news for you: You're not the only one who's a wreck, lover."

The verbal sparring went on in the background, escalating in volume. A scream followed. Margie's mother. The guy must've hit her. I heard a drawer open, rattling of silverware. I called Margie's name, but she wasn't answering. She'd walked away from the phone. Then a male voice, the punk, no doubt, telling her in a low tone to calm down and put the butcher knife away.

"You need to take it easy, Marge."

"No, what you need to do is get the fuck out of my house, Jamal, before I call the rollers!"

I heard the guy say 'all right' a couple of times. "Just give me a chance to grab my suitcase, and I'm gone—and the two of you: *Psycho Ma and Ho Daughter can both go fuck yourselves!*"

Chapter 101

A week later the phone rang. It was Lieutenant Grozewski.

"Is this Fred Reed?"

I mumbled something about him being right. I'd finally resorted to taking sleeping pills in order to get some shuteye and was drowsy.

"Frank Graham is dead."

"What?"

"He's dead."

"Frank? The last time I saw him his condition was stable, with a good shot at full recovery."

"It wasn't from the explosion. We suspect post-explosion foul play."

"I don't know what to say."

"Frank had his quirks like the rest of us. He was a good man."

"Words escape me, Lieutenant."

"We don't know the exact cause at the moment. There will be a complete and full autopsy. We'll be in touch."

He hung up.

Chapter 102

I wanted to phone her. A pay phone made more sense. I slipped into my sneakers, attached the leash to Chambray's collar, and made it out to a phone. I dialed Marge.

"Got a call from Grozewski. Nothing to worry about. Just want you to know everything is fine."

"Talked to the piggy myself. They want me to go in and identify the body."

"Whatever you do, Marge, don't panic."

"I won't."

"Look distressed, but don't fall apart; something might slip out otherwise."

"Don't worry. I'm so happy for us, sweetheart. We've done it."

"Not yet, we haven't."

"There's nothing to keep us apart now, nothing to interfere with our love."

"I love you, baby."

"We'll be able to get married now. Everything will be so great for us, Fred."

"I know it will, honey."

Chapter 103

Not only did I have trouble sleeping, but had developed night sweats. I was worried about Margie, worried she would say the wrong thing, worried Grozewski was onto us. I was drenched in sweat. During the day as well as at night, while doing the pizza delivery. I'd get home. Stayed hyper. I'd pace until it was almost time for Monica to get up, then I'd return to bed and pretend to let the alarm wake us both, lest she wonder what was going on with me, why I was acting the way I was.

Two days later, just as she was ready to leave for work, there was a knock at the door. It was Lt. Grozewski. Troubled and looked it. Something like me. He wondered if he might have a few words with Monica alone.

I waited inside with Chambray, while they talked outside in the yard. Chambray growled and barked non-stop, wanting a piece of that chunky roller.

When they were through, and Monica had left for work, the detective asked me to step outside. Chambray scared the piss out of him and he preferred to stay out of the house. What I got from him was the approximate day and time Graham bought the farm.

"*Thallium sulphate*. That's what killed him. They shot him full of it."

"Who's they?"

"If you don't mind, I'll do the asking."

"By all means. 'Thallium sulphate'?"

"Rat poison."

"Rat poison?"

"That's not all. They discovered *ethylene glycol* in his system."

"Ethylene . . . I don't know what that is."

"Antifreeze."

"No shit?"

He wanted to know if I had an alibi.

"I was Frank's partner. What the hell?"

"Routine. Doing my job."

"I'm sorry, it's just that Frank dying like this . . ."

"I know what you mean. You never expect it to happen to someone near and dear to you."

"Something like that. Yes."

"Like I said, it's routine. The captain's idea, in fact. When the captain says do such-and-such, we do such-and-such." And he still wanted to know where I was at the approximate time of Graham's demise.

What was I going to say? What could I tell him that would stick and make him go away? What didn't occur to me until much, much later, is that he was bluffing—and that it was Bible-toting Rinelle who had pumped plenty of the toxins into Graham while she was in there with Jamal that time. Marge and I coming up later on Halloween was merely the *coup da gras*. Topper. To make sure he was *finito,* and that I was the patsy. Not unlike Lee Harvey & the Kennedy scenario.

Like I said: I had no idea. Sucker through and through. Only what the two of them hadn't counted on, Rinelle and Marge, that is, is that Marge would become addicted to my ability at licking cunt and driving her to screaming spasms with ecstasy. I'd say it was that, basically. But once the initial attraction wore off, and she no longer felt she desired or needed me, I was thrown under the bus. But that was later, way later. I'm getting ahead of myself here.

"At the supermarket buying dog food, a new leash for the dog."

He asked about a receipt. I went and got it for him. He looked at it, then up at me.

"You want more? I even talked to the butcher in their meat department, asked for bones for the dog. I usually did that. They were out."

He nodded. And said he hoped it checked out.

"Want more? I got more: We went to see him. What's the crime? Woman was married to him. She's a widow now. With two kids to raise. I worked for him. He was my employer. Saved me from ending up on some park bench. For a while anyway. Tried to keep me from having to go back to delivering pizza—*for a while, anyway*—until a truck driving gig at the studios opened up. *I got more*: man had enemies. All over the country. From Alaska to Hawaii; from New York to New Mexico. *Want more?* Want me to do your job?'

"You failed to sign in the day you went in to see him. Why's that?"

"Desk was busy; way too busy. Bunch of freaks dressed up like *Freddy Krueger* and other serial killer ass-hats, or else as *Star Wars* and *Star Trek* dipsticks. In Halloween costumes. Made us nauseous. We didn't feel like hanging around, so we went up. What's the crime?"

"How's Marge taking it?"

"Marge? You mean Mrs. Graham? How do you think she's taking it? Hit her hard, real hard. She's a strong woman. She'll be all right in time."

He nodded. "Good looking young gal. It's a shame. Left a widow at her age. Pure shame." Then he took out a roll of *Rolaids* and popped one in his mouth.

"See to it she pulls through, will you, Fred?"

"I'll do my best, Lieutenant."

"Thanks."

Oinker was gone. Cocksucker.

Chapter 104

I dropped two *Alka-Seltzer* tablets in a glass of water and downed it all, then I sat down and didn't do much. Porker had it figured out. I was sure of it.

Marge was on the line.

"You shouldn't be making these calls from your place."

"I'm not. I'm calling from a pay phone."

"Who's with the kids?"

"Don't worry about them."

"Grozewski just left."

"I know. I watched him leave from across the street."

"The hell are you doing sneaking around? They might have a tail on you."

"Don't you think I already thought of that?"

"You should be with your kids, Marge. You're gonna screw things up."

"He asked me what color the van was."

"What the fuck. That's stupid. *He knows what color the damned van is.*"

"Sure he knows. He was toying with me."

"It's routine."

"Same line he uses whenever he gives me the third degree. I strongly suggest you keep that *'routine'* crap to yourself. You're not talking to a high school kid."

"The hell is gotten in you? You never acted like this before."

"Was never involved in croaking anyone, either."

"Relax, will you?"

"I'm sorry, sweetheart. It's just that . . . I'm so tense. I think I'm headed for a nervous breakdown."

"Not another one."

"The pressure is getting to me."

"Just relax, Margie. Everything is fine."

"I have to see you, Fred."

"You will."

"When?"

"I promise."

"When, Fred? When?"

"I'll see you at your place in about an hour."

"You think it's smart to meet there?"

"Grozewski's suggestion. Help the grieving widow, he says. I'm helping."

"I need your arms around me, sweetheart, to comfort me. . . . I need to be with you."

"I'll be there even sooner, just go back to your place. And quit sneaking around. Stay with your kids."

"They're not my kids. They were never my kids."

"Fine."

"The night watchman saw the van that night while on his rounds."

"So what? Maybe we were there to visit, but then realized it was way past visiting hours. Get me? Besides, it's not the only maroon-colored van in Southern California; nor is it the only one with pipes on its roof or signs on the sides. Go home. I'll see you there."

"Hurry, darling."

Chapter 105

Rinelle and her freak had flown back home and it did help. The kids, on the other hand, were a mess and wouldn't quit bugging Margie about their missing dad. Margie's idea of dealing with the problem was to order Butch and his sister Liris to go outside and play.

"You got toys. Got more toys than I ever saw in my entire life. Go play with your toys and stop bothering me already."

Marge and I sat in the kitchen drinking coffee, trying to. We were both all nerves. Then she rose, went about preparing peanut butter and jelly sandwiches for the kids, along with a tall glass of raspberry iced tea for both. I watched her. And couldn't believe it. She placed the plate and the glasses on a tray and carried it out to the front porch. I followed after her. Got there just in time, as the kids reached for their iced tea. I grabbed the glasses and poured the contents out.

"What the hell are you doing, Fred?"

I went back inside without saying anything. She followed me in.

"I'm not the one who's having the meltdown."

"That was raspberry iced tea."

"So?"

"Same shit you put in Graham's thermos that gave him chronic runs. By your own admission. You *hate* those kids. They remind you of him."

"Not enough to want to see them dead."

I looked at her. *And looked at her.* Didn't know what to believe.

"When's the funeral?"

"Week from now."

"What happens to the kids?"

"Been trying to contact his ex. Left I don't know how many messages. She's not returning my calls."

"You got impatient and went for the *raspberry solution.* Jesus, Marge."

"Called Rinelle. No choice. She's in no condition, either. Back on the meds. Thank God, too; I didn't want her to have to be burdened with the brats."

I nodded. It was a problem. One more to add and intensify the load we were already burdened under.

"Look—about Grozewski. You can't let him get to you. He might act like he knows more than he does. Don't let him trip you up. He doesn't know a damned thing." I lied. I didn't know that for a fact.

"I want us to get married, Fred. I want us to start our life together. I want to have your baby."

"You sure about that?"

"Yes. I just never wanted to get knocked up by that insensitive *throwback*. Our baby will have a real chance. Borne out of the love that we have for each other."

"In a while, we'll have it all. We have to be patient for now."

"I thought as soon as the will goes through, soon as that's settled, we could have a gorgeous wedding in Vegas. We'll have a great time there, Fred. Courtesy of Frank Graham."

"We can't rush into anything, Marge."

"I've suffered at his hands way too long. Mental abuse as well as physical. If we waited a month or so, that wouldn't be rushing."

"That's exactly what it is. Rushing. It would be a stupid move, Marge."

"Two months, then?"

"We'll have to forget about that for a while."

"Why? We don't have to. I want to be Mrs. Fred Reed. I want to be your wife, darling."

"We'll just have to go on like this for a while."

"I don't know if I can."

"You're damned right you can."

"It's that slut you're shacked with, isn't it? *Isn't it?*"

I grabbed her by the shoulders and gave her a shake.

"Don't ever talk about her that way! She's a good woman. She's been good to me."

She was crying.

"I can't stand the thought of you shagging someone else. Oh honey, can't you see what I'm going through? Don't you understand?"

I held her in my arms. I didn't want her to cry.

"I love you, Marge. You're talking nonsense. To leave Monica right now would be the dumbest move I could make."

"What do you expect me to do? I can't sit by and be calm while my man sleeps with another woman."

"It's *sleep*. That's all it is."

"I believe you, darling. I just can't help it. I don't want anyone else touching you. I don't want anyone else kissing those lips, my man's lips. Sucking my man's cock and licking his balls. All of that is mine, every part of you—and stays that way."

"You'll have to control yourself, Marge."

"I can't help it, Fred darling."

"*You can and you will.*"

"It's easy for you to say. You're not the one has to come home to an empty bed, while your lover is in someone else's arms."

"I'm warning you, Marge. Unless you settle down, I'm leaving. I'm not going to let you hang me. I'll split town."

"You couldn't do it. It would tear you apart. I know it would."

"It would be hard. What good would we be to each other in prison? Think about it."

She embraced me, hard.

"I'll be all right. I'll be all right as long as you fuck me, Fred. . . . Fuck me. . . ."

Chapter 106

I have no idea why Marge hadn't been able to get a hold of the former Mrs. Graham, because I'd had no trouble at all. Could be her feeling was if the kids were with her when they dropped dead from the iced tea she'd be awarded a greater chunk of the insurance money. I didn't know. Didn't have access to the insurance policy or Graham's will. I was in the dark about this part of it and Marge wasn't forthcoming with the information the times I mentioned it. And the kids? My attitude was they weren't guilty of anything. Kids were defenseless, and whenever I witnessed a child being abused any way whatsoever, be it verbal, physical or mental, something in me goes off, I see red—because it reminds me of the years of hell I'd lived through as a youngster. I hated seeing kids being mistreated by asshole adults. And so I dialed the kids' biological mother from a pay phone and let her know that she needed to come out and get her youngsters away from Marge.

"That bitch. I warned Frank that there was no way it would work. After his money. Mother and daughter, both. Couple of sociopaths. Rinelle is nothing but a crack ho. Evil bitches wrecked my marriage. Frank wasn't perfect, but he genuinely loved his kids. He was a good provider. He may have been a right-wing jerk, but he gave a damn about his kids."

"Graham was abusing her. Saw it with my own eyes. He was a violent drunk."

"That's bullshit, mister. Frank drank, but he never laid a hand on me or my kids. Ever."

"Maybe so, ma'am. But I saw the welts with my own eyes; witnessed the verbal abuse. I'm not making this up."

"She probably had it coming to her, then. Baited him. Her mother is no better. Gutter trash, I tell you. Rinelle is nothing but a ho. Possibly a black widow. That's the rumor around here. You know what they say: Where there's smoke, there's fire. I'd watch my step around those two. In fact, that whole family."

"Do you realize what you're implying?"

"Mrs. Rossi's significant others have a habit of dropping dead."

"Now just wait a minute here —"

"Eight, at last count. Coincidence? You decide."

"You're sure we're talking about the same Rinelle Rossi here? Margie's mother?"

"Margie's *mother*. Yes. *Rinelle*. Crack ho Rinelle. Food stamp scam artist second-to-none, who scammed the state out of thousands of dollars. Look it up."

"If that's the case, why haven't the authorities gone after her?"

"Don't make me laugh. Who's going to go after her? Corrupt cops and government? Spend some time here and you'll know what I'm talking about. Two of the former governors are in prison as we speak. Sanctuary city, to help the corrupt Dems stay in power like forever. So-called gun-free zone where any criminal who wants a gun has no trouble getting not one, but as many guns as they feel like getting their trigger-happy fingers on. We have the highest murder rate in the nation, mister, or haven't you heard. Outfit had nothing on these punks, or even the likes of Rinelle and her ilk."

I admitted I had spent my teen years there, and conceded her take on my adopted home town was not far from the truth.

"Tried to warn Frank he was getting in over his head. Mule-headed. Macho man. That was Frank. Said she claimed he'd got her knocked up. I told him he was being played for a fool. Where was the evidence that he was responsible for the pregnancy; if, in fact, there was a pregnancy. Then a few months later there was the miscarriage. Of course. Was there proof? Did he even bother? Too busy. Said he needed to believe her. Said I was trying too hard to make her look like she had no redeeming qualities. See what I'm getting at? Know-it-all. Wouldn't listen. Had to do his duty as a man and a law-abiding citizen. Sure. Now he's dead. I wouldn't be surprised if the two of them had something to do with it. For the money, I might add. Gold diggers. Only they won't get all of it. There is no way they'll get everything. Oh, they'll try to get their hands on it, but will fail. Only because I have a very sharp Jew lawyer on my side this time. For the kids. Mainly. Not for me, sir, but the kids. They're entitled."

I had to get off the topic. It was pulling me down. Quite a bit of it was pulling me down.

"I'd feel a whole lot better if the kids were with their natural mother, ma'am."

She wanted to know when the funeral would be taking place and where. I told her.

Chapter 107

Days later, at the scheduled time, Frank Graham's coffin was lowered into the ground in a graveyard in the Valley. Marge adamantly refused to pay the plane fare to have the body shipped to the Midwest, and so he was laid to rest in this place that he loathed. Such is life. Ashes to ashes, dust to dust. He would be joining a lot of those peeps he had put in the ground himself.

It was a quiet funeral. Marge and I were there, both in black, so were the two kids. Frank's former wife flew in, pulled up in a taxicab. Stayed long enough to shove the youngsters in the cab, and they drove off.

Marge was not unhappy to see them go. Lt. Grozewski and his younger partner, who reminded me of Frankenstein, and a Capt. Wooster were in attendance. Wooster was another homicide dick with a big head and little gray eyes. Those gray eyes of his gave me a knot deep in the pit of my stomach and kept it there.

There were some other dicks present in plainclothes, several bail recovery agent types. Even a couple of Hollywood producers Graham must have met somewhere along the way, whose productions Frank may have been a tech adviser on, either back in the Midwest or here or both. People may not have exactly liked Graham, but had appeared out of respect and professional courtesy. Who knew? Maybe his kind did get him.

No one said a word to us the whole time. When it was over I drove Margie to her place. She begged me to stay the night.

"How can I?"

I refused to. It would have been a bad move.

Chapter 108

She called as soon as I got home. Luckily Monica was in the backyard tending to Chambray. Marge insisted she had to see me.

"I can't make it."

"Please, honey. I'm going crazy over here. With the kids gone, I'm all alone."

"I was just with you."

"She's there, isn't she?"

"Sure is. She lives here."

"Are you fucking her?"

"What's the matter with you?"

"Don't you start hedging with me, dammit! Yes or no?"

"You're acting like a nut. Get a hold of yourself."

"Don't call me a nut, you two-timing bastard! Are you going to give it to her like you've been giving it to me? Do you tell her you love her the same way you tell me that *you love me*? Do you do all those things with her? Probe her butt with your tool and whisper sweet nothings in her ear while she fakes her orgasms like a typical Porn Valley slut?"

"There could be a tap on your line. Your place could be bugged."

"I don't care!"

"Will you settle down."

"You're a liar, Fred! You lied to me. You don't love me! You never did!"

"It's not true."

"Come see me."

"I can't."

"It's that slut! She's got you wrapped around her little finger. Admit it, *Alfie*. That's why you're not here with me. Admit it, goddamn you, *Alfred*! Admit it! I was ready to off those brats for you, for the relationship—and this is how you repay me?"

I banged the receiver down. I loved her, only the pressure was more than I could take, and Marge didn't want to hear any of it, didn't want to understand.

What had I gotten myself into?

Chapter 109

No sooner was I through explaining to Monica that Marge was having trouble recovering, when the phone rang again. It was the Lieutenant.

"Funniest thing happened. Had a nice chat with a Mex felon we had in here for a while. Goes by Quintero. Fidel Quintero. Name ring a bell?"

"Frank and I picked him up once."

"Come to think of it, that's right."

"What else?"

"Nothing else."

"You called to tell me that?"

"Thought you might want to know: Got bailed again. And skipped—again."

"Think he might have had something to do with Frank's untimely demise?"

"He might have. Then again, might not."

"I'd like to know what you find out. If you bag him."

"You will."

"If he is responsible, I hope he gets the book thrown at him."

"We thank you for your cooperation."

"Anything I can do, let me know."

"We'll be in touch."

I lowered the receiver. The phone rang. I had a hunch who it was.

"What is it, Marge?"

"Are you coming, or do I have to go over there?"

I slammed the receiver down. Monica was looking at me.

"I'll have to go see her. She sounds desperate."

"Go easy on her, honey. She's been through a lot."

"I will. I may be late."

She kissed me.

"I love you, Fred."

I left.

Chapter 110

If Monica suspected something was amiss she was quietly rubbing it in, seeing to it I choked on guilt. Rub salt in his self-inflicted wound until he screams out in agony. Hell, I had to get off that track. Monica had had nothing to do with it.

I bought a pack of Marlboros at a 7-Eleven, and fired up. Tobacco was a habit I discontinued since 'Nam. I was at it again, chain-smoking. I took the long way to Margie's. By the time I reached her place I had (partially) smoked half a dozen cigarettes. I crushed the rest of the pack in my hand and tossed it in the gutter; as I did, I noticed an unmarked Plymouth sedan parked across the street by the entrance to the park. Grozewski and Frankenstein were in it. I waved to them with my middle finger extended and hoped they appreciated the joke. They didn't wave back.

I went inside.

"The hell took you so long?"

"Don't look now, Grozewski is out there."

She made a move toward the window. I yanked her away from it.

"You better pull yourself together, Marge."

"You never used to treat me like this. *Never.* It's her, isn't it?"

"This is exactly what I mean. I don't want to hear another word about it."

"Why do you have to live with her?"

"I told you why."

"You could move out if you wanted to."

"Be realistic, will you?"

"You wouldn't have to stay here. I can deal with that. I can't stand you living in that house with her."

"What have you got to be jealous about?"

"Plenty."

"Bullshit."

"You wouldn't be saying that if I was sleeping with another man!"

"It's convenient, that's all. She has a studio job. I met her at a party I crashed in the ritzy Hollywood Hills a while back. You know all this. Why make me repeat it? Why make me explain things over and over again?"

"Let's find you another place. I'll pay for it."

I had been so shaken at seeing Grozewski out there it had taken me a while to realize she'd had a few.

"You're drunk, Marge."

She slapped me. I slapped her back. She held on, tears streaming.

"I don't want to lose you, Fred."

"That's the one thing you don't have to worry about."

"I'll kill myself if you ever leave me."

"Will you stop talking like that? We're in this together."

She looked up slowly, the makeup running down her face. She was still a looker.

"Do you mean that, Fred?"

"You're damned right I mean it."

Chapter 111

After the Plymouth had left, she grabbed my hand and pulled me to the bedroom.

"I've got something I want to show you." She leaned over the bed, thrusting her rear end out at me, and slowly pulled back her silk robe. She wasn't wearing panties and she had a tattoo on her right cheek. Artistically done, perfectly shaped, were the letters in fancy script that made up my first name: *Fred.* There it was.

"Doesn't this prove how much I love you, sweetheart?"

I stared at the tattoo, dumbfounded. She'd actually done it.

"No doubt about it." After I answered her, I went over and kissed my name; and then I started kissing the rest of her.

We stayed in there a good two hours. Afterwards she wanted to know when I would be putting *her* name on my butt. Just as I was about to explain that it wouldn't be the smartest move in the world for me to make presently, the phone rang. She reached for it.

"The piggy wants to talk to you."

She handed me the receiver.

"Lt. Grozewski?"

"Thanks for helping out. My partner and I thank you for the single digit salute."

"Not at all. You find out anything from Quintero?"

"Enough."

"I see. Couldn't help but notice you were parked out front. Thanks for keeping an eye on Mrs. Graham."

"All part of the job. We'll be in touch."

He clicked off. The fat bastard was playing games.

"What the piggy want?"

"Nothing."

Chapter 112

I showered. Dressed. She didn't want me to go.

"Please, let's not have another row. I don't want us to be like that. Please, Marge?"

"We'll never argue, Fred. When all this is over it'll be so good for us. That's what gave me the courage to have your name tattooed on my butt. Faith. I have faith. With the money I get we'll be free to do as we please."

"This money you keep talking about. What did he leave?"

"Enough."

"That much?"

There was a grin on her face and she was nodding her head.

"Why didn't you tell me?"

"I had to make sure you wanted me and not the money."

"I suspected the man had a few bucks socked away, but had no idea what the amount was."

"*That much.* And more on the way. See why I'm so happy for us, darling? We'll have the world at our fingertips. We'll go on a cruise to South America. We'll fly to Europe. Spend time in Madrid, Paris; Venice, Italy."

"You're sure to get it?"

"I was there in the attorney's office when he had the will modified. My mother had insisted on it. There would have been no marriage otherwise."

"What about the kids? Don't they get anything?"

"Enough in trust for their education, the rest is ours. It's still quite a chunk, you know. Not to mention his life insurance policy. The insurance company is balking at the moment, but they have no choice: they'll have to pony up eventually."

"How much?"

"Enough to make the bucks left in his will look like walking around money."

"*How much, Marge?*"

She refused to say. She seemed to enjoy keeping me in the dark about this part of it. I told her I'd call her in the morning, and left.

Chapter 113

I walked in. Monica had the receiver in her hand. She looked upset.

"I think she needs help."

She tossed the phone at me.

"What is it, Marge?"

"Just calling to tell you how much I love you."

"Good-night, Marge."

When I looked up, Monica was standing there, weeping silently. I put my arms around her.

"What is it, honey?"

She shook her head and wouldn't say anything. I walked her to the bedroom, and put her to bed like a little kid. I hated to see her like this. She hadn't deserved any of it. I felt like a louse. I undressed and got in bed with her.

"What did she say?"

"She said the most awful things, Fred. I can't repeat it."

"What is it?"

"It can't be true. I won't repeat it." She clung to me. "I can't believe what she said."

I stayed quiet for a long while after.

"Did you sleep with her?"

I nodded.

"Do you love her?"

"I think I do."

"Do you or don't you?"

"I do."

"Do you love me?"

I didn't say anything. She buried her face in her pillow and wept. They were tears of pain. I hated myself for it.

"I was a fool. You never loved me."

"I did."

"*You never loved me.* You used me. I was your hooker all this time."

"Don't say that."

"Nothing more than a hooker. My friends warned me about getting involved with someone younger than me. I was a fool to think we would ever have a life together. I was such a fool."

"You're a good person. And I care for you; I do. . . . It's just that . . ."

I wanted to reach for her. She jerked away from me, her face buried in the pillow.

"*Don't touch me. Don't ever touch me.*"

"I don't know how to explain it. This thing with Marge . . . it just happened."

"Nothing just happens. You let it happen. You let it happen and that's why it happened. You were looking for something else and you found it."

"I feel lousy."

"You should. You're a creep, like all the rest. I believed in you. I thought you'd be different. You're no good; just no fucking good."

We both stayed quiet the rest of the night. Neither of us said a word, neither of us slept. She rose at 5:30 and left for work.

I got up and kept drinking coffee until I had it coming out of my ears. I was trying to contain my anger, but it wasn't working. Marge had a hell of a whipping coming.

I dialed her number.

The phone kept ringing at the other end. No one was answering. I was boiling inside.

Chapter 114

I didn't dare go over there that day, or the next from fear of what I would do to her. Finally, by the morning of the third day, without attempting to reach her, I walked over. My ever-present shadow, Grozewski in his car, crept behind me as I walked north. Got to the house. Noticed that both the van and the Fiesta were gone. I knocked on Margie's front door. There was no answer. I called over there throughout the day, as well as the next. I got nothing. Not even so much as a message on her answering machine. If she'd left it hooked up I'd have left a few choice words of my own, but she hadn't. That's three-plus days of frazzled nerves and worry.

Where was she? Locked away in some loony ward somewhere? In jail? Staying with a neighbor to hide out from me from fear of what I'd do to her for the way she'd treated Monica? I didn't know. Could be she was back in the Midwest. Maybe with her mother. That had to be it. Only there was no way I'd be calling over there unless I absolutely had to and was convinced that she, in fact, was with her.

As I turned away from her front door and walked on through the gate, Grozewski got out of the Plymouth and approached me.

"Morning, Lieutenant."

"She's out of town. Visiting family."

"I see."

"You're up and about mighty early these days."

"Concerned, that's all. She sounded desperate the last time I talked to her. Threatened suicide."

Grozewski popped a *Rolaid* in his mouth. "When was this?"

"Several days ago."

He pointed out that Monica didn't appear to be her usual 'upbeat' self lately. None of that was any of his business. I let it go. It was best to.

"Mrs. Graham's unpredictable behavior is starting to get to us both."

"You're rid of her for a while."

"Hope she stays away, to tell the truth."

"You don't mean that? Your having been a partner of Frank's and all."

"Monica has threatened to leave me."

"Tell me, Fred: Who stuck the needle in him? Was it Marge, or was it you?"

"I beg your pardon?"

"It was the work of two people. Apparently Frank came to prior to being injected. Someone rapped him on the head a couple of times and put him out."

Yeah, well, I only recalled rapping him on the head but one time. That was neither here nor there. For now.

"Frank made lots of enemies—all over the country. It came with the territory."

"You been sleeping with Margie?"

"You're going just a little too far, Lieutenant."

"I don't think so."

"You want to say I murdered Frank Graham? If that's what makes you happy, go ahead. I don't mind telling you, Lieutenant, you're out of line.

I don't think you realize the seriousness of the charge."

"I've seen some good actors. You're goddamned convincing."

"Margie and I have nothing in common, for Christ's sake. She's a good looking woman. A man would have to be blind not to see it. I've got what I want. Monica and I plan to get married."

"Since when?"

"Since none of your damned business, Lieutenant."

"I'm looking at the pieces and they don't fit. Yet."

"Not much Margie's done has made sense since her husband died. What do you expect? She's a nervous wreck. Dealt quite a blow. Lost her husband and the kids. All things considered, she's holding up pretty damned well, if you ask me."

"She hated those kids."

"What makes you such an authority on Marge Graham? I know you've known Frank practically your whole life; you never got close to her."

"They were Frank's kids. She couldn't stand them." He popped another *Rolaid* in his mouth. "I'll keep hounding her until she cracks. And when she does, she'll spill enough to incriminate the both of you. When that happens, your ass is mine."

He drove off.

Chapter 115

It was a good thing to have Marge out of my hair. The flip side of that was I couldn't keep an eye on her. I bought a pack of cigarettes, found a park bench and chain smoked for an hour. What remained in the pack I gave to a homeless couple with three kids.

At 2 p.m. I made a long-distance call from a pay phone. Rinelle Rossi, Margie's mother, answered at the other end. She wanted to know who was calling. She knew, but there she was pretending that she didn't. I told her that a friend was calling long distance from Los Angeles.

"Margie's not home."

"Please, Mrs. Rossi, I have to speak to her."

"Why do you need to speak to my daughter?"

"I was Frank Graham's partner."

"His partner? Frank's partner? God rest his soul."

A minute later Margie was on. She seemed ecstatic to hear from me. She was nearly whispering, to keep her mother from overhearing.

"I knew you'd call, darling. I knew it."

I asked what it was her mother had against me. She said she couldn't talk. Couldn't go there. I could hear Rinelle trading insults with a familiar-sounding male in the background. Jamal. Was my immediate guess. I pretended to ignore it.

"I miss you, Margie. Why didn't you tell me you were leaving?"

"I was scared you'd be angry with me, Fred."

"Why would I be?"

"After what I'd said to Monica."

"Oh that. Think nothing of it."

"You mean that?"

"I know your feelings for me are strong."

"I love you, sweetheart."

"I need you by my side. Get on the earliest flight possible."

"When can we get married, Fred?"

"We'll talk about it when you get here."

"I'm sorry about what I said to Monica. She's a beautiful lady. I know your love for me is true and that I have nothing to be jealous of."

"Don't worry about it, honey."

"Are you sure, Fred? You're not angry?"

"Angry? Of course not. Water under the bridge. Get your reservation and let me know."

"I will, Fred."

"Call me back right away."

"I will."

She called to give me the flight number and that it would be taxing in at 8:15 the next evening. It occurred to me to mention the Fiesta, and to ask if she knew that it was gone.

"Got rid of it."

"You were actually able to get someone to buy it?"

"Not exactly."

"What exactly?"

"I'm not able to talk about that at the moment, honey."

"Okay, then. I just hope you drove yourself to LAX in the van, Marge, because it's not in front of your house."

"Sold it to the neighbor. You know the one. I couldn't stand to look at it for another minute. It was Frank's van. I hated it; I hated that damned van. Hate anything that was his. That goes for that house out there that he picked without talking to me first. I rented a storage facility and moved my valuables out: clothes and shoes, movie-related publications; my books and tabloids. Got it out of there. The rest that's there? I don't really give a shit what happens to it. Goodwill can come and pick it up."

"You sold the van? The Ford was a piece of crap, we both agree there. But the van, that was some nice van, Marge. I hope you got a good price for it."

"I did okay. Could've done a lot better if the shotgun and all that other stuff hadn't gone missing: bullets and the guns."

I wasn't about to own up. Those weapons were paid for in heavy sweat and toil and a good chunk of my sanity. I kept mum about it. Instead I asked what she got for the van.

"*I am not currently able to discuss that particular topic.* And you know very well why."

I let it go. Had no choice.

"Have a nice flight, hon."

"*I love youuuuuuuuu.*"

"I'll be there to pick you up."

Chapter 116

The actual decision to dispose of the only witness to Frank Graham's murder didn't occur to me until much, much later. To hold it off, anyway, until she actually had her hands on some real money, but I kind of think it might have crossed my mind during that long-distance phone conversation.

I wasn't one hundred percent sure how I felt about her at this point. I'm not saying I knew for certain she was going batty, only that there was something about a possessive, emotionally disturbed woman that turned me off sexually, no matter how attractive. I can't speak for others, that's the effect it's always had on me. Like I said, I thought she was just upset, nervous, resented Monica. I wanted Margie close to keep an eye on her, and to straighten her out, if possible—and if that were not possible, I knew I was in deep shit.

After hanging up the receiver, it dawned on me that our relationship hadn't been such a prize after all. The physical need for her was still there, I had to admit. I didn't think she was such an angel anymore. Of course, she never had been. I'd have bet my last dollar that this woman had had a history of emotional problems that she had kept from me. Lookit how fucked up Rinelle was. Look at the dysfunctional environment Marge came from. As bad as mine. Easily. Possibly worse. My instincts may have been there all along attempting to warn me, only I hadn't been paying attention. Failed to heed. And I knew I had my hands full now.

Chapter 117

Monica came home two hours late that day. She'd stopped at a bar near the studio and had a couple of cocktails with her girlfriends she said. She'd gone straight to bed.

The next evening she was late getting in again, drunk. She pretended to be searching the house for another woman.

"Where is she, Romeo?"

"Where's who?"

"You disappoint me, Freddie. No young bimbo sleeping in my bed? Why isn't she here? I'm in the mood for a *ménage*."

"I didn't want to hurt you. She was distraught."

"Do not explain. Do not say anything. I need sleep. In the morning I shall know whether or not to kick your butt to the curb."

She plopped down on the bed and slept.

I found the car keys in her purse and drove to LAX.

Chapter 118

Margie looked as radiant as ever. It was almost enough to make me want to believe she was as normal as she looked. We embraced and walked like that to the parking lot. When I touched on the subject of the van again and asked her to tell me what she got for it she refused to give me a straight answer. What I got, instead, was that she let her mother have a substantial sum to keep Jamal and his thug buddies off her back.

"What about the rest of it?"

She wasn't talking.

"Marge, that was a nifty looking van that Frank invested a lot of time and coin in. There is no way you gave Rinelle all the money you got for it. No way in hell. *Especially knowing what she fucking spends it on.*"

She was grinning. Dug around inside her tote bag and came up with her purse. Opened the purse and held up a Polaroid of a Camaro the color of egg yolk.

"What's this?"

"Camaro."

"I know it's a fucking Camaro."

"That's where the rest of the money I got for the van went. Traded the Fiesta in for the *Camaro*. My dream car. Now I won't feel insecure when I go out on interviews. I'll be able to compete; truly compete."

She kept on and on how this was what she had needed all along, except Graham had never wanted to hear it.

"Know what I feel like at the moment? That I actually have a chance. I upgraded my wardrobe and had pics taken for the new portfolio before I left. Wait till you see 'em."

We had to watch the money, and this out of control bitch was spending like crazy. And she couldn't shut up about the Camaro. It was at the dealership. She was having the stereo system replaced and new carpeting put in.

"Should be ready by now. Oh, Fred, I can't wait for you to see it."

I shoved her Polaroid back at her. She couldn't stop gazing at it. Couldn't stop yakking about it.

"It's too late to go get it tonight. We'll pick it up first thing in the morning."

She reminded me that it wasn't new, but ran like it and looked it, and felt a need to remind me that it had chrome wheels, brand new tires and relatively low miles. I wasn't interested in the least and let her know it. I was pissed that she had squandered the bucks and managed to cause me problems at home. The sheer stupidity of it had me seeing red all over again. The pressure cooker was boiling over.

"That van was paid for. You had months, in fact, the rest of the year left on the car insurance."

"All I had to do was transfer the auto insurance from one car to another. Nothing to it."

"There's no getting through to you, no way to make you see how downright reckless the whole thing is."

She claimed she had always wanted a Camaro. "Ever since I can remember. A boy I dated in high school had one—fully loaded. That was the reason I went out with him."

"So you gave a pussy-hungry dork some pussy because you liked his car?"

"Something like that."

"He the one knocked you up?"

"No."

"You got any idea how bad it looks? Huh? To go out and buy a shiny new short right after your husband got put in the ground?"

"Camaro is not new."

"Are you that fucking dumb? Are you? *You can't be.*"

"I'm entitled to some happiness after years of taking his bullshit."

"It's your timing that I'm talking about here, Marge. Your timing just plain sucks."

Chapter 119

When we got in the car, I slapped her hard, twice.

"You disturbed, bitch!"

She screamed, and raked her fingernails across my face.

"YOU BASTARD! YOU'RE LIKE HIM! YOU'RE NO GOOD!"

She reached for the door handle and had it open, when I pulled her back in and gave her two more harder than before. What bothered me about it, she seemed to enjoy it. It seemed to confirm something in her: I really cared now, because I had slapped her. I was in trouble.

She was weeping. Crocodile tears. No doubt. Looked like. Hard to tell with psychotic bitches like this.

"I shouldn't have come back. You don't care for me."

"You're talking nonsense."

"I didn't help you get rid of that shit-heel to be treated like this, to be taken for granted by you."

"*Help me?* Was I the one who stuck the needle in him?"

"I just want you to care, to show a little affection."

"You make it impossible."

I drove the car out of there.

"I'm tired of being treated like dirt."

"Seems there's no other way for you."

She grabbed at the wheel, screaming, nearly causing a bad wreck on Century Boulevard. I shoved her back. I didn't hit her anymore. I couldn't chance getting bagged over a stupid thing like that. She shook her head and giggled. We were bug bin-bound.

"A delivery boy. To be stuck with a delivery boy."

"Knock it off."

"The new man in my life, Rinelle. He delivers pasta."

"Pizza."

"What's the difference?"

"Stop it."

"Rinelle might say something clever like: You got to fill that boy with some ambition, Margie. Can't let word get to our friends and neighbors that my girl's married to a loser who delivers meat balls. We'll tell people he has plans to open a pizzeria. He's working his way up, learning a trade. Getting his foot in the door. No, Ma. I tell them the truth: He does deliveries—*for tips*. What he did before he hooked up with Frank. Now that the asshole's dead and buried, Freddy's back to his true profession: *pasta delivery*."

"Your mother's a crystal meth addict, Marge. You think I care what she thinks of me? Running around with hypes like Jamal. She ran your father Mario's bail bond business into the ground soon after he died. She's fucking evil. Should've heard what Frank's ex said about her, too. All them missing husbands, huh? Bitch is some kind of Black Widow. That's right: Rinelle. Scammed the government out of thousands. How about them *food stamps*, sugar-pie? Want to name-call? Diss a model citizen like me? I'm a *professional driver*. I'll be driving *for the studios. Union job*. That kind of gig pays real bank, for your information. Bein' a pizza gopher is temporary. To tide me over. I'm too good for a shit job like that."

"Since when do you have a studio job?"

"It can take years to break in. Comes down to who you know. Takes patience. It's a tough nut to crack. Like that's news to you. Tryin' to get your foot in yourself."

"Don't worry, Fred honey, I'll take care of us both. I'm loaded now, remember?"

I got on the 405 and took it north. Fired up a smoke.

"But how could you forget? It's what drew you to me in the first place, wasn't it?"

"You're nuts. I never knew he had any real money. I was out to get laid. Saw the tits and *culo* and wanted some."

I glanced at her. Then did it again a couple more times. Was it worth it, anyway? Craving pussy and the butt crack, sucking on those tits. The price we paid.

"You had me over a barrel. Threatened to rat me out to Graham about Chambray attacking his son. Yeah, I wanted your ass that night, and I was ready to walk away. You know I was walking away, but you stopped me, kept me from leaving. Now I'm getting this shit from you?"

That twisted smile on her face remained. I didn't like looking at it, and tried to keep my eyes on the traffic in front of me.

"Truth is: we both needed to get laid, Fred. Bastard was old and he was either too exhausted or too drunk to do me any good. Then he had the bullshit with the prostate. Fact is, I just plain didn't like him putting his hands on me, or try to shove that short dick in my face the rare times he could get it up."

"Short dick?"

"Macho assholes like that always have a wide ass and a short dick. Explains why he was attached to his shotgun. Loved to wave it around. Wouldn't go to bed without it. Some of these right-wingers are like that: their dick is their gun."

The thought of that macho blowhard forcing his dork in her mouth was not a pleasant image to deal with. I did my best to shove it aside. Got nowhere.

"And don't bullshit me about not knowing he had a few bucks saved up, either, babe. Spare me."

Maybe she was right. That was part of it, only I didn't want her to know it. Maybe I suspected the man had money socked away. Sure. He'd mentioned it in one of his stupors. Add the bling on top. In safe deposit boxes.

She fired up a smoke herself and continued to cackle.

"Know what I can't figure out? I need you. You beat me, you use me, treat me like dirt—and I love you. I wish I didn't, but I do."

"What you're in love with is the way I use that cat o' nine tails on your healthy *culo*." I looked at her for the reaction. Bitch was into rough sex and couldn't deny it. There was road ahead I needed to pay attention to.

"I never treated you like dirt. That was Graham's style."

"Do you intend to keep your promise, or was that just a move to get me to come back—so you can keep an eye on me? Make sure I don't say the wrong thing to the wrong people?"

"Both."

She studied me for a long moment without opening her mouth.

"I meant it. I'd like for us to marry."

"You do mean it, don't you?"

"Just like you, I'm hooked. *I wish I wasn't, but I am.* I wouldn't have to marry you to spend your money, so that's not the reason behind it."

She clung to me and wouldn't stop kissing me. I stayed on the 405. Took it up to the 101, and got us headed east.

Chapter 120

We took the Vineland offramp and decided to drop south a stretch and pull into an X-rated motel on Ventura Boulevard, instead of the Howard Johnson's. It was then I spotted the ugly green Plymouth in my rearview. I didn't say anything. Margie noticed it just the same. She became a wreck all over again.

"I can't. Not with that fat shit following."

"Let him. He hasn't got anything on us."

"I can't, Fred. He's ruined the mood. It wouldn't be smart, not this soon after Frank's death."

"Why didn't you think of that when you said all those things to Monica?"

"I said I was sorry."

I looked at her. It was pointless.

"We'll get you a room. I'll leave you here. I'll tell him you couldn't spend another night in that house." Not that there was any need for it. Grozewski knew. But Margie didn't know that Grozewski knew. So I played the game to keep her from falling apart.

"Why did I come back?"

"Got a nice chunk of change coming from the insurance company, Marge. Process was initiated in their LA office. Makes good sense to stick it out right here." I mentioned the Camaro. "Then there's the matter of your childhood dream to act, remember?"

"The acting?"

"Yes, the acting. Main reason you bought the Camaro, ain't it? So you wouldn't feel 'insecure' when you went to see casting directors."

She wasn't saying.

"What? Desire no longer there? All of it laid on me to justify getting rid of a perfectly good van and spending the money on an overrated, gas-guzzling hog of a muscle car?"

"It's there."

"Don't sound like it to me."

"That ugly van of his was the guzzler. You know it's true. It felt like pouring money down a bottomless pit whenever we had to gas up."

I walked her to her room and left.

Chapter 121

I found a pay phone and dialed the motel.

"I don't know how much more I can take of this. He's out there."

"It's routine. That's all it is, Marge."

"I'm really beginning to hate that word."

"What word?"

"You know what word: '*Routine*'."

"Look, he's out there because he has to be."

"Does that mean we're going to be hounded the rest of our lives?"

"Of course not."

"*I came back to be with you. I'm stuck in a motel room all alone.*"

"I'll be back later tonight. He has to go off duty sometime."

"Not him, Fred. He never goes off duty. We took out his best friend."

"He doesn't know that."

"He does."

"You're getting hysterical again."

"He was just in here, Fred. He told me about Quintero."

"He what?"

"The Mexican told him how you tried to set Frank up, while pretending to be the partner's friend."

"The fat bastard is bluffing. Don't let him rile you, honey. I'll be back later."

"Will he ever let us be?"

"I'll call later tonight."

Chapter 122

When I got to my place there was no room to park the car in the yard, my clothes and things were strewn all over it.

I walked in. Monica had been hiding behind the door. She held a screwdriver in her hand and looked like she would have used it. I don't think it was the screwdriver so much that shook me up, as the look in her eyes. She had undergone a total transformation: from a mild, never raising her voice woman to a potential murderess. I'm not saying she didn't have every right, because she did. The change did get to me.

"Leave my car keys."

I did.

"Now get out."

I stepped outside.

"You're a good woman. I didn't mean for this to happen."

I knew I was at fault and meant what I said. She slammed the door. I waited a while. I could hear her weeping on the other side. This was why bars were invented. And Fred Reed went looking for one.

I don't know, but my causing our split like that I felt was a break for Monica Frances Gooch. I really hadn't been worthy of her. I'd had so many run-ins with so many warped and psychologically off bitches over the years that I'd had no idea how to treat one that had actually been kind to me. Now she would have a chance to find someone halfway decent, someone more stable. My life had been one long screw-up, and the scene with Monica had been the topper. I'd had something *so good and near-perfect* there that I just had to destroy it. I wasn't used to things working out.

Chapter 123

As I said before, they won't sell you booze after 2 a.m. in LA, so with my remaining bottle I started the long trek down toward the motel. When I reached the motel, about an hour and a bunch of squares later, the Plymouth was sitting parked in the lot across from the front entrance. Grozewski was alone. Seemed like he was asleep. His window was about half the way down. I crept up, nice and quiet like. When I was close enough, and had begun to raise the liquor bottle over my head to strike him down with, his eyes opened and a .357 Mag was aimed at about the center of my face. He cocked the hammer.

"I'd love you to do it, dirtbag."

"Do what?"

I put the bottle to my lips and took a long pull, as though this harmless motion had been my intention all along.

"Your yellow streak is showing, Reed."

"Care for a hit?"

Bruno Grozewski didn't say anything.

"You wouldn't shoot an unarmed man?"

"I'm thinking about it."

"So how are you any better?"

"I'll get you nice and legal."

"Sure you can wait that long?"

"You killed a man in cold blood."

"To use your own word, he was a *'dirtbag'*—and I didn't kill him."

"Keep pushing, Reed."

"Face it, he was a homicidal maniac. He was decent to his kids from time to time, but it hardly made up for the ugliness; trail of blood he left behind. I worked with him, remember? Put me in the hospital years before—for no reason, other than it gave him a boner."

"Nothing would please me more than to pull this trigger."

"You know, you're a lot like he was: a man for law and order, no matter what it took."

"The slut is waiting for you."

"That's what's bugging you, isn't it? The fact that I'm getting it and you're not. Such a fine piece. Loaded, too. Will be soon. You should see her in bed. Insatiable. She's got moves I never knew existed."

"She'll crack. You won't always be there to watch over her. Then I'll get you. I'll get you good."

"Go home, Bruno. Don't waste your time around here. Go home."

I made it to Margie's room. She was in a stupor. She'd been drinking, too.

"I've got good news, baby. Monica kicked me out."

We passed out in each other's arms.

Chapter 124

Sometime later that night the door to the motel room banged open and Grozewski, with Frankenstein toting a camera with a bright flashing light, burst in and snapped away. Then laughing hysterically, they left. I spent the rest of the night cradling Margie in my arms. She cried until the wee hours of the morning.

When she finally quieted down and dozed off, I washed up and bought us some breakfast in the motel's lounge. She didn't want anything to eat, just a drink. I resisted. She insisted. I gave in. She pulled away at the bourbon until it knocked her out. I spent the rest of the day taking care of her. She couldn't stop vomiting. The manager kept coming around to see if everything was okay. I told him it was.

He wanted us out of there pretty bad, especially after the Valley afternoon papers came out. The story was on the front page. We didn't get the headline treatment. Both of our pictures were on there. The article didn't come right out and say we murdered Frank Graham, it was close enough. We were *persons of interest.* I guess it would have been sufficient grounds for a lawsuit if they had. They had been careful in their wording. A picture of Grozewski was also on the front page. I kept the paper from Margie for as long as I could.

The long-distance call did it. Grozewski had apparently contacted her mother. Now Rinelle, that Loony Tunes mother of hers, wanted to know if it was true: *Did she kill her husband?*

"Ma, how can you say that?" Margie pleaded. She sounded pretty damned convincing. Thanks to the booze. I almost believed it myself.

After the phone call Margie went to pieces all over again. I was barely holding up myself. The strain of it all was getting to me, too. It wore me down. In an effort to pick up her spirits, I reminded her that that fancy yellow Camaro of hers must've been ready and that we ought to go get it.

We took a cab to the dealership. The Camaro was ready. I had to admit, what a beauty it was. Shiny and impressive enough. I looked at Margie, too much of a wreck to show real interest and handed me the keys.

"I'm too depressed to drive."

The only reason we stopped by her photographer's to pick up the latest version of her portfolio was because I suggested it.

Chapter 125

We moved to another motel in Studio City, stayed a night, and moved on. We did that for two long weeks, with Grozewski no more than a few yards away at all times. The guy didn't sleep. I wondered if he was still on the force? He couldn't have been, not the hours he kept.
On the second Friday, it was there on the front page, his mug shot again. Dismissed from the force. Something about disobeying his superiors, going against his commander's orders. It made it all the more tense. This guy was out to nail us. He was putting everything on the line to do it.

Margie's money, the portion she was due in Frank's will, came through. Some of it, anyway. It wasn't exactly in probate, but something like it. She stayed mum about what was going on as well as the amount. I hadn't cared for the secrecy, but had to show patience. I was not a virtuous man by any stretch of the imagination, but was capable of patience when called for. It was called for here. *Five-0,* no doubt, wished they could've put a freeze on Frank's accounts, accept they didn't have a leg to stand on. Still this was all she was going to see for the time being until certain things got ironed out between the participants. And the life insurance? What she got from the slick type she talked to at the insurance company was double-talk and no set date of release. It was being 'looked into,' they told her. Frank was covered. Payout depended on circumstances. And this remained to be determined. Sometimes these probes lasted a while.

It took everything I had to keep her from falling apart. I tried getting a job in Graham's line of work, but the people Frank Graham and I had done business with, the bail bondsmen, wouldn't have me in any capacity. I was recognized everywhere I went, and for the wrong reasons. Then there was my track record, runs-ins with the law. It got to be hopeless.

I let my hair grow, wore fake eyeglasses, and got another job delivering pizza, trying to bide my time long enough for the big money to come through or maybe a studio driving gig.

The pizza delivery didn't last long. Either someone would recognize me, or Grozewski's calls to the employer got me canned or both. He was also badgering Margie with random calls when I wasn't around. He kept trying to fill her head with ideas, trying to get her to 'come clean,' by insinuating that I had talked with them about a deal; that I was looking to plea-bargain at her expense. It was too much for her to take. It was about this time that he really started in with the verbal assaults by phone. Sometimes he would have his cop buddies do it, other times the calls resulted in long silences and hang-ups.

The first call we got from the fat cop had to do with the rat poison.

"I've got a witness named Pee-Wee says you were asking about cyanide and SUX. Claimed you had a suicidal pal wanting to go with SUX as a second choice."

"Bye-bye, Bruno."

He had a few things, but this was pure bluff. He was fishing, trying real hard to rattle the cage Marge and I appeared to be trapped in. Not a doubt in my mind he was pulling the same bullshit on her. And then the phone rang again.

"Succinylcholine. Neuromuscular paralytic drug. SUX for short. You were asking around about it, trying to bribe people to get it for you. Then there's KCL that you were interested in."

This pig was no dummy. Never mind that he didn't have anything solid, just yet. It was enough to make this mofo nervous.

"Is that it?"

"I'll see you dirtbags dead."

"Another call like this, and I'll have you picked up for making obscene phone calls."

I hung up.

Chapter 126

We followed Grozewski's story in the papers. His wife had left him. The Pee-Wee call had been the last one like it for a while. The rest of the time the phone would ring Margie would pick up and the party at the other end would click off. It did exactly what Grozewski intended. It frazzled her nerves. She was a far cry from the Margie I used to know. She was drinking. She'd turned into a lush. We didn't argue anymore. She seldom made any sense. I seldom ventured outside, afraid she might babble a confession, or worse, sign one.

We were low on cash, a week behind on the house rent, when Monica showed up at the door. Margie was out cold as usual.

Monica and I went for a walk in North Hollywood Park. We talked. She wanted to know if it was true, that I had murdered the man? She wanted the truth.

"I gave you the truth. I had a hand in it. I knocked him out —"

"But you didn't stick the needle in his arm?"

"Nonetheless, made it possible for her to do so. I even stopped her from offing the kids. Yes, she wanted to get rid of them for the sake of the relationship. I refused to go along. Phoned the biological mother long distance. She flew out and got them. How does that help me? It doesn't."

"You wouldn't have done it, Fred, helped take that man's life, if it hadn't been for her."

"Why are you here?"

"It's obvious. I wanted to see you."

"Are you working with Grozewski?"

She didn't reply, just looked down sadly.

"I'm sorry. I didn't mean that. You're still in love with me, aren't you?"

She nodded her head.

"I screwed things up, didn't I?"

Her eyes welled. "You were it for me. We were going to make it work. My shot at happiness."

"As much as I know there's no hope for us ever having a future together—I know it's hard for you to believe—and I don't expect you to, not after what I've done—I feel the same way."

She wiped the tears away. "I know you do."

We stopped walking.

"We had it, didn't we? What I went looking for somewhere else, and participated in a murder for it needlessly. We had it all along."

"We did, didn't we?"

I watched her walk to her car. Why did this have to happen in order for me to realize how much Monica meant to me? Why?

I walked back to the house and the lush lying on the sofa. She had put on twenty pounds. A steady diet of doughnuts and *Cheese Balls* and general junk food will do it every time. More and more I thought about removing her from my life, the way one might remove a pimple from one's ass by squeezing the puss out.

Chapter 127

It was wishful thinking on my part. To have done away with her right then and there would have dug my own grave.

Instead of outright homicide, I decided I would help Margie drink herself to death. Since she was already so determined to accomplish it on her own, I'd only be cheering her on. By then, the rest of that money Frank left should be coming through; maybe even the big insurance payday. I still had no idea how much, but I had this innate feeling it was going to be some jackpot. Then of course, it's the sort of thing that results in fantasies swirling in your head: wine, women, song. Trips to Belize, Costa Rica, Copenhagen, Amsterdam. The life. With money to spend. I made plans for us to get married.

Margie came up with cash and wouldn't say where it came from. Source had to be the bling in Graham's safe deposit boxes. Made me wonder if that was the real reason she'd gone to the Midwest that time: Graham must've had more than one safe deposit box for all the bling he'd been collecting from skips over the years. Or maybe I was wrong. She wouldn't say. We were married in Vegas a week later. It had been one of those no-event, fast weddings, with Margie soused to the gills through the entire thing. She had barely been able to get the 'I do' out.

We stuck around another day or so while I dropped a few bucks gambling. Margie stayed in her room. I picked up some cash by unloading the gold chains I boosted on that East LA roof while playing Graham's flunky and videographer and saw to it that my 'better half' had enough to drink. To release the tension caused by the fact I'd probably made the mistake of my life by marrying the woman, who weighed over two hundred pounds by now, I paid the *Hen House* a couple of visits. I picked out a light-skinned Latina and a Scandinavian type with huge tits and wide hips from Minnesota. Both times. There was frolicking in the jacuzzi, as well as elsewhere. Something I'd always wanted to do. It was also a way to keep the trip from being a total bust.

When I stepped out of the place, after my second and last visit, to take a cab back to the motel, Bruno Grozewski was sitting there in a rental.

Even in Vegas he was on my tail. This guy just wouldn't let up. Playing the slots in Sin City, doing some small-time gambling can be fun, but not when you're being hounded. I decided it was time to drive back to LA before all of our money was gone.

Chapter 128

To keep our overhead down, and because Margie insisted Gone With the Wind had been shot literally across the street, we ended up staying in a seedy residential hotel in Culver City a stone's throw from Laird Studios. Building was V-shaped, sat on a v-shaped corner. There was a dive of a bar across the street to the east of us. A family from India managed the depressing state of affairs that the hotel was. Retirees on fixed incomes and down-and-outers like us were the tenants. Some had even worked as extras on *Hogan's Heroes* and years later *Ilsa—She-Wolf of the SS* that had been shot on the same sitcom set that Margie couldn't shut up about. I didn't give a shit about any of it. My mind was on other factors that kept pulling me down into a funk I feared I might not be able to climb out of.

Room was no bigger than a closet. We had a bed with a metal frame, shower, a mini fridge. It was hell, a prison cell. Walls and ceiling that may have been painted white originally had turned a sickening yellow from decades of heavy tobacco use. Spiderweb cracks from quakes and age were everywhere. There was a bargain basement dresser, what passed for a small table, and a single chair that you feared might collapse if you didn't lower your butt on it with a considerable degree of caution. Our present cribby and building reeked of pesticide and who knew what else? Payphone was in the hallway. I'd spent my share of time in a few shit holes like this in different towns in the past and it never got any easier. Felt like the walls were closing in and the ceiling might drop on your sorry ass at any minute—and that would've been the only positive aspect to the entire soul crushing enterprise.

Marge kept calling the lawyers handling Graham's affairs. The lawyers kept stalling. A couple of grown kids of Frank's from his first marriage, and not Butch's mom, that Margie had never met, had their hand out and were extremely pissed that they had been left out of the will. The insurance company continued with their version for not coming forth with the payoff: Corporate bureaucracy. Technicalities. They had ways of inventing so damned many.

"Investigation still pending into the death of Frank Graham."

Then wife #2, Butch's mother, claimed she and her kids had a right to a substantial amount. Things like that kept happening.

I couldn't find work. Marge was tight with what money she had access to. I was running out of ways to keep my bloated 'better half' in booze. If I didn't do that she wouldn't die, and if she didn't die not only would I not see any coin, chances were she would have chirped like a canary about all of it. Boozing her to death seemed like the only clean way out, the perfect way to do away with her.

We thought we had accomplished a clean job of it with Frank, but we hadn't. Sure, we hadn't left any real clues (other than the coroner's claim of having discovered rat poison & antifreeze in his system); they still couldn't prove who fed it to him. Graham had had so many cons and ex-cons who hated him in and out of prison from New York to LA, from Alaska to Hawaii, who could have hired anyone to knock him off. Law had nothing they could nail us on, no actual witnesses—except the two we had forgotten about: each other.

We were witnesses to a murder we committed. And she knew it. And she probably knew I wanted to get rid of her. It must have crossed her mind. Sooner or later I was going to do it. The only way to stay out of prison and get the money, and maybe make it across the border to Mexico. A man could really live it up in South America with the kind of windfall she had coming, make a new start. And if Monica and Chambray wanted to, they were welcome to come along. It was up to them.

Chapter 129

One night when I staggered into our room with a bottle of T-Bird she brought it up.

"I've been sitting here, wondering how you'll do it."

"Do what?"

She laughed. It was a pitiful wino laugh, saliva drooling down the side of her mouth. "What do you mean: '*Do what?*'"

"Brought you some vino."

I held the bottle out to her. She didn't take it.

"I'm on the wagon."

"Since when?"

"I want to know how you plan to do it."

"Do what, for Christ's sake?"

"Make me disappear."

I didn't say anything.

"You don't think I know what's going on inside that head of yours? I won't take another drink, until you admit it. You want to get rid of me, don't you? *Don't you?* You hate me."

"Don't be ridiculous. We're in this together."

She cackled some more. The saliva covered her chin. She grabbed the bottle, unscrewed the screw-cap and hit it.

"I'll tell you something, Fred . . . if I die, you're a goner."

She swigged it again. Like father, like daughter. Her step-daddy had died of it. Cirrhosis of the liver. From what I heard. I could only hope.

"How's that?"

"There's a manilla envelope out there someplace with enough evidence in it to give you a thousand years, or the death penalty. Either way, you're fucked —"

"You're kidding?"

"Try me and find out."

"Why'd you let me marry you?"

"I didn't."

"Why didn't you stop me?"

"I got a good laugh out of it."

Although she hadn't been able to finish off the Thunderbird, she had consumed plenty, and slept real good that night. I lay awake, figuring on a solution. I was trapped into spending the rest of my life with a lush. I couldn't leave her, I couldn't kill her. I was chained to a crazy woman who didn't bathe, or comb her hair. I was dumbfounded at what she had done to her once good looks. Chained to a crazy woman.

Chapter 130

I was tired and stretched out next to her in that bed that was hardly big enough for one person, let alone two people. I closed my eyes. Thought about Chambray and how much I missed her, and then Chambray snapping at Frank's kid Butch somehow superimposed itself over that. I didn't want to think about it, tried to shut it out. Maybe if the damned kid hadn't been so pesky it wouldn't have happened, none of it would have happened: I wouldn't have been obligated to work with Frank Graham and I wouldn't have met this whale lying next to me. And it wasn't just her weight that bothered me, it was her screwy mental state that I wanted no part of.

I didn't dream that night. One needs to be asleep in order for that to happen. But the nights I slept I dreamt mostly of Margie and the many ways I could ice her ass. I attended her funeral so many times I lost count, but in each dream she would pop right out of the grave, blood spurting from her eyes and mouth; just gushing. Many a night I'd wake up in a cold sweat. Some nights I dreamt of Frank Graham stalking me through the streets of Hollywood wielding his favorite pump-action shotgun. I'd come close to getting away from him, but that damned Doberman pinscher would always track me down; and after the dog was through mauling me, Frank would make his appearance, macho 'Dirty Harry' style, blast me away with the 12-Gauge, shattering my skull to pieces.

They were just bad dreams, I know, but they took their toll. One night I had a dream that was a little more pleasant. It was a wedding in a garden of flowers and palm trees with many happy people attending and having a good time. *Monica and I* were in white. It was our wedding. After the ceremony we flew to Hawaii for our honeymoon. And what a honeymoon. We were the happiest couple. The sex was great. Monica was a wildcat in bed now. What a change in this woman: from a shy, less-than-exciting prude, to a sex-starved hellcat with a hunger to explore and please.

I was shaken awake. Wine trickled down my face from above.

"You're dreaming about that slut again."

Marge was holding the bottle above my face as she spoke.

"I was dreaming about us, the way it used to be."

"Shit."

The wine splashed my face. I yanked the bottle away from her. She clawed at me. I held it back.

"That's it. You're on the wagon."

"Have you taken leave of your senses?"

"I can't let you die, remember?"

"I lied."

"I don't believe you."

"Gimme the bottle."

"Prove it."

"How? There is no manilla envelope, no evidence. If there was, I'd be incriminating myself, too, remember? I was there."

"You don't care what happens to you."

"Who needs you, Alf?"

There was a half-eaten box of day-old doughnuts on the dresser. She staggered out of bed to reach for one. I pulled her back and let her have the wine.

There was a knock at the door. I opened it. It was the drunk, Joey 'Gone Withe the Wind' Butts, who had one of the rooms on our floor. Rummy couldn't shut up about having appeared in the civil war soap whenever you saw him.

"Phone."

"Who from?"

"I was in *Gone with the Wind*—and that makes me better than you, dog dip."

"You were in *Plan 9 from Uranus*. Effing geezer."

"Not *my* anus, *yours*."

"You can't answer a simple question?"

He walked away without turning. I got to the pay phone. Monica was on the line.

"Can you talk?"

"Sure."

"How much longer are you going to keep doing this to yourself, Fred?"

"What do you mean?"

"You're letting her drag you to your grave. You're killing yourself."

"I'm chained to her, Monica. I'm chained."

"Bullshit, Fred. That's pure bullshit."

"She's got evidence stashed away. I can't leave her; I can't do anything."

"I looked into it. It's called plea-bargaining. By turning state's evidence you can get off with a light sentence."

"How light?"

"A few years."

"How light, Monica?"

"Six or seven."

"Too many."

"I'm wasting my time."

"I'm glad you called."

"I'm wasting my time, aren't I, Fred?"

"When you tell me to throw away six or seven, or eight years of my life, you are. You don't know what prison is like."

"I won't bother you anymore."

"Let's get together."

"What for?"

"I'd like to see you."

I heard her weeping quietly.

"Why did you have to get involved with her? This wouldn't have happened to us."

"I wish I'd never set eyes on her. I could blame it on Chambray. I know better."

"She assaulted another old woman. Got her in the kennel. I don't know what to do about that dog."

"Woman press charges?"

"No."

"I'd like to see you. If it's no, I'll understand."

"When can you get away?"

"How soon can you be here?"

Chapter 131

I returned to the room to wash my face and comb my hair. Not that it would've made much difference. Only I couldn't find a comb. I started going through the drawers in the battered dresser. Nothing but moth-eaten panties and boxers in the first one.

"Where's your hair brush?"

"That slut is trying to take you away from me."

I yanked on the lower drawer and got nowhere. I did it again, and the damned thing came out all the way and dropped to the floor, and something caught my eye. Looked like a torn piece of tie-dye cloth, maybe part of a T-shirt that had been wrapped around something and the ends tied on top. There was a visible knot. I untied the knot, unwrapped the cloth. There was a finger inside. Christ.

I held the cloth up and the finger that was in it. It was a thick, middle finger with the same type of deep red nail polish that Margie and her mother both were partial to on it and had been slapped on carelessly.

Rinelle, I thought right away. Only the finger was clearly too thick to be one of hers. Besides, there was no tat. The tattoo was missing. Either the letter "R" or the letter "N" should have been on there. Not to mention some type of ring. Broad liked having all sorts of rings on her fingers, the better to punch peeps with.

Was I disgusted? *Thoroughly.*

"What's this?"

She wouldn't look.

"The fuck is this, Marge?"

Finally, she did turn. Squinted.

"Looks like a finger."

"*No shit.* What's it doing here—and whose is it?"

"Rinelle's. I believe. You weren't supposed to see it."

"Was there a note? Who sent it?"

"Your guess is as good as mine."

"Jamal?"

"Kind of what I concluded."

"What was it sent in? Box? Envelope?"

"Box."

"Where is it?"

"Threw it out."

"You threw it out?"

"*I threw it out.*"

"You take a look at the postmark to see where it came from, at least?"

She shook her head, not looking at me.

"Couldn't make it out."

I got the idea the bitch was lying.

"How much she owe them?"

"Big. Why I was pushed into staying with the redneck throwback. Resented her for it for years and I'm still not over it."

I cursed. Jammed the cloth the finger was in in my pocket.

"Try my purse. Brush should be in there. If you still want it."

I had the door open. Brushed my hair back with my hands.

"Fred! Where are you going with my mother's finger? *Fred!* Goddamn you!"

"I need air."

Margie was muttering at this point. Incoherent. I could hear her as I walked down the hallway. Sounded like she was about to pass out.

Chapter 132

I had a bit of time before Monica showed. Looked up the address of a local funeral home in a phone book I found in the lobby and walked over.

The guy was old and bent and reeked of graveyards and death. The Grim Reaper himself. I unraveled the cloth and showed him the finger. The old dude confirmed what I suspected: it was a man's finger. More than likely. The polish painted on to make it appear that it was a woman's. Then he said he couldn't be certain.

"It's quite old."

How old didn't matter to me. So long as it wasn't a recent amputation.

He held it to his nose. What was he looking for? Trying to detect? Embalming fluid? Formaldehyde? He wouldn't say. Lifted his head, then rubbed either side of the cloth against the finger, and we both saw that either a type of brown dye or makeup came off the skin to reveal that the corpse the finger came from could not have been a person of color. Some revelation.

Dumb-ass Rinelle. Hadn't been able to find a finger to match her own complexion so she'd attempted to disguise it to make it darker than its original tone.

He was looking at me again.

"This is the kind of makeup we use when we prep a body for viewing. This finger came from a light-skinned and/or white individual, and someone wanted it to appear otherwise."

"To make it look like it came from a person of color."

"You got it."

Not only that, the bitch always had a bunch of rings on her fingers, and this finger had zero markings that indicated that any type of finger had been on it recently. She hadn't even been clever enough to leave one of her rings on it, or just plain had been reluctant to part with any of them. Effing loser. Like Margie.

He asked where the finger came from. Where did I get it?

What was I going to tell him? Instead, I answered his question with a question, which I normally hated doing as well as detested those who liked to pull that shit.

"Sir, you sure about the finger having come from a white person?"

He was done talking to me. He had work to get back to, and simply held the rag with the appendage my way, offering me to take a closer look for myself. I declined, and suggested he do whatever he felt like with it, and got out of there.

Chapter 133

Monica pulled up in a new Mustang in front of the fleabag as I walked up. She had a deep tan and she'd had her hair done, a streak job. It looked a lot better than the plain dishwater it used to be. I got in. She failed at concealing the shock in her eyes.

"Don't say it. I look like shit."

"Have you been eating?"

"Who can eat?"

"What are you doing to yourself, Fred?"

"Get me away from here."

She shifted, and got us out of the area.

"You're doing pretty well for yourself."

"Personal secretary to Sonny Sheldon."

"Not bad."

"He's only the hottest writer/director/comedian working in pictures today. I make a good salary."

"Nice to see you, Monica."

"Sheldon is looking for a chauffeur. It won't pay as much as a union driving job; it's a good start for you. I think I can get you in."

"Six years from now?"

"Whenever you get out."

"You would wait that long?"

"We had something, Fred; you and I."

"You would be 42 when I got out, Monica—if all I got was six years."

"I would wait."

"Who did you talk to about the plea-bargain?"

"Someone in the D.A.'s office. Don't worry, I didn't let on it had anything to do with Frank Graham."

"I can't go to prison."

I'd had my taste of being locked up in a cage and hadn't liked it. I'd never told her about it. But I'd been naive enough to *spill my guts to Marge. Go figure.*

"Do you want to spend the rest of your life like this?"

"I could go for some new clothes—if you can afford it."

She took me to *Fred Siegel* on Melrose Avenue. Bought me a couple of pairs of slacks, couple of dress shirts, socks, underwear; a windbreaker.

Chapter 134

She drove us to her new place in Burbank. A shower usually helped some, no matter how defeated and/or disgusted you felt. I shaved, showered, even brushed my teeth with a new brush that she had made available.

Monica had certainly moved up. She was a stone's throw from the equestrian center on Riverside Drive. She was paying five hundred bucks a month for a one bedroom; a hundred dollars more than the house we'd lived in in North Hollywood.

"It's cozy. It has your touch. Too expensive, though."

She shrugged. "I can afford it."

We drove to a steakhouse for dinner across the street from NBC.

Chapter 135

We were both surprisingly relaxed and comfortable with each other, considering what had happened between us. I pointed it out to her.

"Are you really surprised, Fred? You shouldn't be. It could be like this all the time."

"As long as Marge is passed out."

"The D.A.'s office would work out a deal with you."

I didn't say anything.

After the meal, I said I had better get back to the hotel. We headed south through Hollywood. I didn't look forward to going back up to that roach-infested, smelly room, which in fact, was nothing more than a brick coffin. I had no choice.

I warned her to keep her car doors locked before I got out. Area was not bad during the day, only nighttime was a different story. Culver City had decent neighborhoods to be sure, but this hotel, and a few others in the vicinity, was the pits. Bottom of the barrel. End of the line. If you lived here you already had one foot in the grave. Young or old. Didn't matter. Probably was a good place to call it quits in. Why else stay in a terminal dump like this?

"Thanks for the evening, the clothes."

"For what we once had."

"Will I see you again?"

"Think about what we discussed."

"I take it that means yes."

"Maybe."

"You don't know what you're asking."

"I'm prepared to sacrifice six years for a lifetime of happiness. I would wait longer than that."

"I'd go crazy in the joint."

"What do you think is happening now?"

"I'm not behind bars."

"Oh no?"

She drove off.

Chapter 136

I hurried to the fourth floor; two, three steps at a time. The drunk, Joey *'Gone With the Wind'* Butts, was standing outside our door pulling on a bottle. It didn't look right. His room was at the other end of the hallway. I shoved him out of the way and went in.

Grozewski was sitting on the edge of the bed and he had a cassette recorder. Margie was still passed out, but she was mumbling in her sleep. I dropped my clothes on top of the dresser, yanked the recorder out of his hands and flung it at Joey Butts, then I did likewise to Grozewski. He came at me with a blackjack, swinging. He rapped me real good once on the forearm and back of my neck. I went for his throat, forcing him to the floor.

Joey Butts scurried down the hallway threatening to get 'the bulls.' A second later a bottle exploded against the back of my skull, and I had to let go. By the time I'd recovered, Grozewski was up on his feet.

I staggered to the bed. Margie still held the bottleneck in her hand.

"You'll never shake me, dirtbag." Grozewski felt a need to remind me.

"I ever catch you with my wife again, I'll kill you."

He laughed, and left.

Chapter 137

My skull throbbed. The death stench of the whole place and the way she looked made me want to puke. The back of my head was bleeding.

"Why'd you have to do that, Marge?"

"He never got anything out of me. I was faking it."

"You sure?"

"Sure as I know you were out with that strumpet."

"Strumpet?"

"Slut, whore, *strumpet.*"

"Ran into a buddy of mine. Sonny Sheldon's bodyguard."

"I need a drink."

"You don't believe me?"

"I read you like a book."

Her head dropped back, hanging over the edge of the bed as she laughed that annoying laugh. I'd begun to hate the sound of it more than anything I knew. I felt dizzy.

"I married a loser. With Frank I had security. With you I get heartache. Keep her soused, Alf. Let her pass out. Cheat on her when she's too drunk to keep her eyes open. Don't underestimate me, Freddie Reed. And most of all, don't lie to me. I hate being lied to. Don't deny it. It only pisses me off even more."

I got up to close the door.

"Don't do that." She sat up. "Want you to meet someone. Mr. Scheitz?"

A bald-headed black guy walked in. He was in his 40s, my height. He carried a shoebox under his arm.

"Fred Reed, meet Mr. Barney Scheitz, private investigator."

Mr. Scheitz brought the shoebox over to the bed, in exchange for a regular white envelope he got from her. He counted the money in it and left without a word. She took a cassette out of the shoebox. Tossed it at me.

"Play it."

I got Grozewski's tape player off the floor, and played the tape. There were two voices on it, mine and Monica's. Our entire conversation in the restaurant had been recorded.

"Real smart of you. All that has to happen is for Grozewski to get hold of it. We're sunk."

She giggled. "He won't." Then she took some photos out of the box. They were shots of Monica and me kissing.

"All I ask is not to be lied to."

"Where did the money come from for all this?"

"What does it matter?"

"Private eyes don't come cheap. Who paid for it?"

"Beat it out of me."

"You'd like that, wouldn't you?"

"I'm blackmailing you, Fred. I want you to take me to a sanitarium before it's too late. I was killing myself with the booze, and you were helping. Now you're going to help me get well."

"Not until you tell me where the money came from."

"Rinelle."

I leaped at her, my hands clamped around her jaw. I squeezed.

"Kiss me, you fool."

I let her go, and fired up a smoke.

"Your money came through, didn't it? Unless you were able to get your hands on more bling in another safe deposit box."

She nodded. "Some of it came in. I was wondering how long it would take you to figure it out."

"Why didn't you tell me?"

"I wanted it to be a surprise."

"It is, believe me."

"I needed time to think; figure out what I wanted to do."

"You're forgetting: half of it is mine."

"Says who?"

"Says who?"

She had to let me hear that horrible cackle again.

"I love to tease you, darling. Of course half of it is yours. We've made it. We have done it, Fred!"

"Not until the insurance pays off."

She ignored that. Sat up, embracing me. The odor of her was bringing my dinner up. I had to pull away. Pretended to be closing the door.

"I want to look like I used to. I want to start over again. Help me get on the wagon, and stay on. Help me kick the booze, Fred. Get off the *Twinkies* and bad food. Start eating right again. Working out. Get the figure back. I want to be the Margie you fell in love with."

"All right. But none of this *Scheitz business* anymore. Grozewski's badgering is more than I can handle. I don't need a private eye bird-dogging me."

"Anything you say, Fred honey. Now come here, and give your baby a kiss."

Chapter 138

AA wasn't good enough for Margie. She wanted a sanitarium. And got one. At $1,000 a week in Pasadena. She was going to have to stay until she was cured. She kept me on a weekly allowance so that I'd have to go see her every week. The weekly visit was more than enough for me. The rest of the time I spent with Monica. She arranged for a leave of absence and we flew to Reno, all expenses paid by her boss.

She was required to check out some of the comic acts, jot down anything worthwhile, report anyone who was up-and-coming in the smaller showrooms, anything her boss could cash in on, use in one of his productions. I made every effort to enjoy myself, but Marge and Grozewski were like a razor-sharp pendulum swinging back and forth inches above my Adam's apple.

We gambled, played the slots, took in a couple of shows. Buddy Hackett was funny, Toni Tennille was nice, but too middle-of-the-road for my taste; mostly we made love in our suite on a waterbed.

We flew back to LA. Monica wanted to know what I had decided.

"I can't do six years."

Chapter 139

When I went back to the sanitarium for the second time Margie was in a rage. She threatened to quit the program.

"You've been with the *ho* again!" And threw a stack of color snapshots at me of Monica and me in Reno.

"She knows about Frank Graham. That's why I went to Reno with her. It was a business trip for her. Sonny Sheldon sent her out."

"How does she know?"

"She's not stupid."

"You told her."

"She put 2 and 2 together."

"I can't go on like this! I can't concentrate on what I'm doing knowing you're out there balling her, Fred. I can't do it!"

"It won't last."

"You promised you wouldn't see her."

"I'm doing it for us."

"Don't con me."

"She wants time to prove I still feel something for her. That's all it is. After the agreed upon period of time she'll let go. I got her word."

"I don't trust her, Fred. She'll never let go. You're my husband, goddamn it! You're my husband. . . ." She wept. "I can't last another two weeks in this place."

"You sure can. It's going to be like it used to be for us, remember? When you get out it's going to be real good for us."

"I need a drink."

"Don't talk like that."

"It's costing."

"What's four grand when you've got a hundred and fifty? That's what you got, wasn't it?" I was guessing; trying to trip her up into revealing the amount they'd laid on her. She didn't fall for it. Instead switched the subject.

"Grozewski's been snooping round."

"What's he done?"

"Keeps calling up, asking about me."

"You don't have to talk to him."

"I don't."

"Let's plan on that trip to Hawaii when you get out."

"She'll always be in the way, Fred. Let's get rid of her."

"Come on."

"I'm serious."

"I am, too."

"What would it take?"

"We got each other, for Christ's sake."

"We don't."

"We do, honey. We do."

"She won't quit until she's taken you away from me. She wants to get back at me. I know a little bit more about women."

"It's wasted energy. Concentrate on what you're doing here, nothing else."

"While you're out there carousing?"

"We have no choice."

"Let her go to the cops. She hasn't got anything on us. Grozewski knows as much as she does, more; we're not in jail."

"She can prove it —"

"Bull."

"Grozewski can't."

"Let's get rid of her."

"Forget it."

"We can hire someone."

"It's out of the question."

"You didn't say that when we had to get Graham out of the way."

"It's not the same thing."

"The hell it isn't."

"I'll see you next week."

"I'll have it figured out by then."

Chapter 140

We were lying in Monica's bed, drinking beers. *Merv Griffin* was on tv. He was interviewing a professional hit man whose face you couldn't see. The hit man's name was 'The Weasel.' Some name for a professional killer.

It dawned me just then. Something had been amiss all along about her new place: the dog wasn't around. Chambray. I asked about her.

"She's run off."

I turned away from the tv screen, looking at her. Evidently a Chatsworth rancher had adopted her.

"She attacked his teen daughter and took off."

I didn't know what to say.

"She'll be put down this time."

"If they find her."

"If they find her. I wouldn't have been able to move in here with her. Landlord won't allow dogs. Cats yes; no dogs."

My eyes were back on Mr. Weasel.

"She wants you out of the way, Monica."

"She's a basket case, Fred."

"*She wants you dead.*"

Monica finished her can and cracked the top on another. We watched the tube. The Weasel explained the facts behind hit number #6. He'd forced the man at gun point to wash down enough sleeping pills with

Southern Comfort so he'd never wake up; and he never did.

"It would be nice if something like that were to happen to her."

"That's out."

"She's neurotic enough to do it."

"She's got money she'd like to live long enough to spend. If she dies, I do, too. The evidence, remember?"

"She love you?"

"Yeah. So what?"

"Get her to destroy it."

"She's not that stupid."

"We'll think of something. . . ."

Chapter 141

The third visit to the sanitarium gave me chest pains. More painful than usual. I was too young for chest pains. I'd had to deal with Margie's mother, too. She was one chunky tweaker with a nasty mouth. She'd flown out with that wasted junkie fuck to give her daughter *'the support she wasn't getting from me.'* I was accused of having put Margie in the sanitarium.

"She needed to dry out, Mrs. Rossi."

Woman wouldn't hear of it. The sun was out, haze not bad, and it should have been close to a perfect day, instead the three of us stood under a palm tree on the grounds and argued. The junkie, for the most part, stayed out of it. Thank god for small favors.

"It's not his fault, Ma!"

"Of course it is. You never touched alcohol when Frank was alive."

"*Goes to show how much you know, Rinelle!* Don't blame anyone. It's my fault. Maybe it's Frank's. Could be it goes all the way back to you and your husbands!"

Little did I know at the time this was a bogus row. Total sham. It had to do with me, but not entirely what it seemed. Margie was tied to me emotionally and Rinelle hadn't cared for it one bit. She was about to lose all influence over her own daughter.

It was then I noticed it: the middle finger on Rinelle's right hand was heavily bandaged. She hadn't offered an explanation and Margie, conveniently enough, didn't mention a thing about it. I decided going there would be a waste of time and would only result in lies and excuses from them both.

Yeah, could be someone tried to sever that finger: Jamal, or one of his drug-addled goons, or else it was Rinelle herself. I was willing to lay odds it came down to the latter. Repulsive Rinelle had to be the culprit. Only hadn't been able to follow through & sent the one she got somewhere.

The bickering went on; it always would go on. This was how they expressed love for one another; better yet: loathing. More like it. The deep-rooted kind that never went away. Not only that, I was being dissed by the mother. This was her style, after all. Shit on him behind his back, as well as to his face. It took some balls. Loose cannon ball-buster had balls to spare.

"Margie, he's a loser. He's going down. He'll take you down with him."

"My stepdad was a juicer. That's what killed him, Ma. And you had some others who weren't any better. That's why I've got this problem. It runs in the family."

"You don't know what you're saying. This man is no good for you!"

"We've gone over this before. I love him, Ma. What am I supposed to do? Spend my life with somebody I don't give a damn for? Been there. Remember? I'm supposed to be miserable like you and Mario? You took his abuse. Never loved that man/never had the guts to leave him. The creep you replaced him with was no better. And the creep you replaced that creep with was no better, either. And this guy? Jamal? *Why?* I can't believe this is the best you can do, Ma. Now you want I should do like you? Throw my life away? That's not what love is about!"

"You love that?" And she would point the finger at me. She only heard what she wanted to hear. I'd been getting some pretty good hints all along why Marge was such an out-and-out neurotic. Further proof of it was right in front of me.

"I love him, Rinelle!"

"Love is overrated. What is there to love? You love a bum? *Drifter.* You love him the same way Jamal loves me! Love is a laugh; one big joke!"

"Fred is a professional truck driver. For the studios. They make real good money."

"Since when is he a truck driver? He hasn't even got a CDL. Where's his commercial license? *Show it to me.* I'd like to see it."

"Any day now."

She was stretching the truth here. I kept mum about it.

"I raised you to be a truck driver's wife? No, Margie; I don't think so. Call me when you have made arrangements for an annulment, otherwise I don't want to hear from you."

"You're just pissed because Frank's money spigot suddenly went dry, now that he's under ground! There went *your booze and crack money!* You sold me to him, before I knew what was going on! I was too young to know what you were up to, bitch! Was it my fault you refinanced the house not long after Mario died and spent it all on *stud muffins* half your age like this guy Jamal, and meth! I felt sorry for you and went along; married the asshole! And paid a heavy price! Something you never gave a shit about! My welfare, you effing heartless bitch! Anything for meth! Right, Rinelle? Don't matter what it does to your kids! Fuck you, loser! You're the loser, and that druggie pusher you dragged out here, *not Fred! You! You're the fucking loser, tweaker! Go through men the way I go through Tampons! Step daddy was what?—Hubby Number 5? I've lost count! Can't keep track! What you said he was: Five, or was it six? Or do YOU even know? I can't even keep up with all the kids you got out there all over the country, by an army of different men: legit and otherwise!*"

"You are about to get your ass kicked, young lady, if you don't shut that filthy mouth of yours! You got no right! I adopted plenty of those kids to help them, get them out of miserable orphanages they were stuck in!"

"For state aid and food stamps. To get over."
"YOU HAVE NO RIGHT WHATSOEVER TO RUN YOUR MOUTH THIS WAY! NONE!"

At least this was what was happening on the surface. What the battle was *supposedly* about. Like I said, it took me a while, but I put it together eventually. This was exactly why they'd walked away from me and the junky and took it up for round two behind the building. I wasn't the most astute cat on the block, but I picked up enough snatches of the screeching and screaming to put two and two together: Rinelle was after her cut of the pie. That was it: *money.* She wanted the dough, and she wanted Marge to ditch the worthless lost cause: me, emotionally. See, the emotional attachment hadn't been part of the initial scheme. It was the old tune: *Throw the asshole under the bus.* Why I'd been chosen. No other reason. Only Rinelle and Margie had no idea that Marge would fall for me, and fall she did. Hard. The other thing I picked up on was that Graham had already had a substantial life insurance policy out, and that Margie and Mommy Dearest had either convinced him to double it or else they took out a second policy on him for twice as much. Nice. And who stood to benefit and/or collect? *Bingo!*

Problem was the insurance company continued to stall and both Margie and Rinelle were getting real restless. Rinelle more so than the daughter, obviously. She needed her drugs and fast life style, so did her gigolo beau, who was living off of her. What a lovely bunch of coconuts.

Chapter 142

Well, the rage heated up, and the two of us: the pusher and I both made it over in time to see the *Battle of the Bulge* escalate. This was the encore from that hospital room catfight. Continuance.

"What's up with the finger, Rinelle? What'd you do?"

"I can't talk about it."

"You can and you will."

"You know what my situation is, Margie. Why badger me? What good does it do?"

"Was it Jamal?"

"What do you care?"

I couldn't help it, and yelled from where I stood.

"Where'd you get the finger you sent?"

If looks could kill. Rinelle shot me one of those. That was her response. Best way to avoid an issue. Refuse to address it. I looked at Jamal.

"Hey, I don't know nothin' about no finger. This crazy bitch be into shit that never make no kinda sense."

"You sent the finger, Ma. Without a name or return address, to make it look like it came from Jamal and his crew."

"You're nuts; you're all nuts."

"Asshole, Ma! I nearly vomited when I opened the box and saw what was inside. I was worried sick."

"Good."

"What a despicable cunt you are!"

Rinelle spun around and slapped her, hard; then again; and more. And it would have gone on indefinitely if Margie hadn't grabbed her by the wrist and yanked on it, pulling her mother to the ground nearly. When that failed, she grabbed her by the hair and yanked with all her might, and down went Rinelle and screamed. She gripped Margie by her skirt and pulled and yanked until she had it torn down the middle. Blows were exchanged, hair pulling picked up; both women rolling on the ground, screaming and cursing. It was pure venom and vitriol.

At one point Margie was furious enough to smack her mother with the cast. I did what I could to pull them apart, and got punched in the mouth for my effort. The older woman managed to get her hand on her tote bag and smacked the daughter across the face that left her momentarily stunned. The mother took the opportunity to rise to her feet, straighten herself and step back and away.

"It's your money he wants, Margie, not your heart. Why he married you." Mama Rossi muttered as she walked away. "Pretty soon Frank's life insurance will be coming through. That's what the truck driver's after."

She was wiping her eyes with a white handkerchief, then blowing her nose. With my help, Margie recovered to the point she was able to stand up. She parted her legs some and urine poured out of her.

"Quite a bit of that money goes to his kids, bitch, and you know it!" Although Margie was done pissing, she was clearly far from done with her share of the yelling. "You'll never understand what love is about, because you never loved dad; you never loved any of them! You don't know what love is! Couldn't even fake being distraught at his funeral! *Cold-blooded ho!*"

Then she quieted down some, and was talking to herself, it seemed. Noticed there was a thin crack down the center of her cast. Cursed under her breath. "Bitch knows how to piss me off. I'm always wrong/she's always right. Just wet myself, too. What the crystal meth-addicted slut does to me." She cranked up the volume again. "I got my shots in. Feel real good about that. Effing cunt. Learned to fight back. Used to take it; just let her beat on me. No more. Got to fight back with a bitch like that."

The widow Rossi, and her emaciated, scab-faced companion were gone from sight.

Chapter 143

After Margie had calmed down, the first thing she mentioned was Monica.

"We gas her to death. In her own apartment. While she's asleep. We can buy gas masks for us. Hold her head down in her bed while she inhales the gas. Or else stick her head inside the oven until she goes out; then we tuck her in. Say *beddy-bye*. Sleep tight, lovely." She was proud of herself. "Not bad, huh?"

"She dies and I get nailed for it. Your private detective, one Mr. Scheitz, has seen me with her, or have you forgotten?"

"Why can't it be suicide?"

"It's not suicide, not the way you got it figured."

"Got anything better? *I'm all ears.*"

"Why don't we change the subject?"

"You falling for her again?"

"You nuts?"

"You are, aren't you?"

"Didn't I leave her for you?"

"Is there any way you can get me a drink?"

"Cut it out."

"I'll have a backup plan next time you visit."

I kissed her on the forehead, got my allowance, and left.

Chapter 144

I finally got to meet Sammy Higgins, Sonny Sheldon's bodyguard/sometime chauffeur in his office on the studio lot. Sammy was a six-one black belt in Karate; an easy-going guy with a red beard. He'd worked as a bodyguard for a few celebrities over the years. Sheldon and Higgins wanted to meet me before Sheldon would approve.

Since Higgins was a 'Nam vet there was enough in common there. As far as everyone was concerned, I had the job—if I wanted it. Three hundred a week to start. It wasn't big money, but it was a beginning. I said I would sleep on it.

Chapter 145

Later that night, even though Monica and I wanted to celebrate, it certainly was cause to celebrate—we didn't. I knew there was no way I could hold down a steady job with Grozewski and Margie constantly on my mind.

"I can't take the job right away. We both know why."

"Sleeping pills."

"You make it sound easy."

"It worked for the Weasel."

I guess I couldn't get over this woman, too, so eager to become a killer. How could I have read Monica wrong? I never thought she had it in her.

"I know people who would do anything for a chance to work for Sonny Sheldon. How often does an opportunity like this present itself?"

"I want the job. It's what I've been trying to do for over two years now. You know that. I was hoping I might be able to get into stunt work eventually. It's why I came out west. You know how I feel about all of it."

"Let's find out where she's got the evidence hidden, Fred, and do it. If you want—I'll do it alone."

"You mean that, don't you?"

"I don't think I could stand to be away from you for six long years, after all."

"We'll have to trick her into revealing whatever it is she's got stashed away."

"I've got an idea. She wants me dead, right? You go along with her. We fake my death, in exchange for the evidence. You'll have to make sure it's *the* evidence, and that she comes through. The trick won't work the second time. She's too shrewd for it. That's it. We fake my death. Get the evidence, and get her out of the way."

So far so good, I thought. I didn't mention anything about the money Margie had had and that I wanted to get my hands on it, too.

"She thought we could gas you in your sleep."

"Good. She's doing our work for us."

"I'll get the details straightened out with her. I'll get back to you."

Chapter 146

The day Margie left the sanitarium she was looking like her old self again, almost anyway. We found a motel on the Strip and worked out 'the details.' Tried to. Two days later we still hadn't decided on how to do it. Margie was getting impatient. She wanted Monica dead in the worst possible way.

"What the hell is it, Fred?"

I blamed it on Grozewski's snooping around.

"I can't think when I know the son of a bitch is watching."

"You're worried about the evidence, aren't you?"

We were sitting by the pool. Grozewski had taken a room at the same motel. He was sitting across the pool from us, while peering over the top of the *Hollywood Reporter* from time to time. He had a headset over his ears and appeared to be pointing a listening device in our direction.

"There's a thing you can get: it's called a shotgun mic. He's got one. It can pick up at a distance of —"

She sprang to her feet. "Don't tell me what a *'shotgun mic'* is."

She called us a cab. We discussed the rest at the beach, facing the waves. Grozewski remained behind, by the hot dog stand. He was stuffing his face with a footlong and watching us through a pair of binoculars.

"Can you relax now?"

"I am relaxed, Marge."

"You're worried I won't destroy the evidence, aren't you?"

"Something like that."

"I love you like I've never loved anyone, ever. I want us to remain together, nothing more. After she's gone, the evidence is yours to do with as you please."

"That's no guarantee."

"We'll have to start trusting each other . . . all over again."

"Before we do anything, I want that money transferred to a joint account. We're husband and wife, remember?"

"It always was in a joint account."

She showed me her bank book to prove it. One hundred grand. Had been. At one time. Before the cost of the sanitarium. Ninety-six Gs. Give or take. Not that it really made much difference when it came to how I felt, because I was ready to kill this cunt for ninety-six cents—just to be free again.

"I never stopped loving you. Not for a moment, Fred."

"You heard what Rinelle said. She hates my guts. She's convinced I'm no good for you."

"Fuck Rinelle. She's not running my life these days."

We took a cab to Westwood, rented a car, and ditched Grozewski. We picked up a couple of gas masks at the *Supply Sergeant* on Hollywood Boulevard.

Chapter 147

I called Monica from a pay phone.

"It's set. You check out tonight."

"Did you see the evidence?"

"Yeah."

"You sound uncertain."

"Like you said: She's pretty shrewd."

"I don't expect her to destroy it. Should at least see it."

"I tried."

"Try harder. We won't get a second chance, Fred."

"I'll call you back."

Chapter 148

"We'll have to do it some other night, Marge."

"I'm not waiting another minute, Fred."

"She's got people coming over this evening."

"I'm through stalling."

"What's another day?"

She had to have a drink. I took her to a bar. She had her drink. Looked at me. "It's the evidence, isn't it? You'd like to see it first."

"We'll have to start trusting each other, remember?"

She had to have another drink.

"It's in a safe deposit box. Same one Frank kept the bling in. The bank won't open 'till 10:00 a.m. We'll get it in the morning."

"Good enough."

Chapter 149

The Camaro's bright yellow paint job made it far too easy to follow, it seemed to us, and so we did our best to keep from using it for errands we wanted Grozewski not to know about. Ditching the fat fuck took some effort and we were able to pull it off from time to time. Not often enough, though. Our run to the bank was one of those times we managed it.

I opened the envelope. All it contained was a taped conversation of the two of us discussing how to take Frank Graham out, a signed confession by her. It would have been enough to start another investigation into Frank Graham's death, I guess. I wasn't interested in how or when she'd had the opportunity to get it on tape, I just wanted to get rid of it. We burned the material.

"How do I know this is all of it?"

"I kept my end of the bargain. I want her out of my life."

"We'll need alibis, like before. We'll have to shake Grozewski, too."

"He's the least of our problems. We got our alibis: each other."

"Not good enough."

"Grozewski is our alibi. He'll testify, if it comes to that, that we never left our motel room."

"Run it by me again."

She did. She got the idea to make a duplicate of our motel room key.

"The clerk won't know it's missing while we're getting a copy made because we'll attach the same key chain to another key, any key; he won't know the difference. Then tonight, while the original key is in the slot, we sneak out the back. He'll never know we left. When *Five-0* come snooping around, if they do, he'll show them we haven't left, because our key will be in the cubbyhole."

I told her I didn't like it.

"Got anything better?"

I didn't at the time.

We got a copy made. I told her I had to go off by myself for a while and think. She said okay.

Chapter 150

I went to see Monica.

"She thinks I believe her about the evidence, that she's got it all destroyed."

"Great."

"I don't see what the point is in going through with the rest of it."

"She wants to get me out of the way. It'll make her happy."

"It's not worth it."

"It'll be a lot easier to get the pills in her, when she finds out that I'm not dead after all, and that we're still carrying on. She'll start boozing harder than ever. As long as she's alive, you'll never be a free man, Fred. You don't have anything to worry about. I'm the one who's doing it, or have you forgotten?"

"I don't want anything to go wrong."

"What can go wrong?"

"It's getting complicated."

"Who said it wouldn't be?"

"I wonder if it's worth it."

"You don't mean that."

"I don't."

Chapter 151

We put on some soft music and Monica, for the first time since I've known her, revealed a secret fantasy she'd always had. She'd always fantasized about being tied up, treated like a sex slave. She wanted me to do it to her: take her clothes off and tie her to the bed, take her by force, make her do things and do things to her. This is what had been missing with us before. She told me that when she was a kid her mother's common-law husband would from time to time discipline her, turn her over on his knee and spank her behind. She wanted me to do this to her. The more she talked the more I wanted her. It made me want her like I had never wanted her the whole eight months we'd lived together in that house across the street from the park. I strapped her down to the bedposts and fondled her and teased her until she couldn't stand it and begged me to do it to her, to put it in. I refused, and wanted to prolong the teasing. She kept saying she wanted to be spanked. I spanked her buttocks with my hand a few times and watched her butt turn red, then I got my brown leather belt and gave her several strokes, not hard enough to hurt her, just enough to sting her cheeks and leave crimson streaks across it. She liked it, and kept moaning. I abused her verbally, called her my whore, my slutty bitch, and that I was going to do with her as I damned well wanted.

Of course, it escaped me at the time: the two babes had more than me in common; they favored it on the rough side. Being spanked, dominated. So much for being independent and in control. Feminists. What did I care?

She wanted me to put it in all the more, to give it to her. My groin wanted to accommodate, but I made her wait. I told her she wasn't going to get it until I wanted her to have it.

"If you want me to give it to you you'll have to do as I say. Talk dirty to me, admit you're my sex slave, my sex tramp. My bitch to be used and abused as I see fit."

She played along. Got hotter. We both screamed out together toward the end. It was by far the best we'd ever known together. We laughed afterwards. I asked why she had never been able to reveal her fantasies to me before?

"Too shy. I was just too shy, I guess."

Before leaving, I reminded her again that it was going to happen later that night, and to leave her window unlocked, and shut the gas off.

Chapter 152

Margie was on the phone when I walked into the room. There was a flask on the end table. She lowered the receiver and fired up a smoke.

"Had to have one last fuck, didn't you?"

"Had to make sure there was a way for us to get in without having to break in; by either leaving a rear window unlocked or maybe the door facing the back porch."

"I get the idea your heart isn't in it—but your cock sure is."

I ignored that.

"You're wasting money on that gumshoe."

"*My* money."

"*Our money*, dear."

"*My share.*"

I fired up a butt and sat down. It was five minutes after seven. She got up and put her arms around me. "After this, we'll be free, Fred."

"Sounds like a song I heard once."

"It'll be our song, the song of the love we have for each other. I've never been to Hawaii, Fred. Always dreamed I'd be going there some day. Me and my dream man . . . making love on the beach in Hawaii." She squeezed me, nibbled my ear. She reeked of whiskey.

"I can hardly wait." I wasn't lying, either. She was the only witness to Frank Graham's murder. The sooner she was dead, the better.

She continued to hum and maneuvered herself onto my lap. She had unbuttoned the top of my shirt and played with my chest hair.

"Did I ever tell you you have the sexiest chest?"

"Not as sexy as yours."

"I just love a hairy chest."

I thought about knocking her teeth out.

She had a wild look in her eyes, and kept glancing at the clock. She was trying to tell me we had enough time for a roll in the sack. I made like I was too preoccupied with what we had to do later that night. She didn't buy it.

Barney Scheitz appeared knocking at the door, and the inevitable argument got temporarily postponed. She gave him a couple of hundred dollars, and he left without a word.

"Doesn't he ever say anything?"

"I asked him not to."

"Something you've overlooked. He could easily blackmail us later."

"I doubt it. Frank knew him."

I didn't pursue it. It would have been pointless."

Sure he could have blackmailed us. There would have been nothing to it; just like I knew he could easily blackmail me once Margie had been done away with. But I had little to worry about. Monica had volunteered to do it on her own. It was going to be her problem.

Since there was plenty of time left and I didn't want her to start thinking about sex again, I talked her into going to a bar. I made sure she didn't overdo it. I didn't want her to get too soused.

Chapter 153

At around 11:30 we drove out to where Monica lived on Riverside Drive. Grozewski was already waiting there, parked on the Equestrian Center side.

Margie glared at him.

"Look at him, Fred. Fat bastard. Doesn't he ever give up?"

It was then I realized there was no way around it: Bruno Grozewski was going to have to be eliminated. I kept the car rolling and didn't stop. He followed. I drove up to Alameda Avenue and took it west. At Cahuenga we made a left down toward Universal Studios, taking Lankershim over to the Universal Studios Tours Entrance. We made it up the hill to the Universal Sheraton.

Chapter 154

In the basement lounge of the hotel over beer and pretzels, Marge and I talked about ridding ourselves of the fat man as the fat man sat at the bar looking over his shoulder, eyeballing us. After I'd had a couple, I walked over to him.

"You haven't got anything on us, yet you persist."

"Sooner or later I'll nail you; I'll nail you both."

"Would it do any good to make an offer?"

He didn't say anything.

"I didn't think so. You haven't got any proof. It's all speculation. You think we did such and such. We didn't."

"The big gal is holding on a lot longer than I thought she would. It'll be over soon."

"She's trying to pick up the pieces. You're making it impossible. I don't like what it's doing to her."

"Take me out."

I laughed. "It's illegal."

"Is it?"

"Last I heard."

"You'd be surprised how many guttersnipes get away with it."

"Does it worry you?"

"No. You won't be one of them."

I pulled back with a fist and was about to let him have it. He drew his piece. "Another time, Grozewski."

Chapter 155

Margie and I returned to our motel room. There wasn't much else we could do. After she'd gone to sleep, I called Monica from a pay phone in the lobby and explained.

"Some other night then, Fred."

"Some other night."

Chapter 156

I returned to our room, got the bank book out of her purse and stared at it, just stared. *Ninety-six thousand dollars, and I owned half of it—and soon would own all of it.* Graham's young kids got some of it, which was acceptable; the older ones, adults, got left out entirely. The big payday, life insurance—remained the great mystery that I was quite unclear on and wondered if it would ever come through. Knocking off Margie for the ninety-six grand alone certainly would have been worth it, but it wasn't what convinced me to follow through on it; it was the thought of having to spend the rest of my life with her, and from fear she might run to the rollers one day with what she knew. The solution seemed to be in those sleeping pills Monica had suggested. But just so that I wouldn't be getting myself in a similar bind again, I was going to let Monica handle it. All of it.

She hadn't told me how she was going to get Margie to swallow a fistful of sleeping pills, and I decided I wasn't going to ask, either. Just let her do it. I remember sitting in that chair and holding that bank book like it was the Holy Grail. At the time it seemed like it. Thinking about all that money and what it could buy made me restless. I knew I wouldn't get any sleep that night. I got on the phone in the lobby and called Monica back.

"What took you so long? There's beer in the fridge. Hurry over."

I did.

Chapter 157

Later, after we'd made love, and it had been just as kinky and great as the other night, I felt a need to point something out.

"I still can't get over at the way you've changed. It was never this exciting. I mean it was good before, don't get me wrong. It never had the thrill it has now. I can't get over it."

Monica shrugged, smiled. Proud of herself.

"I realized if I didn't want to lose you again I better get rid of my inhibitions. And it worked."

"Did it ever."

We were lying in bed, drinking beer. I asked her how she planned to keep Margie's mouth open long enough to shove those sleeping pills down her gullet. Monica said that she was going to think of something.

"Like what?"

"I'll think of something."

"What if it backfires? Like you said, with her there may not be a second chance."

"You're worried I may need your help."

She hit the nail right on the head. I didn't want anymore, if I could help it. I'd had my share with Frank Graham.

"All I have to do is wait for her to pass out. Hold some Night Train or T-bird near her nose. She'll open her mouth all right. The rest will be easy. Pills will be in the swill, in powder form. Cheers."

I asked about the gas in her place. How were we going to fake that? "There's usually a slight hissing sound when you turn on the range, unless of course you left some soft music on before you turned in."

"Hissing sound? Only in Hollywood movies."

I guess she was right.

"Are you nervous about something?"

"No." I was lying, and swallowed beer. I couldn't put my finger on it, but something bothered me. Maybe it was knowing deep down I would never get to spend any of that money, not as long as Grozewski was around; maybe it was just the plain fact it had all gotten out of hand. Pumping that rat poison into Frank Graham and putting him six feet under made me feel bad enough, and it hadn't been the end of it. Margie was next, and Grozewski after that, and what had started it all in the first place had been lost so fast it made your head spin.

I think mainly I wanted to be able to do things with the cash, live a little. I'd never been to Hawaii, or even Rio or Acapulco. While in 'Nam, I had toyed with the idea of going to Honolulu on R&R, then changed my mind and flew to Sydney instead. Didn't regret it. Hoes were hot, and they were willing. They loved dollars. I had to work on an angle so that one of these women would get Grozewski out of the way.

I mentioned his name again to her; and that as long as he was around there was going to be trouble. No peace for either of us.

"He'll figure it out the same way he figured out what happened to Graham."

"How's he going to prove anything?"

"He hasn't been able to up to this point. He's a persistent son of a bitch, though, I'll say that much for him."

"What's to keep us from moving to the Caribbean? Or Europe? Or Asia?"

"You'd give up your job?"

"Just like that."

"You worked so hard to get it."

"Just like that."

She was still primarily a secretary, but had worked her way into a very good position, a good salary, and if she stuck it out there was no telling how far she could go. Sonny Sheldon had liked her enough to take her under his wing. And she was willing to give it all up for me.

"Fred, if this guy bothers you so much, get me a roscoe."

"Roscoe?"

"What happens when you read B-movie scripts for a living."

I looked at her good and hard.

"You mean it? About the gun?"

"Nothing is going to come between us, ever again."

"Wait a minute, Monica."

"You'll have to show me how to use it, of course."

"No problem there."

Chapter 158

At around 2 a.m. I returned to the motel. Margie hadn't moved a muscle. She snored. I couldn't sleep, not in the same bed with her. She snored like a pig and smelled like one, too.

It was incredible, how quickly the transformation had taken place. Barely a year before she had been one of the sexiest bronze goddesses I had ever laid eyes on. I had wanted her so damned bad back then, had to have her. Could never get enough. No matter how many times a day we had sex, it was never enough. Now this. Rings under her eyes. Halitosis. Those indigo peepers had lost their glow and turned murky. I'd never known indigo to turn a shade of mud. Guess what?

The human body wasn't made if iron. Too much booze and lack of rest, and if you stuffed your belly with too much junk food you turned into a bloated, half-crazed loon. That's what had happened to her. Coming out of that sanitarium that day she had looked a little better, lost some poundage, it seemed. But it had been due to a great makeup job—because the loss of weight hadn't been enough to make any real difference.

Not one bit.

She looked like a freaky bag lady. Never bothered to wash her crotch. The odor nauseated me. The legs that used to give me an instant erection just by looking at them, did nothing for me now. Her butt and tits were too huge, the ankles thick. And her teeth looked like she had been eating scrambled eggs, green and brown scrambled eggs, and hadn't bothered to brush them in quite some time.

No, nothing in the world could convince me to get excited over that again. It's all physical, what I just described that bothered me about her, in and of itself enough; but her heart, I was convinced, was like the rest of her. I mean she had been neurotic all along, only her beauty and sex appeal—when she had it, if she had it—had blinded me to it, didn't let me see the real woman behind the image. Her looks had me convinced I had found an angel, a voluptuous, raven-haired amazon with a golden complexion, and not a gutter tramp. That's what she was from where I sat presently—a gutter tramp.

Heaven forbid I should pass judgement on anyone. I know what I've done. I'm no saint by any means. I'm just trying to figure out 'the affair,' trying to understand the whole goddamn tragedy of it. I couldn't figure out why it had to happen to me. Did I go asking for it? Maybe I did. What are you supposed to do when you are attracted to a good looking member of the opposite sex? Ignore it? I was so convinced that had been the one I'd been waiting for all my life, the perfect one. Nobody told me there was no such thing as a perfect woman, or a perfect relationship. And even if they had attempted to set me straight on it I would not have accepted it. We are what we are.

I wondered where the Margie I had first met had gone off to, or even if there was such a woman left on this planet? Monica had been sweet and good-hearted, too. Look what was happening there.

Well, I thought, if Monica was willing to commit murder in order to preserve our love, I would let her. Only I wasn't going to get myself boxed in again, or so I thought.

Chapter 159

The next morning when all she wanted was a bottle of tequila and a lime to suck on, I made like a delivery boy and got it to her pronto.

I sat there and watched her drink it. I even cut up the lime into six equal wedges, sprinkled just the right amount of salt on the back of her hand. W.C. Fields was right: *"Like blood to a vampire."* He had been so goddamned right. She looked like a vampire. Long, stringy, unwashed locks of hair dangling over half-open, bloodshot eyes. With her tongue, she would lick the salt on the back of her hand and shoot that tequila down her throat, suck on a lime wedge and make a weird kind of grimace like she was dying or was constipated or something like that, then quickly recover as though she'd been given the magic antidote. The days spent at the sanitarium had been a waste. Maybe it had bought her a little time, preserved her sanity a bit longer. Sitting there, watching it all, made me sick to my stomach.

I got up.

"I need some breakfast."

"Where were you last night?"

"Out for a walk."

"You were with her again, weren't you?"

"What the hell does it matter?"

She flung one of the empty liquor bottles at a framed print on the wall. Broken glass covered the room.

"You had better control that temper of yours, Marge."

"*'What the hell does it matter?'* Is that what you said?"

"Want us to get kicked out of this place, too?"

"*What the hell does it matter?* Why do you think we're doing this? You're with that slut when you should be with me! *That's what it matters!*"

"You're a lush."

"You want a divorce?"

"Shape up. That's what I want."

"And you'll ball no one but me?"

"How many times have we gone over this?"

"When was anything settled?"

"A bottle of booze always settled things for you."

"When was the last time you so much as touched me?"

"Let's forget it. Right now. Just forget it. Drop it."

"When was it?"

"Drop it, goddamn it!"

"When?"

"I said —"

"I don't want to drop it! When? A month ago? Two months —"

"Don't be ridiculous."

"I can't seem to remember."

"You're exaggerating."

"*I'm not exaggerating.* You haven't got any goddamn lead left, do you?

She gets it all. She drains you every fucking time! She sends you back empty! Nothing left for me! And you say I'm exaggerating?"

"Keep your voice down."

"Why should I? *I'm exaggerating?*"

"I didn't want her to suspect anything."

"If this is what's in store for us, I want a divorce."

"No one is getting a divorce here. We're gonna get you sobered up when this is over. We're going away."

"I killed a man for you—and this is what happens." Tears streamed down her face.

"You killed him to free yourself of his temper and abuse."

She cried. I went over and kind of put my arms around her, and waited until she had quieted down. I have to admit, I thought about snapping that goddamned neck for her.

Chapter 160

I waited until she had dozed off. Then I went out for breakfast. I was so exhausted I fell asleep in the booth of the restaurant. A man's chuckles woke me. More accurately, it had to do with a hard to miss odor that only a certain type of pig gave off.

Grozewski. Sitting across from me at my table, sipping coffee. I was too tired to do anything about the condescending look I got and closed my eyes.

"The final stretch, eh Fred? Think she'll make it?"

"Is it worth it? What you're doing?"

"I don't think she will make it."

"You loved Frank Graham that much, did you?"

"You left two young kids without a father."

"And you lost your family over it."

"I'll take care of my own. You've got enough to worry about."

"What's your angle? No one could have loved a son of a bitch like that, no one; his kids included. There. I said it. No doubt, even his kids lived in fear of him. The man was a menace. He treated people like dirt."

"You mean Margie?"

"Everybody."

"Mainly her."

"You're blind if you didn't see it."

"Oh, I saw it. The option was always there for her. Frank's first wife left him, so did Carol, wife #2. Left him after half dozen years. Margie could have done the same. But no, not opportunistic Margie. You see, Margie had dollar signs in those violet eyes of hers; dollar signs and homicide. To be expected. Having been raised by someone as disturbed as Rinelle Rossi. And you walked right into that web like a real chump. In a way, I feel sorry for you, Reed."

I opened my eyes. Had to. This guy feeling sorry for me? I wanted to knock him senseless. He could feel me tensing up.

"Don't. Just don't."

"Don't feel sorry for me."

"Look at the way you've boxed yourself in. Only one way out. You'll have to take her out."

"You must have been a chubby son of a bitch when you were a kid, too. Chubby and loud. With a short weenie. Got pushed around a lot, huh? Got beaten up a lot, didn't you? You were the punching bag for every wise punk on the block. Then God-like macho man Frank Graham comes along and saves you from one of these beatings. You idolize him the rest of your life, not wanting to face up to the fact he's a bummer, a ruthless bully—but he saved your neck once, so he can do no wrong."

I was guessing, but I thought I had him pegged. He'd reminded me of some others like him.

"Close. It didn't quite happen that way. He was always a bully. I got picked on a lot; you're right about that. I got beaten up. . . . It was mostly by Frank. The other kids thought it was funny. Frank kept it up. He was sort of like the neighborhood leader, among the punks. They looked up to him. It got him laughs when he shoved me around, so he did it—that's why he did it."

"Then one day he shoves a little too hard, hurts you pretty bad, puts you in the hospital. He's worried. You're tight-lipped about it; don't rat the creep out. You come out of it okay. Earn his respect. From then on you're like brothers. Am I right?"

"I'll tell you something: no one laid a hand on me after that. No one."

"He was a *redneck throwback*. He died a *redneck throwback*."

"He had problems."

"Latent homo."

Grozewski ignored the remark.

"Just couldn't function as a husband."

"Yeah? What's that mean, Grozewski? He couldn't get wood?"

"Few years back some punk black kid from the projects up for triple homicide stabbed him in the testicles with a pocket knife. Frank saw doctors. Nothing worked."

"Not that he wasn't impotent before that."

The dick shrugged.

"And Margie knew about it before they were married?"

"It happened after."

"Her take on it is you two have had more than a bro-mance going on for years. Had she had a hint early on she never would have ended up with him."

"She married him for his earning potential; security. He knew it. Married her anyway. He loved her. I did my best to talk him out of it. So did Carol. He claimed to be in love with Margie and did what he did and it got him put in the ground."

"This thing has more twists and turns than *Scheherazade*."

"Difference being it won't bode as well for you—as it did her. Scheherazade was spared by the king—and lived. You, on the other hand, are going down. *Chump*."

"I think I got it finally. Except for one minor technicality. Which is: Who was top dog in your close encounters. I suspect it was Graham. Who gave? Again: Our man Frankie. 'Bachelor Number #1'; except in this case he was married to a (once upon a time) smoking hot, mixed race bombshell named Marge Rossi."

"True friendship is a rare commodity these days. Something a rootless type like you would never understand."

"He was a killer. Cold, ruthless. *Killer.* And he was probably that way before he got his *nutsack* sliced—*if it ever took place.* I don't believe a fucking word you say, by the way. I worked with him. Not only saw the sadistic streak with my own eyes, but was one of his vics. Lots of peeps hated his guts. I don't. Got over it. Plenty refused to. Graham getting half his face and other parts fried in that downtown hotel explosion is one prime example. I'll tell you what threw me, though: bounty man taking his kids to the zoo that time, that I was aware of, Universal Studios. Buying them toys. Hardly makes up for all the beatings and taking skippers out; ugliness."

There was a stretch of silence.

"You look like shit, Reed."

He rose from the table. Walked toward the exit.

"Take a look in the mirror if you think I look like shit."

I don't know that he heard me. He was out the door by then.

I didn't want to go back to the room that reeked like a brewery, but I headed back. Got as far as the sofa in the lobby and lowered my weary bones down on it.

Chapter 161

From Grozewski's point of view I had killed his hero. From my point of view, I was David who had pulled down Goliath (sort of); and yet from a third point of view, I was a murderer. I tried to justify it and I didn't. I had taken a life, at least participated in the taking of a life. There is only one good reason for that, I believe, and that is in order to save the lives of others, the killing of a ruthless heel has to be the right and only thing to do.

He'd been abusive with Marge all those years, and I'm not so sure that was reason enough alone to do it. Frank Graham had been a mean SOB who enjoyed brutalizing and killing people. Though I never saw him actually kill anyone, he did admit to it on his own. Sure, there were skips that he took out, like the twins on that rooftop in East LA that time, but it had been self-defense. Who could fault a man for that? Not I. Looking for reasons to justify why I participated in his demise, other than the true and real one, was pointless.

Truth is, if I dared admit it to myself, I had helped do him in for something altogether different. I had done it for the love of a woman and for money. I had done it for a better life than I'd known, great sex with a hot chick. Driving for a living had never gotten me anywhere in the past. I'd had my share of it: paint delivery, bread delivery, paper delivery. Not to mention all types of trucks that I drove while in Viet Nam: supply and troop transports. It was no way to get ahead. I'd come out to LA in hopes of a better future, a break—and had only managed to hit rock bottom, delivering pizza to hopped up, tightwad porn-addicted insomniacs in the Valley.

All I had wanted was a break, a chance. Everybody deserved a chance, I thought.

The job offer with Sonny Sheldon, Monica's boss, would have been nice, only it was pie-in-the-sky, the timing all wrong. It was frustrating. And now I was working on taking another life, maybe two. I wasn't looking for Easy Street anymore, just freedom. I had to be freed of that psychotic lush in my room.

Chapter 162

When next I looked up at the clock on the wall, I realized I had spent close to an hour on the sofa in semi-shuteye. I dreaded going upstairs, dreaded having to look at her again, smell her. She wanted to get laid. And she was going to bring it up again. I was so goddamned sure of that.

I made it up the steps. The door was locked. All the pounding in the world didn't make any difference. The door remained locked.

"Let me in, Margie."

I kicked at it and continued to do so until the assistant manager came hurrying down the hallway wanting to know what all the racket was about. I explained that my wife had locked me out.

He let me in with a pass key and hung around outside the door to see that everything was all right.

I went in, glass shards crackling under my shoes. The room was empty. I heard a door close and hurried back out into the hallway to see her run down the stairs. I made it to the lobby, following. Saw her jump in a cab parked at the curb. Grozewski was in the back seat with her. My blood was boiling and I didn't care. I ran outside and pulled him out by the collar and threw him down on the sidewalk. I told him to stay down.

"Or you had better be ready to use that piece."

He didn't move.

I slid in the back seat with Margie and told the cabbie to take us to an all-night coffee shop in the area, any coffee shop. And to move it.

Margie was in a state of frenzy, as usual. She started to babble something about not being able to go through with it. I told her to keep quiet. It would not have been wise to let the cabbie pick up on any of it. For all I knew, he could have been a cop working undercover.

Chapter 163

We got out in front of Ben Frank's.

"What happened, Margie? What's going on?"

"I wanted to confess."

"What's the matter with you?"

"I wouldn't have done it. I just thought I did."

"Why? What about us?"

"There is no *us*. I'm killing myself and you're balling that bitch. There is no *us*."

"If I didn't care I wouldn't have taken you to the sanitarium, for crying out loud."

"It's a joke with you. That's all. A joke. Tell me something: How much longer do you plan on letting me go on?"

"I'm not getting into that again. We're getting a fresh start. We can do that now with the money."

"If I die, you get it all. The greedy look. I know that look. I know it well."

I took her inside.

"How about some soup, Marge?"

I knew one thing: I couldn't wait. I couldn't afford to. I wanted it done fast. And I was desperate enough to do it myself.

Chapter 164

To prove to her that there was still an 'us,' I offered to get Monica alone.

"You'll need help, Fred."

"If you insist."

Later that night, after we'd both gotten some rest, and made sure Grozewski wasn't around, we drove to Monica's apartment on Riverside Drive. We had to walk along the concrete gangway to the rear without being heard or seen. We climbed up the wooden stairs to Monica's second floor porch; this was the side her kitchen was on. I handed Marge a pair of latex gloves, slipped into mine. I had the key in my hand and happened to glance back at Marge as I unlocked the back door. The lack of surprise on her face that I should have a key took me aback a bit. Not much, just a bit. She had never asked and I had never mentioned that I had access to a key. This should have been a red flag right there. It stood out. And I didn't add it up until later, much later. By then it was too late for me.

We donned our gas masks, and entered, closing the door quietly behind us. We tiptoed into the bedroom in back. I taped Monica's mouth with duct tape, and the rest of her had to be secured to the bed. It had to look like the real thing. Then I helped Margie tape all the cracks in the place: all around the front door, all three windows in the living room, the two windows in the bedroom. I shut the bathroom window. It looked tight and taping it would have been a waste and I didn't bother.

There were the two windows in the kitchen that faced the back porch and backyard. We got those, plus the top and sides of the rear door that we had walked through. It was a lot of work. Margie hadn't expected it. I paused at the stove all dramatic like, because Margie's eyes were on me, and turned all four jets on, plus the oven—with the oven door open all the way. There.

After the deed was done, and Monica dozed off again (to her demise, supposedly), we untied her. I checked for a pulse and assured Margie that she was gone. Margie wanted to make certain. I shoved her away from the bed.

"Goddamn it, she's dead. Let's get the hell out of here."

We made it back to the kitchen. I opened the rear door, waited for Margie to step outside. I followed. Closed the door, then locked the deadbolt, and we made it down the wooden porch steps, quiet as a couple of church mice.

The look on Margie's face. Something bothered me about it. She was ecstatic. That's what made it all the more puzzling. That weird feeling I'd had earlier like a sixth sense, like my guts trying to tell me something was off kilter. I couldn't put my finger on it. I recalled reading Spiderman comics as a kid. Spidey had a thing like a *sixth sense*. If someone ever attempted to sneak up on him from behind, if there was danger in the air, he could sense it.

That's exactly what it felt like. Someone was trying to sneak up on me, figuratively speaking, and I don't mean Grozewski, either. Leaving Monica's place that night, I kept turning my head, never seeing anything; no one was tailing, not even Bruno Grozewski.

Margie wanted to celebrate with coffee and doughnuts. Fine, I thought, although I was wired enough and barely touched my joe and pushed my doughnut her way, which she did not waste time gobbling right up. Then it was on to the *Palomino* in North Hollywood.

Chapter 165

The country/western venue was packed. The headliner was piano playing wild man Jerry Lee Lewis. One leg in a cast, top of his head wrapped in gauze, the gent sang his heart out for the rowdy crowd. A couple of killers were watching and enjoying a legendary entertainer whose nickname was *'Killer'* rock the house. Margie joked, she laughed, thoroughly enjoyed herself. I knew I wasn't going to have any qualms about putting her away.

Chapter 166

I waited for her to go to the john before I called Monica from a pay phone.

"Is everything all right?"

"Of course."

"She's so happy you're dead."

"I can imagine."

"I don't know if I can wait, Monica. I think tonight's a good night."

"She drunk?"

"Damn near. I'll call you from the motel."

"I'll bring the pills."

"No problem there. I can get pills. I want *Roofies*, instead."

"Rohypnol?"

"Far quicker and deadlier than sleeping pills. Sleeping pills they make these days lack the potency of sleeping pills of old. I want Roofies. Makes it sweeter. Why fuck around?"

"No, you stay with her. The Roofies I can do."

"You sure? You can get your hands on Roofies?"

"You forget: I work for a Hollywood celebrity. I can get anything."

"Anything?"

"Anything at all."

"In that case, how about cyanide? That would be best of all."

She hesitated.

"Cyanide, Fred? Are you sure?"

"You said anything. I'd love to see the bitch go down. Dead within minutes."

"Sounds lethal."

"Extremely."

"I could try. It would take a while."

"If you can get the Roofies, get the Roofies."

Chapter 167

Now *that sixth* sense was working overtime. I tried to shake it and couldn't. I tried telling myself it was nothing, nerves, being pursued by Grozewski and the adrenalin pumping caused by what was about to transpire with Margie. I would finally be rid of her. I wouldn't have to kiss that booze mouth anymore. And the money would be mine. At least the part that was in so far. And as far as the life insurance motherlode was concerned? Who knew? The widower was bound to be the recipient once it came in, the way I had it figured. If not, so be it.

I took Margie back to our room. She passed out on the bed soon enough. I dialed Monica from the lobby.

"Got the cyanide?"

"I couldn't. I thought you said —"

"Forget it. Got the *Roofies*?"

"Yes."

"Let's do it some other time."

"What's the matter with you now?"

"I feel *funny*."

"I don't understand, Fred. What is it?"

"I can't explain. Did you ever read Spiderman?"

"What?"

"Never mind."

"See you in fifteen minutes."

About twenty minutes later she was in the lobby. She wanted to know what was the matter with me?

"I can't put my finger on it. Jitters."

The clerk behind the desk dozed in his rocker.

Chapter 168

I walked Monica to the second floor. We went into the room. Margie was snoring as usual. Monica took the bottle of Night Train out of her purse and unscrewed the cap, and stared at the bottle in her hands for no real reason. She walked over to the bed, and stopped. Everything she did seemed to take forever. Why was she stalling? Why was she taking her sweet time about it?

Then she turned, looking up at me.

"This is murder. Isn't it, Fred?"

"That just occurred to you? She murdered you, too, didn't she? Let's get it over with."

"This is for real. . . ."

"Ninety-six thousand dollars. All ours."

"She may not know my death was a phony. But it was. This is the real thing."

"How could you go lame on me at a time like this? At the last minute?"

It infuriated me. I yanked the bottle out of her hand and proceeded to pry open Margie's jaw. That booze breath was overwhelming.

"Remember one thing, I didn't kill Frank Graham by myself. She'd had a good hand in it."

Chapter 169

The details of what followed isn't exactly clear. We hadn't bothered to turn the lights on when we entered and what moonlight had slanted through the curtain over the glass door on the balcony side and window to the left of it had been enough for what we needed to accomplish, although the room had remained fairly dark.

I remember hearing the closet door bursting open and a man's voice declaring that it was the police and not to move. Then someone tackled me, forcing me to the floor. It was Grozewski. I smelled him. When he punched me in the jaw and saw it was not going to do the trick, he drew his piece. I went for it, trying to wring it out of his hand, and failed. Even after I gave that son of a bitch a head-butt, he still refused to let go of the piece. Then it happened: gun went off. Grozewski got real limber like. I scrambled toward the glass door on the balcony side. I heard Grozewski, clearly in pain, order whomever else was in that room with him (probably his buddy Frankenstein), not to shoot. He wanted me alive. I was *his*. The entire incident had taken seconds, but it was enough for me to realize what had happened, that I had been out-conned by Margie and Monica. Hell hath no fury like a woman scorned. Except in my case, I had two women pissed off at me, possibly three. If you counted Rinelle.

I knew that pool was below that terrace somewhere, and there was the glass door I needed to get past. No way would I be able to break the thick glass it was made of and there was no time to grab the handle and slide it open, but I had no choice. Groggy head and all, I did my best to crawl toward it like a demon on speed, the way we'd been taught in Basic. I spun on the floor, dug inside my pocket for the .380 and fired off a couple of wild shots, not giving a shit who or what I hit.

I reached for the handle to the door and yanked it open, and leapt out, collided with a potted plant on my right that lacerated my face and neck. There was partial blindness in the right eye. Had to be blood. I imagined. Swiped at it with the back of my hand. Glanced down. There was plenty of blood on it. Knuckles and the rest of my hand.

The scuffle with porky, then the run-in with the plant. What the fuck? What was I doing? Where was I going? Top of my skull ached. Face in pain.

I scaled the handrail that was part of the balcony, and leapt into the air. No clue where the fuck I was headed. I wasn't sure when Grozewski had fired or that I had even been hit, because when I came down and clipped the edge of the diving board with the same side of my face that stung from the encounter with the plant and subsequently hit the water below, the incredible pain I felt just then temporarily numbed all of my senses: *skull and body*. Numb. Throbbing.

I had a deep gash under my chin; I had cuts along my neck and along the right side of my jaw from bouncing off the diving board. At this point it didn't matter. I was half-dead and woozy, but it made no difference. The .380 was gone, too. Lost in the process. Did it matter? Didn't mean jack at this point. Because the numbness took a hike soon enough and agony wasted no time moving in.

I had to get out of the pool and find the Camaro. Did so. With great effort. Wet and bleeding, near effing tears, I made it to the sidewalk and realized I'd been hit in the left leg.

Chapter 170

Wooster tailed me in an unmarked car with another roller in uniform. I drove toward North Hollywood, took Lankershim to the Hollywood Freeway, and headed south, the speedometer needle hitting the 100 mark.

I took the Hollywood Bowl offramp, and lost Wooster and his buddy by pulling into a motel driveway on the corner of Hollywood Boulevard and La Brea Avenue, and by coming out at the other end and cutting across La Brea down a side street. An LAPD chopper flew overhead with a search light. I drove down Highland Avenue, turned on Hawthorn. I found a spot under an owning in back of Hollywood High, and killed the engine. Sirens wailed, a helicopter circled overhead. I remained slumped in the seat, examining the calf the bullet had gone through. To stop the bleeding, I tore a shirt sleeve off and tied it round that part of my leg. It did some good. Not much. Some.

Chapter 171

I stayed put the rest of that night, soaking wet, shivering, fighting a fever. I think being wet and miserable bothered me a lot more than the wound, the wet boxers especially, that clung to my groin and bunghole and caused great discomfort. No matter what I did to ease the pain in and around my crotch it did no good.

I thought what a sucker I had been, what a fool, to be out-slicked by a couple of ballbusters like that. My instincts; I should have been paying more attention to my instincts. Was I angry? I was angry. Angry enough to want to kill them both. First finish the job on Margie, and then knock off Monica; the frosting on the cake. They'd ruined my chance at all of it: *money, freedom.*

Everything was shot to shit now.

I was pissed beyond words. What a sap I'd been. What a sucker.

Chapter 172

Rollers continued to prowl the streets until the sun came up the next morning. Then after a short pause, the manhunt continued. *Black-and-whites* were zipping up and down the main drags. I could hear them. Anyway, that break the chopper took must have been because they had to change shifts or something, or maybe the pilot had to go take a dump. It had given me enough time to get out into the open, hide behind a dumpster in an alley there, and let the sun dry my clothes.

Chapter 173

What followed was uneventful. I had passed out from the fatigue and the pain, and was discovered by the garbage collector, some Mexican kid with bloodshot eyes and a cocaine nose. Could hardly speak the language. He had the sniffles and kept wiping his snout with the back of his sleeve with the one arm, while his other arm probed at me with a dirty shovel.

I remember yanking that shovel out of his hand and whacking him across the mouth with it, and I blacked out.

Chapter 174

I woke up in a hospital bed with a gloating Grozewski looming over my face.

"You don't feel so slick now, do you?"

Hell, I closed my eyes.

Later, after I'd recovered and was read my rights and was taken downtown and stuck in a holding cell with three members of the Crips gang up for as many counts for murder, Grozewski paid me another visit.

I noticed a limp in the fat fuck's walk. There was no way to tell where it was he got shot during our motel room scuffle. My guess was the bullet had entered somewhere in the groin region, not that it mattered. Point being, he was in pain and should've been laid up, instead he was up and about. Determined to rub it in.

"She's getting off light, real light. For turning state's evidence."

Then he went on to name all the charges they had on me: murder in the first degree, attempted murder, assault on an officer with intent to kill, resisting arrest. He even brought up the incident with Chambray, the fact that I had run off. About the only thing he didn't mention were the two wild shots I'd managed to squeeze off prior to making the jump and my subsequent encounter with a diving board. Must not have hit anything worthwhile. Too bad.

"By the way, how is Chambray? They ever pick her up?"

He ignored me, and said that he was going to see to it that I got something for that, too. It was funny to him the way I had been conned. He was proud of it. He'd never been fired by the department. His family had never left him. It had all been part of the con.

I let him do all the talking, while I asked around for a light. None of the Crips had a light. It was not allowed. They didn't want a *white bread motha-fucka'* like me near them.

The fat cop had parting words for me. "I'll do my best to see you end up on death row."

This last comment of Grozewski's was what kept the members of the Crips from wanting to cripple me in that holding tank. I had earned enough respect to be left alone.

Chapter 175

Between briefings with my lame-brained court-appointed attorney and visits by journalists, Lt. Grozewski would come by just to show me the headlines. Somehow the whole thing had gotten turned around and I had been made to look like I had planned Frank Graham's murder all by myself, that I had coerced Margie into it, that I had beaten her, abused her, forced her to have sex with me, and threatened to kill her, too, if she didn't go along. According to Grozewki's testimony, I had been the one who provided the rat poison and the syringe. Marge was intent on going for the jugular: mine. I was the reason her right hand ended up in a cast. I'd squeezed her wrist so hard while forcing her to inject Graham that I had broken her hand *and* wrist and was the cause she had to wear a cast. Money having been the main motivator for all of it. Frank's money. That she stood to inherit as the widow and I would've had access to.

It was plenty bothersome.

It wasn't good enough for her that she had gotten off almost scot-free, and that my chances looked slim at best. Seeing to it that I got dropped six feet under wasn't good enough for her. It irked me plenty. I knew what I had done, but she'd had a hand in it, a good one. I had attempted to end it for her because she had sought to do the same to me.

She paid me a visit. When I mentioned the papers, she denied having talked to any journalists. She was lying, of course, because she knew about the letters I was getting from Monica. She was clearly enjoying what it was doing to me. What she did to me was no different from what Rinelle did to Graham. Like mother like daughter. Like I said: Hell hath no fury. . . . Add greed on top . . . and you've got a recipe for *vengeance à la carte*.

Monica's letters said that she would always feel something for me, for the way it used to be with us, and that she had gone along with the cop's ploy because I had shattered her dream, that I had tainted a love that could have been so wonderful and pure, a love that should have and certainly would have lasted, and because the police, having caught up with Chambray at last, had threatened to put the dog to sleep unless she cooperated fully.

I guess it was her way of getting back at me for acting 'like a man,' for destroying something that came along once in a lifetime. In one letter she said she would be moving back to Phoenix to live with her parents, and then in another letter she said she was not sure. Men in this town were so flaky and not worth bothering with, lousy marriage prospects, and that she must be a poor judge of character even at her age for having gotten involved with someone like me. She said I belonged behind bars because of what I'd done and to not try to contact her again.

Some of it I understood. Some of it, frankly, made no sense to me. I think the fact I had put her down for not being sexually interesting initially really got her to want to see me hang. I thought I was only being honest. She didn't see it that way, I guess. So she turned on me, plotted my demise with that screwball Marge.

What were they going to do now? *Board a cruise ship together with all that money and head for Mazatlán?*

Chapter 176

They're selecting the jury presently. My attorney tells me that could take weeks. Weeks, days, I don't care. It doesn't bother me. He also said I could be getting the death penalty. It was possible in a capital case like this. He mentioned my troubled background, the encounter with Graham.

Well, I would hope it's either the death penalty they nailed me with or as brief a sentence as possible. Maybe fifteen to life, with parole in six years for good behavior. You never knew. It was wishful thinking.

My greatest fear in prison is of being gang raped. Once that happens to a man he is no longer a man, but something a lot less: a punk; nothing. I'd been there before, you see: having had to fight off toothless homo freaks obsessed with the male *culo*. So it weighed on a man's mind. You learned to sleep with a hunk of pipe or a shank under your pillow, within easy reach. It was a fucked existence anyway you looked at it.

Third month into the trial they caught me trying to cash in my chips and put me on around the clock suicide watch. I wanted to be transferred to the psych ward, from which escape might have been possible. They didn't do that. Grozewski made sure that it didn't happen.

For weeks I had been asking for writing materials, possibly a typer, and finally was able to get my hands on a used one. To help in my own defense, I wrote it all down, the whole thing, the way it had happened, and made every effort to deal with it as honestly as I knew how. I also hoped to sell it to Sonny Sheldon, Monica's boss, and hoped to use the money to hire a contract killer on the outside like that Weasel guy we saw on tv to take care of the people responsible for putting me here.

Chapter 177

My manuscript was titled *Night Sweats*, not that it matters, because it was inadmissible and was rejected not only by the court, but as well as everyone else. It was at this point I decided to plead guilty to all of it; every damned charge they could level at me. There was no way to get a break, I knew, why should my life start changing at this stage of the game? By pleading guilty I also avoided death row by a hair, and was given life, without possibility of parole. Only because no matter how hard the DA's office tried to prove I was the one who had injected the bounty hunter with rat poison, they couldn't. In the end, what they had was Margie's word against mine. Her sitting there the whole time in the courtroom with her forearm in a cast further underscored what a heel I must be.

What I wanted to know was why the antifreeze was downplayed to the extent that it was? That was simple, according to my state-appointed dingbat defense attorney: That wasn't what ultimately caused the man's demise. Margie had been feeding it to him long before I came along. Fine. How did the DA know that it wasn't, *ultimately*, the accumulative effect that, alas, did it?

"You're not going to get anywhere with it. You forced her to pump the strychnine into him."

My mouthpiece was playing devil's advocate.

Just as I had suspected during that argument with Margie what to go with: antifreeze or rat poison. The clock had been ticking, time slipping, although on the surface not that crucial, but crucial enough: the choice what to go with was just another straw that tipped the whole kit and caboodle in their favor. It was the poison that did him in, and not the antifreeze at all. Had we stuck him with the antifreeze he would not have expired. The way the prosecutor saw it and played it up to great effect. Milked *it* and other *myths* he conjured up for all they were worth.

I was out after fifteen, an old man, pushing 50. I won't go into those hellish years, the two shank attacks I survived by the skin of my teeth. If I was cynical when I went in, I was one bitter motherfucker by the time I got out. My goal, my one and only goal in life was to get back at those who tripped me up and took those precious years from me: the trio: Piggy, Marge, Monica. I would hunt them down. They would be dealt with. They would be deep-sixed. They would be cut down. They would be made to pay for the years of suffering, for the betrayal, with the same type of indifference and lack of compassion. Since I was not human in their eyes, they, too, would be less than human in mine. Tit-for-tat. Eye for an eye.

I hadn't deserved one third of what I had been given. There were times you had to take matters into your own hands if you wanted justice, fairness. Nothing else mattered to me. There would be a price. I was prepared to pay that price.

End of Book One

BACKLASH

Love, Lust & Murder

Book Two

KIRK ALEX

TUCUMCARI PRESS

TP

Tucson — 2018

ISBN: 978-0-939122-56-1 (6x9 pbk)
ISBN: 978-0-939122-57-8 (ePUB)

Dedicated to Sean Chercover for writing a couple of
private eye thriller masterpieces, namely
Trigger City & *Big City, Bad Blood*. Kudos.

Chapter 1

The stalking phase of the hunt was on. I worked my way back to the North Hollywood area. And I had a real partner with me this time, a mixed-breed pit bull stray I befriended along the way and named *Payback*. *Redd Dogg* is what I went by this time. Couple of mutts; that's what the current incarnation of this team was. And the trio? Well off now. Graham's life insurance policy had paid off a while back, big time. And Rinelle? Long dead. Murdered. By assailant and/or assailants unknown. Until the mook, Jamal, to avoid Death Row, confessed. He'd beaten her with a ball bat, chopped her up with a meat cleaver and fed parts of her to animals at a zoo. And he'd done the same to some other peeps. Swell fellow. He'd been the major motivator, the punk who'd initially pushed Rinelle (who pushed Margie) into pumping the antifreeze into Graham. How nice. Until he busted Margie's mother spiking his *Night Train* with same. Even sprinkling his corn flakes with roach killer.

"Hear what I'm sayin'? Boric acid. Claimed it was powdered sugar. Gimme nose bleeds and runnin' shits. Belly cramps." He lost it. "Took her ass out." His claim. What he said. According to media. "Good riddance to bad rubbish." His own words. "Ho was a Black Widow. Owed me big time."

Turned out to be true: Margie's demented mommy Rinelle had poisoned her first few hubs the same way she had buried Margie's step daddy Mario, by lacing their Gallo with antifreeze, at times resorting to other means. Nobody really knew what her final tally was. When Margie's stepfather—of *Rossi Bail Bonds*—kicked the bucket, the house had been paid off; no mortgage—until Rinelle decided to refinance and blew most of it on crack and meth that she got from Jamal and his pals; the rest on one-armed bandits wherever she could find them: Vegas, Nevada; Gardena, CA; Atlantic City.

Monica was the primary force behind a legit production company and was producing cable tv specials, documentaries and motion pictures. She did docs on Sam Adams, Harry Truman, Honest Abe. Quite successful. Worked with the biggest stars. Margie? The other half of this dynamic duo and co-owner of said showbiz enterprise? Acted in substantial productions; their own as well as those initiated by others. She never carried a film playing the main lead, although she did just fine playing second or third principles. Was also co-producer with Monica on some things, as well as screenwriter; living together in an exclusive part of Receda in the San Fernando Valley.

Now, anyone in the know will tell you: San Fernando is the main hub and center of the multi-billion dollar a year porn industry. It is also a known fact that more than a few major corporations have a hand or two in this money-making machine. And like so many on the mainstream and legit Hollywood side who got their start this way, put together their grubstake to make it in Hollywood in this fashion, by dabbling in smut, so did ambitious Monica and her enterprising honey. No, they didn't appear in these films; they were far sharper than that, in that they were catalysts behind their productions and owned them outright. This was the only way to go—if you intended to make bank. Of course this was how they had funded their maiden mainstream pet projects that got them in the door, that and some of that money the insurance company paid off. Furthermore, they continued to dabble in porn, using pseudonyms—as everyone in porn did, simply because it was not easy to walk away from easy money that smut was and continued to be.

Chambray? Long dead, one supposed. Her presence and memory traded in for a couple of cats, as Margie had never cared for dogs to begin with. Dogs had been Frank's thing. Monica had wanted to make her 'life-partner' happy and got her the felines.

Gay? Is that what they were? A couple? Sure. Stranger things have happened; and this turn of events was not what had bothered me at all.

Far from it. Even Grozewski had divorced his wife, retired from the police department and moved in with some actor who played a detective on a tv series that Bruno was technical advisor on. Nothing unusual about any of it. Stranger things have happened in Tinseltown.

Chapter 2

Tailing them was not a problem. None of them knew what I looked like these days. The years in stir had left their mark. Hair had turned white. Face was lined and speckled with liver spots, what you could see of it, as I'd grown a full beard. Spots and wrinkles came with old age. Nothing to be done. My sight was not what it used to be and I was wearing eyeglasses now. Also, I drank a lot more. Mostly beer. Had to do with nerves. Life took its toll. You couldn't hide it, only fools denied it.

I got around in a used van, lived in it for the most part, took on what jobs I could find. Still suicidal, as always. I came to terms with this a long time ago. My fate. Damaged from the get-go, and certain things you just couldn't shake. Thoughts that my life amounted to nothing persisted. The way it was for most of us. I might've gotten somewhere early on, but hell, some handicaps were tough to overcome. But that didn't matter anymore. Rage fueled by a fucked-up beginning was no longer there, not an issue—that I could tell. Oh, the damage I certainly accepted at this point, but I was living with it. You had to, or else your skull exploded with the frustration and anger.

About the only thing that kept me going still was contemplating how to nail them, these cretins who wrecked my life to the point I no longer wished to go on. No ambition, no desire—for anything. I was no longer interested in driving for a living or pursuing stunt work. What a joke that was; the fact that I ever considered doing something like that for my bread and butter. I couldn't stand tv, movies and the assholes who made them. In this respect, admittedly, I was not different from the late *mother-humper* himself: Frank Graham.

I didn't want to own a house or get married or have kids. None of it. Other than *payback*. Plain and simple. I was not a complicated man, after all. All I wanted was to see them pay the piper, and pay they would.

Meanwhile, there was tailing to be done, meticulous records of their every move recorded on video tape as well as in my notebook, comings and goings, who the friends were, where they ate breakfast, lunch, dinner, the clubbing and whose parties they liked being present at to be kept track of.

The biggest irony, I thought, the three were in the midst of turning the documentary about me into a feature film, with an actual narrative thread this time. So you knew right away, it was not a stretch, that they would fictionalize quite a bit of it. This irked me. The doc had been full of half-truths and outright lies and fabrications to begin with, now they were going to push the envelope even further in this area. Well, it was Hollywood. They did whatever the hell they felt like doing and called it *dramatic license.*

"When it comes to war, truth is the first casualty."

Who was it that said that? Not that it matters. But, yes; they were in the process of casting, and when they consulted their lawyer to see if they were legally obligated to get my permission, my consent, it was there that he informed them it would be wiser to change certain names, and that, also, I had been released.

Chapter 3

Did this bit of news make them nervous? Sure. Grozewski, more than the women, but they were apprehensive about it enough. There was no way to deny that I had been short-changed, mistreated; sent up the river for their gain. The spiteful bitches were concerned at last. And had hired a PI to look for me.

I took jobs that paid cash money, so there was no way to track me down. I didn't use credit cards, didn't have a phone of any sort. And my license? In another state, where I picked up the used ride, a van that resembled the one owned by Monica's son Modi: down to the same shade of tan and mag wheels. I added, to either door, the red lips and tongue hanging out, which was the Triple-Threat Divas/M&M logo.

Modi also had one of those idiotic *I heart LA* bumper stickers on his rear bumper. It pained me to do it, nearly made me vomit, but yes, I stuck one on there. Changing my license and registering the van at the Southern California DMV would only have alerted them, so I didn't go that route. I counted on accomplishing what was needed before I got pulled over by the rollers and aided this scheme along by getting around on a bicycle quite a bit, and by using public transportation the rest of the time.

I let my gray hair grow long, grew the beard; wore dark shades over the specs during the day and hats, all types of hats: wide brim, ball caps, that concealed quite a bit of my face. And what would I do for a gun? Weapons? I was willing to spend my own hard-earned cash on a few items, but thought to return to the park to see what I might dig up. Had no real idea that the late Graham's arsenal I'd buried years before would still be there or that I'd even be able to locate it.

Find the upper case 'G,' I reminded myself over and over. *Find the 'G.'* And take it from there.

It did require some doing. I showed at the park early one dawn and started probing and searching around, looking for the tree with the marker. And should I have failed to locate one or the other? So be it, was my attitude. I'd buy what I needed. Guns were not difficult to come by if you knew where to look. The average law-abiding citizen had a hard time, especially around these parts, but not peeps like me. Not that I gave serious thought to using a piece on them. A piece would have been too easy, too quick. I preferred something else; something more. I wanted these fucks to suffer. I wanted anything but a gat: claw hammer, screwdriver, ice pick, butcher knife, shovel, tire iron, cyanide, antifreeze, anything but a bullet that entered your vic's body and dropped them soon after.

So, I wanted suffering. I needed to see and watch them die. I wanted to make sure that they took a long time to expire, that it was painful and protracted, so that I could savor and enjoy every minute of it; hear the cries, pleas, begging. . . . I wanted maximum suffering. I wanted the bitches to taste fear and experience pain: psychological, emotional, physical. The gamut. Pain. Agony. Anguish. And I wanted that pig Grozewski to scream like the cunt that he was and beg and whimper for his life.

Extreme? By someone who rarely behaved this way? Yes, long before I got bagged and did the long stretch, I'd been in and out of the joint for this and that offense; theft, usually. As a kid even, I'd been far easier going, even with all that crap I'd been exposed to: mental abuse, beatings, starvation, but life warps you eventually, damages you eventually to the point your anger builds and escalates and ultimately boils over. Because it must. Because it has no other recourse.

And this is what was taking place here: a boiling over. Explosion. *Tsunami of hatred.* I wanted to crush the trio for the vermin that they were; I wanted to dispatch and grind into the dirt all three because they were insignificant turds in my eyes, just as I had been insignificant to them years *before, during, and after.*

Want to *punish?* Feel like being *cruel?* Okay. *I can play this game. What's good for the goose. . . . The wrath of Fred Reed. . . .*

I located the tree, and dug up the tool box soon after. Opened it up. It was all there, wrapped in plastic as I'd left it: the pump action 12-gauge, several guns, and plenty of ammo for the works. I would clean and oil all of it thoroughly; get my hands on fresh ammo to play it safe. I would also pick up a few unrelated items: camcorders and sundry doodads: remotes and plenty of video tape.

Make a snuff flick? Was that the idea? Yes and no. The notion was to make a doc of the events as they unraveled in real time; a true doc. What a doc should be, as opposed to the one they had manufactured, by omitting facts and playing loose and free with motives. Most documentaries were like that: made by assholes with an agenda, trying to convince you to look at scenes and/or situations as they saw it, whether it was skewed bullshit or not. They rarely gave you the truth. Why? Why the need to manipulate? Because punks and pissants were warped in their take on things. Because the twisted punks and pissants were insecure and feared the truth and did not want you to be able to think for yourself. I say give it. Put it out there. To include every bit of detail in its gut-churning glory and let the gods decide who is right and who is wrong. Let the chips fall where they may.

Images, in this narrative, will be devoid of edits, slick or otherwise. Nothing ends up on the cutting room floor . . . but a body or two. Footage will be raw and real. Not unlike life itself.

Chapter 4

This is where I went after them, where the meticulous stalking commences. I got myself hired as dishwasher at *Pinocchio's Pasta*, one of their regular eateries in the Valley, and a couple of other places where they liked to get together and talk shop, plan productions, yack with actors and art directors and script writers and cinematographers and other porn and mainstream vermin of their ilk.

Things were going well, as far as I was concerned. I was in no hurry. It was fine, until late one night the *Pinocchio's Pasta* kitchen manager asked me to help the busser collect dirty dinner plates out there in the dining area. Problem was Monica and Margie and Grozewski and their pals were staying late, long after we had closed, drinking and yakking, and I was going to be busted, found out, if I went out. I had to come up with a reason why I couldn't do it, something legit.

Wearing dark shades over my eyeglasses at midnight was out. All I had to cover up with was my ball cap, which I pulled down low over my eyes, and kept my face turned away, plus the bifocals. Someone in their group called out to me; one of them, Grozewski, I think it was, or maybe his actor boyfriend, asking for another beer. I nodded my head, without turning. Returned to the kitchen with my tub full of plates, relaying to the manager their request.

"Go get it to them, then."

"But we're closed. They need to leave."

"They're regular customers. Generous tippers. We can't ask them to leave, and can't tell them they can't have their beer."

He ordered me to go in the walk-in cooler and get the beer. I hesitated, then finally went inside. Got the bottle of beer, and just stood there, sweating. What now? I was dead. If I went out there they were sure to recognize me. If I didn't, I got fired. I didn't care for the job, but felt I needed to stick around a while longer. I was a man on a mission, not from god, but someone far more legit: someone who'd been slighted, backstabbed and discarded. Nothing short of slaughter would do; my kind of slaughter. If I left the job on my own, I'd still be good, still be able to follow through on my plan.

I stepped out of the walk-in, slowly. Let the door close shut behind me. I could feel the manager's eyes on me. He knew I didn't want to go out there, but what he did not know was why. Still, he offered to take it. I said I'd handle it.

I picked up my tub, propped it on my shoulder before I stepped through the swinging aluminum door, and walked over to the table, making sure the plastic tub kept my face blocked and concealed from sight the entire time.

I paused at the table, placed the beer in front of Grozewski's boyfriend, who said thank you. I kept walking, collecting the other plates at the other tables.

When I returned to the kitchen, the manager gave me the look.

"Now, was that so hard?"

I shook my head. Didn't say word. I could have twisted his mellon right off. I had to stay calm, collected. To use an old, very old cliche: I had bigger fish to fry.

Chapter 5

With all the beer they were drinking it was just a matter of time for the twats to have a need to use the john. What I hadn't counted on was both going at the same time. Yes. To the 'powder room,' as the ladies like to say in classic Hollywood flicks.

What now?

I watched them go. Kept my eye on the door. I risked too much if I went in there with the two of them. Had to wait and hope that one came out alone. It didn't happen. Finally they emerged, and it was my loss. Until next time. Eventually one would go in there by herself. Either Margie or Monica, by herself, was fine.

At last it happened: Monica. Grabbed her purse. Hurried to the back where the restrooms were. Went in. I gave myself a reason to go in the back area and the short corridor where the water fountain was and johns were located, and slipped inside the women's crapper.

She was in the stall, talking on her cell phone. I looked about for where her purse might be. On the floor in the stall with her? And it very well might've been if the floor hadn't been littered with balled tissue, cigarette butts and general debris. She'd had no choice but to leave it on the vanity counter along the wall to my left.

First thought was to turn out the lights and take the keys, all of them: house and car, instead of making impressions with the clay kit I'd brought with, which had been the original plan.

I had to nix the idea soon enough. Missing car keys would've created the type of situation I didn't want when it came time for them to leave. So that was out. And should she have noticed that her house keys were gone? Too bad. It was the sort of chance I was willing to risk. Like most peeps, she was sure to have a spare set or two back at her and Margie's cribby. Besides, the fact her significant other would have hers with solved the issue. Tough shit if it didn't.

Now or never, I thought. Before actually turning out the lights, I played with the switch on the wall a few times, flicking it rapidly, to make it appear like an aftershock was about to cause an outage, then left them off. It was plenty dark. What light her cell gave off was a minor concern. The door to her stall was closed and it had to be good enough for what I needed to do. I was at the purse. Stuck my penlight in there.

"What the hell?" Monica was clearly buzzed on wine. "No, the light just went out. I should be used to these things by now. You would think." Then she said something else. I heard her laugh. "At a time like this, too. Would you believe it? I'm in the bathroom. Yes."

I found the house keys. Damn near went for the car keys, too. That's when I spotted what appeared to be a gun butt. I shoved a bankbook out of the way, and sure enough. It was a Glock. If I could have taken it without risking getting nailed, I would have. It was just as well, though. Now I knew the bitch was armed. Maybe even that other one had a piece somewhere. Why not? Had every reason: the guy they sent up the river was out and they needed protection. Only their guns wouldn't give them that. Too bad.

I left the purse, and was back at the light switch. Did the flicking number once again, as a reminder that the 'outage' had been a minor electrical issue after all, and left the lights on for good before easing out of the john. The manager saw me emerge from the corridor and gave me a dirty look. I wiped my mouth with the back of my hand. I figured my days were numbered.

A while later, while collecting dirty plates, I could hear Monica emerge from the back and walk to the table.

"That was weird. The light in the restroom went out. Thought we were experiencing another quake."

"Really?" Margie looked at her. "Light went out?"

"For a while. You guys never noticed?"

They shook their heads.

Chapter 6

Having access to the compound sure made it easier all around. Wouldn't have to break any windowpanes now. Every little bit helped. I'd be able to walk in through the front door, or maybe the rear. I'd drawn a map of the house. Pretty much knew where everything was. I still didn't have any way to open the gate, but that didn't matter. I'd be able to scale the wall. Small price to pay. From there the place was mine.

Only I had to look out for other people. Her son lived in the Valley. There was Grozewski and his bosom beau visiting on a regular basis; and there was Margie and all those movie phonies she and Monica ran with.

So no, it would not be a cakewalk, but the keys sure made it a lot easier.

Chapter 7

The following night, at the restaurant, Margie, Monica and Grozewski were at it again, rating actors. I could hear them discussing certain Tinseltown mooks who might play me. Brad Pitt was one. Fuck Brad Pitt, I thought. He can't act.

"Kurt Russell."

Too effing old, I thought.

"Jack Nicholson."

No way. Old enough to be my father.

"Not for Freddie's part." Grozewski was talking. "To play me. Maybe Clint Eastwood to play Frank."

"Eastwood?" Margie hadn't cared for the idea from the sound of it. "That decrepit womanizing bastard should've been put out to pasture years ago."

Then the talk was on the female roles and the potential actresses versatile enough, with enough range to portray Margie and her wife Monica.

Some names were bandied about: Angelina Jolie, Laura Linney, Sandra Bullock. Dakota Fanning, and some others. I didn't keep up with Hollywood twats and didn't care. Not only was it pointless (because I would see to it that there would be no movie), but it made me sick to my stomach. Hollywood was a vastly overrated pile of dung—and here was the reason and proof. I knew whatever they did with it would be a lie.

"How about Charlie Bronson to play Frank?" I couldn't tell who made the suggestion. Frankly, at this point it made little difference.

"Part's not big enough. Besides, he dies early on, doesn't he? Like during the first third."

Fuck Charlie Bronson, too, I thought. Fuck all of them: *hoes* and *dogs*. Only the hoes and dogs couldn't stop yakking about it.

"Shouldn't Fred Reed be consulted with regards to some of this? At least offered some compensation?"

"Why? This is not about him. It's fiction at this point."

"The doc wasn't fiction."

"The doc was PD. Public Domain."

"True story."

"Everyone involved was compensated. He got sent up."

"He had it coming. He was a louse. Loser. Not worth bothering with."

Who was saying what I couldn't tell. I was not looking at them and went about collecting dirty plates and silverware. I thought of the different ways I could do the slime in: cyanide was one. I knew where to get it this time. It would have been so easy. A drop in each bowl of soup. They would've died on the spot. I wouldn't be able to get their bodies out of there and make them disappear; and I would've been bagged soon after. I didn't want that.

Chapter 8

I followed the two twats home that night. Even though I'd been there more than once before, thought it prudent to take another look, make certain I knew my way around, got to know the lay of the land better: not only the four-bedroom, five-bathroom Mediterranean style house they lived in, with guest house in back, swimming pool, gazebo, and the rest of it. I wanted to get to know what the neighbors were like a little better, their comings and goings; I needed to know about dogs and security, safest and easiest stretch of the wall to climb over, bind and gag the bitches, carry them out to the car and then drive through the wrought iron gate. These things required planning, not unlike breaking into a home and walking off with the silverware, cash, jewelry and other valuables. You wanted to slip in and slip out, without being detected.

Chambray, as noted, had been replaced by a couple of cats. Margie's choice. She hated dogs, and had pointed it out on more than one occasion years before. "*Dogs* are that *dawg* Frank's thing, not mine. I like cats."

I wore black, everything, down to socks, gloves, ski mask with perforations for eyes and mouth. Found myself in the patio area. Glass door that would have allowed access to the living room was not only closed, but definitely locked. No matter. I had a decent enough view through the curtains. Spied them sitting on the sofa, sipping wine and watching something on cable. Could've been one of their own productions, a doc or movie. Looked like a movie. Titles scrolled up. Monica was the producer, director, co-writer. Margie had one of the female leads. Was also co-producer and co-writer. A couple of *triple threats*, as they like to say in Hollywood (whenever you had ability to do three different things and do them well enough to be recognized in the 'industry' for it).

I imagined even Grozewski was one of the 'triple threats' at this point: tech advisor, associate producer and *fluff girl*. Who knew? In porn, I had come to find out, that's what the chick who got the male lead's cock hard before the cameras rolled, flicked his knob with her tongue until he was stiff enough to get in there and do his job.

What Bruno was to me at this point, after all of it: *fluff twat*. It also came out, just as I had suspected, that he and Graham had had something deeper going than your casual *bro-mance*. No wonder Grozewski felt obligated to hound me the way he did. I had always suspected something of this nature, but hadn't been able to put my finger on it, and when it finally dawned on me, I refused to accept it. Why? Well, for one thing, Frank Graham had been one macho mother-humper, is why. Just like John Wayne. And yet, I'd always felt something peculiar about all that macho posturing. I liked the Duke, mind you, I just didn't care for the macho bullshit.

To me, true macho, the real macho men, never feel a need to carry that testosterone attitude on their shoulder. You knew you were a man inside and that was all that mattered. There was never any need to perch it on the shoulder and keep it there and constantly be reminding the world how tough you were, à la Dirty Harry, and some other phony Tinseltown mooks who went about it this way. Because, to me, usually, these fuckers were queer. Sucked pipe, and took bone up the crapper. Yep. Behind doors. This is the way it went. Tough guy on screen, pussy with a penis off-screen. It wasn't the fact they might be half gay that bothered me, it was the fakery, the phoniness; the three-dollar bill horseshit thing of it.

Chapter 9

Guess what? Fuck Duke Wayne and Magnum PI and Rambo, and the rest of those cocksuckers, because this thing with the twats was going where I expected it to: the wine glasses were lowered and the kissing started.

Pecks, soft and tender, on the lips. Just the way women liked and were always bitching that the men they were with wouldn't take their time on when it came to smooching.

And it was tender and gradual, loving. And as much as I was taken by it, aroused by it, in fact, I loathed the cunts for it, for abandoning me in place of this. Dropping my cock and balls for vagina. How did that work? Why was it this way? How could any woman, especially these two, trade my dick for tits and muff? How was this possible? Was it always this way? Was lesbianism always this rampant and we just weren't aware of it? Am talking about through the ages: *Were bitches always after pussy, as opposed to dick?* And only had sex with us because it was expected and because it was the only way to get knocked up and have a kid? You hoped not. But you also wondered about it.

Margie picked up the remote and turned down the volume on the flick, and turned it up on the stereo system. Something slow and soothing rose up in volume. My groin was hard, and I didn't want it to be. I was not here to get rocks, not here for the sex. I was here on a mission, a mission I'd been contemplating for years, a do-or-die mission that I needed to carry out and then call it quits—forever. End my existence on this planet as I knew it.

So I needed to take my hand off my boner, and stay focused. Only the bitches wouldn't let me. They were at it, back to kissing lips and rubbing tits.

There was no denying who the boss was here. Margie. Margie, the one who'd been demeaned and dominated and mistreated and dissed by Frank Graham, was in total charge here. Go figure. Monica, on the other hand, the one who directed and very often called the shots out there, on set, was the compliant one who preferred to be dominated.

Did I get it? No. And I didn't give a shit, either. Because it was happening and I had no control over it and didn't want to have control over it. The only control I wanted was once I stepped into the scene and took charge and followed through on the payback I had in mind for the malicious she-devils.

Chapter 10

Margie remained seated on the sofa and maneuvered Monica so that she was kneeling before her, between her thighs. She guided her head down so that Monica would be planting kisses along the one inner thigh, then the other; then she had her move her head up, up toward her breasts, while Margie undid the buttons on her blouse. Monica's lips were kissing the cleavage, her lips moving to the right breast, then the top of the left. She had Monica pause long enough to undo the bra clasp in back. The bra was allowed to drop and tossed aside, and Monica was back on the full breasts, sucking in one of the nipples, then moving over to the other.

The way the sofa was positioned and the way the large living room with all its objets d'art from South America, Africa and the Middle East, had been designed, I had to do a bit of straining to the left to see exactly what was going on. The large flat screen tv was on a wall at the left side of the room, Margie and her wife with the capable tongue were on the right. Beyond the sofa was the large kitchen. The problem with where I was had to do with the sofa armrest, even with me standing, it was not easy to make out what exactly Monica was up to. Part of it, or rather, a great deal of it was blocked by Margie's left leg.

Margie had shoved her face down between her thighs. Pressed down with the palms of her hands on the back of Monica's head. Margie's own head was back against the backrest, tilted back, mouth open, grinning and sighing. Then it happened, she'd lifted her feet up and over Monica's shoulders, resting them there, and forced the other woman to go lower, pushing her face down against her nether region. This was a new one on me. Who woulda thunk? This was some wanton and raunchy behavior. Made my Jones go up. And stay up. I wanted to jump in; forget the bloodbath I had in store for them, and just fuck the shit out of both, then slaughter them like the worthless, useless backstabbers that they were.

Only I couldn't. I wouldn't. Because I knew there was no way they'd allow it. These two were certified lesbians at this point; and I was *persona non grata,* as any man would be. When women turned gay like this, if you were male you were out, period. *No ands ifs or buts.* They had no use for you or your penis. Besides, I needed to spare them both the shock of seeing me. Not for their sake, but more for mine. I couldn't afford the disruption and absolute chaos it would have resulted in.

Margie guided the other's mouth back up again. Kept her there. Margie was screaming, her body quivering. She was orgasming; a whole series of orgasms followed, while she pushed the other woman's head down in there all the way and left it there.

Chapter 11

They stopped. Time to take a breather. Monica needed to rest her tongue and jaw, and the other needed to recover from the intense climaxes.

Some mild kissing of the lips followed, hugging. They sipped their vino, draining the glasses. Then Monica rose, walked to the left side of the spacious room where the tv was, reached inside the entertainment console below for a DVD. Popped it in. Porn. Hardcore porn. Monica had come a long way. What I saw of her, taking a stroll on the wild side years before, had merely been the beginning of her all-out transformation that I had just witnessed a sampling of. Porn was the thing for both these days. I was still contemplating going in there, slapping cuffs on both, taping their mouths shut with duct tape, and dragging them out to the garage where their luxury cars were parked and shoving them in the trunk of one and driving out to the desert to the pre-dug graves.

But I couldn't tear myself away from the scene. I needed to see what else was going down, what else they were about to do to each other. I was making up for lost time: years of going without pussy; years of not only not being able to touch and handle and taste, but not so much as look at the real thing. And now, witnessing it up front, the actual, genuine article, was overwhelming. It was way too incredible to do anything that would cut it short. I only wondered if I'd be able to keep myself from going in there and doing something about the craving and absolute thirst to taste those cunts and butt holes. Could I? Was I able? Did I have the will power?

All those years made it seem nearly impossible to pull off, stay away from. I had to have it; I wanted it. *So goddamn bad it was killing me.* Sweat slid down into my eyes. Part of it was the wool hat; part of it, perhaps the greater part, was the practically uncontrollable need and desire. Even considered, if briefly, drawing the camcorder I'd brought with to shoot footy of the action. But then thought: No. *Absolutely not.* Not what this is about. Two over-the-hill broads engaged in intercourse. It was not easy. Far from it.

Monica took Margie's place on the sofa, and Margie now was the one on her knees, between the other's thighs, spreading them, her tongue darting, looking to service her. Monica's eyes were on the tv screen, watching a couple of large breasted women eating each other out, naked on a wide bed, sixty-nine style.

Margie paused, lifted her head and proceeded to unbutton the other woman's shirt. Helped her out of it, helped her take the bra off, and squeezed and nibbled on her average size breasts, the both of them eyeing what was taking place on the screen from time to time. Although both were turned on by it, you got the idea the porn was there for Margie's benefit primarily, just as her need for it had been blatantly obvious during our trysts back in the day. And before Margie could lower her head back down between Monica's thighs, the phone rang.

Monica reached over to pick it up. Sounded like it was her son. On his way over.

"All right, hon. See you in about an hour." She returned the receiver to the cradle. "It's Modigliani. Stopping by with his girlfriend."

It was decided that they would retreat to one of the bedrooms for act two. There was plenty of time before sonny appeared.

Monica walked to the tv, ejected the DVD, and the two disappeared in the hallway on the right.

Chapter 12

I knew I didn't want to be here when the kid and his girlfriend showed, but neither did I feel like missing out on Monica and Margie's boudoir antics. I wanted to see what else they were up to. There was more to experience for both: them, as well as me: the voyeur/peeper. That's what I was: *effing Peeping Tom.* So be it. Also, I had no plans to harm Monica's son or the girlfriend, either. That was out. I was no serial killer and did not kill at random and/or mindlessly. That was for punks like Manson and the others. Fuck that. Ted Bundy and Dahmer and Jack the Ripper. That was not me. That would never be me. Still had some self-respect. I didn't hurt the innocent. All I was after were the assholes who made me suffer; those who caused me so much grief and discomfort over the years. It was personal. Hurting animals, kids, anyone who did nothing to me, did not hurt me in any way, was out. Did this attitude make me a saint? Was I Mother Teresa suddenly? Was I Christ-like? Hardly. Because I still had venom in me, bile, and had a need to taste vengeance. I had wrath that needed release—and nothing short of release would do. And the peeps responsible: Monica, Margie/the two dykes; as well as a porker named Grozewski, would see to it that I got the release. So be it.

I left my spot at the living room sliding glass door, and walked in back in search of access to the bedroom and hoped the window hadn't been locked by them. I could have gone in through either the front or rear door. That would be later. I wanted to watch from the window. Through a crack in the curtain. There was a screen over the window, but the window itself had been left open just a crack, no doubt, for fresh air. When you had cats around fresh air was a must.

I'd never been a cat guy; dogs were my preferred domestic pet, so the odor hit me right away. Had two felines around. Margie's doing. Monica had been a dog lover like me. Stench caused by cats couldn't be mistaken for anything else. I did my best to ignore it. Had to.

Chapter 13

The DVD was inserted into the player here and the image of the naked peeps appeared on the large tv screen as before. Margie and her accommodating lover had shed their street clothes and were in heels at this point, fishnets and the like: crotchless panties. Margie had handcuffed her willing participant to the brass bed at one end and had her positioned on all fours, with the butt sticking out. She had a cat-o'-nine-tails and gave Monica a good one across the buttocks. Monica winced, shaking that muscular rear end. She was older these days, no doubt, but staying fit had paid off. Even Margie looked pretty damned good; had been taking good care of herself ever since getting off the booze and cheese balls. Sure, nowadays she had high end wine during meals, but for the most part, was booze-free and definitely not like she used to be. And that 'Fred' tat she'd had inscribed on her right cheek that time? Modified into their Triple-Threat logo: red lips with the big tongue hanging down I half-wished my own lips were on.

She raised the hand with the cat-o'-nine-tails and gave it to her lover again, putting some force into it this time. Monica's buttocks were streaked red and she was wincing. Not from pain, but pleasure. Or was it a bit of both?

"Are you *cumming* yet, *bitch?*"

"Yes."

"Tell me, then."

"I am, Madam Margie. Do it. Please."

"Shut up and take it, bitch. Take your punishment. Take it and like it, because you have no choice."

"Yes. Spank me; spank me so good. I need this; I so desperately need to be your sex slave . . ." And she was orgasming repeatedly, her body quivering.

Margie may have had the cat-o'-nine-tails in her right hand, but her left was down there between her upper thighs, pleasuring herself with a vibrator, circling and concentrating on that certain area, getting off.

"More. Spank me, baby. Spank me now . . ."

"You want more? Did I hear you say you want more of the same?"

Monica was nodding her head, shaking her hips from side to side.

"Then say so. Say it loud enough; say it so that I'll know you mean it."

And Monica repeated her request.

"All right, then, honey pie. My ever-loving, insatiable ho."

She whacked her across the butt cheeks. Monica's ass jerked, further indication and sign that it felt so incredibly good for her. Margie raised that whip hand and did it again. Down it came. Across Monica's voluptuous rear. Again and again and again, Monica climaxing with each stroke of the cat-o'-nine-tails.

Chapter 14

Margie had taken a massive dildo and strapped it on.

I was so turned on by it and the ensuing action that my balls had begun to ache. What was I going to do now? Rush in there and rape the bitches? Could I control the two of them? Where were the guns? Their purses were with them, and these modern dames knew how to use those rods. You bet. Also, what bothered me: I may be a killer—this was something I could live with—but I was no *rapo*. As much as I craved vagina and those tight *culos*, I could not allow myself to go in there and commit rape. This was out. *Out.*

Then what? I stood there and suffered; I stood there, panting and sweating and rubbing myself, but not too much, because if I didn't watch it, I'd be shooting sperm inside my pants. Fuck that. No good.

I took my hand away from my groin. If I refused to go in and get some tang, and if I refused to masturbate . . . what the hell was left for an anti-social psycho like me to do?

Chapter 15

At last, Margie collapsed, as did the other one, as her neck was on the stiff side from all the work and energy she had just expended.

I was breathing hard myself. Thanked all the forces above for this bit of respite. And I didn't dare so much as touch my cock; because if I had, I would have been shooting a ton of jizz right inside my boxers. Shit. Fuck. Piss. Unbearable.

Control. You had to have control. It was the impossible task.

Chapter 16

When I looked back up, Margie had positioned herself up against her partner's rear and was about to slide that massive strap-on inside her backside. I noticed Monica's wrists were no longer cuffed to the brass bed and she had inserted a vibrator inside her cunt.

Could I even take it after what I'd just been subjected to? Was it possible? *I wanted to go in there. So help me; I desperately needed to go in there and get some hairy beaver and tight bunghole.* Son of a bitch. I was even having second thoughts about deep-sixing these spineless, two-faced hoes. I was. Scene was that hot.

Was it a waste to waste them? Would it be? Of *cunt?* Of female *culo? BJs?* Why not live here with them for a while, get fucked and blown and then do the payback?

How about that? Rape the skanks for a day or two; maybe longer. . . . Yes, but what about Grozewski and Monica's son, and all those other Hollywood motherfuckers who knew them? How would I deal with all that? Ignore the phone when it rang? Not respond to the intercom when peeps pulled up to the gate and pressed the button and asked what's up?— and when they got no answer, went to *Five-0* and filed a missing persons report, or worse: got someone to break into the place. . . .

No. That was out. Hanging around was out. Too bad, too. Ballbusters had to be dealt with. Sans sex. No fornication; no intercourse. Period. About the only kind of intercourse that takes place will be verbal.

Huh?

Yes.

Verbal.

Fuck verbal. I wanted cunt juice on my lips and tongue; butt hole to smell and taste. I needed it so damned bad. To make up for lost time.

Get a hooker. They're all over the place. Wouldn't be the first time. Get yourself a professional whore. Do it. There cannot be rape here with these two double-crossing wenches.

Chapter 17

While they were orgasming and gasping, I was battling my own situation: impossibly painful case of *blue balls* and *gas build up.* Not only could I not take a step without suffering incredible pain in my loins, but a powerful fart escaped my hind end. I froze still, stiff, fearing they might have heard it.

"Was that you, Marge?"

"Huh?"

"You just fart?"

"No way."

Both were lying on their backs, spent and exhausted.

"Modi and his girlfriend Lucy are on their way over, you know? We probably should shower and get dressed."

Then Margie mentioned Bruno Grozewski and that he and his boyfriend had this actor friend named Bix Dixon they thought would make a good Alf Reed."

"Bix Dixon? He's kind of effeminate, isn't he? Fred may have been many things: creepo, misogynist, liar, thief, anti-social, two-timing a-hole, but no way was he ever gay or show any signs of it, Margie. I can't see spending time reading an actor like Bix who is so blatantly gay."

"What're you got against gay peeps?"

Monica looked at her, then looked away with a smile on her face. Both were staring up at the ceiling.

"I can't do that to him, Marge. Besides, Bix is Jewish."

"Jewish? What's that got to do with anything, Monica? I never knew you to be anti-Semitic."

"I am not anti-Semitic."

"Sounds like it. When you talk like that."

"Oh, stop it."

"Just teasing you, hon."

"I feel guilty as it is. He's been punished enough."

"Punished? Fred? What he got he got because he deserved it. *Fuck him.* If this gay kid can act, let's give him a chance. What would it hurt to just have him come in and read?"

"He does gay porn on the side, Marge. If it got out it would hurt the production."

"Gay porn? Since when are you against gay porn? You can't get enough of it. Something I could never understand: a gay woman getting off on watching *men* fuck each other."

"I wasn't always into girls." Monica was back looking at her lover again. "Didn't even know I had that in me . . . until we met and. . . . I'm glad you're in my life, babe. . . ."

Margie turned on her side, slid her right arm under the other's neck and gave her partner a peck on the cheek.

"Is this the best, or what? Are we lucky? To have each other, to be living in this wonderful house and have the wonderful careers we have: respected by the industry."

Monica said nothing for a while.

"We are. We've come a long way . . . but to cast a known gay porn star to play Fred would not only be so wrong, but probably result in irreparable damage to the film. Not to mention . . ."

"What?"

"He wouldn't stand for it. There is no way Fred would let us get away with it. He's out, and we have no idea where he is even. He could be scheming right now how to get back at us."

"I wouldn't worry about it."

"You don't think he's been scheming the whole time he was in prison how to get back at us? He's the type who loves to harbor a grudge, and he's got a temper. Let's not forget that. It's no joke. I saw it, lived with it. At first, didn't think much of it; didn't let it bother me or worry me. In fact, I found it kind of amusing . . . the way he would get worked up about things: if we were stuck in traffic, or if we were in line to see a bank teller or the grocery line we happened to be in wasn't moving fast enough for him; he just had no patience for these things. And living in L.A, waiting is just a fact of life. He had a tendency to snap. It got to worry me; I'd never been around someone like this. And then he lied to me about his background, childhood. Wouldn't talk about it; would never discuss it with me; refused to."

Margie sat up.

"I still have no idea what you're getting at."

"I'm saying I'd feel better if we got a big dog, couple of them. Maybe hire a guard, at least until Grozewski can figure out where he is. Because right now, we have no idea. None."

Margie reached inside her purse. Withdrew a *Glock*. Checked to make sure it was loaded.

"I got my guard and big dog right here. I hope he comes around and gives me a reason to waste his sorry butt. He's a miscreant; just like Frank Graham. Couple of losers. One is dead, and the other should be. The only mistake we made: not smoking his ass when we had the chance."

Monica looked at her, and didn't seem to like what she was hearing.

"I mean it, Monica. The only reason you have that worried look in your eyes: because the asshole is out there somewhere and he's a threat. And he'll always be a threat, so long as he's not where he belongs: locked up behind bars—or dead."

"You just made my point."

"I need a shower."

"Was he scapegoated?"

"Was *who* scapegoated, Monica?"

"Who are we talking about?"

"*Fred?* He was not. He was determined to take Frank out. I did my best to talk him out of it. He was obsessed. Again, some stupid male ego thing. Had to have me all to himself. You know how they are. Got to own you. It's about ownership with these assholes. There was no way to stop him at the time. I was in love with him and had little choice but to go along. Had Rinelle's life been threatened by Jamal and his druggie vermin due to what she owed them? Of course. I did what I could to get Frank to send money. You know the rest. It's psychologically, as well as emotionally draining to keep going over it. Rinelle played with fire and she got burned. It was love/hate with us. There were things, character traits that I absolutely loathed about her; times I wanted to beat the shit out of her, and did my best—and yet, there's no denying woman did raise me; did what she could with me and my siblings. In her own twisted way, mind you. And we don't want to discuss what went on there. It's too much—and does not make me feel good at all, babe. Just talking about this makes me ache for a long, hot shower. I am not kidding, girlfriend."

Margie had delivered that last line with a smile. Stood up. Dropped the piece back inside her purse, and walked out of the room with it.

"I better take one myself."

And no sooner had Monica said it, did another fart escape my backside. I could have died. Saw her freeze. She was certain she'd heard it this time. Walked over to the window, parted the curtain. Slid the window open wide enough. Had her face up against the screen, looking to her left, then the right. I'd ducked down in time, and held my breath. After a while, she closed and locked the window and drew the curtain shut. Since there was no reason to hold back with the gas anymore, I let go with a whole series of emissions.

Chapter 18

I was at their back door. Inserted the key. Went in. I was ready: had the cuffs, rubber mallet, black hoods, .357 Mag—should I need to shoot my way out.

Cat odor was much stronger now that I was inside and it took a lot more to deal with it. I made it down the corridor, walking on the thick, spotless white carpeting. I looked down, to see if my sneakers left prints, anything *Five-0* might be able to use against me later in court (should I fail in my own demise). Bits of grass, tiny gravel pebbles. Fuck it. Nothing I could do there, not that it was evidence of anything, either.

I looked up at the walls on either side: lined with framed posters and stills, pics of crew, Monica and Margie's friends; Hollywood actors & turds alike. Meant nothing to me.

Door on my left was the bedroom where the divas had been fucking a moment ago. I went in. Mallet at the ready. I would have preferred doing this with a real hammer, but the resulting blood might've worked against me: I did not want to leave this kind of evidence behind. I did not want to create a mess—if I could help it. Do it like before, when I whacked Graham in his hospital bed years before: knock 'em out with the mallet, cuff their wrists behind their back, slip the hoods over their noggins & carry them out, one at a time, to one of their luxury cars; drop them in the trunk, and drive off the property. That would be nice; that would be the ideal for me.

Could I do it? Would it happen? One just never knew how something like this would turn out.

Chapter 19

I went in. Could hear the shower going through the closed bathroom door. Monica was in there. I stood there, and waited. Looked at the messed bed, and walked over. Leaned in, had my nose against the sheet-covered mattress, sniffing, taking hard sniffs; inhaling the aroma. I buried my face in it. Lifted my head; grabbed one of the sheets and held it to my mouth. Inhaled deeply. I could not get enough. And as I did it, I was acutely aware that this did not, in any way, help ease the pain in my nutsack caused by the blue balls.

So why then was I being such a *pervert*? Could not be helped. Too many years gone without pussy; too damned many years. Once again, I found myself entering the john, should the door be unlocked, and there was no reason for it to be locked, smacking her across the face or back of the skull with the mallet, and taking her right there in the shower; having my fill, then dragging her out to the bed, and leaving her there long enough to go take care of the other whore.

Would I? Did I dare? Was I a *rapo* at heart? No. Couldn't lower myself to the level of the rapos I'd met in the joint. Fucks were hated; rapos and pedophiles.

They got their asses kicked up and down the fucking yard. More than a few ended up getting shivved in the kidneys or guts. Left to bleed to death.

Fuck this kind of thinking. I was on a mission. Get to it. I did notice their panties on the carpeting. Picked those up, took my whiffs, and jammed them in my back pocket for later masturbatory fantasies. Why not? Jerking it was not a favorite thing, not after having done it for years in the joint, but it still beat sexual assault.

I was at the door to the john. Turned the knob, and went in. Shower was still going strong. I could see her body through the quasi clear shower curtain. The thing had flower patterns on it and it was the reason she hadn't picked up that I was there; that and the fact she was shampooing her hair and face.

I found the piece in her purse. Jammed it in my hip pocket. I reached out with my left hand toward the shower curtain, about to grab it and yank back, while the other that I held the mallet in rose and rose, above my head. This was going to be a beauty: a hard smack down swing that would knock her out and drop her to the bottom of the tub. Except the damned phone rang. And rang. Shit. It startled me. Threw me. I had to get out of there.

Chapter 20

I stood in the bedroom, just outside the john door, listening—as she talked on the phone. It was then I noticed I had failed, better yet, had not been able to close the john door after I'd stepped out. There hadn't been time. I heard her stop talking. It was then I thought I had better duck behind the bed. I hurried over to the far side, and dropped to my belly, just as she stuck her head out through the open bathroom door to take a look around. She must have realized it was odd. She must have thought she'd closed the door earlier, only to discover that it had been left ajar.

I heard her close the john door, and step back inside and continue her conversation on the phone. I had no idea how long she'd be on that damned phone, and got out of there. Walked down the corridor, to a door on my right, another bedroom, and went in. If I couldn't get Monica right now, I'd take care of that bitch Margie first, then return to fix her pal.

"Margie," I heard Monica call her co-conspirator through the closed bedroom door I'd just left. There was a door directly across the way, to a walk-in closet, and I ducked in there in time, leaving the door ajar from fear the noise it would make if I'd attempted to close it. Monica called her 'wife's' name again, as she walked down the hallway to the room Margie was in. I listened intently.

"Phone call for you, Margie hon."

Monica stuck her head into the bedroom, then she returned to the bedroom she had come from. Closed the door.

I eased out of the closet. Entered Margie's room. Neat, clean. Framed pics. All sorts. Friends and family members. Some of her stepfather Mario. Even one or two of Rinelle.

I walked up to the closed bathroom door. Could hear Margie talking on the phone through the noise caused by the shower. She hung up the phone eventually, then stepped in the shower. I had my hand on the door knob, and turned it, attempting to get in there. Only the door was locked. *Locked.* Fuck.

I had a choice, force it in—and risk getting shot—or show some patience? I'd waited this long, what was a while longer? What difference would it make? I'd get them; I knew this for a fact. I'd get both bitches and make them pay. Only I wanted to get in there so bad I could taste it.

I'd had lousy luck in getting to Monica, now I was experiencing the same kind of bullshit with her cunt roommate.

At least I had one of their guns; I had Monica's weapon. All I had to do was get Margie's. That would be it. Unless they had a few more lying around. Just never knew with these modern day violent femmes who loved guns. It was like fucking Annie Oakley or something. Broads never used to go for guns, unless they were old and wrinkled; now those bitches usually packed, on account they had no choice, but these younger babes never did. This was a new one; modern day obstacles for homeys like me to have to deal with. I didn't like it; didn't care for it—but there it was.

Chapter 21

Made me wonder who they'd been talking to? Who else was on the way besides Monica's son Modigliani and Lucy? Grozewski and his boyfriend and their protege Bix? I didn't know; hadn't been able to make out the phone chats through the closed doors.

What now? Take the one out? Monica, and risk undue trouble when Margie starts looking for her? I wanted both—with as little risk as possible. Not only did I want both, but I had to have Grozewski as well. I needed the trio. All three—or nothing. I didn't expect to get Grozewski while here, but at the least, I needed to get the two bitches.

This was a situation now. Also, it occurred to me, Monica would eventually realize that her gun was missing.

I decided to get the fuck out of the bedroom, especially when I heard Monica's bedroom door open again, and Monica calling Margie's name.

I was in the kitchen part, standing there, waiting, listening.

"You take my gun?" They were in Margie's bedroom now. I could hear them both plain enough.

"Your gun? Why would I do that? Why would I even go in your purse? You know we don't do that sort of thing around here."

"Oh, God. This is not good."

"What are you saying?"

"I am saying I am not in the habit of misplacing my guns."

"Could it be possible that this time —"

"No, Margie."

"Okay. What about your keys? You don't recall what happened there, am I right?"

Both were quiet during the next moment, silent. Then I heard a noise like a safe being opened, a gun being cocked. Shit. All I needed; two suspicious ballbusters with loaded guns.

I could have easily shot it out with them, traded bullets and vamoosed. But I didn't want it that way. It would have alerted Bruno, and *Valley Five-0*, and the hunt for an ex-con named Alfred Lester Reed would have been on, pronto. All points bulletin. Get the lowlife scumbag.

I had no choice, but to get out. Scram. Now. The only way I saw it. No way was I giving up. Merely postponing my plans for payback.

As I made it through the kitchen and reached for the side door, I thought: hold on. Just a second here. Kitchen was spotless, counters clean, not a single dirty dish in the sink. To cause them both a bit of confusion, I decided to leave Monica's piece right there on the counter next to the toaster and the knife rack, right after I hit the clip release and pocketed that, including the round in the chamber.

Sure. Let them mull that one over. Then I reached for the door handle to the large fridge, opened it. Jerked it and shot sperm into the 2% carton of milk. Shook it. Returned it. Then I pissed into the OJ. Shook the bottle some. The encore remained. I dug inside my jacket pocket for the narrow jar of *antifreeze*. Uncapped it, poured enough antifreeze into the wine that was the same shade of rosy red. They had a few bottles in there, all types: white, whatnot. Wine drinkers. Monica always was. Now we were all *triple-threats*, were we not?

I zipped up. Helped myself to a can of *V-8* juice, stepped through a doorway on my left that took me into the laundry room, then made an immediate right. Opened the door there, and stepped outside.

Chapter 22

I made it down the stoop. Pressed my body against the side of the house and drank from the *V-8* can. I waited and listened. Margie was in the kitchen. I knew it was her because I could hear her call Monica's name.

"I want you to see something, honey. *Monica?*"

After a while I heard the other ho.

"No way."

"You never misplace your guns?"

"There is no way I left it there, Margie. It was in my purse, I tell you. *In my purse.* My gun never leaves my purse, unless I intend to use it; as well as when we're at the shooting range. *You know this.*"

"It's possible it was right there all along, honey."

"Something weird is going on. The hallway carpet has some grass and gravel on it that wasn't there before, Marge. Something strange is happening."

"Or else it could be a simple case of mild paranoia."

"This is not funny. Not to me. Not funny at all. My *Glock* did not leave my purse on its own to end up on the kitchen counter. Something is seriously the matter here."

"When you figure out what it is, can you please clue me in?"

"I want to check the grounds."

"Before you do that, better check your Glock to make sure it's loaded."

"You know it's loaded. No point in keeping a gun in my purse unless it's loaded."

"Just check."

Sounded like Monica did.

"Shit. What the fuck is going on? *The clip is gone.* First my keys disappear, now this."

That was the last bit I heard, because I got out of there. Made my way toward the back, all the while thinking: Yes. Let them mull it over.

Garage looked pretty large to me. Big enough for four vehicles. That's what was in there: two M. Benzes, a Vette; one big ass SUV. I needed to find a place to hide out for a while. Maybe for the rest of the night.

Chapter 23

Monica cased the grounds: gun in one hand, flashlight in the other. I could have easily wasted her, then gone inside and taken care of the other twat.

What stopped me? What kept me from doing it? Her son. I didn't want him to see his mother in the kind of condition I was determined to leave her in. Nothing more to it than that. I wasn't about to spread misery beyond my payback plan. So you see, the FBI pros, and other profilers, have it all wrong. Not all anti-social types are alike; not all of us kill in the same manner or for the same reason.

Was it blood lust? To a certain degree. In this case. Some of that in there. And because of my attitude, I couldn't do anything to her . . . unless she left me no choice. Unless it came down to: *her or me*. And if I got cornered, was left without a way out, I'd have to put her butt in the effing ground. Then take care of Margie. And that still would have left fat ass Bruno to deal with.

The other thing that made it worse: I didn't want to have to go back to the dishwashing job; I didn't want to have to listen to any more talk of movies and casting and budgets and locations; I didn't want to have to listen to them talk about how they needed to *'tailor the story'* in order for the movie to work. My own demise would've been easier to take than having to return to *Pinocchio's Pasta*. And I was determined not to. I had no idea how I was going to stick with this resolve, all I knew I was determined.

I kept peeking from behind the SUV. Monica walked cautiously, aiming that flashlight from side to side of the vast yard: the pool area, lounge chairs, barbecue. Then the door opened, and the other lesbian was out, Margie. Had her gun with her, a flashlight. So now I had both to contend with. What chance did I have of getting out without having to put them in the ground right here in their own backyard? And when would Monica's son and his girlfriend show? Wasn't it about time? And who else was on the way? Grozewski and his boyfriend? And that actor they called Bix Dixon?

I had no idea; all I knew was these backstabbing bitches that I hated and loathed and despised were bound to locate my hiding place. As if I didn't have enough to cope with, more gas was struggling to escape my rectum. I needed to fart. Holding one or two farts back, without major consequences was possible, but when you had a series struggling to leave your asshole, it became a pain.

What the fuck was I going to do? Not only about the gas, but the armed bitches who were ready to shoot on sight? They knew how to use those effing rods; I saw the paper targets from the indoor range. They hit the Bull's eye more often than not. Far better shots than me. It was not easy to admit, but hell, it was true. And a guy with a black ski mask on, and the rest of him in black attire, was not about to be mistaken for Saint Nick, especially not this time of year.

I couldn't help it, and released another fart. And a beam of light, probably Monica's, drifted over to my part of the garage. Was I fucked? Would I have to open up? Kill them both, and the hell with the rest of it?

My biggest screwup, miscalculation, so far, since setting foot on the property, was not killing them while inside. This was going to be much tougher. A gun fight was sure to alert the neighbors, and *Five-0* would be on their way. And I'd have a much tougher time getting to Grozewski.

The beam of light shifted away from my area, and was on other parts of the garage.

"You heard that? Margie?"

"What was it?"

Monica said nothing.

"You just make sure you don't shoot me by mistake, Monica. Or the cats."

"*Cats?* Didn't know they were out."

"They got out. Or one did."

"Great."

"Just be careful."

Chapter 24

Either Margie's or her wife's cell went off. Sounded like Margie talking into hers. The cat they mentioned earlier walked past me, startling the holy shit out of me. Not having been able to determine what it was initially, I'd been ready to fill it full of holes. Could have been a raccoon, a dog, possum, anything. I'd had no idea. It was a good thing I'd have been able to keep calm.

Margie was talking. They were both a good distance away, but I could make out some of it. The damned cat walked back this way, and I was able to hiss at it. And it scampered off with a yowl. Then ran out of the garage, toward Monica. I could hear Monica give up a sigh of relief. She scooped the cat up in her arms and walked back toward the house.

"Bruno. Wants to know if it would be all right to stop by with Bix."

I could see Monica shake her head.

"Well?"

"I don't mind doing favors for people, Margie; helping out. . . . I just don't like having my arm twisted to cast someone in a role they're not qualified for."

"How do we know that he's not qualified?" Marge had the phone covered with her free palm, to keep the party at the other end from hearing what was being discussed.

"We've gone over this, Marge. I'm tired of it. It's getting late. My son is coming over. Why can't Bruno's friend stop by the production office instead? Say sometime tomorrow? Why does he need to bring him by here tonight?"

"Feels he would get lost in the shuffle. Hates cattle calls."

"It wouldn't be a *'cattle call.'* We don't treat people like cattle and never have. He can come in by himself and we can read him then."

"Can he at least stop by to pick up the sides?"

"He wants pages? Tonight?"

"So he can prepare, before we have him come in. Bruno is convinced this kid has real talent."

"Where have we heard that one before? Town's full of geniuses."

"Yes or no, Monica? I will go along with whatever you say on this. I can't keep him waiting all night."

I heard Monica curse under her breath.

"Okay. Have them stop by."

Margie spoke into her cell, then ended the conversation.

"Know what this is, don't you? Bruno hung up on another one. By giving him a break, he figures the kid owes him, and he's in his pants. And I get tired of it, Margie."

"Come on."

"How many times has he pulled this? He doesn't seem to give a damn that if an actor is wrong it can kill the movie. Shitty movies get made all the time, and this is just another reason why: *actors who can't fucking act.* I'm sick of it. And besides, looks like we're going to have to go back to producing porn for a while to replenish the coffers."

"I was afraid of that."

"See now why I get upset when Bruno pulls this shit?"

"You're also being unfair about him. He's brought us some pretty darn good people, too, over the years. Male and female talent."

"Know what? I'm tired of discussing it."

It was at this point that a tan van drove up to the wrought iron gate. Margie chin-gestured in its direction.

"Looks like Modi's here."

Chapter 25

The sliding gate alone looked like it must've cost a few grand by itself. Way more than the crappy van I owned, that was for sure. They were doing all right. I should've been impressed. Truth was very little impressed me at this point. That gate was on a rail and you could hear it crawling along, sliding open. There was Modi in the fancy van with the big ass mag wheels waiting for the gap to widen enough to drive through. It took a while, but the opening was finally adequate and the son drove on through and took the road in and pulled up to where Monica and Margie were waiting.

The driver climbed down. Modigliani was in his late 20s these days, a healthy looking, handsome dude. Chick magnet. Like I used to be. Way back when. A blond stepped down from the passenger side. She was in heels, long legs. Had some type of sexy dress on with a slit. Woman was stacked, from what I could tell.

I could hear Monica's son introduce the woman with him to his mother, then to Margie, and the four of them went in the house.

There was a door on my right with a sign on it that said: **Studio**. I hadn't noticed that before. I'd taken this part of the structure to be the guest house or maid's quarters, and maybe at one time it could have been—but the sign said it was a studio. It made sense, in that Monica and her partner were filmmakers. Well, let's say they were involved in it. To call them 'filmmakers' might be giving them more credit than they deserved. My take on it. The way I saw it.

I turned the knob, and went in. Turned my penlight on, and waved it around. Carefully, cautiously. There were video cameras on tripods, a Nagra audio recorder on a table and some other video-related equipment: slate boards, rolls of duct tape, markers. One section of the set-up was made up to look like a bedroom, in that there was a brass bed and three false walls. Wall on the left side, and one on the right. Plus the one directly behind the headboard. Front of the bedroom was wide open for camera access. There were some fake plants, framed crappy paintings, end tables, lamps. There was a unisex john to my right. I noticed a Coke machine. Your average kitchen type refrigerator. Had me wondering if there was anything edible in there. Also had me wondering if I might be able to hide out here for a while? Long enough to take care of business: hammer the trio in the skull, dump them in one of the vehicles and drive them out to the desert. This way I wouldn't have to return to the furnished room, wouldn't have to put in another day at the Pinocchio diner. Just stay here and take it easy. And if there wasn't enough food in this fridge, all I'd have to do is wait for the bitches to leave the house, and make myself at home. Eat their food, shit, shower and take it easy—all the while working out how to carry out what I needed. Work on perfecting the plan. Execute it when I was ready.

I walked over to the fridge. Had my hand on the door handle. And just as I was about to open the door, I heard voices approaching. The lot of them were walking up to the studio, not through the garage, but the other door that was in the front.

Shit. I had to scramble and hide. Where? I hadn't really had enough time to scope out this part of the joint. There were plenty of places to duck and hide, only I hadn't been able to consider; and now I did not have the needed time. So I dove under the bed. Crawled under and away, toward the back wall.

I'd remain balled up in my all black attire and wait to see what happened. If I got found out I got found out. I'd crawl out and let the fireworks commence. Fuck it.

The front door opened.

Chapter 26

Monica and Margie walked in. One of them flicked the light switch on the wall. The place lit up, everywhere but under the bed. I hoped so, anyway. I could see them, all of them; from their feet up to their heads.

For the time being. Once they started to walk toward the center the heads went, got cropped, then shoulders, and so on, until all I could see of them was from the feet up to as far as their knees, then even lower than that.

That blond with Modigliani was built like a brick shit house. She was a coed interested in doing adult flicks to pay her way through college, from what I gathered. Could be it was bull crap, but this was the line she stuck to. So Monica's kid was a procurer now, unless Lucy, the coed's name, was not a true girlfriend, instead merely Lay of the Week. Didn't matter. Because they were discussing her maybe doing a masturbation video at first, to see how she liked it. If she felt comfortable, then take it from there.

Monica was doing the talking. In charge. At least here. Playing the in-control director. Back in the bedroom with all those carnal antics, she was the slave, taking orders from Marge. Not here, not now.

"What do you think?"

Seemed she was asking the woman her son had introduced as Lucy earlier.

"I would like that."

"So long as it's understood: You will never be asked to do anything you're not comfortable with. I know certain unscrupulous types out there behave that way. We don't. Marge and I don't care for any of that underhanded bullshit that certain video companies like to pull on those new to the industry."

"That's what Modi was telling me. And that's exactly why I'm here. I feel good about the whole thing."

"Have you considered a stage name, honey?"

"Not really."

She asked where the woman was born.

"Anchorage."

"How does Lucy Ice sound to you?"

"Why not?"

"You will not be asked to fuck anyone you don't feel like fucking, Lucy Ice. You will not be asked to eat out anyone, blow anyone, you don't absolutely feel comfortable with. You need anything: like lube, to drink;

whatever, you don't hesitate to let us know. People who work for us, rather in our productions, are treated fairly and with respect every step of the way."

I got it. This foxy, hot cunt was going to take her clothes off and masturbate on the bed, and I wouldn't be able to see it. It bothered me; I think it bothered me even more than having to hide out in this chicken shit manner from the hoes I'd come to abduct and haul off to the pre-dug holes in the ground I had waiting out there for them.

Chapter 27

Okay. There were mirrors throughout the place, all types: on casters, framed, you name it, as well as other props. Mirrors made trick shots possible, as well as certain porn performers liked to watch themselves while fucking and/or chugging sperm. I understood; and just wished they'd taken the time to adjust one of those mirrors so that I might be able to watch this babe play with her tits and pussy.

But they were at it, and didn't give a shit about my needs one damned bit. Guess I was still human, after all; vengeful, blood lust on the brain, slaughter-bound—and yet I still wanted to see what was about to go down with this hottie and her steaming cunt.

They got some kind of easy beat going; the usual synthesizer porn mood music. Coed Lucy stood on the floor, doing a slow dance number. It was pretty much easy to surmise: swaying those hips from side to side, bending over, cupping those large hooters, and then squeezing them together. Only all I could see was the lower part of those tanned calves and the feet in those black stiletto heels. Her toenails had been painted with cherry red nail polish. Monica was giving gentle instructions: Turn this way, honey; now that way.

"Stick your tongue out, sweetie. Now lick your lips. Upper, then lower;

slowly . . . take your time. That's it; take your sweet time. You're making love to the camera. Actually you're getting the middle-aged jerk with the beer belly watching this horny as hell." Then she corrected herself. "I shouldn't be saying that." She laughed. "You're enticing a really hot, studly guy with a major boner right now. . . . Your hands are inside your upper thighs; gently, gradually, rubbing . . . not quite on your cookie, but near it, around it: above, along the sides, and below, but not on it . . . not yet. . . ."

They were destroying me. I couldn't see it, but it was easy to imagine what was going on. Then the thing I dreaded might happen was taking place: Monica was asking her to bend forward, all the way, and touch her ankles. . . . While the blond did this, I could see her face. . . . Had she been paying any attention at all, she would have spotted me, discovered me, and I would have been in deep *crapolla*.

Monica asked her to turn around, so that her ass was to the camera; run her hands up, up up along the sides of her legs, lift the dress up and over her buttocks, to reveal the thong panties. I couldn't see that; all I could make out was the back of the woman's head and all that blond hair hanging there.

"Slow, always, slowly run the palms of your hands over your buns . . . have them linger there. Gently, caressing your butt crack with the tips of your fingers. . . . Please take your time. Keep the tips of your fingers there, up and down, slowly, slowly. . . . Now, take that hand and rest it on your right hip. Take your other hand, and slide it from in front of your pelvis and gently rub the mound. . . . Rub the cloth over the pussy. . . . Rub it . . . rub it. . . ."

My cock was hard. There was no way to keep it from happening.

Chapter 28

She was done stripping and needed to take a pee break. That's what was heard. And me? I had a far worse problem: my bowels needed evacuating, on top of the gas situation. Yes, I needed to take a shit, bad. And there was no fucking way.

Some goddamn vengeful, tough-ass mofo. That was me. Stuck under a bed in a makeshift porn studio in somebody's backyard needing to take a dump—and not able to budge. Huh? While everyone else took their break, drinking *Perrier* or *Pepsi* or root beer. What?

They were discussing the second phase. What to do next. She was going to be inserting an impressive dildo in her cunt, and maybe something up her butt, too. Some type of butt plug, something. And then, for phase three, they wanted her to shave her *vagina*. That was their word, not mine. I rarely use 'vagina' when talking about pussy. I prefer cunt, twat, beaver, snatch or snapper. Anything but vagina.

But yes, they were going to have her shave, especially if that effeminate actor friend of Bruno's was coming over. Maybe they could have him do a scene with this Lucy hottie. Maybe. Yes, the guy appeared in gay male films, but you never knew: it was possible he'd be able to get it up for Lucy. There were types who swung both ways: did men and babes. They'd have to see.

Lucy Ice was back. I could hear those high heels hitting parts of the cement floor. Some of the cement was covered with rugs, not all, but some of it, especially in and around the bed.

Monica's cell went off. She spoke into it. Bruno was at the gate. Somebody needed to go out there with a remote and let the man in. Modigliani volunteered. His mother handed him the remote and he left.

The music was back on. Lucy was on the bed. I could hear her writhing and moving about up there above me. Monica wanted sighs and moans, but nothing fake.

"Keep in mind, hon, less is more. Always, darling. *Less is more.* Tone it down. It can be intense, so long as you're feeling it and are able to convey this to us."

The whore's moans decreased, but the movement went on, the vibrator was humming.

"In and around the clit, sweetie; slowly, gently, mouth open; you're looking at the camera. . . . Look into the camera, not me, the camera. That's it, sweetie. Mouth stays open, head back some. . . . It's on the clit. It stays there. . . . Now, gradually, gradually . . . down, down, lower and lower, slide it inside. . . . Slowly, in . . . and slowly, out. . . . That's it. . . ."

The door opened, and in walked Bruno and his protege, the gay porn actor. Yes. Quite the stud: tall, dark and handsome. Only it's going to be interesting to see if he can get it up for this Lucy hottie. I wished I was in his shoes so I could fuck the shit out of her right now; jump her effing bones and drill her asshole, then her snatch, up into her mouth, and back down again . . . way inside that rectum. My dick was hard, and the gas wanted out; as did something else.

Now the talent was being told to reach for the butt vibrator and insert that up her shitter. Damn, I wanted to see this. It was a real bitch not being able to move, not being able to do something about it.

I could see Bruno and his boy Bix standing out there, expressionless. It didn't work for them. Big tits; sweet, tight twat meant nothing. Zippo. Zero. They were into something else. Effing Bruno's mind was on what this guy Bix was packing down there.

What a topsy-turvy world we lived in. A hot ho like Lucy up there probing her tight asshole with a vibrator, another in her moist cunt, and these guys were *nonplussed*. I didn't get it. I mean I did—but I really didn't.

How could they not be interested, at least to some degree? How was that possible? Bruno had even been married, with kids! Forget it, amigo. You ain't about to solve a damned thing.

Chapter 29

Lucy Ice was instructed to take the vibrator out of her cunt and slide it up across her belly, between her tits and up into her mouth. Run the tip of her tongue around the crown, always taking her time, then slide the thing into her mouth and suck on it.

"That's it, dear. Suck it. . . ."

After a while, it was back down at her pussy. She was instructed to turn over, on her knees, ass in the air, and continue . . . and take it home. Monica requested a prolonged and protracted orgasm, a series of them. She wanted Lucy's body to quake and quiver; she needed her to wince.

Lucy was wincing and something additional: gasping and groaning, moaning. I got the idea Monica was having her replay her very own orgasms back in the bedroom with her partner Margie—by proxy.

And then it was over. This part of it, anyway.

Monica thanked the girl, and suggested she was free to shower. Lucy walked off toward the john, and Monica and Margie turned to Bruno and his young pal Bix. Intros were made all around.

He was handed his sides from their upcoming crime drama 'loosely' based on my life, and given time to go over them, before doing a reading with either Margie or Monica, maybe even Modi.

Chapter 30

Lucy was back, still in those stiletto heels, and she had a white terrycloth, knee length robe on. Hair combed, lipstick red mouth, and smelling like tulips. She sat in one of the chairs at the far end, legs crossed, smoking a cigarette.

Bix seemed to be ready. He sat in a canvas chair across from Margie. Margie would be the one doing the scene with him. Monica was directing, as usual. Her son was running the camera. They were videotaping the reading.

Well, Bix delivered his lines and he was so effing bad that I nearly cursed out loud and jumped out from under the bed. Fuck this gay porn actor. *Fuck him.* He sucks. And I don't mean dick, either. Not this time. Can't act. And I didn't want him playing me. Period. He was awful. Just plain awful. Yes, it was merely a cold reading; I knew a bit about these things from having been around Monica and Margie listening to all the chatter at the diner; still, even I knew enough to know that the punk was a dud.

Yes; okay; he was probably hung like a rhino, but he couldn't act worth a shit. Get rid of him, I nearly blurted out. Tell him to take a hike. Now. Please. Please don't let him play me. Anyone but him. *Anyone.*

Chapter 31

The scene was over, thank god. Over. Even Monica, bless her, could see that the guy was no good. As an actor, anyway. So did Margie; so did everyone in the room except Bruno.

"What do you think, Monica?"

People were quiet. This was the way it went when someone was lousy; didn't have it. Bruno needed his answer. Reminded Monica she ought to give him one.

"Well?"

"Bruno, you're a friend, a great friend. We've known each other for years . . . ."

"But what?"

"The best we can do is offer him video work."

"Porn? He's trying to get away from it. He wants to be a legitimate actor. That's why I brought him over. I thought you'd understand."

"I do. We do."

"Who's *'we'*?"

"Margie and I."

"I don't hear Margie saying anything."

"I back her, Bruno."

"Just like that. It's *cold reading*, for Christ's sake. He didn't even have a chance to prepare, Monica."

"You wanted it this way, Bruno."

"He's under pressure. This is real pressure here. Bix is good. I've seen him work. And I don't mean what he does in those smut videos. He's great in them; but I mean the kid, Bix, can act. I think he's a real thespian. Maybe not in Olivier's league, or Brando's, but in there somewhere, for sure."

"You see, exactly why I was against this. I did not want this, my friend. Bruno, this is no good; this is not right. Sorry, Bix."

The fat man sighed. Yes, Bix didn't look happy, but whose fault was that? He had talent in a different area. Let it go at that. Should have been pleased. I mean, the motherfucker had a big dick, from all accounts. Be happy. I wasn't small myself; wasn't huge, but this guy certainly had to have more than me. So why not take it and cheer up? Make your money, if you're doing smut, or else get the fuck out and go deliver pizza or wash dishes. I did it; many of the dead-end, low-wage shit jobs. In and out of prison. Was he too good? Evidently.

Margie had an idea: why didn't they take a break? Go in the house and have a sandwich, a cocktail, and talk it over like adults?

Yes, I said. To myself.

Chapter 32

As soon as they left, turned out the light, I was out from under that bed and rushing into the john. Dropped my pants and shat like a champ. Goddamn. What a relief.

I mean, yes, sex was great, and love was great (the rare times it worked) and other things were great and mattered, but if you couldn't take a shit when you really needed to, you were effing dead. Same thing if you couldn't whiz. I remembered what Graham went through at the VA that time. Stuck in a nightmare of escalating agony. So, this was the best break I'd had in a while: being able to empty my bowels and ponder my next move.

There was a shelf, 20 feet wide or something and looked about 6 ft. deep, right above the bed, where a bunch of props were kept. A wooden ladder ran up from the floor along the right side wall. What if I explored that part of the studio to see if I could find a place to hide out for the time being?

I wiped, showered, got into my skins. There were toothbrushes there, but I didn't dare use any of them. Hey, they had effing porn stars in this place, peeps who licked each other's cornholes—and I sure as hell was not about to use a toothbrush used by these mooks.

I pulled the ski mask over my face and stepped out of the john. My belly reminded me I was both: hungry and thirsty. I was back at the fridge. I didn't care for Perrier, but that was what was in there, so I grabbed a bottle, uncapped it, and took a long pull. There was a brick of Swiss cheese wrapped in plastic that looked inviting. I grabbed it, tore the plastic cover off and took a bite. A couple of slices of bread would've been perfect, but you can't have everything. Cheese hit the spot. I chased it with another pull of Perrier.

I walked over to the ladder. Paused there. Looking up at the shelf. Could it hold me? Could the shelf support my weight? On top of all else that was up there? And what if one of them should appear looking for something, dildos and whatnot, and discovered my ass hiding in there? Simple: they'd get their ass shot off. Bang bang. No worry.

I could hear them out there, walking up to the door. What choice did I have? Back under the bed, or upstairs? I'd had enough of being under the damned bed like a rodent, and climbed up that ladder as fast as I was able.

The door opened and the bunch entered. I ducked down, crawled along the creaking, dust and cobweb covered boards to a spot behind a cardboard box full of all sorts of porn paraphernalia and froze and hoped the racket I'd made hadn't been heard by them.

Chapter 33

If I'd thought I was in a precarious situation, and no doubt, I was: concerned that the boards might not be able to support my weight, or that if I moved so much as an inch, the creaking would alert the Hollywood geniuses below—someone else was experiencing a far greater dilemma. The big, bad stud horse couldn't perform. He got out of that robe he had on, stood there: 6ft 3, 18-inch arms, narrow waist, washboard abs; all that, plus the thick hunk of meat, and he couldn't get it up. Had to hand it to Bruno, though, in that he never wavered in his support.

"Give him a chance."

So they did. Let him climb on the bed and try to make it with the voluptuous Lucy. Margie and Modi videotaped what was taking place. Only not much was going on, in that the 'Great Adonis' Bix Dixon stayed limp.

Monica was cursing under her breath. Bruno was about to open his mouth again, and she raised her hand to tell him to zip it. But they continued taping. This bastard couldn't even fake liking to lick pussy. *WTF?* I could see the expression of disgust on his face. What kind of porn actor can't even fake liking beaver and tits? Lucy was frustrated. Took offense. Who could blame her? Not I.

Finally Bix Nix (what his name should have been) sat up, apologizing.

"I'm sorry. I truly am sorry, Ms. Gooch. I wanted so much to do my best for you, for my friend Bruno. I . . ." He shook his head, and began to cry. His face in his hands and he wept.

Fuck. I felt sorry for the gay Terminator. I did. What could you do? Pussy was not his thing. Some men, like this stud, were into dick. Dudes. Cock and balls.

Someone handed him a tissue. I think it was Monica, who walked over and put her arm around his shoulders.

"Now, now. . . . None of that."

She walked him away from the bed, and for something to do, they resumed shooting more footy of Lucy jerking herself. Yes, get as much as we can of this young ingenue, and the goddamned boards beneath me, even though I hadn't moved a fraction of an inch, cracked by degrees and gave, and down I dropped, right beside the blond bimbo; and the legs on the bed broke, and the bed hit the floor. Miraculously enough, I'd managed to hold on to the Perrier and Swiss cheese. Proved how empty my belly was. And for lack of a better idea, as I was stunned myself, just as Lucy and everyone else was, I rolled over and dug my face between Lucy's thighs and began lapping cunt as if my life depended on it. Because it did. I was scared shitless—but there was nothing else I could think of.

Lucy had screamed and screamed some more. Monica, had the situation under control, and demanded that her son and Margie continue filming. She was acting as though the whole thing had been planned.

"Remember, hon: *less is more*. You're doing just great, Lucy. Keep doing what you're doing."

Lucy settled down, and her moans by this point were genuine, because I'd pulled the ski mask back, off of my face, and was eating the hell out of her. I was desperate, and what kept me desperate was knowing that both Margie and Monica were packin'. And I had no idea how I was going to talk my way out of this.

Chapter 34

The young ingenue was orgasming, one after another. Enough of that, I thought. I needed to get mine, and I maneuvered myself up toward her mouth, slid it in there. Fuck it. If I was busted, I might as well bust a nut.

She went to it. Dumb blond college bimbo, was sucking with enthusiasm. And they were getting it on tape. That was all that mattered; and I knew I'd have to have some kind of explanation when it was all over. What was I going to say? I had no idea, either.

I made sure Ms. Ice didn't overlook a bit of the region. I had a bite of that Swiss cheese, pulled on the bottle. She worked the helmet. Ran her tongue over and circled. Now, I thought. Here it is: I'm blasting. A Fred Reed *tsunami*. I unloaded. And kept going. The ingenue was desperate for this job and future work, and never wavered on the enthusiasm. Good. Great.

I screamed. It was amazing. Nearly choking on the chunk of cheese in my throat. Managed to recover. When I looked up, I could see that Bruno was too pissed to appreciate what had just taken place. He and his young stud muffin walked to the door and were gone. The scene was over. Lucy asked the director for permission to shower.

"Of course, darling."

Monica waited for the girl to go in the john, then turned to me. I made a half-hearted attempt to pull the mask back down, but it didn't work. She had her gun in her fist, so did Margie.

"Now, who the fuck are you, buster? And what the fuck are you doing hiding out in our studio?"

I was ordered to ditch the ski mask. Did that. Then pulled down my collar, to reveal the prison neck scar. Silently requested pen and paper in order to write. Was given it, and I jotted down that I had been desperate to break into porn and thought this would be the only way that I could show that I was capable; I was also homeless, and finally asked for their forgiveness.

Due to the heavy beard, and deep sunburn, they hadn't been able to figure out who I was, or could they? I figured it wouldn't be long before they finally got it. Of course, if they didn't, there was always Monica's son, who might. True enough, I'd met him years ago and the kid had been in his early teens back then and we had spent next to zero time in each other's company the times he came by to visit his mother, still. . . .

"You're good, did a nice job there, but who are you? We still need to know who you are, what your background is, before we can even consider signing you. You can't just walk in off the street and expect to be hired."

Margie was shaking her head. "Fuck all that." She demanded to see some ID.

I was screwed.

Lucy emerged from the restroom, and I pleaded for them to let me use the john, that I desperately needed to take a leak. They couldn't refuse me. I had some more of that Perrier, another bite of cheese, and placed both gingerly on the night stand. Gesturing with my hands, I promised I'd answer all of their questions right after I took care of business in the john.

Chapter 35

I hurried in there, opened the small window, and crawled through. It was a task, because these things are usually narrow. But I managed somehow. The only thought on my mind was to get to the wall, scale it, and jump to the other side and scram.

I got to the top, when I heard them yelling for me to stop. All were out. Margie and Monica aiming those Glocks. Would they fire? *They wouldn't; they couldn't.* Neighbors would hear the shots and call the bulls. This would not make them popular. Add the fact you're making porn in a residential neighborhood. Not against the law necessarily. It was private property after all, but just a bit uncouth—even in uber liberal Porn Valley. About the only thing that kept my ass from taking a bullet. These wenches were good shots. I made it over.

"We don't want to wake the neighbors." It was Margie. Reminding her wife.

"It was him."

"You sure?"

"It's fucking Fred! It was him!"

"But the beard. I couldn't tell. I mean there was something about him but I . . . I don't know. . . ."

"Call Valley PD. The asshole is back. He's the dishwasher at *Pinocchio's.*"

"Redd Dogg?"

"Yes."

"Exactly! That's why that face looked familiar."

"He was there all those times, ever since his release, snooping around, scheming how to get in here, cause us trouble."

"He said he had no place to go."

"He also claimed he couldn't speak. When you and I both know he can. Sounded hoarse, caused by whatever happened to him in prison, but we both heard him talk in the diner, Margie. *You know we did!*"

"Why did he have to come by here? Why couldn't he stay away and leave us be? We want nothing to do with him and he knows this. And yet, he had enough balls to come by and harass us. Unreal. The way he fell through the boards like that. *Fucking too much.*"

"We better stock up on ammo. With that asshole around. He's trouble; always has been. He'll do his best to turn our lives upside down. I know him. What did I tell you about his vindictive nature? He holds a grudge. He's blaming us for his problems. All the problems he caused for himself, all the trouble and prison term that he brought on himself. Blames us for it. That's why he's here."

I was on the other side of the wall, waiting, listening, to see what else they would do. The only one doing the talking now was Monica, into her cell phone, telling the police operator to send cops over; they had a break-in. She gave the address. I decided it was time to get out of the area.

Chapter 36

It was going to be a lot tougher now to carry out what I had in store for the bitches. It didn't mean I couldn't pull it off, just that it would be a real task to carry out.

When I looked up, Bruno's car was still sitting there at the curb, Bix Nix crying. Bruno doing his best to calm him down. He was rubbing the back of his neck. Bix was actually crying in the other man's shoulder. Sobbing like a baby. What the hell kind of man was this? All that muscle, major tubesteak; thick neck, Mr. Olympia physique, and he was blubbering like a baby, because he hadn't been able to get it up to shag that bimbo back there.

What was I going to do now? Walk away? Pass up the opportunity to deep-six Grozewski? Here he was. *Right in front of me. I had him.* But if I took care of him, wasted his sorry ass, Bix was a witness. I'd have to take him out, too. And I didn't want to do that. I knew I'd hate myself if I killed the punk. Punk had done nothing to me. Absolutely nothing. In fact, I had him to thank for making it possible for me to lay that blond hottie back there. It was true. If he'd been able to get it up, I would have been fucked. Big time.

What was I going to do? Rollers were on their way. *Rollers.* And I had Bruno sitting in his car no more than thirty feet from me. They had no idea I was behind them, crouching next to a parked car, gun in hand. Waiting. Deciding what to do.

The whole thing made me ill. I didn't want to take out an innocent bystander's life. I didn't. So help me. This was not me.

Would I? Was I going to? What choice did I have?

Anyone reading this is going to say: *Reed killed the guy because he was gay.* Didn't matter that it wasn't true. This is what they would be saying. He killed the guy out of jealousy; because the sissy had a big dick and the looks and body—and Freddie hated that about him, and wasted his ass.

It was a dilemma, in a long life of dilemmas. One after another. Waste Bix Dixon, and have Bruno drive us out to the pre-dug graves; chain him to a tree out there by the shack, bring the two wenches out, then turn them loose, wrists cuffed behind their backs, turn them loose and let them take off. Well, I wouldn't cuff the wenches' wrists behind their backs probably, cuff them, not together, but leave the cuffs on. But in Grozewski's case, cuff his behind his back, and let the fat *tub-of-shit* try to outrun me this way.

Bix was crying still. And Bruno was the comforting Daddy. He had the hots for the young stud with the impressive *chorizo*, but now he was being extra supportive.

Shoot him. Shoot Bix, and get it over with, and hit the road with Grozewski. Do it. Just do it. Time is running out. Rollers are on the way. You have no time to lose. None. Get it over with.

I was scared. Sick to my belly and scared. Because of what I was about to do.

Chapter 37

What I really wanted was to go back in there, grab the rest of them: Monica, Margie, Modi and the dippy blond. Get them all. Take them with. Out to the desert and deal with them out there. Because if I didn't, Monica and Margie would blab about me to the rollers. And if it got out, if my name got mentioned, they'd be after me. There would be nowhere to run after that. A former pig (Grozewski) iced, and how many people all told? Bix, Modi, Margie, Lucy and Monica? How many was that? I was too nervous to count, add 'em up. I had to make my move.

And if I did go in, how was I going to get the bitches to drop their guns? Couldn't be done. Not this way. There had to be something, a move I hadn't thought of, a move that hadn't occurred to me.

Chapter 38

The gate was sliding open, and Monica stepped through, and walked over to Bruno's car, driver's side. She still had that roscoe in her hand, and kept looking around while addressing one annoyed Grozewski.

"You didn't happen to see him? He leapt over the wall back there."

"Who are we talking about?"

"Who did I say?"

"Fred Reed? What makes you think he's even in California?"

"It was him, I tell you."

"Bullshit, Monica! See what you and Margie have done to *him?"* Grozewski was indicating his pal Bix. "He's distraught, so distraught— and for what? You couldn't give him a break. The one person who desperately needs a break. You shot him down without so much as a real chance."

"He couldn't get it up, Bruno. Why lay blame on me and Margie? You saw it. And you also saw Redd Dogg—*Freddie,* rather—jump her bones like a thoroughbred; never having appeared in a porn video in his life. Why? Because he enjoys fucking women. Your friend here—no offense, Bix—is used to shagging men. Nothing the matter with it. We can offer him work in our next all-male epic. Only there is no way he's playing Fred Reed in our mainstream version of what took place there."

"This is too much. You're obsessed with him, you and Margie. Can't seem to get Fred Reed out of your system. Doesn't matter that he's been away, locked up, behind bars all these years. You never heard from him; he never badgered either of you, but you insist on bringing his name up. Make the film, but stop imagining things. I don't need you to pretend that he's on the premises, simply to cover up the fact that you and Margie were rude to my friend. You broke his heart in there; and owe him an apology."

"Fuck you, Bruno!" Margie had walked up. "That goes for your boyfriend there: Bix!" She held up her middle finger. "Monica is too nice, but I'm not. Here! *Fuck the both of you!* I saw him with my own eyes; and

she's not imagining anything! Freddie, the certified *nut-job asshole* is back! To cause us trouble. And if I were you I'd watch it. Keep this in mind: You were just as responsible for sending him up the creek. The three of us had an equal hand in it. You want to pretend it didn't happen, go right ahead. We're taking extra precaution, because we remember what he's like; what he's about! And what he's about is *payback*! That's why he was hiding out in the studio."

"He's been in the house." Monica was getting her two cents in. "*Sniffing around.* Took the Glock that I keep in my purse, changed his mind and left it on the kitchen counter, *after he'd taken the bullets out. That's not something I imagined or made up. We're giving you facts, Bruno.* Take heed. Cops are on the way."

"You called Valley PD?" From the way he reacted it sounded like he felt they were wasting their time. They wouldn't answer. "Wouldn't hold my breath."

According to Monica, they were definitely on their way.

"Knowing how they work, you'll be lucky if they get here under two hours."

"We'll wait."

Chapter 39

"It just occurred to me, he never signed a release."

"What are you talking about, Margie?"

"Fred never signed. We can't use the scene we just shot with him unless he signs a release; otherwise we risk getting sued."

"At a time like this, Marge? You're bringing this up? Who cares about a goddamned release, hon? We use it. If he decides to pursue legal action, let him. He hasn't got a pot to piss in. How's he going to retain a lawyer? Besides, all he has to do is come in to get compensated. And we get him to sign when he does—and have him thrown back in jail where he belongs."

Grozewski's cell went off. I couldn't make it out exactly, but it didn't sound pleasant. I was guessing his live-in roomie Percy was pissed because Bruno was spending too much time with Bix Dixon.

"He was tested. Yes, they read him, Percy. Then he did a scene with this *'ingenue.'* Well, tried to. It was a flop." Then: "What am I still doing here? It's a long story that I don't feel like getting into." Bruno stopped talking to do some listening. For a moment. "He took it hard, Percy. Real hard. When am I coming home?" His eyes were on Monica and her roomie. "Are we staying, or are we leaving, ladies?"

Monica and Margie looked at each other.

"He'd like a chance to make a couple of bucks. Main reason we're here. The least you can do to help out; after what he's just been put through. He's flat broke, why Percival and I let him stay with us. Can you please put something together, Monica?"

"Now?"

"I realize it's short notice."

"After all that's happened? You want us to put something together right now? At this hour?"

"Please? Would you consider it? For old time's sake."

Monica sighed, then shook her head. She cursed under her breath.

"We can try. Sure."

Bruno was back on his cell, relaying this info to his partner at the other end.

Chapter 40

I needed to climb back over the wall. About the only option I had at this juncture. If I attempted to hightail it on foot in a quiet residential neighborhood like this where no one walked, I'd get bagged for sure. It would take a while to get to where I'd left my ride parked with Payback in it. Rollers were on their way. Get back on the property, hide out, and wait for the opportunity to make my move.

Grozewski and his protege had stepped out of Bruno's car. He'd given the kid a Kleenex to wipe his eyes with, then a comb, while talking on his cell. Sounded like he was communicating with some of his piggy buds at Valley *Five-0* headquarters.

Monica had walked away, and was waiting by the gate. So had Margie, until she heard what the former piggy was saying to the party on the other end.

"Just what do you think you're doing, you fat fuck?" Margie was the one doing the screaming. Like mother/like daughter. She walked up to his side of the car.

"Calling them off, Marge. We can't have cops coming around when we're getting ready to shoot a gang-bang."

"Who gave you permission? Who gave you the okay? We had our home invaded by a stalker, goddamn you! What is your problem? Are you that fucking dense?"

He looked at Monica, who walked up.

"You want cops coming around now? After what we decided to go ahead with?"

The dick-obsessed former piggy couldn't wait to see his protege get reamed by a gang of thugs with large tools. Didn't give a rat's ass about anything else. He couldn't get into the Idaho spud's crapper, so he'd settle for the next best thing: watch him get drilled by others. Effing lowlife. This was the *bottom-feeder* who sent me up. Made my life a living hell for helping get rid of another *bottom-feeder* named Frank Graham. Go figure. Better yet: don't figure. Anything.

I still needed to get back over that wall, and hide out somewhere. I needed to nail the bitches, nab them, and bury them. Those shallow graves were waiting. Hated to see all that hard work it took to dig the holes go to waste.

"Your call, Monica."

"No one gave you permission to cancel the police. It would only make sense to have them at least write up a report of the incident."

"No need to have them show for that. I'm saying this as a former detective: on the force here, as well as in the Midwest. All you—and Margie—do is drive to the station in the morning and fill out a report. But if you do that, he'll never sign the release. Up to you. It's still not a good idea to have cops stopping by for this. It really isn't. They'll talk to your neighbors. It's negative publicity you don't need at this point. You've had enough of that, don't you think?"

Monica stood there, staring/glaring at him, as did Margie. It looked like they'd had it with this portly loser. It seemed they were finally, at last, seeing him for what he truly was: dipstick idiot of a has-been fat fuck doughnut eater. I could have told them as much. Look what he was doing, just to see the young stud take prick up his rectum and/or see him suck pipe; chug sperm. It made you sick. At least it did me. I hoped I didn't have to see it. If I had to hide out on the property, I hoped it wouldn't have to be back in the studio.

Margie was in his face. "All this, just to get your *jollies.* That's it, isn't Bruno? You motherfucker. Explains why you and Frank were so close. Explains why he never had any lead left for me when he got home, after spending time with you."

"Now, wait just a minute. No need to be disrespectful here. I thought we were friends."

"With friends like you, who needs vipers?"

I recalled the line. Used by Graham in his tête-à-tête with Rinelle that time, years before. Monica was quick to second what Margie just said. And Margie wasn't done. *"I read you like a book."*

"Cancel, or not?" Grozewski was looking at Monica. "Your call."

"At this point? *What difference does it make?* Freddie's long gone by now."

Chapter 41

I had climbed over the back wall and landed between it and back of the garage. I could hear them out there, in the front yard. I inched my way up alongside the far wall, peeking from behind a hedge. Percy, Bruno's boyfriend was the first to arrive, and the two were arguing. Jealousy. What it came down to. Bruno was spending too much time with the 'hero' from Idaho, and Percy didn't like it. It made him feel insecure, evidently.

"Just trying to help him get back on his feet, Percy."

"Not without me. You don't come over here and pull this shit without me! It was *agreed!* This is *betrayal,* Bruno!"

"Percival —"

"*Don't you Percival me!* It was *agreed*: You would not come over here without me! And you did exactly that! Now you're acting like you don't get why I'm pissed. *Give me a break!*"

"They were all here the whole time! Nothing 'sleazy' took place! Monica, Margie, Monica's son and that new girl: Lucy Ice, I believe her stage name is. All here. So why am I being chastised, Percy? It's uncalled for—and I refuse to take blame for something I'm not guilty of."

"This isn't the first time you've pulled this kind of shit, Bruno!" His partner was screeching. "Where is the *honesty? Trust!* This was supposed to be a *monogamous union* here!"

"It is."

"I don't like it. Furthermore, I refuse to take it."

"So you're willing to toss the relationship over a perceived slight, that it? You image a wrong was committed, and that's it? Flush the relationship away? Makes no sense. To flush away, what—8, almost 9 years? Why?"

"Because you can't be trusted!"

The other cocks-for-hire were showing up, pulling up in fancy wheels: Jeeps, Vettes, Benzos and what-not. One or two, of course, drove up in absolute junkers. Most of the bucks they made went up the ol' nose. Both Monica and Margie decided enough was enough of the sniping duo.

Monica was the first to put her foot down.

"This bickering needs to stop. And I mean right now."

"She's right." Margie couldn't wait to get in the fray, as usual. So much of the way she acted and the loud way she had of talking reminded me of her dead ho mamma. Rinelle. "Take it home; take it wherever you want, but not here. Not now or anytime, as a matter of fact. We've got work to do—and a positive atmosphere *is-a-must,* lest we give the wrong impression to the talent."

The bickering gay men couldn't/wouldn't stop.

"*Enough!* You're not putting the director on the spot. Shut-up, or get banned—for good. I mean it. There is work to be done. Monica needs to focus on that, and not your bullshit bickering."

"What bullshit?" Was it Percival? It was Percival. "It's not *'bullshit.'* This is my life! I've taken as much as I can off this two-faced fag!"

"Okay." Margie pointed a finger at him. "Get in your car and drive off. Leave. *You're gone.*"

"Wait —"

She held up her cell. "Percy, leave—or we call *Five-0. Now.* We've had it up to here."

Bruno's boyfriend cursed under his breath, got in his car, and pulled out.

The talent, five studs: white and black, climbed out of their vehicles. Couple of them dressed in suits, others casual: in jeans, shorts, etc. Bruno's eyes lit up. He went around glad-handing those he was familiar with, then he did the same bit with those he was *not* familiar with.

Chapter 42

I couldn't stick around. No matter how hard I tried to convince myself that I needed to. As curious as I was to see how many of these fucks would end up drinking the antifreeze, it just was not reason enough. My idea of a group-grope and/or gang-bang would have been: Monica, Margie and Lucy Ice and me. Or, if possible, a couple of other good-looking built wenches with tight *culos* and dripping wet twats, and not a bunch of low-life bottom-feeding Porn Valley mooks reaming and creaming all over a healthy looking and naive kid like Bix Dixon.

The only alternative to finding out who drank what, would be to return to Pinocchio's the next day and see who shows up. There was also that other incentive: money owed to me for the decent tongue job I laid on Lucy Ice. Sure. Why not? Money always talked. There were always ways to spend it. Didn't matter that you had a death wish and intended to check out. And who knew what Monica and Margie planned on doing with the scene? Make it part of some kind of anthology. Call it: *Daddy Knows Best.* Or: *Daddy Taught Me the Ins & Outs of Shagging.*

I didn't care what they named it or what they did with it. All I knew: If they wanted my autograph, they'd have to fork over some decent bread. And what if after I signed and got paid, Monica and Margie decided to press charges? Report my breaking into their place? I'd get what for that? Deny it? I could. It would be the two of them, against one of me. I'd lose. Would I get jail time for it?

No. There is the video footage that would 'prove' I'd gone in with permission. Even Grozewski had been under the impression the whole thing had been set up beforehand by Monica and her partner as backup, in case his boy Bix failed to deliver the groceries.

So what did I have to fear? Instead, I stood to gain: with the money I'd be able to buy a few more things, as well as food for Payback, and then give what remained of the money to someone to take care of him after I was gone. I scaled the wall and got out of there.

Chapter 43

It was a good thing, too, because when I got back to the van it was obvious my four-legged pal was eager to go for a walk. I grabbed the box of dog biscuit treats and off we went for a stroll in the ritzy neighborhood. It didn't take him long to go. We must've been in front of some rich showbiz mook's house when Payback decided to take a dump. It filled me with great joy to watch him drop a big load on the perfectly manicured lawn. Payback was in no hurry, either. It did not take long for some ancient fuck with uncombed, long hair, a reject from the 60s hippie era, in a bathrobe and slippers to come rushing out, waving his index finger, cursing at us. I looked up, calm as could be. So was Payback, releasing log after log. The pissed Tinseltown loon came on. I held my middle finger up, knowing it would only intensify his rage. Then when he got close enough, I drew my piece. That stopped him cold. His arms went up. Rich and spoiled, he still had gall to bitch, though. Fucking scumbag hippie must've been on a cocaine high. Had the red nostrils and sniffles.

"You got no idea how much it costs to keep this lawn looking like this. Dog urine destroys grass. Property value goes down when there's dog shit around."

"Is that so?"

"I'm in real estate. I'm telling you. Dog waste depreciates property. It's tough enough to keep it off the grounds as it is."

"I can think of one way to keep it off, asshole: *make you eat it*. If you're not back inside that over-priced cribby of yours by the count of three, that's exactly what you'll be doing: *ingesting* my dog's *turds*."

I started counting. Suddenly something made me stop. There was what appeared to be a joint stuck between a couple of his fingers, left hand.

"That a bong?"

"Cocoa puff."

He started to explain.

"Shut the fuck up."

I took a good hit, and commenced the countdown.

". . . One thousand one . . . one thousand two . . . one thousand . . ."

He was inside and slamming his door shut. I finished the bong, unzipped, and watered his grass like a 'Russian race horse.' What we used to say—as young punks—back in the Midwest whenever we had to take a leak: *"I gotta piss like a Russian race horse."*

Payback responded with his final opinion on the matter: one last log, and was ready to continue our stroll. I gave him a couple of dog biscuit treats, and we resumed our adventure through this high-toned hood.

Chapter 44

Yep. They were there the following night. Chipper. Smiling. Well, with the exception of Bruno's boyfriend. He especially didn't seem to be happy that Bix was sitting next to his soulmate Grozewski. I only refer to Bruno as being his roomie's 'soulmate' because that's the word his roomie kept using. Soulmate.

"I thought we were *soulmates*, Bruno."

"We remain so, Percy, honey."

Monica was looking at me, while I walked from table to table tossing plates into the plastic tub.

"Surprised to see you here. I must confess, Fred."

"Why is that?"

"Because of what took place last night."

"Exactly why I'm here. Somebody owes me a good chunk of cash. For services rendered."

She pulled out a contract, then waved a check. I went over to take a glance at the amount.

"You're joking."

"Three hundred is a fair amount for that scene."

"Twice that would be closer to what I had in mind."

Both Marge and Monica appeared to be taken aback.

"You wouldn't want to screw an old friend."

"We could've filed a report, but never did."

"Only because you liked the scene so much and needed me to sign on the dotted line, Monica."

Neither of the wenches said anything.

"Pay me what I'm worth, and we'll do a few more—and you've got yourself a series: older, handsome gent/younger wench hottie. Call it what you like, but I thought something along the lines of: *Daddy Was My First,* or else, call it: *Seduced by Uncle Sly.*"

"Five hundred." Monica's counter offer. She had come a long way since I knew her back in the day when she was a lowly secretary to Sonny Sheldon.

I stuck with six. Six seemed like a nice round number to stick with. I'd been a sucker too often in the past. I needed money. Dog food wasn't free, and neither was gasoline—and where I intended to take them was way the fuck out in the sticks, away from the city, miles and miles away. Besides, who was going to look after Payback? I'd talked to someone out there, a desert rat living in an RV who was willing to take him on after I was gone. I'd give the man what was left of the money for the dog's upkeep. Seemed like the right thing to do.

I kept moving about, performing my bussing duties. If I didn't get what I wanted, they didn't get my John Hancock. That simple. She waved a new check around. I insisted on cash. They scraped it together. This time I signed the release.

Chapter 45

"She'd like to do another scene with you." Monica was intent on talking some more shit, no doubt.

"Lucy. She's in love with you. Well, your tongue, anyway. You make love with such zeal. It was memorable for her."

"And for me. Only because I'd gone years without."

"What do you say?"

"If you and Margie joined in. For old time's sake." Why I'd said it I couldn't tell. Must have been half-joking. Better yet, fucking with them. To see what the dykes would come back with.

"We don't fuck males." It was the big mouth. Margie. Couldn't wait. Her loathing of the male runneth over. "Especially jerks named *Alf Reed.*"

She knew I didn't like being called Alf. I let that part go.

"Venom so thick you could cut it with a knife."

"Venom? *Venom?* Fuck you. You came back to disrupt our lives. Only reason you're not back in jail is because you're good at eating pussy; about the only thing you're good for. It saved your ass. You made some decent money for getting that young babe off. You're offered even more money for an opportunity to turn your life around and ditch this nothing shit job you got here; and what's your response? How do you react? Like the typical asshole we've always known you to be. Born loser. I can see this is a waste. Next time you break into our place, you're going down, fucker. You're effing toast. You don't set foot on our property unless we give you permission; unless you're invited! Get it, *chump?*"

"The '*chump*' gets it. I'd also like to point out that you're sending mixed messages. She wants me for another scene, and you want to send me back to Q., as if I didn't do enough time; as if I hadn't paid enough dues."

Margie was about to say something else. Monica placed her hand over hers, to calm her down.

"Margie, if your goal is to get me shit-canned, you're doing a pretty damned good job of it."

"You'll get shit-canned with or without our help."

"Will you do another scene with Lucy Ice?"

"Maybe. Toss in another hottie like her, someone stacked, with a great ass—and I just might consider it. For the right price."

I really was not interested in pursuing porn as a career. The only thing I was interested in was seeing the three '*triple-threats*' drop down into the graves that waited for them in the desert.

But if a scene, the possibility of another scene taking place on their property presented itself, and it seemed to be . . . I had a thought, well, the notion had actually occurred the night before, when I saw Monica's kid pull up in that fancy van: the perfect vehicle to carry the three out to the holes: Margie, Monica and Bruno. (Only because Modi's van was much nicer and had a good strong engine in it, as opposed to what was under the hood of my junker.) But yes, his van had made me think along those lines: knock them out, or wait until they consumed some of that antifreeze, carry them inside his van, and drive out. But then what about Modi? And whoever else happened to be there: what would I do about them? Take care of them somehow?

I knew Modi would be there; if Lucy was there, so would Modi be, as he appeared to be pimping the chick. Should it happen this way, what about Grozewski? What would I do there? I'd have to drive out to his place, knock his ass out, and carry him inside the van. This piggy weighed plenty. There had to be an easier way. *There had to be.*

Figure out how to get him back to Monica and Margie's studio. And the only way to do that, would be to have a reason for Bix to show. If Bix was there, it was almost guaranteed that so would be the former roller.

Chapter 46

The wine connoisseurs were drinking their wine and I wondered when the effect would take place, or would it be like before? Nada.

I was at the far end of the diner when I caught my first sign out of the corner of my eye that something was not right with our happy and ambitious Hollywood players. Monica was the first: stomach cramps. Nausea. It was beautiful to see. She had her arms crossed across her lower belly. Clutching that part. Not unlike Frank Graham whenever he took a sip of that 'healthy' raspberry iced tea from that thermos years before, not unlike yours truly that time I had my first and only sip upon Graham's insistence. Margie took notice and wondered what was up.

"What's the matter, sweetie?"

Monica appeared to be in a trance, not saying anything, just staring straight ahead. Not blinking even. I watched her wince; eyes closed.

"Oh God."

A sigh. One of discomfort. Clearly. Margie proceeded to pat her on the shoulder. Monica brushed her hand off, stood up and staggered to the john in a kind of hurry. Moments later one of the most beautiful sounds I ever heard was so loud that it hit all of us in the dining area.

Both Margie and Grozewski had a concerned look on their mugs. Yeah. Worry. I didn't recall them having these looks and/or expressions on their effing kissers when the judge threw the book at me. Oh no. Nothing remotely close to it. In fact, what I saw was smugness. Yessiree, Bobby. They were smug and pleased.

I wondered who would be next? I didn't have to wonder for long: because Margie was vomiting on the floor. Making grunts and pleading, once again, to a god who never existed, and vomiting her guts out.

If Monica's little turn of events was a joy to witness, this was better. Oh, this was way better. The loud mouth was making all kinds of loud noises and gasps. You'd have thought the over-the-hill shrew was dying. When in fact, there was no way. Not here; not now. Because I hadn't poured enough of that antifreeze into the bottle. Nope. Didn't want them to croak here. Merely wished to see them suffer a bit. Call it the *pre-death preview. Trailer.* Of things to come. They were in the film and tv business. Wasn't that what they called those things? Take a quick gander of features to come.

She rose, with Bruno's help, needing to get her to the john, only Bruno wasn't going anywhere himself, because he released a series of farts, and started not only vomiting, but was shitting his pants. Antifreeze had given him the runs. *Deja vu.* Where had I seen this before?

Oh, this was too beautiful for words. If only I could have had a video camera right now for this. Surely, I would have taped it—for posterity's sake.

Margie, bent over, staggered to the ladies' room. And Bruno? He couldn't budge, the diarrhea continued to run down his trousers. And his heartbroken boyfriend? Pleased as punch. So happy and thrilled. The look on his face saying: *You had it coming to you, two-timing faggot!*

"Shut up, Percy."

"I never said a word, honey."

"Just shut-up!"

Bruno didn't want to hear it, whatever it was. I watched him leap from the table and hurry to the men's room, farting every agonizing step of the way.

Chapter 47

The manager of the place, Aldo Picasso, finally came out to the dining area. I made like I was busy; and, frankly, I was: dirty plates and silverware needed to be collected and dumped in the plastic tub on my shoulder.

"What's happened here?"

Bix, the teetotaler, was shrugging. Percival could not give up that grin no matter how hard he tried. He shook his head like he gave a damn, but failed there as well.

"Something they ate. Or drank. They're in the john, puking their guts out. Bruno soiled himself. What a sorry state of affairs."

Aldo was speechless. What did this mean? Lawsuit? If not a lawsuit, it still meant plenty of trouble for Pinocchio's.

He walked over to me.

"Redd Dogg, can you tell me what's going on?"

Instead of going with his typical belligerent tone, he was using a hushed approach. Sounded almost human. It threw me momentarily.

"They doing drugs? Toot? That's it isn't it, Redd Dogg? Did you see them *snorting*? You can level with me."

I looked at him without saying a word.

"I'm talking to you, *Redd Dogg*. You give them drugs? That's it, isn't it? Didn't matter that you risked my job. I got a family, asshole. That don't mean shit to you."

"I didn't see anyone abusing illegal substances, Mr. Picasso. Besides, I was busy tending to my duties here: cleaning up, picking up plates."

"What'd they have to drink?"

"I don't know, sir. I never served them anything. That's not my job. That's the servers' job. I keep my nose out of other peoples' affairs."

"Bullshit. *Fucking transient.* Trouble-making *mook.* Should fire you on the spot. Got this feeling you're behind this somehow."

I said nothing.

"Only reason you're not fired is because I don't have all the facts. Once I put it all together, you're out of here, buddy. Like that other jerk I canned. Got that *Redd Dogg?* You're gone. Same as Henry. Buncha losers."

"Do what you gotta, Mr. Picasso."

I walked away with the full tub of dirty china and utensils. I heard him curse under his breath, then walk over to where the restrooms were and started calling their names in quick succession. Only nobody was answering.

Chapter 48

Good, I thought. Maybe the mothers are dead. All three of them. Save me the trouble of the rest of it. Sure, I'd feel short-changed, cheated—but what the fuck?

Only the assholes weren't dead, on account we could hear all three vomiting through the closed doors of the restrooms.

He knocked on the women's door. And I heard Margie scream. "Don't come in here, motherfucker! You got a lawsuit on your hands!"

"Lawsuit?"

"Food poisoning and tainted wine! You're in deep shit, mister! You're effed. Big time!"

Aldo said nothing. Sighed, then moved over to the men's room door. Went in. Bruno could be heard shitting up a storm. He had a super bad case of the runs. Sounded something like an elephant in there taking a violent and painful dump.

Oh, it was worth it. Wished I could stand beside them and watch and chuckle my ass off. Only I was glad that it wasn't possible. Bruno smelled up the joint. Bad. It was tough to take.

Aldo closed the door. Stepped away. Took a few steps toward the kitchen in back and froze, just froze, glaring at me. I pretended like I didn't notice, like I had my mind on work. Only I think he was smart enough to detect/pick up the smirk on my face. Not that I'm in the habit of smirking, or having anything like a smug look on, but this time, *this one time*, I believe I was the proud owner of both.

He pointed his index finger at me, and held it. I mean he just held it like that—without uttering so much as a syllable. Then just as suddenly, continued on to the kitchen.

Chapter 49

Did I actually care? Did I? I'll tell you how much I cared. I felt like dropping the tub full of dishes and forks and spoons and knives, instead I lowered it onto one of the tables, untied my apron, and casually unlocked the front door. That's when I stopped, and retraced my steps. I lifted that tub and spun with it, and watched all those plates and chunks of food and forks and knives and glasses go flying all over the floor and tables. I took my time walking back to the front door. I heard Aldo emerge from the kitchen.

"What the fuck, schmuck?"

My middle finger shot straight up, and I waved it around; then my other finger went up, and I waved them both—with a nice grin on my face to accompany the gestures.

"Kindly choke on excreta, punk, and expire."

"You cocksucker. Redd Dogg."

He moved toward me. In a real hurry like. Good, I thought. I reached for my shoulder rig, timing it. By the time he got to me the business end of my .357 Magnum was up against the hair in his nostrils. Pretty much ended his mobility.

"Now what, dick snot? Who you gonna *blow* to get out of this fix? *Who you gonna call?* Kojak? Go ahead, *punk*. Tell 'em I pitched your plates all over your grimy floor—on account your abuse was hard to take."

He kept his mouth shut. Scared shitless. Hell, I thought he might do a Bruno Grozewski number and take a dump in his panties. Only he didn't.

I stepped outside. Made it toward my ride. Oooh. If you've ever walked away from a soul-sapping shit job, you would know exactly how this felt.

Chapter 50

I got in that rattling junk heap of a van, affixed the muzzle to Payback's snout, politely requested that he keep his growling down to a minimum, and took it around to the front. Not near the entrance, but not so far away that I wouldn't be able to see who drove up to get the vomiting vermin.

I figured an ambulance would draw too much attention and result in negative publicity and Aldo would call a cab. And the cabbies I knew, had known, didn't like cleaning up vomit in the backseat. All I had to do was wait and see what happened.

A Valley cab eventually pulled up forty minutes later. Cabs around here took their time. And the Three Musketeers limped out, moaning and groaning, threatening to sue Pinocchio's. I reached for a camcorder and did my Bertolucci bit.

Bruno was still farting, you could easily hear it even from where I sat parked and watched the whole pathetic situation. Was there a taxi driver alive who would let a guy with stained pants get in his cab and soil the interior and ruin his night for him? Doubtful.

And then Margie, the biggest mouth in Porn Valley, had to pause to expel some more bile. She wiped with the back of her hand, cursing and screaming and wanting to know why there was no ambulance.

"He begged us not to . . ."

Monica's explanation was feeble, between wiping tears and snot from her face.

"Who the fuck is *'he'*, Monica?"

"Aldo. It would look bad."

"*Fuck Aldo! We* look bad! There must've been something in that lasagna, or the salad, or Caesar Dressing."

"The wine."

It was Grozewski's turn to groan. Tripped on his own feet. Bix came up from behind to hold him up.

Well, my cinema geniuses got as far as the cab's rear door, one of whom grabbed the door handle—only it wouldn't open. They tried again. Margie cursed, and demanded that the cabbie unlock it.

The driver stuck his head out through the rolled down passenger window.

"I don't take drunks. You peeps are dunk. And that gentleman there? Looks like he shit his pants."

"*You're not taking us?*" Margie stayed with the incredulous tone. Not that it got her anywhere. "We just want to get home. *You're refusing to take us?*"

"There's a big tip in it for you."

"Ain't a tip big enough to get me to take you, sir."

On that, the cabbie pulled away. Margie was cursing up a storm, like the Margie of old—and flipped him the bird. This was music to my ears. Scene gave me a certain satisfaction inside. Dirtbags. Self-centered, disgusting sacks of horse dung. I didn't blame the cabbie; I couldn't. I would've done the same, I thought, as I turned the key in the ignition and pulled up. I was still shooting video.

Chapter 51

"Get in, Margie."

"A human being. At last. Endangered species." She must not have recognized my voice right away, from what I gathered as a result of what I heard next.

"Is that you, Modigliani? *Modi?*"

The van did look enough like his. It was dark out. It was late.

"Sight for sore eyes." What she thought. Until she opened the passenger door, and then her expression changed. I lowered the camcorder.

"I'm here to help. Reconsidered your offer. You're right: Chance of a lifetime. Up to you, Margie."

She stayed put. I got out. Went around and slid the side door open for the others.

Bruno staggered in and plopped down on the mattress, followed by Monica. Margie remained standing. Undecided. I reached for the open passenger door and opened it wider in an effort to help her decide.

She finally went for it. Climbed in. I closed her door. Even managed a smile while doing it. Bix slid the side door closed without climbing in himself. I guess he'd had enough of it: the puke, stench, screaming and cursing. For all of his prowess in the sack, as a gay stud, he was a mild-mannered type—and who could blame him? In fact, I was okay with Mr. Bix Dixon not going along. It meant one less human to have to deal with. It meant less worry. It also meant one less life I'd have to take.

I returned to the driver's seat. Payback handled himself beautifully. Knew to maintain when he was ordered to. The muzzle helped, no doubt.

I was looking at Margie.

"Be happy, don't worry."

"How about if you zip it and drive, *jag-off?*"

Jag-off was the Midwest version of jerk-off. Not that it mattered. Meant the same thing.

"Get us the fuck out of here."

"Yes." It was Monica. "Please." Polite to the very last. Cold-blooded, heartless, but always polite. Even when she was being spanked and having her backside drilled by a massive dildo. Polite through and through.

I turned my head to see how the two in the back were doing. Out. Snoring and moaning. Margie still awake, bitching and cursing, but her eyes were open. No problem. I'd take care of her in a moment. I had plans.

I got us out of there.

Chapter 52

Margie was having a tough time keeping her eyes open.

"Are we home yet?" Inquiry came from the back. Sounded like Monica.

Bruno was muttering Bix's name. Something about being in lust with him. "It's not love, Bix. It can't be. I'm hurting Percy. I can't betray Percy. I can't, Bix."

"We there, Margie?"

"No, we aren't. Because we seem to be going the wrong way, taking a route that makes no sense."

"What did you say?"

Monica was aching, and she had the dry heaves. She'd vomited so much back at Pinocchio's that there didn't seem to be anything left to puke.

"I said we are going the wrong way, Monica." Margie was looking at me. "What's up with that, *Alf?* Where the fuck are you taking us—in this serial killer van? This is the kind of van a serial killer would own."

She leaned out the open window and threw up. Wiped with the back of her sleeve, and kept looking at me. I had the camcorder going. Had it down at waist level and was shooting footage of her. Margie noticed and it seemed to increase her ire.

"Are you taping this? Goddamn you!"

My response was to grin.

"Stop this fucking *serial killer* van and let me out."

"Sure, Margie. No problem."

I stopped the van, reached under my seat for the rubber mallet, got out, and walked to her side. I opened the passenger door, all the while shooting footy. It didn't take much; didn't take long, but I drove that hammer right into her jaw. It was fast, like lightning quick, and she slumped back against the seat.

"I hate, *hate* serial killers. And dislike being compared to them."

That really stung. Being called a shit-bird serial whacko. In fact, if I had the time, if I could ever make it happen, I'd go after them myself. Go on a world-wide hunt for serial turds. But I was too old for it. Time was running out. I had a mission to accomplish, a job to do. My hands were tied.

I stowed the camcorder. Dug into the pocket of my cargo pants and fished out a pair of cuffs. I drew her arms behind her, and cuffed her wrists.

"Serial killers are *punks, pedophiles, rapos. That's not me.* I don't molest kids, I don't rape bitches. I don't harm animals. I play *get back. Payback. Get even. Steven.*"

"Hey." Sounded like Bruno moaning. "What's going on?"

I closed Margie's door. Slid open the side door, and stood there. Stench was incredibly bad. Vomit and waste.

"I'll tell you what's going on. You ruined my van, is what."

I climbed in, bashed him in the face, twice, then gave Monica a solid one across her jaw. I cuffed their wrists behind their back, climbed down, slid the side door closed. I climbed in the driver's seat. Margie was moaning. In and out of it. Face was bleeding. Tears and snot and blood oozed down that loud snout of hers, that was no longer cursing and/or threatening. The other two did their share of moaning as well: sounds of pain and discomfort. I think those cuffs may have been clamped on a bit tight.

Pre-dug graves waited out there for us.

Chapter 53

Margie continued to moan and shake her head, mumbling, cursing and threatening. The only thing that kept me from driving that mallet into her big mouth again was the fact I needed her to have enough strength and stamina for later on and the plans I had for her. So I let her moan; I let all three moan and plead and beg to be un-cuffed.

"Sure."

I pulled up to the curb about a third of a block from a mini-mart. I reached inside the glove compartment for the roll of duct tape. Tore off a strip and taped Margie's yap shut. Then I tore off a couple more. Took care of her pals.

I draped one of the worn blankets over Margie, urged her to stay down in the seat, and pulled into the minimart parking lot, parking in the poorly-lighted right side of the building that was devoid of cars. The few cars in evidence were parked in front of the store.

I went in. This called for a celebration of sorts: beer, cigar, something to eat. Burger or hot dog. What I ingested no longer mattered. Junk food? In a world that was crawling with *junk humans*? Bring it on. What difference did it make what you consumed and/or exposed your system to?

No difference.

Besides, everything was full of chemicals. GMOs. Corporations were committing murder on a grand and massive scale. And got away with it. *Mental illness, Alzheimer's, cancer.* All for *profit.* That's how it worked. You killed one human or two, you went to jail. You killed thousands, no sweat. Because it came down to the reason—and *murder for profit* was the best and most excusable reason of all. And yes; there's that other one. Called *war.*

I added potato chips to the lot, peanuts, box of ginger snaps. Paid for the items, and returned to the van. A transient approached me. White dude in his 30s. Slimy, grimy and bearded. Strung out, no doubt. Asking for 'spare change.' He smelled as bad as Bruno and the two bitches.

"Sure, homey."

I gave him two singles. He was grateful. He stood there looking at me, while scratching his crotch.

"Don't I know you from somewhere? You ever do time?"

"Did time with your mama."

"My mama's a ho."

"Welcome to the club, bro."

I got in, yanked the strip of tape off Monica's mug, then did the same for the former law enforcement flunky. I pulled back the part of the blanket that had been over Margie's face, but did not remove the duct tape. I didn't want to have to hear her utter a single syllable for a while. Then I pulled out. We had a long drive ahead of us.

Chapter 54

I took a bite of the hot dog, stuck a few chips in my mouth. I looked at Margie. Coming to, her eyes doing the eyelid batting number: *I can't believe the nightmare I'm stuck in.*

"Believe it."

Then I asked if she was hungry. Not sure why. Maybe just to fuck with her. I got no answer.

"S'matter? Cat got your tongue?"

She wasn't talking. Shook her head, but didn't say a word, or tried to— or maybe she did. The gag made it tough.

"Even a ball-buster like you deserves a last meal."

My eyes were on her crotch and the urine stain there. Margie had pissed her jeans. Healthy ass, domineering Margie had wet herself.

Just as well. The piggy had shit his pants, one bitch was covered in puke, and this one had wet herself and soiled the seat. Did it matter? Make any difference? Nope. None of it. I'd been headed this way my whole life. Sealed fate. From the day I crawled out of my mama's contaminated womb. Sure, I'd tried to walk that straight and narrow. I did. Did my best. Only it wasn't in the cards. Wasn't meant to be. It took a bit of luck to have any kind of happiness, things to go your way. I just didn't have it. I used to be bummed about it. It used to frustrate me, make me angry; caused me so much anxiety. But now? I accept it. None of it matters anyway. Not much made any difference.

I kept the beer inside the sack, out of sight, in case I got stopped. And then it occurred to me: if I got pulled over by the rollers it didn't make sense to have a bloody-faced Margie G. sitting in the front with me like this.

I stopped the van, grabbed her by the collar and dragged her in the back and dropped her on top of her pals, where excreta belonged. All three: slime. Not even human, as far as I was concerned. They'd taken great joy in seeing me suffer. I remembered all of it, as if it happened yesterday. Every smirk and dirty look. I was worthless. Not even human. Well, this is what I felt toward them now: nothing. I was looking at a pile of dog shit. And they would be treated as such. The only thing that kept me from smashing their skulls in was that I wanted to see them suffer. I needed to stretch their suffering out for as long as possible.

Spiteful? Who? Me? No shit. For years I was in denial about that. Face it. Admit it. I was one spiteful motherfucker. I never forget a slight; I never forget having been dissed, offended, put down and swept aside—especially after I'd been kind.

Her cell went off; then a moment later so did Monica's. The first made me jump, the other made the hair on the back of my neck stand straight up. I was getting rattled. Just a bit. Fear my plans would go awry. That was it. Mainly. Made my guts get tight inside. I liberated the aging bombshells of their phones. Considered relieving Bruno of his, but the former oinker smelled so bad I thought I'd put it off until I had no choice. I made it back to my seat, and drove.

Chapter 55

Adrenalin was up there, way up there. Talk about rush. I had it. Natural high. Better than a beer buzz and/or toot, Ex or reefer. I just had to remember to keep checking my mirrors. Had to remember that Percy had been back there at the pasta joint. Also needed to remember that Margie had initially thought it was Modi pulling up when I drove up in the van. My conclusion? Somebody must have called him from inside Pinocchio's before they came out.

Maybe, too, I was imagining things. Nerves. It felt real good to be finally doing it, but the fear of being stopped or having someone interfere with my plans before I could finish the project I'd spent years dreaming of and planning could be yanked right from under me. So close; so damned close—only to have it cancelled by some unforeseeable entity . . . like pigs in a squad car, or . . . who knew?

I had to slow down. Watch my driving. Play the law-abiding, conscientious citizen. That was me. Mr. Reed. Three vics in his van. On the way to the killing fields of Joshua Tree. Where the desert sand will run bright crimson with human blood.

The moaning and farting went on back there. The wenches were moaning, Bruno was the one doing the other. As usual. The former piggy had a gas problem. I rolled my window down; then I reached over and rolled the other one down at the next red light.

Chapter 56

One of the cell phones went off in the right pocket of my cargo pants. Now I couldn't remember which was which: whether Margie's was in that pocket, or if it was in the other pocket. On top of that, I had a new dilemma on my hands. Who could be calling? Some porn actor friend of theirs? A crew person looking for work? Pinocchio's? Aldo fearing a lawsuit was on the way? What was I going to do? Answer? Or not answer?

I let it go. The hell with it. If they were desperate to get in touch they'd call again. I did reach inside and fished the cell out. Modigliani. He'd hung up, with a message. He'd also texted a few words:

Where are you? Why did you leave in that other van? Call me back. Modi.

Had me wondering if Aldo might've caught the number on my rear plate.

It was then Bruno's cell went off. Percy was calling, no doubt, wondering what was going on. I let it ring. I'd hoped for a cleaner escape/get away with my vics than this. But what were you going to do? When did things ever go one hundred percent for anybody? When? Like never—that's when. Especially not with a place full of flotsam like this one was. Porn Valley was hopeless, and I was just another hopeless case.

I'd have to remember to get Grozewski's cell. Stench or no stench. I happened to look back just then, and the fuck had the cell in his hand. He'd somehow been able to reach inside his pocket, even with his wrists cuffed that way; he'd been able to reach inside and get his hands on the cell phone, and Monica was attempting to text with her nose.

Son of bitch.

I pulled over. Got back there, kicked the phone away from them and backhanded the fuck across the side of his face.

"You think I'm playing some kind of game here, porky? That it?"

I looked down at Monica. There was fear in her eyes. No way to hide it. She feared me. At long last. And it was plain enough to understand and get and see: She knew; I mean the ho knew what she'd done to me, put me through, her and cunt Margie.

"You're afraid huh? That's good; that's real good, Monica. You not only shredded my heart, but thoroughly enjoyed my suffering. You were the Judas, if there is such a thing as a female Judas; responsible for my crucifixion. I was crucified—for something most men and women get away with with a slap on the wrist. I was wrong, I admit it; I betrayed you. But it was also nothing more than a shag, sex; what I'd been guilty of, and hadn't deserved what I was given. Humans err; we make mistakes; all of us—except you and Margie and this *shit bag* over here. All of us are flawed, except the three of you."

I kicked her in the face, hard. Watched her head bounce against the other bitch. I knelt down, grabbed Margie by her hair, then grabbed Monica by hers—and banged their faces together. Watched the blood ooze from their noses and mouths.

"Want to talk about wrath? *Hell hath no wrath like a woman scorned?* That it? Is that how that goes? Hell has no wrath . . ."

I looked at the former pig. Gave him a kick in the belly that resulted in more flatulence escaping his big ass. While fatso was farting I was searching for his cell phone that had gone flying off somewhere in the back a moment earlier. Finally found it inside the plastic bucket I'd used to wash the van with and/or change the oil from time to time. I sledged the cell with the mallet and tossed the bits outside.

"Motherfuckers."

I returned to the steering wheel. Pulled away from the curb.

Chapter 57

Go home, was my text to Modi. *Sleep tight.*

Mom, Where—Are—You?

I was tempted, so tempted to respond with: I'm tied up at the moment. Love, Mommy. And it took a lot not to.

I drove on through the night. Lightning flashed off in the distance. Thunder roiled. Rain was imminent. I couldn't tell how much or how hard, but it was on the way. I actually wished it wouldn't rain too much, on account it would be tougher to carry out what I had planned. I didn't want to have to track after the bitches in mud, having to wear heavy boots and parka.

It was a thin drizzle for starters, and who knew, maybe it would continue on this way. Well, you dealt with things in life, didn't you? You just dealt with it. I'd been through far worse; I'd been through plenty.

Chapter 58

Dawn was breaking by the time we reached the area. Rain had eased up way back, miles back there. Joshua Tree was barren, for the most part. I got out to relieve myself. Made it possible for the ladies to do the same. Gave them their privacy. So you see, I was not so far gone.

I had the cam going again, wanting to record the next step: drive over to the first grave. Phase was valid enough. I parked the van right beside it, so that once I slid the side door open, all I had to do was grab Grozewski by the belt buckle and heave him out. And this I did, and the former roller rolled right into the muddy grave, landing on his back. Ah, he looked a mess, but those eyes were wide open and he was looking up at me.

"Know what, Bruno? This just occurred to me. Not exactly sure where it comes from, but your first name should've been Bondo. *Bondo* Grozewski. They should have named you *Bondo*. Missed an opportunity there. I prefer Bondo over Bruno any day of the week."

He was still lying on his back, eyes open wide. Huffing; straining to speak through aching teeth.

"Let's hear it, *Bondo*. The usual. How wrong I am to do this."

"You can't. I did what was expected of me. I had a job. You took a friend's life."

"Can't tell the truth . . . even at this late stage, *Bondo?* You're hopeless. Your whole life a waste—something like mine. There is no other way this could end. You fucking die. It's *karma*. I've considered all other possibilities. And all of them come up short, in my estimation."

"Percival . . ."

"What about him?"

"This will destroy him when he discovers that I'm gone. Missing. No body. Nothing to bury, or any way to say good-bye. My kids; my kids should know . . ."

"The plan is to leave certain details in the confession I've been hard at work on; where your bodies can be found."

"Why not just shoot me?"

"Want to give you a chance."

"Burying me alive is giving me a chance?"

"Crawl out. Claw your way to freedom. If you manage, you're a far better man than I figured."

"Un-cuff me. Give me a real chance. Take the cuffs off, Reed. *Take them off.*"

I couldn't see myself doing that. I did un-cuff one wrist, had him place both his hands on his belly and clamped the cuff back on. He claimed he was dying of thirst. I placed a jug of water a few feet from the grave. Suggested it would be there when he crawled out, if he managed to crawl out.

"I'll even leave one of the shovels behind, should a bobcat appear, or a gila monster—to defend yourself with."

"Nice."

"Nicer than the three of you were to me."

I then dropped one end of a three-foot-long hose within easy reach of his mouth, and suggested he suck on it for air, then I un-cuffed the ladies in order to put them to work. Retrieved a shovel from the tool box in the van, detached the entrenching tool from my pack and let them go to it, while the cam recorded it.

They shoveled the dirt in. Some of it mud-like from the rain earlier, the top layer anyway. As weak and as sore as they were, they stayed with it. They were fairly good at taking direction: scooped a full shovel, held it over his face, turned it, while I watched the dirt drop down on his eyes, mouth and nose. I had to remind them that the other end of the hose needed to be unencumbered and poking out, so that the former piggy could take in air—once he was able to get his mouth on his end down there. They did that. Stayed with it, rotating. While the one poured the dirt over him, the other was digging her shovel into the mound beside the grave. Like clockwork.

Eventually I wouldn't be able to see that dirty effing mug, nor be able to smell the stench of him. Stench of a smelly pig. When the grave was full, I had them pat the flat ends of their shovels over it. From one end to the other. Now, this was still fairly loose dirt, and all he had to do was suck in air through the hose, then start clawing and scratching his way with his hands, and moving his head, jerking it—and he had a chance to crawl out. Slim; still a chance. Better than what I'd been given by them. Up to him. Entirely up to him.

But I'd had enough of the fat turd, and needed to concentrate on the twats.

Chapter 59

I secured the folding shovel to the pack, and thought to leave the other where it lay, as promised. I'd given my word, and my word still accounted for something.

Then it was time to address the babes, while the vid cam registered every delightful detail. Like the Uni-bomber, I'd never been a fan of electronics and/or high-tech in general: Sci-fi, machinery, computers. Bunch of shit we had no business fooling with and would surely do us in one day. A blind man could see we were moving in that direction. And yet, having stated thus, there was no denying I was happy to be able to capture what was taking place in this handy manner.

"We're going to do the tango, my ex-lady loves; my former *ménage à trois* bitches. Fred Reed's version of the tango: you *running*, and me *pursuing*. Me giving you both a head start, and you hoping to stay alive by outrunning me and Payback. Or . . ." Here's where I paused. Some scribes, in certain books I read while in stir, like to call this a 'pregnant pause.' Not me. I never would. Well, I read a lot of shit while in stir, especially by a certain overrated horror schlockmeister, and others of his ilk.

"I give you a choice: Go out the way *Bondo* Grozewski just went. And see if maybe you can last long enough to dig your way to the top. What do you think? I give you both that choice."

I yanked Margie's tape from her face and she started in, cursing; the big effing mouth as always. I handed the camcorder to Monica, and did the only thing there was to do: smacked the high yellow in the face with the butt end of the rifle. And she flew; the *over-the-hill shrew* flew like she had wings. Backwards, so hard, that she landed into the large grave, the one big enough for two bitches. She was down there, stunned, silent; weeping, but not running that yap of hers. A chunk of both, upper and lower lip torn off; some of the teeth in front no longer there. Made her look like a crystal meth addict. Something like Rinelle.

I pulled out a second camcorder and got it going. Saw to it that Monica continued shooting hers as well.

"I dreamt of this . . ." Ooh, I did. Exactly this, thousands of times in my dreams; fantasies I had while lying in my bunk thinking, planning how to get back at the two man-hating, spiteful she-devils.

I gestured to Monica to help her 'life partner' up and out of the hole.

"Put the camera down for a minute. Give her a hand."

This she did. It was work, and took effort, but she managed.

Chapter 60

I had them get out of their stained and smelly clothes, then re-cuffed their wrists in front. "You're going to tiptoe through the tulips without any clothes on, and no footwear."

I tossed a pocketknife Margie's way. She caught it, then looked up. Afraid to open her trap to ask what it was for. That was fine.

"On the outside chance you have a close encounter with Bigfoot."

"Already have."

"Yeah? And I had mine with a couple of toxic vaginas." I looked at Monica. "You like *documentaries*? Exactly what we're going to do here: make a documentary. A real one. None of that fake, contrived shit, either; you know? Where you withhold footage, manipulate what's included. We're going for the *Real McCoy* here."

"This is sick." Marge could not resist the need to interject. "Your male ego can't accept the fact that two women fell in love and don't like being involved with men. You're behind the times, Fred. *Throwback*. No different from the way Frank was. This is a new world we're living in. Times have changed. There's no stigma attached to women wanting to be with women, and men with men. Accept it. You'll have to. Whether curmudgeons like you like it or not."

"I'm really going to enjoy seeing Payback tear your pee hole to pieces, bitch. In fact, that's the main reason we're putting it on video, for the playback. Multiple viewings later on."

"So you can jag off to it, no doubt."

"I'm getting a boner just thinking about this."

"Fuck you."

She spit on the ground.

"Give me a reason to put a hole through that stone heart right now, cunt, or start running for your life. I've got to take a dump. Eating that over-priced slop at Pinocchio's that they like to pass off as 'gluten-free' Italian food never did agree with me. You two ought to know about that. Should give you a head start. Between now and by the time I'm done wiping is exactly how much time you got to disappear and save your psycho ass."

Monica promised large sums of money. Whatever I wanted.

"Name it. You got it. New car, house with a pool; leads in adult features, or star in your own life story. You wanted a *ménage* with us and Lucy Ice. It's doable. She liked your style of giving oral; you know that."

"Truth is, you're an over-the-hill old ho, Monica. Both of you. Old hoes I got no use for. I got zero interest in balling a couple of bitter dykes with nasty *culos*."

"You liked Lucy. There's others like her. It can be arranged. Killing isn't always the answer."

"It sure seemed to be when Marge managed to draw me into her and her mother's scheme to do Frank Graham in, didn't it?"

"That was then. He was beating her."

"Or else she wanted it to look that way. And it worked. I was the certified chump. Scapegoat."

"It was the only way out for her. He was thoroughly abusive. You have no idea what that's like, to live under a chauvinist's thumb."

"I'm a man, therefore I wouldn't have a clue. My gender never suffers; ever."

I indicated the scar on my neck. Before she'd had a chance to say something else, I shoved a couple of pieces of paper in her face: Dog-eared newspaper articles I'd been saving since before having been released from my state subsidized cribby.

"Lower the camera and start reading."

Before Monica had so much as unraveled the one, Marge was tossing up some more lies out there.

"Let me guess: Jamal's last resort confession. How he got his career criminal ass off death row. Not much to be believed there."

Monica read in silence.

"I was standing outside your bedroom window when you asked Margie if it were true: that she and her mother had been looking for a patsy all along? And if I had been that patsy. She had denied it, just as she's denying now."

Monica looked up.

"Her mother risked losing her life if she didn't cooperate. Two wrongs don't make a right. How will taking another life solve anything?"

"Judge threw the book at me. I stood there in the courtroom listening to him list the actual offenses, then added a few imaginary ones for good measure. I was stunned. Speechless. The only thing they didn't seem to nail me for was jumping into that motel pool in my street clothes and contaminating the water with the blood from my gunshot wound. When I pointed it out to my court-appointed mouthpiece, his response was that maybe the prosecutor had overlooked it somehow and to leave it at that."

"You're out. Free to start over. Why look back? Why throw away the rest of your life? It's never too late to start over. Appreciate what you have, Fred. This takes you nowhere. Murder is wrong."

"I'm too old to give a shit about any of it."

"*Suicide* is what he's after." This was Margie's two cents worth of wisdom. Could be she was not that far off. "Once he kills us there's no going back. He'll have to take his own life, or else it's back to being caged like an animal."

"I was misled. Used. Abused. Left to die. I didn't deserve what I was put through. It seems to me you two care more for cats and dogs, four-legged creatures in general, than you do for my gender. *C*unts like you are ruining society. Didn't used to be this way. You've gone too far. All you *snapper-lapping twisted sisters* have gone way overboard with this warped agenda of yours. You think I'm the only one who feels this way? I am not the only one who feels this way. Far from it. *Got an ax to grind?* So do I."

Chapter 61

Monica looked at her best friend and soulmate, waiting for answers, at least one answer that might resolve some of it. Margie, at the moment, had nothing to offer. I had Monica fold that article and hand it back.

I told her to take a gander at the other. This was the one that contained testimony from some of Margie's half-siblings: sister Tezlyn, brothers Lorenzo and Thalmus; an uncle or two.

While she read, I thought of a couple of other things. Stuff was coming at me: images mostly; words also, that echoed from deep within some chamber inside my skull. I recalled the *fracas* between Margie and Rinelle and the *faux reason* that fueled it at the Pasadena drug and booze recovery facility.

"Margie was drying out, out there in Pasadena. Rinelle showed with Jamal. There was a vicious falling out between Margie and her mother: hair-pulling and pissing; screams and creaming. Well, they were screaming at each other, while I practically found myself creaming in my boxers. That's neither here nor there, because the battle was over Margie falling for me emotionally. It wasn't supposed to happen—and her mother was freaking. I didn't get it at the time. It came to me later, much later. Added it up. It meant they'd have to start searching for another sucker to take the rap for Graham's murder. Finding the right type of sap took time and time was the one component they were in short supply."

The two exchanged glances. When Margie had nothing to offer in her defense, Monica resumed reading. She finished. Handed it back.

"Is this true about your mother, Margie?"

"I don't know. And besides, what difference does it make at this point? Fred got dumped and will find a way to justify killing us for it, out of spite; spite and vengeance. You heard him: it's about payback. Nothing else. What Rinelle did or didn't do has nothing to do with Fred's agenda!"

"Rinelle was the personification of the term Black Widow. Poisoned who knows how many of her hubbies and/or unfortunate gentlemen callers. Graham was just another worthless 'male loser' who needed to be put out of his misery for the cause. Cash was in short supply. It's always in short supply, no matter how much of it dope fiends get their hands on. Rinelle and Jamal's craving for crack and meth was out of control. You read the articles: Jamal was a pusher who didn't know how to keep from getting high on his supply. Owed plenty to those he got his shit from. Graham's life insurance, plus bank account and property he owned was clearly the bull's eye on the bounty hunter's back."

Monica said her 'life partner's' name, desperately waiting for another denial. It came, but it was as lame as those before it.

"Lies, Monica. Jamal created this false confession because the DA's office promised him a deal. It saved him; the so-called confession spared his miserable life. Got him off death row, like I said and been saying: *He saved his own ass with a pack of fabrications.*"

I saw an opportunity to jump in.

"What reason did your siblings have to *'fabricate'* anything, Marge?"

"Pay off."

"By whom, Marge? How?"

"Jamal's book contract with a major New York publisher. He won't get a dime, but they sure stand to."

"Were Jamal's nosebleeds fabricated? Or were they caused by boric acid he caught Rinelle dumping into his *Wheaties?*"

"Lies to save his ass. Shave time off his sentence."

"Hardly."

"Got him off death row."

"Bodies were unearthed, re-examined. Antifreeze was discovered in Mario and others. Your stepfather never died of a heart-attack, did he?"

Margie said nothing.

"Prison shrinks had an expression they were partial to: *Cognitive dissonance.* Ever heard of it, Margie? Any idea what it means?"

"No. Why don't you enlighten us? Since you're the one who entered the big house a dumb-ass and came out a wise-ass."

"You know the truth, yet insist on deceiving yourself."

"Deceive this."

Margie stood there defiantly. Middle finger raised. She was good at it. Feisty Margie of old was back. Her true nature tough to shake, after all. Not unlike a rattlesnake taking on a new skin after it had slithered out of the old. The poison remained. It was still a venomous reptile. What had been my immediate reaction to Rinelle years before, pretty much. And twisted Margie had been contaminated by her. So had plenty of others out there, no doubt. Society. Scrambled and fried. Welcome to the carnival of warped minds and disfigured anatomies. You had a choice: tolerate and learn to exist in it, or opt out entirely. I must've been leaning toward the latter, like Marge said.

"What it was always about: you and Rinelle giving a worthless fuck like me the finger. Getting her off the hook with Jamal and his source. I happened to come along. Ready-made heartsick sucker. Scapegoat. It was perfect."

". . . No."

"Took you a while."

"You were and you weren't."

"Which?'

"Initially. Then I fell in love."

"For a while."

"You saw the battles I had with Rinelle. We bloodied one another silly."

"Granted; it was awesome burlesque. Some of the best. Motive appeared muddled, but it was entertaining to watch."

"The reason for my attempted suicide. I was conflicted. Didn't want you involved. Rinelle kept pushing, insisting. She had no choice, really. She owed. What the battles were about. She was under pressure to pay up. I sent what I could; what I was able to get Graham to give up. It wasn't enough; it was never enough—no matter how much was sent."

"Indecisiveness that lasted about, what?—five seconds?"

"Weeks; months. You know this."

"Bullshit."

"They threatened to start amputating her fingers—one by one—unless I got with it and delivered. Frank had to go. Jamal and his low-born thugs sent that finger and threatened to do more unless I did as they asked. I did what I could to keep it from you, hoping you wouldn't see it."

Who sent the finger was questionable at best. I let that part of it go just then.

"No, you left it where I was sure to find it."

"To what purpose?"

"To make it easier to justify to yourself the double-cross you planned to pull off later on: You stabbing me in the back. Exactly what this is about. It didn't work. Actually, it's laughable."

"You would find humor in it."

"Finger was a phony. Either you or Rinelle must've greased some underhanded undertaker's palm along the way to provide said male finger, then painted it with nail polish to make it look plausible."

"How was I to know where it came from?—who sent it?"

"Oh, you knew. This was worked out between you and your mother. I'd stake my life on it. I'll go so far as to claim that you were glad she was offed finally. Made it possible for you to lay your hands on the entire pot of gold—at the end of the blood-stained rainbow. *Bingo*. Your way of finally getting back at her for shoving your underage ass at degenerates old enough to be your grandfather."

"Finger may not have been hers, doesn't mean that the threat on her life wasn't real. You saw Jamal, what he looked like. We both know how it ended for Rinelle and what he did to her."

"When he caught her trying to feed him roach killer. Still doesn't explain the lies at the end, ratting me out when it was *you* who *stuck* the needle in Graham. It was you insisted on rat poison, not me. It was *you* who put *antifreeze* in his thermos long before I happened on the scene. Like I said before: I was a Johnny-come-lately in all of it. Certified chump."

"I told the insurance company what they needed to hear—for the payout. Only by then it was too late to save her."

"In that case, how come I never saw my slice of the pie? Not that it excuses the betrayal."

"What good was it going to do you in prison? I had a life to live. You were in a cage. Well provided for by the state."

"*Goddamn, you're ignorant.* It was life and death every minute of every hour of every day of every week of every excruciating, mother-fucking month of every year I was inside."

"You're not satisfied with my answers, the truth as I know it, then all I can offer up is this. Choke on it, fucker."

She had balls. Because the finger was back. Where the backbone came from, I had no idea or was even able to come close to explaining. Was I amused by the gesture? Some. Payback wasn't, and went at her, digging his fangs into her right ankle. Margie smacked at the dog, hard. Not with the knife, but her free hand. Had she used the knife at this juncture she would have been dead on the spot. End of story. But she hadn't and her reward was she got to go on breathing. *For the time being.*

"Don't like dogs, bitch? He's way better than a pile of shit like you."

I stowed the camera. Slung the rifle over my shoulder and had the shotgun up, aiming. At this close range I preferred going the shotgun route. Marge did not hesitate this time, and limped off.

The dog barked, vicious mother that he was. Wanted Margie's hide. I rubbed the back of his neck to calm him down. He did. To a degree. Then noticed Monica, and would have settled for her easily enough. I held on to Payback's leash. Monica jumped back, her face streaked with tears and blood.

I undid my belt buckle, and squatted.

Chapter 62

I reminded Monica to get the video camera going. Did suggest to keep it wide and that I didn't want jarring once we began our trek after her lesbian pal. She was sobbing, shaking uncontrollably.

"Get a grip, or I'll bury you right now."

I wasn't raising my voice. There was no need for it. She knew I meant business. My rage, my hatred/loathing was one hundred percent pure. The only problem in this area of loathing came down to trying to decide which one of these *'femme fatales'* I loathed more.

"See, that was the one thing that was tough for me: concluding which one of you I resented and wanted to deep-six ever deeper: *Her* or *you*? *You* or *her*? It went back and forth like that all those years while in the joint. Everything else was worked out. I even had backup/contingency plans, but had never been able to decide which one of you ball-busters I wanted to see scream out the loudest; which one deserved the greater intensity of suffering. I'm still at a loss, years later. Standing right here, looking at your worthless fucking face, can't decide."

Then it occurred to me: the long strands, filthy and dangling over her eyes might interfere with her ability to get good footage.

I drew the dagger from the scabbard. That got her to stop sobbing at least.

"Lower the camera."

I held the blade up, near her face, then holding clumps of hair in the other hand, cut quite a bit of it all around. Chopped it off. She looked like shit. Well, she looked like shit lately anyway, but this made her appear atrocious. So be it.

"I want some *decent footage* of this."

She nodded her head.

I double-checked the items: shotgun, rifle, rope, handguns, ammo, rubber mallet, duct tape, water, biscuits for Payback, power bars for myself. I'd been able to stuff quite a bit of it into the backpack. Payback continued to growl at Monica and it was clear enough to me he wanted a piece of her, possibly more than a piece. Seemed like he wanted to tear her apart.

She was naked, no shoes. I looked at my watch. How much time had I given Margie? Twenty, twenty-five minutes?

"Should we give her another five, Monica dear? What do you think?"

She wasn't saying.

"Don't you think she deserves five more minutes?"

"What difference would it really make?"

I nodded. Had to agree.

"You'll kill her the way you killed Mr. Grozewski."

"No, I'm afraid it's going to be a lot more painful . . . for the both of you. It's going to be excruciatingly painful. Because, you see, I was emotionally involved . . . and felt some sympathy should have been forthcoming; felt I was owed something, a little more than what I got, at least. What I got, in fact, was zero. Nothing. That's what you're going to get here from me. *Exactly. Nothing.*"

She didn't say anything.

"Well, then, we got us an old whore to find. The hunt is on."

Chapter 63

I let Payback take a good whiff of Margie's panties, and off we went. He tugged and yanked and growled, pulling on the leather leash. It was all I could do to hold him back, keep him from causing me to trip on my own feet. There were rocks out here, crevices, cacti, twigs, branches and a few dead Joshua trees that had been uprooted by a vicious storm or two over the years, or else old age had been the real culprit. Possibly both.

I reminded Monica that I didn't need to be in the shot. Mainly I wanted footage of her lesbian friend, once we got close enough.

"Depending on what Payback does. Try to stay in front of me, better yet—off to the side. I don't need to be in any of the shots."

"When do I start?"

"I'll let you know."

She was to my right, walking alongside this way. She was holding the camera in her hand, waiting for word from me. I happened to look down at her mud-caked feet. There were cuts.

Now, I had no idea what Margie might attempt to retaliate with. Yes, she was a woman, but she was no meek little chickie, either, not at 5ft 11, and those strong thighs and buttocks. She didn't have powerful shoulders, this was true, but I also knew she could throw a punch. Saw it with my own peepers, many moons ago, when we were young and pretty and she and her mother were engaged in fisticuffs. Then I remembered the time I stopped her from poisoning Graham's kids. Fact was both of these twats were twisted. Then you had me: with a crack right down the center of my psyche too blatant to ignore. I used to be in denial about it. No more. No point. What for? We were 'triple threats' all right. These hoes were at the end of their rope, and if they wanted to stay alive you knew they had to try to pull something, anything. It behooved me to stay alert. Like in the fuckin' jungle, or as you drove a transport through some village. You never knew when that sniper's bullet would pierce your helmet and park itself in your scared shitless brain.

Anything was possible.

It was then I thought to look up, at the trees, all around. That's what you did: kept looking around, all the time. Left, right, in front of you—and up into the trees. Came down to you or Charley.

Was she dumb enough to actually climb up a tree? She'd be dead meat for sure if she did that. There was no way Payback would miss it.

My good buddy continued to tug, but then he'd go off to the left, double-back, go to the right; then returned to where I stood and headed on in a straight line—as if he was walking point. Well, could be he was. Point dog. Wanted her ass. Wanted blood. Payback could tell they were no good. That simple. I'd got taken in years before: by the curves, tits, pussy and *culo*. And with Monica? It was even more than that; she'd been far more conniving: when she laid all that fake sweetness on me. And I'd thought: *Lifesaver. Hope.* The light at the end of the tunnel. A way out; a way to rescue myself and have something like a clean and normal life. She was sane, and I'd needed someone normal and sane. She appeared to be, anyway. Good-hearted. Fair-minded. Fuck. What a chump. That *facade* had me conned; suckered me in, and I'd let my guard down. Never up to that point. Had always managed to stay alert when dealing with humans. I knew it was a world of smiling two-faced snakes. The *T&T* reeled me in. *Tits and Tang. BJs.* It was more than that. A state of serenity. Peace of mind. Sure.

I looked at her just then. Easily hated her more than ever. Despicable? She was that—and some. I despised the off-kilter *effing lesbo* more than I could ever state here. It wasn't so much that she had turned gay and taken up with that other duplicitous witch; as stated before: I didn't give a rat's ass who was gay or what people did between the sheets. None of that shit meant a thing to me. Women liked to eat pussy? Their business. Men enamored with the penis? Their call, not mine. Was zippo to me. Waste of time to even think about. Saw it in stir: males doing the nasty with each other. Who gave a good goddamn, man? The whole effing sex thing was not only overrated, but utterly moronic. I said it: *Moronic.* With a capital *M.* Very often— *or at the least*: more often than not—we were mentally defective creatures and carried on as such. So, no, the fact they devolved into lesbians, or say, always had been, though it was latent, it was the fact they'd *turned on me*—and not only TURNED, but treated me as though I were less-than-human, simply for having been born with a pair of balls and a prick. This was exactly where my disdain came from, this rage that had been brewing and escalating over the years. To say I had loathing wouldn't come close to stating how much hatred I harbored toward the two ball-busting sacks of female waste.

And as far as women went in general? This world wouldn't be much without them. Hell, it wasn't much anyway. But am saying, life would be just about a total waste of fucking time without the female to spice things up and make existence interesting.

So there you have it: for all those man-hating bull dykes out there. You know the type am talking about. The pig ugly, perpetually angry wenches with the hairy upper lip, who can't seem to get through a day without blaming all that ails this universe on the male. Those worthless, hateful *bags of hog snot* I can do without. Those are the bitches this world would have been way better off without; those are the *hate-filled shrews* who cause so much grief among the average male and female who merely wish to get along and know how to appreciate one another.

But types like Margie and Monica? I got no use for. In fact, nothing would make me happier than to slice them up; make them suffer like no one has ever suffered. Their type like to talk about: *Hell hath no fury like a woman scorned* . . . Really? Get ready, because I'm going to show you what real fury is about. Fasten your seat belts, motherfuckers, because the *Freddie Reed Wrath Express* is headed your way.

Chapter 64

Payback got my attention again with all the tugging and jumping and growling. He wanted to sink his fangs into flesh.

I didn't know what sense it made, but I suppose he knew what he was doing. Could've been the way Marge had been scampering along: undecided. *Zig-zagging.* Then thought her chances were best if she kept on in a straight path. So this is the way we trudged on, straight ahead, but after I'd taken a look at the cell screen to see what, if anything, the hidden video cam aimed at Grozewski's grave picked up. No movement, that I could tell. Didn't know if he was alive, or dead—or if he had a real shot at clawing his way to the top. It was up to him. All of it. Entirely up to him.

I followed Payback's lead. It was a nice crisp morning. After all that rain. Clear blue sky. *Azure.* Unusual for usually hazy Southern California.

Chapter 65

Monica stubbed her left foot and winced and had to stop. I let her. In fact, I did better than that: I had her sit on a boulder, lifted the foot to take a better look. Poured water on it to wash the mud and blood off; then I took out a Band-Aid and applied it to the cut. She looked at me without saying anything. The expression on her dirty face said plenty: *Why do this if you intend to kill me later?*

"I especially need you to run the camera for this portion of it. Would really like you to stay healthy long enough to nail the temperamental twat. Of course, I'd like you to stay fairly fit for when we start your phase of the adventure."

Didn't mention that I had other things in mind for the duo—to test this bond that they had between them; this love and loyalty and dedication. What would take place between them when it came time to decide, choose between life or death? Would they turn on each other? Go for blood? It would be interesting to see. I'd be running the cam for that part of it.

She fought back sobs.

"Psycho bitch from hell. Two of them. Never shed a tear when I was hurting and being sent up the river; but your dyke friend gets a scratch, or you stub your toe and it's cause to go on a crying jag."

The dog wanted a chance at her. I held him back.

"See, even he knows you're dung." I turned away, spit, then looked at her. "Cry me a fucking ocean, bitch. Move your ass. Let's go."

We moved out.

Chapter 66

Payback tugged another time, hard, nearly causing me to trip on a log that had been lying diagonally across our path. I cursed, staring at him. He seemed to be saying he hadn't meant it, but merely wanted to sink his teeth into the ho we were chasing after.

I kissed him on the snout. "Forget it, pal. I understand."

I happened to look at Monica. Tears were flowing again, snot. She wiped with the back of her forearm.

"I risked going to jail over that dog of yours that time. Chambray? Remember that psycho dog. I never knew why Chambray was so angry and fucked up. I mean, I understood, I related because that was me; my whole fucking life—but I didn't get what had caused her to become like that. I don't know why I felt that way about it, because there was no mystery to it: she had you for a mistress. You, and whoever else had been abusive to her."

"I'd had to leave her back in Phoenix with some people for a few months. Something must have happened to her. I never mistreated her. I saved her from a trailer trash family as a pup."

"Or else your own family fucked her up, the same way they fucked you up. Wished I could have spotted your hatred toward the male early on. I would have bailed. Right away. Would not have stuck around. Nope. I suspected you had plenty of bitterness in you . . . only I kept hoping my gut instinct was wrong."

I spit on the ground, took a sip of water. Poured some down Payback's throat. Gave him a dog biscuit.

"I loved Chambray. . . ."

"Love, Monica? What's that? You loved me, too, as I recall."

She said nothing. Tears rolled.

"Margie means that much to you?"

It took her a while to answer.

"You know she does. That pocketknife isn't going to do her much good out here, with all these wild animals roaming, snakes."

"We'll see how much she means to you. . . ."

The dog jerked on the leash; impatient to get going. I held him back, just a second. I needed to take another look at my cell screen and the image being picked up by the vid cam back at Grozewski's grave. It was a decent enough angle, shooting down from high up in a nearby tree. Although the camera was primarily pointed at the grave the former dick was in, I'd left it wide enough to cover plenty of the area. And just to be on the safe side, I had a backup cam aiming at the general area from a different angle.

There was movement. And then some. Looked like fatso had managed to burrow his way to the surface finally. I watched him yank the hose out of his jaw and toss it. Had to give the man credit. Cuffed wrists, many pounds of heavy dirt on top of him; dirt in his ears, nose and eyes, and he managed to make it to the surface.

I stood there appreciating the effort. He lay on top of the grave, on his back, gasping for air, sobbing; covered in grime and whatnot, gasping and sobbing.

After a while, he stopped the blubbering, looked around, making sure I wasn't anywhere near, and crawled toward the jug of water. Uncapped it and gulped down plenty, recapped it and reached for the shovel. He staggered to his feet, and limped out of sight.

Okay. Fine. Earned it, didn't he? I wasn't sweating. Let's see how far he gets. About the only thing that concerned me was Monica's kid, and maybe Bruno's boyfriend. Not Bix, but Percival Balsley. I also wondered what Aldo, the Pizzeria manager, might think up. I had no idea.

I played the footy back for Monica, to let her see. She looked up afterwards.

"Will you let him be now? Will you let him live?"

I said nothing.

"After all he's been put through, after all the pain you caused him . . . doesn't he deserve a break?"

"Sure. He deserves a break; the same break you three gave me."

"So you're showing it to me just to torment me."

"Showing it to point out how *determined* and *resilient* humans can be at times. This was exactly the kind of determination that kept me going all those years in stir: wanting my taste of vengeance."

"Was it worth it?"

"You have no idea how sweet."

"Margie was right. Only this is beyond sick."

"Because you're the ones being subjected to it. When it was being done to me it was par for the course; nothing unusual. I didn't rate. When you were rending my heart to pieces . . . it was no big deal. . . . It was, in fact, entertainment. You were amused by it. I saw the doc you made afterwards; saw the footage. I was the laughing stock in the joint because of the lies you and that cunt spread about me. This scar . . ." I yanked on my collar, as I had before in their studio. This time I held it a while. "Shiv attack, as a result of your documentary. Punk decided to test my mettle. So don't talk to me about breaks, asshole, and how sick someone is. Turds like you, and her, is the real reason this world is so fucked up. On the surface: nice and calm, so decent. But below—once you look below the thin veneer— is where the bile lies."

I flipped the lid to close the video screen, and we headed in Margie's direction. Payback was happy about that.

Chapter 67

The cell phone in the right pocket of my cargo pants went off. I dug it out. Modigliani. Texting. Again.

Mom, why won't you answer? I am worried. Where are you? Please respond. Let me know that you're all right. Love you, Mom. Modi.

I showed it to Monica. She choked back sobs.

"Let's stop this. Fred. Now. While you have a chance. Bruno is alive.

You won't be tried for murder, at least."

"I won't be tried for anything. That's the plan. I paid. More than my share of dues. *I paid.*"

"Enough is enough."

The second I stowed her cell, the one in the other pocket went off. It was Aldo, of all people. *Aldo.* What did any of this have to do with him? Pizzeria manager. Yes, the name of that greasy spoon was *Pinocchio's*, but this did not excuse him sticking his nose in it.

Margie, we need to know that you're all right. Margie? Please let us know. Something. Anything. People are worried.

I thought it made better sense to respond than not to:

We're on our way to see a doctor friend of Bruno's. We both have a terrible case of the running shits. Thanks to you. Hoping the doctor will be able to give us something for it.

Then the text signal sounded again. This time it was her son.

What's this doctor's name, Mom?

My comeback? *Dr. Feelgood.*

Where are you, Mom?

I wasn't going to respond after the above, but then thought: What the hell. The kid is worried.

Beverly Hills. We're fine. And quit worrying so much. Love, Mom.

I closed it, placed it on a boulder, reached for the mallet—and smashed the cell to bits. Cops had a way of tracing these things, even when not in use. In case Modi had attempted to file a missing persons report. I dug the other cell out, and did the same to it: crushed the crap out of it, then swept the pieces into the wind, hard, with the back of my forearm. Watched them scatter.

The texting had become annoying. Made me wonder if the kid had gone to the rollers. I was being pushed into actually turning into a serial killer—and this was the last thing I wanted. My conclusion: if they showed; if the busybodies appeared: Monica's son Modi, Aldo—and, possibly, Percival. If those two were up in arms over this, so then was Percy.

Had to be. I'd have to deal with them—and whoever else they had with them. *Five-0*? I didn't know. This would make me a serial killer. For sure. That many bodies? That many lives snuffed? Yes. *If it went that far.* I had no idea that it would—or wouldn't.

"You can't kill all of us, Fred. They did nothing to you. My son, and Mr. Picasso."

"Let's hope they don't get out here and find us, before I've had a chance to take care of you two shrewish wenches. On the other hand, should they appear . . . who knows what might happen."

"You're seriously ill. You know that, don't you?"

"Let's see: I'm ill, and you're not? You and that other twisted old crow are perfectly normal. What was done to me—the *'scrotum sack'* in this ménage—is acceptable to you. That how you see it?"

"You broke my heart. I loved you. You took that love and tampered with it, testing my trust, until it finally turned to contempt. No different from what my mother was put through by one heartless cad after another."

"And your ex-hubby, no doubt."

"Yes."

"That's how it is. At last. The picture comes into focus. That's how you justified what I was subjected to?"

"The last one conned her out of her house, cleaned out her bank account; broke her heart and took everything she had. Disappeared. Never to be heard from again. She had a nervous breakdown. Was in therapy for years. She died a broken old woman."

"That might explain why you turned out the way you did. Doesn't excuse it, but it'll do. Or else you had *lesbo* tendencies all along. *Latent.* Bitter. Spiteful. Toward my gender. Waited for the slightest reason to excuse unleashing it. Doubt you ever had genuine love for that kid of yours. Modi? Should've been born female. Females are superior to the male in every way. Your take on things. What's the other psychopathic female's reason for being the way she is?"

"Her stepfather was a skirt-chasing whore monger. He drank."

"All the blame falls on daddy. Her mentally imbalanced, drug addicted

Black Widow Mommy had nothing to do with it. That how that old song goes? Blame all of it on the male of the species, that it? No matter how many dudes took a dirt nap as a result of her one of a kind, Rinelle Rossi concoction."

"You had a lot coming to you."

"Not half as much as you two spiteful *culos* were so eager to mete out."

Chapter 68

There was a boulder about two hundred feet up ahead of us. Gut instinct indicated it was time to have the camera back in action. I gave the nod, and turned Payback loose. What sounded like Margie giving up a shriek on the other side soon after was followed by a yelp that made chills crawl up my spine.

We hurried over to discover Payback lying on his side with the knife hilt sticking out of his left temple. Next to zero life left in the mutt. Marge stood over him, pure rage in her eyes. Arms and legs streaked with blood.

There was no choice but to shoot him. Add this hurt on top of all the others.

I had her retract the pocketknife. I detached the folding shovel from my pack and tossed it at her feet and had the over-the-hill ballbuster dig a hole to bury my friend in. I relieved Monica of the camcorder and had her help out. Payback was lowered into the ground and covered up. I retrieved the shovel.

"There's only one way out of this for either of you. . . ." I tossed the same type of pocketknife to Monica. "Go to it. Carve each other up, or . . . take your chances with this." I indicated the shotgun. It was also time for the camcorder to be back on. Footy would be needed of the ensuing segment. I waited. I grinned, and I waited.

"Got a choice. . . . Up to you."

Chapter 69

There was some superficial slashing and non-life-threatening stabbing and kicks and hair-pulling and spitting, even peeing. Lots of screaming and tears. But Margie, having been assaulted and bloodied by Payback earlier, turned out to be no match for Monica.

She was down, on her back, out of her mind, but not so crazy that she still did not wish to live at this point. Monica was kneeling beside her, frothing mouth and face over hers, knife held against Margie's throat. It was tense, good and tense. I had a boner. Nothing like witnessing two naked psycho bitches going at each other. No denying my need for it: *blood lust*. Only I wondered what the bitch was waiting for.

"Finish her."

She wouldn't. She couldn't. Tears flowed. She was sighing. Gasping.

Tossed her knife aside, clutching her belly. Then rolled over on her back for a while, trying to catch her breath. Then a moment later she was embracing the stunned and wordless (for a change) Margie, sobbing in her bosom and kissing her face: tears and dirt.

"I am so sorry, dearest Margie. Can you ever forgive me?"

It was touching; and it was also comical. Because Margie was a *woman* she was *worth* crying over; she was *worth* empathy, *worth* being embraced and supported. I, on the other hand, hadn't been worth a damn when I'd been down, hurting, struggling to hold on by a mere thread.

Fuck 'em. Men can be wrathful. My actions here proved it. Many times over. Freddy's wrath. *A Dead Man's Wrath*. Would have made a nice title for this tale. Even better than *Night Sweats*. But enough was enough. I'd had my fill of the dykes and their all-too-sentimental affection for each other. I pitched the heavy rope at her, had her tie it about Margie's upper torso and then I had the shaken survivor drag her loving pal back to the grave, where both were dumped, not unlike refuse that they were, and covered up— without benefit of a hose to breathe through. I made myself scarce.

Chapter 70

I monitored quite a bit of what followed on my cell. Grozewski leapt out from behind bushes with his shovel and water jug, and started digging in the general area Monica had been buried.

After a while, feeling frustrated by the cell's less than adequate image of what unfolded, I did reposition myself, although remaining concealed, close enough to the action to be able to capture more of it with the camcorder in my immediate possession. Here's where I got bold to the point of temporarily abandoning the oft-sought wide angle and zoomed in. I wanted detail. I'd read, or heard, somewhere along the way that 'detail was god.' So be it. I fooled with the zoom. Moved in for a bit, and kept it there; then I zoomed out some. I was no filmmaker. Certainly had no desire for it. Now or ever. But I was also fairly certain experimenting with the zoom in this manner would meet my needs.

Growzewski had tossed the shovel aside and had started in with his bare hands, clawing and scraping at the dirt with his trembling fingers, sobbing the entire time. I watched snot, sweat and tears drip from his chin and cheeks.

He got to her face. Helped pull her out. Handed her the jug of water for a quick gulp while he dug away to rescue their pal.

Monica was one anxious wreck, looking around constantly. The fact that Bondo was ignoring her unsettled state enervated her further. This only resulted in underscoring his own shaky demeanor and he reminded her to calm down, that they needed to help Margie get out.

"He'll kill us."

"He's gone."

"He is just waiting for us to help Marge so that he can murder all three of us. That's what this is about. Whole purpose. He's *psycho*. *Sadistic*."

"No. He won't. He's gone."

"How do you know?"

"Why do you think he left the shovel behind?" Grozewski pointed to the jug. "*And that!* Would he want us to have water to drink if he intended to kill us?" Then producing a pair of car keys on a keyring, he dangled them in front of her stunned face. "That's right: keys to his van. Left on the seat. *Would he want us to have the van if he didn't want us to live?*"

She looked at him, while he resumed shoveling dirt.

"That's right. It came from Fred."

"How do you know those are keys to the van?"

"How do you know they're not? Even if they're not, it would be easy enough to hot wire."

"Makes no sense. What's he going to do out here in the middle of nowhere without transportation?"

Bondo shrugged. "He's suicidal. Let's hope he kills himself. Who cares what he does?" He urged her to help him dig. "Please. *Monica.*"

She snapped out of it, and assisted. Frantically.

"Thank you."

"The nightmare is finally over. We get my sweetie out, give her some water to drink, and get her some help; get all three of us some help. And turn him in. Throw him back in prison, where an animal like that belongs."

"You talk too much."

"*I talk too much?*"

The former dick looked around. "You're saying way too much."

She bent down, started brushing/shoveling dirt aside with her hands. Then just as suddenly, yanked the shovel out of his and pushed him away. She had to be the one to rescue her best friend and lover, not some male, even though he was gay and really had been a good pal of theirs for years.

Margie's face appeared. Frantic, panic-stricken, in desperate need of oxygen. Monica wiped dirt and pebbles from her face and neck. Leaned in to give her mouth-to-mouth. Helped her sit up, then gradually, allowing Bondo to lend a hand this time, pulled her up and out. Offered the jug of water. With their additional assistance, Margie managed to stand on her feet. Coughed, non-stop. Disoriented. Had no idea where she was, or who the two people beside her were. Monica embraced her. Bondo attempted to. Margie wanted nothing to do with either one. Cursed in a mixture of Spanglish at them, as well as the dirt in her eyes that she had a difficult time getting rid of.

I was at the rear of the van at this point, where I stayed put, eyeing the proceedings. I'd had no idea, none, that I would let them walk . . . until it happened; up until this very moment. I always claimed I was no serial killer. Was this proof enough? What I wanted, above all else, was payback. And this I got. And then some.

Chapter 71

I watched the scene transpire. Not sure why exactly, because I'd had enough of it. There wasn't going to be any killing. I didn't want to go down that path, after all. It was time to call it quits. And when I saw how manic Margie had become, I knew it was the right decision. She attacked him, then Monica. Margie had gone insane. Monica nearly there, same as Bondo. Batshit crazy. She grabbed at Monica's hair and yanked and wouldn't stop, until Grozewski stepped in to break it up. Shoved them apart. But then Margie screamed, cursing, and scratched at his face, pummeling him with her fists. Then it was Monica's turn to come between the two of them. It went on. They ran away from her, down the path, toward where the van was parked, and Margie went after them, picking up rocks to pitch at them. She picked up a sizable switch, slashed at the air with it, and tore after her friends.

Chapter 72

I stepped out from behind the front of the van, aimed the shotgun at Bondo, and let go with a blast. Blood and bone and waste spattered Monica's upper body and face. She screamed. I aimed at her torso, squeezed the trigger, and she disintegrated into way too many grisly pieces herself.

Margie walked over, cursing at her 'stepfather': *Me*. Now *I* was her *Daddy*. I aimed at her skull to shut that motor mouth up, and let go. The first volley took her head right off. I followed it up with another aimed at her torso before her body hit the ground.

I retrieved the camcorder from where I'd had it perched atop a nearby stump. Scraped their pieces up with a shovel and dumped the viscera and limbs into that old bucket I had and then dropped the mess in a hole I'd dug not far from there. It took so many trips that I lost count after the first dozen or so, but I got it done.

Initially I had considered planting them in the same grave Payback (presently re-christened *'Debt-Free'*) was in simply because it appeared to be closer, or was it? Blame it on exhaustion. No way was my friend's final resting place closer. Not only that. Why insult the dog? He deserved better.

The physical labor part of the task over, there appeared a need for this avenger to take a dump, but before doing so another need, more urgent than that one came into play: I had to urinate. And so I did. Whipped it out and pissed over their remains. Yes. I made sure to spread it around, giving all three their equal share.

I filled the hole back up. Well, you had to treat the dead with some respect. Why not? Then, of course, number #2 was on: a need to take that dump. Yes, I'd crapped earlier, but you know how it goes: some days you had to shit twice. Life.

I undid my trousers, squatted over the area where Monica was down there, squeezed out a good one, then I moved on over to where chunks and limbs of her female friend lay in the ground below me, and liberated another sizable log. *Coup de grace*, I believe it's called. The ultimate kiss-off. You might also say there had been a need to 'autograph' their final resting place. This was Hollywood, after all, the 'Dream Factory'—and the Dream Factory always was full of shit anyway.

Chapter 73

I drove the van toward the edge of a cliff, shoved it in 'P' and got out. Opened the rear door, poured lighter fluid over the mattress and set the mattress on fire, and closed the door. I walked to the driver's side, climbed back in, shoved the shifter into 'D', and watched the van roll toward the edge. Flames billowed in back of me. I couldn't think of a more perfect way to go out. I'd always had this fear of heights, fear of flying, fear of being burned alive—and this was my way of overcoming and facing all three of my fears head-on.

I stayed calm, collected. Truly. At peace. The van inched closer and closer to the edge. It rolled, gradually, but it made progress, as did the fire, crackling. I could hear the wheels going over and crushing what sounded like glass shards and dry clumps of mud and gravel. Just as we reached the very edge, and the front end was over the cliff and began tipping downward and the front wheels cleared the edge itself, I shoved my door open and leapt out and watched the rest of it go over, and nose-dive to the abyss below, where it was engulfed by flame. Front end crushed like an accordion, and the rest billowing: fire and black smoke. I may have waited for the explosion that never happened. Hollywood movies were so much bullshit and outright lies. Cars rarely exploded. Sure, now and then. It was fairly uncommon. But the mother did burn. I have to tell ya. All out. Fire.

Why hadn't I stayed in the van? Simple: Depredation. Scavengers.

Vultures, lizards, scorpions, coyotes and other scavengers would have appeared eventually to pick at my bones. I couldn't allow that sort of thing, not after what I'd been through. Nope. Still had a bit of self-respect left. Some. Not much. Some.

Chapter 74

The deed is done. The Piper was paid. Some will tell you revenge is a dish best served cold. I can't comment one way or another. The Germans have a word for it: *schadenfreude*. The Italian version is *contrapasso*. All I know is it felt good. Gave me a certain satisfaction to bury these sacks of manure. That's what they were to me. Not even human. Could be I'm not much myself. Could be none of us is. I would let all those idiot philosophers that I read over the years while in stir contemplate that pile of worthless turds.

Me? After retrieving the tree-cams, as well as anything else connected to what took place out here, I made my way to the pre-dug grave that awaited—far from there. I hadn't wanted to be anywhere near them and I thought this was fine. All I had to do now was decide the way I wanted to check out. Options were available. Too many to go into. Alas, it came down to cyanide, or shotgun blast (à la Ernie Hemingway). Now, my sole purpose of contemplating the shotgun route is to circumvent any pointless suffering. I figure I've had more than my share of it already. Should this make it difficult to ID the body later on, match DNA? Depends how long it takes them to locate my bones. That basic & that simple. Buy it or don't buy it.

I have a plywood board rigged to the left of the grave that the dirt is banked against so that all I have to do is lie down in the hole, kick the two-by-four that supports the plywood out of the way a moment before the blast, and the dirt will pour in over me and fill the hole up. My purpose for this phase of it? As before, at the edge of the cliff and why I leapt out of the van before it went over: to prevent depredation. That is a postmortem diss I have no use for. On the other hand, should it happen anyway, so be it. Nothing to be done there.

Chapter 75

In the end, I'm just another peckerwood with my pecker in one hand and a shotgun in the other. I will stroke my groin for one final blast of Twinkie filling, while replaying the footage in all its grisly and gruesome detail on the camcorder screen, then—hopefully, in tandem—squeeze the trigger for the best orgasm of all.

You see, the narrative was always moving in this direction. What more could any man hope for? Well, he might hope for something else, something in addition, even better—but he wouldn't get it.

If you're holding the stack of paper that contains the full disclosure regarding the ménage and how it imploded, then someone has found my remains, or at least discovered the manuscript. On the other hand, if you have yet to come across the confession, and that's what this screed is, after all, a confession, then the fools are still searching.

THE END

LUSTMORD:

Anatomy of a Serial Butcher
Book One (of Two)

By KIRK ALEX

Blurb & Novel Excerpt

*Who knew the minister next door
was also a sadistic predator?*

Cecil Omar Biggs is not your average man of the cloth. By day, he appears to be a hardworking preacher, but once night descends upon the quiet Southern California neighborhood where Biggs resides, his darker self emerges. Living a double life as a sex fiend and brutal murderer, he enjoys luring innocent victims into his basement lair by any means possible.

Converting an old house into a church, Biggs becomes the perfect wolf in sheep's clothing, which also puts him in the ideal position to attract his unsuspecting prey. He lives to satisfy his sinister appetites without remorse or limits, indulging in his more violent tendencies as soon as the sun goes down by torturing and killing the women he abducts in his dungeon of doom.

But how long can Biggs keep up the nice-guy-next-door pretense while secretly living as a homicidal maniac? And what happens when the locals start suspecting that there's more to this seemingly harmless Bible-thumper than meets the eye?

Chapter 1

They were into it. Heard more than he wanted to.

"J.J., don't!"

"Shut your mouth, whore!"

"I'll be good! I promise, J.J.!"

"I told you to shut your hole!"

"Don't hit me, J.J. You better not hit me no more!"

"I'll beat you to death! Filthy heifer cunt!" Slaps and screams followed. "Why, you ain't even a good whore! Where's my whiskey money, bitch? Spent on shoes and ice cream for that worthless little shit? Why come? Since when are the little bastard's wants more important than mine?"

More slaps followed, screaming. The next sound was the male's, a deep grunt, as though on the receiving end himself. Furniture was thrown, dishes. The woman shrieked.

"We're out of ass-wipe, over-the-hill heifer, and you got nerve to waste money on ice cream and shoes for the little pissy!" Dogs barked; a real ruckus was in progress up there. The boy pretty much ignored it all. Went about in a calm way burning his spiders, tearing wings off flies.

The view from where he stood at the grimy rear window on this tenement landing between the third and fourth floors gave one about as much hope and peace of mind as the hell going on up on the fourth floor: a back parking lot with cracks in the pavement, pot holes and loose cement chunks and gravel that had, over time, become the unofficial dumping site for neighborhood wrecks. Autos of all makes and sizes, pickup trucks, vans, gutted. Some without doors and windshields or wheels, had been abandoned to rust on wood or cinder blocks, bricks, piled rocks.

Knee-high weeds grew from fissures in the pavement. There were scattered stacks and piles of threadbare tires and strips of black rubber throughout; rusted out mufflers, gas tanks, radiators and grills; engines that had long ago been stripped of anything useful.

Down, toward the right-hand part of the parking lot-cum-junkyard, where the dumpster was located and over-flowing to capacity with refuse, dead foliage, and an assortment of fractured and discarded bargain-basement, low-rent coffee tables and nightstands, sofas and chairs, toasters, crock pots, washers and dryers, refrigerators and other appliances, large and small, with additional mounds of plastic trash bags bloated and splitting at the seams, that surrounded it at the base, were a couple of stray dogs engaged in the act, something the boy had been exposed to enough times in the past, so that in and of itself held no real interest; only these two were caught up/entangled in such a way that he had never witnessed until now. Stuck, they were, ass-to-ass, literally; on all fours, heads at opposite ends. Evidently attempting to separate, to untangle, and not able to do so.

One would pull one way for a while, dragging the other with him, then the other mutt would pull, or try to, in his direction, forcing the other dog to back up, neither getting anywhere.

Mexican standoff? He couldn't say. All he knew was it was the Latino part of town. East LA. What was going on?

It was only moments earlier that they had been in front of the building. Fucking, to be sure, but doing it the way they were supposed to: the male, forepaws atop the other's hind end, while he pumped away from behind. The boy's mother, with whom the boy had walked up, having been thoroughly disgusted by the sight, had flung one of her pumps at them. The dogs hadn't bothered to separate—maybe even then had not been able to—instead had hopped the short distance to the left of the tenement to where the driveway and entrance to the lot in back was. And here they were, still at it, only coupled in this baffling manner.

What was it J.J., his dogcatcher step-daddy had said to him about it that time? Couldn't recall the exact words. "Ever see 'em stuck, boy, it's 'cause the bitch has got her snapper locked on the male's prick and he ain't gettin' out until he shoots his load in her. Then the head of his prick, fat like a light bulb, goes down; only then can the male take his dick back. Now, them young males don't get it; and it's fun to watch 'em panic, an' struggle to pull out. Ain't happening, no way. What a man who knows dogs does then is to calm the asshole down. Only thing that works. Calm the motherfucker down."

Cecil wondered if that's what was going on, if only in a casual way. Because the mongrels, the junkyard, and the heaps hardly mattered beyond what went on in them at night, as well as during the day: local prostitutes, some who lived in the building, sneaking about with their johns, junkies in a crazy frenzy to slam a needle somewhere, bums seeking out vehicles with missing seats to take a dump in.

He'd taken more than one girl to one of the forgotten sedans himself, gotten them to pull their panties down and show him what they had.

None of that rated this mid-morning. No. What mattered and preoccupied his thoughts were the spiders and fat flies he enjoyed burning to a crisp on his side of the window, the flies who threw themselves mindlessly against the pane, and the spiders lying in wait in various corners of the window frame and the traps they had spun for the purpose of snagging a meal.

The boy stood at the window, book of matches in hand, doing the thing that sent the familiar sensation through him: setting things on fire, living or not; fire did it for him. Even though it was beyond his comprehension how or why the mere sight of fire and destroying things in this fashion had the effect that it did on him, it did not stop him from yearning for more of the same.

Drawing his attention above his head, in a web in the upper right corner of the frame, a newly trapped fly struggled to untangle itself, to no avail. Spiders knew what they were doing. The web was sinewy, tough, and this spider's latest victim was not going anywhere.

As expected, the spider emerged soon enough from within its lair. Moved toward the prey. With bated breath, the kid waited until the predator was practically upon the doomed insect before striking the match, reaching up, and roasting them both.

There were other flies he pounced on, clutched in his fist, and dealt with. Large, glistening green flies, who made the loud buzzing, grating noise that added to the thrill, he caught and relieved them of their wings. They were incredibly easy to grab: dumb flies who kept throwing themselves against the grime-streaked glass as if they expected to be able to drill through somehow and escape out there to join up with thousands of their ilk at the dumpster below and anywhere else throughout the lot.

The boy snatched them up, yanked the wings off, and watched with something like inner satisfaction as they kicked out with their spindly legs on their backs, on the sill, kicking out frantically, that enhanced the experience for him. There was no denying it, no explaining it: the combo, fire and subsequent death, not only heightened the senses all around, but clearly left him in a state of arousal, just as there was no denying he felt responsible for what was taking place up there on the fourth floor.

Coco Garcia, the gap-toothed, obese Mexican woman who lived across the way from them in the other apartment and everyone knew to be a prostitute, who had, in fact, turned his mother on to some of her johns, poked her head out through her partially opened door.

"They're at it again, huh, kid? I wouldn't take that off no man. I hope she beats the shit out of his fag ass this time."

The boy said nothing. Looked up at her, then turned away to mind his spiders and flies. He was down to his remaining match and that bothered him. The big woman shook her head at the ongoing racket. She withdrew back into her place and closed her door.

"Lemme get this straight, bitch: You stayed out all night and a good part of the morning, and all you got to show for it is a handful of change? Why, you ain't even good at whorin'! To call you a whore would be an insult to all the hard-working whores out there! Hear what I'm saying, bitch? You ain't even good at whorin'! You don't rate!"

"It's the boy's birthday, Joe. I wanted to do something for the boy this once."

"You ain't even got enough coins left here for a bottle of *rotgut*—"

"He needed shoes, Joe. It's his birthday."

"How many times I gotta hear about the bastard's birthday, *goddamn you!* I ain't got enough here for a taste, and you got nerve to spend on shoes and birthday cakes and ice cream!"

"Can't you do without this one time? We'll get some money later—"

"Why should I have to do without, bitch? Why should I have to suffer? Didn't I tell you to abort the bastard? Didn't I?"

"There was no money for it, asshole! You drank everything I brought in—like you're doing now!"

"You're blaming me? *It's my fault?*"

There was a loud slap. The woman screamed. There was tumbling. Someone being thrown against a wall. More screaming and yelling. Mad dogs barked inside the apartment.

Eight-year-old Cecil Omar Biggs stood at the landing between the floors, struck the last match and burned a plump spider with it. Through with that, he was back on the green flies: easy to catch, while they kept at the filthy windowpane, buzzing away. He'd sever their wings and lower them on the window sill on their backs. Liked to watch them kick wildly this way.

He had an unusually large one now. Was desperate to burn it. Went through his pockets in search of matches. Dug up a book. No matches left in it. Kept searching, found another. A single match left. Struck it. Lowered the flame toward the frantic fly: the fat fucker. He wanted to kill them all. Nothing gave him more pleasure than killing these fuckers. And then he got him but good. The last match. That was it. Gone. All of them. What would he do? Keep catching them and tear their wings off. He'd have to find some more matches somewhere soon. While happening to look up toward the top of the windowpane at a couple of flies banging their heads against the glass, his eyes wandered up toward the ceiling, up there in both corners, large cobwebs, too, but he couldn't reach those. He wished that he could. There were also plenty of dead moths along the window sill that he felt like frying . . . but he needed matches for that.

The landing was littered: beer cans and soda bottles, cigarette butts and empty cartons, bologna packaging and candy bar wrappers, used condoms and Tampons. He shoved his worn sneaker around in there, in search of a possible match, a lighter . . . and found nothing. He cursed. Needed fire. The yelling and fighting in their apartment kept on: more things being broken; his father's dogs barked. Then he heard John Joseph release a deep howl. The apartment door opened like a cannon shot, and his mother, heavily made-up as usual, both eyes swollen, mouth bleeding, with all that wild dark hair flying and not a stitch of clothing on her, scrambled down the flight of stairs toward him.

There was panic and terror in her peepers; even, incredibly enough, to some degree, a kind of glee. He noticed, too, a couple of her front teeth were missing this time.

She descended the stairs in her clumsy, harried way, with John Joseph, drunk and slobbering, nose and jaw bloody, in his soiled OD green army boxers and worn, mis-matched white socks, staggering in the doorway, the birthday cake haphazardly balanced on the palm of his left hand, while he held onto the doorjamb with the other to steady his aim. He cursed and hurled the cake at her, the birthday cake that she'd only bought moments earlier. J.J. sent the cake flying through the air as she neared the landing where the boy stood. The youngster turned his back in time. The cake grazed the top of her head, and a good deal of it deflected and spattered the back of the boy's neck.

"Half a whore!"

"Up yours, faggot!"

The boy's mother continued on down the next flight to make her way toward the lobby below.

"I'll kill you, bitch! Kill the both of you!"

John Joseph ducked back inside, to reappear seconds later with the box the boy's new footwear was in and pitched the shoes, one at a time, at the eight-year-old.

One shoe bounced off the top of the boy's head and went sailing through the windowpane, causing him to pivot enough for the second shoe to nail him between the eyes. The blow sent the kid spinning into the corner, his face buried in his hands. He wasn't crying, merely doing his best to deal with the throbbing pain.

ZOOK

By KIRK ALEX

Blurb & Novel Excerpt

Some very strange things are taking place at the New Pueblo Funeral Home . . .

War vet, Ray Zook, a PTSD afflicted former grunt, is about to regret that he ever set foot in Tucson, Arizona.

All he wants is to gain the courage to face his inner-demons and somehow explain to the widow of his best friend what *really* happened to him during their stint in the military. But when Zook is mugged and takes a temporary job working the night-shift at a crematory run by a couple of unsavory employees, those plans get derailed.

After witnessing a series of disturbing incidents—like the shady "after hours" business taking place—that hurl him into an immoral world of grave robbing, coffin swapping, and even disappearing bodies, Zook finds himself caught in the middle of a twisted power-struggle to control ownership of the funeral home.

If Zook hopes to escape this utter mess with his sanity intact, he must rise above his fears and confront the dark deeds before he ends up back in the looney bin . . . for good this time.

Chapter 1

I had just gotten off the bus and the two of them followed me: the dim-witted young chick with the dishwater hair and the beastly two-hundred-pound butch dyke with her: all tats and rings and studs and chains. Lots of black leather. Blue/black crew cut. Demanding money.

"For what?"

"BJ."

The other one was quiet. Just wasn't there mentally. Didn't seem like it mattered to her, either. It was the bitch built like a dozer who was after my cash. I dared her to take it, which hadn't been a wise move at all. She cold-cocked me. By the time she was done I was on the ground, nearly out. She'd flipped me over on my belly and sat on my back. I could hardly breathe, let alone do much of anything else at this point. She'd taken my wallet, extracted the bills, tossed it back at me. Spit in my direction, and they walked off. With close to eighty dollars of my jack. My roll. A good chunk of it. If it hadn't been for the paper money I'd kept stashed inside my sock I'd have been up the creek. I was, but at least with what remained I'd be able to rent a room, buy something to eat, a newspaper, and look for work.

I had been sound asleep, as comfortable as one can possibly be on a Greyhound bus. Been pulling on a bottle of hooch all the way from Phoenix. The idea was to stay on in Tucson long enough to beef up the roll and continue on to Ft. Worth. The ex had family there and I hoped that's where she'd ended up. I didn't have a need to connect with her. It came down to my kid. In her early teens by now. Hadn't seen her in years. I'd been to LaFayette, Indiana; Bowling Green, Kentucky; Lawrence, Kansas, and dozens of other towns, large and small. I stayed on the move; perpetual motion seemed to keep the demons at bay—at least I had myself convinced of it. I had war-related nightmares I couldn't shake, and some other things I was trying to live down. Staying on the move seemed to be the answer. Only how in hell do you get away from yourself? I'd been given the boot by more apartment managers and motel desk clerks for kicking the floor and walls in my sleep than I cared to remember.

It was usually some indiscriminate setting, me unarmed, being chased by the enemy in some far-off land. Commies? Mid-East zealots? Your run-of-the-mill America haters? Who knew? Or maybe I was in denial. Unwilling to face my demons. It took a lot to deal with that shit.

That was where they got on, though: Phoenix. The young one: couldn't tell how old, didn't look half bad in tight jeans, pink blouse, although the heavy one with the butch cut made me want to retch. This was one unappealing broad. And wouldn't you know it, she was the one who dropped her sweaty and mean ass in the seat next to mine. She wanted a hit off my hooch. I told her to piss off. Took the occasional nip from the bottle, pulled the blanket up to about my neck. I had no idea how long I'd be staying in Tucson. Didn't know a soul in town, not really. It was just a place to drive through, or maybe spend a week in, look around. Been in the 'Old Pueblo' before. Worked as a busser at some sports bar some years back, did a bit of panhandling.

What nudged me awake was the two of them switching seats. Now the young one was sitting next to me. Before the fat one gave up her seat, she whispered in my ear: "My cousin gives great head."

"How much?"

"Forty bucks."

I told her to get lost.

They switched seats, and before I knew it, 'cousin' had her hand under my blanket. Inched it slowly toward my crotch and was rubbing it, just running her fingers gently over it, and I'll be damned if my groin didn't begin to stir. All that vino, and there I was: getting wood. She proceeded to unzip my fly. I let her; pretended I was asleep, and let her do what she wanted. I figured if I acted like I was dozing, they wouldn't be able to claim I owed them money later, her and the beast she was with.

She had it out, stroking, slowly, taking her time. Then she ducked her head under the blanket. I let her. Of course, I let her. It had been a while. No love, no sex. Traveling the country on buses, when the money was there, hitching when it wasn't.

She had her tongue on it, licking; then she had the shaft inside, all of it. I didn't have a tremendous whole lot, but it was all right; there were some poor bastards who envied what I did have. You lived with the hand the Dealer laid on you—and this time the Dealer had shown me some kindness, I thought. That head of hers bobbed up and down, not fast, gently, gradually, taking her time. And the fact that it was night provided adequate cover. Passengers were zoned out, with the exception of some punk in his teens, across the aisle, watching out of the corner of his eye. Let him. Probably wished he was me, the big shot, getting his nuts off on a Greyhound bus to nowhere.

The licking went on. She played with the head, flicking it thoroughly. This chick had been around, knew her business when it came to licking balls and sucking cock. It had been such a long time, too. Probably did this to get by: sucked off strangers for whatever they could pick up. Who knew? Did it matter? Only I'd had too much wine. Couldn't make it. It was no good. Wine and sex didn't mix, not for me.

She lifted her head. I pulled out my wallet. Extracted a tenner for her effort. She did what she could. Not her fault. Before the young hooker had had a chance to even take a good look at it, the beast, her freakish 'relation,' stuck her hand in and snapped up the sawbuck. She sniffed it. Looked it over. She was not pleased. Tough, I thought. That was a ten-dollar try.

"My name is not Bill Gates and I don't own *Microsoft*. Besides, I never got off."

"You're lying." She yanked her 'cousin' out of the seat, and lowered that wide posterior next to me.

"We agreed on forty."

"Like hell we did."

"That was a forty-dollar BJ. You never had anything that good in your life."

"How would you know? Maybe I had better." For a fact. Only my ex-wives wanted nothing to do with me, especially the last one. I had no idea where she was. Ft. Worth was nothing more than a guess, a vague one, like all the other towns I'd been to. She'd taken the kid and disappeared off the face of the earth. Could explain the roaming. If I admitted it to myself. I didn't need the exes back, only ached to see the kid. A girl. Must have been six years ago I saw her last. I didn't blame the wife for leaving me. Couldn't take the screaming in the middle of the night, the kicking at the floor with my feet, the times I was stationed out of the country, or stuck in some bug bin here in the states. I drank to fight the demons. Only made everything worse. They had me on *Prozak*, then *Paxil*, at the VA. While I was in the whack ward the wife dropped the bomb: wanted out. I couldn't stop her, didn't try. She never mentioned custody, only because she figured she was entitled. She'd given birth to the child and that was that. Frankly, I was in no shape to take care of a kid, couldn't even take care of myself. I let it go; let them both go. The ex had a man, in fact, had been shagging a neighbor while I was stationed overseas. The way it usually went. I'd had it done to me once before. Kid could be his, biologically. Probably. Don't matter. I treated her like she was my own. You get emotionally attached. Kids are all right. Always wanted a family. Always did. Things kept going wrong somehow. Something would always happen to turn things upside down. This was divorce number three. You know what they say: three strikes and you're out. Three marriages, three divorces. I was defective, a loser. Something was seriously the matter with me. It was the war; it was other things.

"I doubt it." She looked at me. "Not with that nose and those teeth." My nose was bent, both ways, in bar brawls that I usually started and lost, so were my teeth—born with them that way—the ones still there: black, yellow. Of the uppers in front, I had but one left. In the middle.

I pulled the blanket up, and pretended to go to sleep. Only she wouldn't let me.

"Thirty bucks. You can't deny that was worth thirty bucks."

"You got what it was worth. And that's the end of it. I never got rocks. You bitches came on to me. Before I knew what was going on, your nympho girlfriend was molesting my privates."

"You owe us money."

"Fuck off, or I go to the driver."

"He's our friend. That wouldn't get you anywhere."

"What does *he* pay for it?"

"That's a different case. He gets a discount—and has nothing to do with you."

"I feel drained for some strange reason and crave rest." And this time I shut my eyes and kept them shut. I could feel them switch seats again. As she got up, I turned my head, and caught her cousin going down on some geezer way in the back. I guessed the freak was on her feet in order to collect payment, and before I knew it, the young bitch was back sitting beside me. It wasn't long before she had her hand under my blanket again. This time I slapped it away, and she left me alone.

We got off the bus. I had my old backpack; walking down in search of a cheap motel along Drachman. Then I turned down an alley. Big mistake. They'd had friends waiting for them. Indians. Looked like. I was jumped, knocked down. She stood on one side, while one of those drunk Indian friends of hers stood on the other, and they took turns delivering a couple of very effective, if unsteady, kicks to my kidneys. The beast had emptied my wallet, rummaged through the backpack, spat in disgust and left me lying there in the puke and blood.

Welcome to Tucson, Arizona. To be fair, this was no slam against the Old Pueblo, and besides, the bitches had hopped on in Phoenix.

I was up, wiped vomit from my chin. Dug my hand inside my left sock. At least I still had that. Jammed the spare socks and underwear, photo album, toiletries, back in the pack. Checked into a motel, washed my face, showered, then plopped down on the floor and slept the rest of the night and most of the next day when I had to go out and find a bar, or *Circle K*, to buy a can of *Spam* and a 6- Pack of *Red Dog*, a newspaper. At this rate, my money wouldn't last long and I'd be stuck here indefinitely. Taking a look at the job ads was in order.

* * *

ZIGGY POPPER AT LARGE

14 TALES OF GENERAL DEGENERACY, OF MAYHEM & DEBAUCHERY – FOR THE MORALLY CONFLICTED & BORDERLINE CRIMINAL

– Not For Prudes Or The Easily Offended –

Raw & real, filthy & funny gutbucket dispatches from the gritty streets of LA by Kirk Alex, author of the acclaimed & controversial **LUSTMORD: Anatomy of a Serial Butcher . . .**

It's a hot mother of an afternoon in seedy East Hollywood. Ziggy Popper is fresh out of the joint, sitting in a dive bar nursing a beer and minding his own business, when a scrawny loser walks in & parks his skinny butt on the stool next to his . . . and offers him cash money to shag his shack job. Even shows him a faded still of a wench tied down to a bed, spread eagle, with nothing on but a blindfold. The bitch of it is the female in the photo resembles Ziggy's ex a great deal, the one who helped send him to prison.

It's more than enough to make Ziggy want to take this on. From there, Kirk Alex's story takes a wild and unpredictable turn. Hardboiled and packing a punch of LA attitude in its gritty realism and black humor, "Ziggy Popper" shows what can happen when a man's past catches up to him. Even in the middle of a steamy sex scene.

About the Author

Kirk Alex's novel *Lustmord: Anatomy of a Serial Butcher* was a finalist in the Kindle Book Review's Best Book Awards of 2014. He is also the author of *Zook, Fifty Shades of Tinsel,* the story collection: *Ziggy Popper at Large,* the *Love, Lust & Murder* series: *Throwback & Backlash,* the Eddie "Doc" Holiday Private Eye Series, and a few other novels & shorts.